Winery

Drake Wines, Volume 2

Chelle pimblott

Published by Chelle pimblott, 2021.

This is a work of fiction. Similarities to real people, places, or events are entirely coincidental.

WINERY

First edition. June 18, 2021.

Copyright © 2021 Chelle pimblott.

Written by Chelle pimblott.

DEDICATION To my book bitches without you I wouldn't be writing xx

To my editor in chief, thank you for all that you do and it goes way beyond editing and being a sounding board. Love ya guts! To my family, thank you for allowing me to write and forgetting to cook for you sometimes. Love you always xx

***** **Please note ** WINERY: was written by an Australian Author, in Australian English. As such you may assume there are some spelling errors within, however it's just how we spell things downunder. *****

Chapter One
LOGAN

"Logan, you have to tell them. I'm tired of living in the shadows. I'm tired of our relationship being a secret to those who matter the most. I know how much Makenna and Caleb mean to you, especially since your parents died, but you need to do this." He gets up and moves away from where we'd been cuddled up together on the couch. "I won't be your dirty little secret anymore Sweets."

"You're not my dirty little secret Jules. They know when you're here. They know how often you stay here. Jesus! It's not like we can hide any of that, I live on the family property." I say in frustration.

"Ohhh, I know. Believe me Logan I know! Except they think I'm here on business and we end up working so late that I crash here." Jules shakes his head like he can't believe it. "Or they think we drink too much, making it unsafe for me to drive myself home." Jules sighs and walks back over to sit down next to me. "I need more than that Logan. I need a relationship that people know I'm in. I was understanding in the beginning, truly I was, but Logan it's been years. I know you love me, but I'm not sure that's enough for me anymore. I think I've been pretty patient but even I have my limits. I think you forget that I've known Kenna, Brady, and Caleb, almost as long as I've known you. I don't think they're going to react how you think they will. I think you're more worried about how the people you deal with for Drake Wines are going to take it, and that hurts more than anything else. That you're more worried about strangers than you are about *my* feelings."

"You know that's not true Jules." I say, shaking my head in frustration. "I'm nervous yes, but not for the reasons you think. Look, you've had years to get used to how you feel and how people perceive you. *So* many more than me, to understand who you are and where you fit in. When we met I was ready for us, but it was still like a sledgehammer to my heart and brain. I love you and I don't want to lose you, but you do have one thing right. I have a business to run, and it's not just me that relies on it for a living. I have to take a lot of things and people into consideration."

Standing up Jules says, "I think you need to work out who *you* are Logan, and I can't help you with that. I'm not giving you an ultimatum Logan, because they never work well. I know you'll make a knee jerk decision if I do and I don't want you to do that. I'm going away with work for a couple of weeks, and I think we can use that time for the clean break that we need after so many years together. You need to decide if you want to be who you think everyone else wants you to be or do you want to be your true self? Even if that's without me, I'll be happy for you."

"You mean you're breaking up with me?" I ask, not believing him, needing him to clarify what he's saying.

"Yes. I'm going out of town for two weeks, so there's no chance we'll run into each other, I'm sure that will make it easier."

"Right. How long have you known about this trip and when were you going to tell me about it?" I ask, angry at Jules, and myself. "When did you make the decision to use it as an excuse to leave me?"

"I only found out yesterday. I didn't tell you because we couldn't see each other last night if I recall." Jules says, angrily. "And why couldn't we see each other last night? Oh that's right! Your sister set you up on a date. A *date*, Logan! A fucking *date*, because your sister is unaware that you're already in a relationship. *With me!* Do you *know* how insane and insulting that is? Do you? I do. I also know that if Kenna knew you were dating anyone, me included, that she would have never set you up with someone else."

"Jules. Please don't leave. Not like this." I beg him. I don't want him to leave, not when he's not going to be around for a couple of weeks.

Looking down at the floor so he doesn't meet my eyes Jules says, "I'm not staying here tonight Logan. I can't. I'm too hurt." He shook his head, taking a step back when I reach out for him. "No. My emotions are too torn up Logan, I can't take anymore. Plus, I need to pack for my trip. I'll talk to you when I get back."

"What do you mean, 'when you get back'? You mean we're not having any contact for the next two weeks while you're away?" I ask, shocked. We've never gone that long without talking to one another, not even when we first met, when nothing had happened between us yet. We were friends first and foremost.

Without looking my way, Jules heads for the front door and says, "I think it would be for the best, Logan. I think you need the clarity of not talking to me to make a decision, and I know I need a break from feeling like I don't have all of you."

"But you do. You *do* have all of me. Please, don't leave like this." I'm not above begging. "Please? Jules, don't leave me."

"I can't have all of you while you're hiding us from your family. I can't Logan, and you know it. This trip was thrown at me yesterday, and I didn't want to go because it meant leaving you. But the more I thought about it, the more I realised that this might just be the break that we need."

"I love you Jules." I say, my voice is barely a whispered raspy version of my normal voice.

"I know Logan, and I love you too, but I don't know if that's enough anymore, Sweets."

I watch as Jules walks out my door, for what is perhaps the last time, willing for this all to be a bad dream. I close my eyes as I hear the rumble of a car start, and then slowly disappear down my long driveway. I sink down into the couch we were both just sitting on together and drop my head into my hands. When the first sob racks my body I slump further down in the soft cushions of the couch.

What the hell am I going to do without Jules for two weeks? Two fucking weeks without the love of my life!

As I sit there, I realise that my family think they know everything there is to know about me, Logan Jack Drake, but the truth is, I have a secret so big, that it will blow their fucking minds when they find out. When I *tell* them, that Jules is so much more than 'just' my best friend. How the hell am I going to tell Makenna, Brady and Caleb that Jules is everything to me. He *is* the love of my life. I know one thing for certain, and that is, if I don't tell them soon, I risk losing Jules forever, and that is something I can't live with. While the thought of losing Jules forever gives me heart palpitations, the thought of losing either my brother, *or* sister may actually give me a heart attack.

Now, my conundrum with the situation is that I would usually talk something like this through with either Jules or Makenna, and for reasons that are obvious, I can't talk to either of them about *this*. Jules made it clear that I need to make a decision, and I am sick to death of living a lie, without a doubt, but it also makes me feel sick thinking about telling my family the truth.

I just watched Makenna walk down the aisle and marry her high school sweetheart, the love of her life, Brady almost a month ago. It made me realise just how much I'm missing by not having Jules by my side, as my friend *and* my partner.

I've asked myself some hard questions since Jules walked out my door without looking back.

Do I believe there is something *wrong* with our relationship? No, I do not, I love Jules with every part of my being. I don't doubt that for a second.

Do I truly believe that my family will disown me when I tell them the truth? No, not really, but I still carry some doubts about telling them. I don't want to put the family business at risk in any way, because of my personal life.

What I do know is that I've been living two lives for so damned long, that I'm not sure I know how to bring them together without hurting someone in the process. Whether that's Jules, Makenna, Caleb or myself.

I SPEND THE FIRST WEEK of Jules' business trip texting and calling him. When I don't get any responses, I have to come to terms with the fact that he's deadly serious about this break, but I have to tell myself that it's not permanent, otherwise my mood will become unbearable for everyone around me. Including myself. I keep asking the empty house why my love can't be enough for him?

Who the fuck am I kidding, I know exactly why my love isn't enough and he's given me more than enough time to pull my head out of my arse, to tell Makenna and Caleb the truth about our relationship, but it never seems to be the right time. I always find an excuse not to and it hits me like a brick as to why he's so pissed with me!

Jules and I met before my parents were killed in that fucking accident and Jules was by my side for the whole thing, but that didn't seem like the right time to tell my siblings about my relationship. Then, when we finally moved on from all the ramifications of their sudden deaths, legal and emotional, we managed to get Caleb to go back to university, so I didn't want anything to disrupt him. Once he came home from his studies, I thought I'd give him some time to settle back in to being back in the fold of the family and the business. I wanted to give him time to decide what he wanted to do within the family business without my life getting in the way. That's taken a little longer than I expected to be honest.

Kenna and Brady were already engaged before the accident but all their wedding plans got put off indefinitely afterwards. Once everything settled down, and they announced they wanted to move forward with the wedding and finally get married, I was behind their decision one hundred percent. Their wedding became my priority and I didn't want to ruin their big day by making my own relationship announcement, but I realise now, that was the last straw for Jules.

Me putting our relationship on hold once again for a sibling, even though Jules loves Kenna and Brady as much as I do, must have been frustrating to watch, even more so to not be able to be by my side to share in it. Not in the same way two people in a relationship share that kind of event anyway, we were just mates to anyone who looked on.

It's Friday night and normally I would have been making a move to leave my office to go out with Jules, but he isn't here. Instead I'm staring off into space, still sitting at my desk, once again wondering about how the hell I got myself into this mess and wondering how the fuck I'm going to get out of it! If I'm honest with myself I know exactly what I have to do to fix the situation I find myself in, but I'm not really sure that I *want* to. Maybe Jules was right.

Maybe he's right and love just isn't enough. I'm pondering this depressing thought when there's a noise at my door.

"Knock, knock." I look up to see my sister, Makenna standing in the doorway. "What are you still doing here? I thought you'd be out scouting for fun with Jules." I know what they think of our relationship, all they see is friendship. It's so much more than that.

"Jules left at the start of the week for a two week business trip." I reply, barely looking up from what looks like my paperwork, but really I'm just scribbling on some paper.

"Ahhh well that explains why you've been grumpy all week and why I haven't spotted the gorgeous Jules around here this week." She smiles, as she walks uninvited into my office, and deposits herself in the chair opposite me.

"I haven't been grumpy all week." I snap at her and I realise that just confirms what she's accusing me of and now she's laughing at me as I frown.

"Sure. You're as happy as a fairy riding a unicorn. Right." She laughs, while nodding her head in agreement. "Maybe I should call Jules myself and find out when the happy traveller will return to our midst."

"No!" I snap a little too quickly and aggressively. "I'm sorry Makenna, I know I'm being a cantankerous old bastard, but that's not a good idea. Jules is working and doesn't need either one of us interrupting him. OK?"

"It was a joke, Logan." I know I've upset her by the look on her face, but I can't have her calling Jules up and asking if everything is all right. "I just wanted to come and check in on you, make sure you're OK. You've buried yourself in work this week and now I know why." She stands up to leave, but stops at the door, turning back towards me. "Just a word of advice big brother. I know you've got this sexy grump vibe going on that's all the rage these days, but if you don't start thinking about how you treat the people around here, you might find yourself needing to hire new staff. Not to mention, your siblings may start to give you the cold shoulder."

"I'll take that under advisement Makenna." I try to smile, but I think it's more of a grimace if I'm being honest. "I'm sorry if I hurt your feelings, I didn't mean to." I don't know how to explain to her what's going on. "I'm trying to work some things out. Personal things, and I'm not sure what the right thing to do is. For anyone."

"Is it a relationship kind of thing?" She asks, sitting back down, and I nod. "Does Jules not approve, is that why you haven't spoken all week?"

"How the fuck do you know we haven't spoken all week?" I ask, amazed.

"Because I know you. Now answer the question, doesn't Jules approve of the new relationship?" She repeats.

"It's not new but no, Jules doesn't approve of the relationship as it stands." I answer cryptically.

"Do *you* like the way the relationship stands at the moment?" It's a good question. It's one I've avoided asking myself because I fear the answer. It takes me a minute to think about my answer, but Makenna waits, she always does.

"No. I really don't, but I don't know how to fix it Makenna." I say, exasperated, and rubbing my hand over my face. The week old scruff on my face scratching my hand. "I think I screwed up. Actually, I *know* I screwed up big time, and I'm not sure I can fix it."

"Do you know what you have to do to fix it?" More questions.

"Yes." I answer, so quietly I'm not even sure she heard me until she's standing beside my chair and turning it so that I face her.

"Logan, if you know *how* to fix the problem, then do it. You deserve some happiness big brother and I think you know who you want to have that happiness with. Don't let your big brain get in the way of what your heart wants." She smiles at what I can only imagine is a bewildered look on my face. "I'm not a young dumb kid anymore Logan and I know you think I don't have real relationship experience because Brady and I have been together forever, but it's still a relationship that we work at every damned day."

"I know that Makenna." I'm astounded that's what she thinks I believe about her relationship. "You're an amazing businesswoman, partner and wife. Brady's a lucky son of a bitch to have married you and he knows it too. Why do you think he grabbed on tight and didn't let go?"

"Thank you. It's always nice to hear that your big brother thinks so highly of you and your choice of husband." She hesitates for a few seconds before continuing. "I just want you to know, to understand really, that no matter what, you can talk to me Logan. Not just about work, but about life as well. Caleb and I appreciate everything you've done for us since Mum and Dad died, but you're allowed to lean on us as well. You don't have to be Mr Stoic all the damned time. You're allowed to need us too. You're allowed to live your life however you choose to. We won't judge you, we just want you to be happy."

I'm choked up with emotion and I can't trust myself to speak. I know this would be the perfect opportunity to come clean about my relationship with Jules, but for reasons I can't explain I just can't. Seeing the disappointment all over her face kills me. Almost as much as it did when I saw it on Jules' face a week ago. "Thank you Makenna, I appreciate that." I manage to get out around the emotions clogging up my throat.

"You're welcome Logan. The offer stands for whenever you're ready to tell us what's going on." I still can't speak, so once again I just nod. "Did you want to join us for dinner tonight? Brady's cooking up some wonderful feast and with his track record, you and I both know there will be too much food and we'll be eating the leftovers for days. He doesn't know how to cook for two, which is incredible given how long we've lived together."

I laugh along with her, grateful for her ability to lighten the mood. "He never ceases to amaze me with how much food he cooks, but I think I'll pass tonight if you don't mind? I'm not really fit for company, and I need to think about a few things. Make some decisions about what I want and my future."

She leans down and kisses me on the cheek. "I hope you choose Jules. He makes you less of a grumpy bastard. He's also good at making the weight you seem to think you need to carry alone, somehow less." She whispers in my ear and I'm too stunned to answer, before she's gone.

Does she know? If she knows, does that mean Brady knows too? What about Caleb?

How could she possibly know? They can't, because if my siblings knew about my *real* relationship with Jules, they would have said something by now. Wouldn't they? I mean, none of us are shy about telling each other things. Except I haven't been telling them the truth about me, have I? Maybe they're just respecting my privacy and waiting for me to say something.

Holy fuck! What if they *know*? Maybe I haven't been as discrete as I thought.

No that can't be it, Kenna just had the perfect opportunity to ask me point blank, and she didn't. She doesn't know anything, not for sure anyway.

I pack up my stuff, turn off the computer, hoping like hell that I saved everything as I watch the screen go black. I need to go home, eat, pour myself a glass of whiskey, and think all this through.

When I get home five minutes later, I sink into the cushions of my couch, with some stupid movie on the TV and a glass of whiskey in my hand. I know I should make myself something to eat, but I don't want to get up to do it.

Instead, I send one last text for the night to Jules, hoping that I finally get an answer.

I miss you. Logan xx

I'm not sure why I put my name on the end of the message, except that I'm making sure that Jules knows where the message came from.

I stare at the TV not even seeing what's on the screen, and think about Jules. Wondering what he might be doing tonight, who he's with, if he's having fun. Is he thinking about me as well?

"Fuck!" I scream out into the emptiness that is my house and my life. Without Jules here I feel like I'm not living and I know my life shouldn't be wound up in one person making it worth living *for*, but I miss him. I pour myself another glass of whiskey, and by the time I'm halfway through it I decide that I definitely should have had something to eat.

The last thought I remember having before drifting off to sleep was, Jules was right, this couch is comfortable!

Chapter Two
JULES

Walking away from Logan a week ago was the hardest thing I have *ever* done but I needed to do it for my sanity. I love the man, but I can't live in the shadows any longer.

When the opportunity to leave town for work came up, initially I didn't want to take it up, because leaving Logan for two weeks was just unfathomable to me. That was until his sister, Makenna, set him up on a date. A date! And even worse than Kenna setting him up on a date, was the fact that he *agreed* to go on it! He told me it was because he didn't want to upset Makenna and he assumed I would be understanding. All I heard when he said that was that hurting *my* feelings was OK. All because he couldn't bring himself to tell her the truth about us.

That was the last straw for me. I refuse to be his dirty little secret any longer. Not when it means saving Kenna's feelings over mine. Not to mention I know that if the tables were turned and I went on a date he would have been outraged, but I was supposed to just accept it? Nope, enough is enough!

I told him a white lie when he asked me how long I'd known about this trip. I told him I only knew about it the day before, the truth is I knew about it for quite a few weeks. Back when my boss first mentioned it though, I didn't put my hand up to volunteer. The day before the trip, my boss told the office that they needed one more to go, and his eyes turned to me. I knew then I was going whether I wanted to or not. Therefore, I told him a little white lie, after all I *was* only told I was going the day prior.

Then, while we snuggled up on his couch he started laughing and regaling me with stories from his *date*! I didn't find anything funny about my boyfriend, the love of my life going out on a date with someone that wasn't *me*, and I'm at a loss as to how Logan thought it was so amusing.

When we first got together I could see the funny side of Kenna fixing him up with her friends. I knew he wasn't interested in the dates and he wasn't ready to tell anyone about us. Then Jack and April Drake died. Then Kenna and Brady got married and here I am, still sitting on the sidelines. I couldn't be with him properly at the funeral to help him mourn. I couldn't stand beside him at the wedding to celebrate with the family either, because no-one knew about our relationship. They thought we were *friends*.

That's why even though I didn't get a choice about going on this business trip, I'm quite relieved to be going away. I don't want to leave Logan but maybe some distance will help both of us understand what we need. I guess what I really mean is, that *Logan* has time to think about where he wants this relationship to go. I think the distance will be good for both of us, we can clear our heads without the other one around to distract us and hopefully get some clarity. Have we broken up for good? I hope not, but I can't say for certain.

Leaving Logan that night was damned difficult. I didn't give him an ultimatum though, they never work out well for anyone and I don't want to *make* him make a choice. I need him to decide to join his worlds, not keep them separate.

"Hey Jules, can you come over here and look at this report for me? I'm not sure I'm reading it right, but if I am, this place is in more trouble than we first thought." Sighing, I go over to join Gavin at his makeshift desk and start looking over spreadsheets and reports for the rest of the afternoon.

After spending the rest of the afternoon confirming Gavin's suspicions, I pack up my stuff. I've already turned down the invitation to join him and the rest of the team for dinner, which will no doubt turn into a few drinks as well. It is the weekend after all and we're all away from our families, and friends, but I'm not up for company.

"Are you OK Jules?" Gavin comes over to ask me quietly as everyone else gathers their things getting ready to leave.

"Yeah Gavin I'm fine, I just don't feel like socialising tonight, that's all." I smile at him.

"That would be why I'm asking if you're OK, you're always the first one ready for dinner, with a few drinks at the end of a rough week, but tonight you said thanks but no thanks."

"I know. I just don't feel like it tonight. Maybe I'm coming down with a bug or something, who knows." I shrug my shoulders not looking him in the eyes.

"Is everything OK between you and Logan? Has he hurt you?" He asks tensely. I appreciate his protectiveness but I don't want him to blame Logan for my down mood, even if he *is* half right.

"He just has some decisions to make and I'm hoping he'll make the right ones." I shrug my shoulders again. "Being away from him is hard, you know?"

"I get it, I didn't want to leave Jilly for two weeks either, but she knew what she signed up for when we got married. So did Logan. Still, it doesn't get any easier." Gavin says, resting his hand on my shoulder, he leans in a little closer so that he can ask really quietly without anyone else hearing him. "He hasn't told his family yet, has he?"

"No it doesn't get any easier and he *does* understand. That's not the issue at all, even though I kind of did spring this trip on him out of nowhere." It feels even worse this time. That's probably got something to do with the fact that I'm actually dreading returning home to talk to Logan. "No, he hasn't told them yet. I told him before I left that he had to make a choice, I can't go on living in the shadows of his life."

"I'm sorry Jules. You shouldn't have to ask to be a part of his life if he loves you." Gavin says, pulling me in for a man hug. "I don't doubt his love for you Jules, but you guys also can't hide forever."

"I know and thank you. Now get out of here, they're waiting outside for you. Honestly, I'm just going back up to the room, have a shower and order some room service. I might even find a ridiculous chick flick to watch."

"OK, but you take care of yourself, you hear me? I'm worried that you're getting sick." He says louder so that if anyone *is* listening they'll think I'm unwell.

"I promise." I tell him, then Gavin joins the others to go to dinner, while I lock up behind us and make my way up to my room. We're working out of a conference room in a hotel to sort out where a business connected to the hotel is losing money. Like I said, an exciting job for all involved.

When the door to my room clicks closed, I strip out of my clothes and head straight for the bathroom. A nice hot shower will help me to relax, that's the plan anyway. I've read every message that Logan's sent me since I left his house. I haven't answered or even acknowledged his messages. I know he loves me. I know he misses me. The only message I need from him is saying that he's spoken to Kenna and Caleb or when he plans to. Until I get *that* message I'm not interested. I'm not even close to wanting to go back to his house. I don't even know if I'll let him into *my* house.

I've sent him one message to let him know that I got here and I'm safe, that's it.

In the shower, I close my eyes, letting the water that borders on too hot to wash over my head, over my shoulders and down the rest of my body. Enjoying the soothing heat and pressure. My mind drifts to Logan, it always does when we're not together and I imagine him joining me in here, begging me to turn down the heat, his glorious body naked and slippery wet. I can feel my body reacting to thoughts of being with him again and even though he's not here with me, I let my mind wander. My hands stroke up and down my chest and abs. I suck a breath in as my thumbs graze over my nipples. In my mind I see Logan smiling, enjoying watching me as he fists his cock, stroking it until the tip is glistening.

My phone starts ringing, jolting me back to reality. Instead of answering the call, I wash myself all over, refusing to relieve the sexual tension that has me rock hard and highly strung. It's my punishment for getting carried away and thinking of Logan. He may be the love of my life but that doesn't mean I can't control myself.

Out of the shower I dry myself off quickly and wrap the fluffy white robe from the back of the door tightly around me and walk out to sit on the bed. Flicking on the TV to find a RomCom, I pick up my phone I've put off checking because if I see Logan's name on the screen, I might be tempted to call him back. Just to hear his voice. Only it's not his name on my screen, it's Makenna's. My heart starts to beat wildly, thinking that maybe something has happened to Logan and it's so bad his sister has to call me. There's only one way to find out, so I call Makenna back.

She answers on the second ring, "Hi Jules, how are you?"

"What do you mean, '*hi Jules, how are you?*' Is everything OK? Is Logan OK? What's happened?" I ask in what is effectively one long word.

"I told you if you called Jules he was going to panic." I hear Brady say in the background, but Makenna still hasn't answered me yet.

"Makenna Harris, spill now!" I say, the panic in my voice obvious. I'm ready to spring into action and start packing everything up while I'm talking to her, so I can leave as soon as I hang up. Job be damned.

"Everything is *fine*, Jules." She stresses the fine and I relax a little, until I realise that's how people start a sentence when something really bad has happened, so you don't stress and that causes me to tense up all over again.

"Are you sure?" I ask cautiously.

"Positive." She says, then sighs loudly. "Except that my big brother has been an absolute grumpy arsehole without you around. I mean I know he's got that grumpy bastard thing that all the ladies seem to love these days but he's even grumpier than usual and I was just wondering if you guys have had an argument?"

"Yes, the ladies do seem to love a grumpy bastard these days. They seem to think they can change him, make him happier somehow. Maybe they have a magic vagina?" The irritation and sarcasm in my voice, even though I'm trying to make a light-hearted joke, obvious.

"The guys seem to like it too." She quips.

"Well, in my experience most guys do enjoy being grumpy bastards, yes." I respond, not allowing myself to be baited into biting back.

"No, I mean they're attracted to the grumpy bastards just as much as their female counterparts are." She says, no hint of disgust or malice in her voice. "Aren't they Jules?"

"What the hell are you asking me for? I'm sure there are plenty of guys around the world that love their share of the grumpy arseholes of the world. Figuratively and literally." I say, with a bitter laugh. "It's not like I'm *the* expert."

"If you're sure Jules, it was just a question." She sighs, long and loud. I feel like I should apologise for my bad mood but I'm pissed off at the Drake's. Well, only one but she brought him and his damned love life up, making me pissed off all over again. So, I don't speak I wait for Makenna to just get to the point and say what she called me to say. She rarely bites her tongue for long, so it must be something good. "He misses you Jules." She says quietly, then pauses, and I hear Brady mumble something in the background. "When do you get back?"

"Next week." I answer, short and sweet.

"When next week? Will we see you around Drake Wines when you get back?" She asks, her voice soft and full of concern.

"I'm not sure when I'll get back just yet, to be honest with you Makenna and I'm not sure if I'll be welcome at the winery."

She gasps, obviously shocked. "So, you two *did* have a fight then?"

"You'll have to talk to your brother about that Makenna, he has the answers you're after, not me." I know I'm being short with her, but I'm not going to do Logan's dirty work for him.

"I've already tried talking to him, Jules, that's why I called you." While I can hear the frustration in her voice, I can't give her the answers she wants. I also understand that she just wants to help her brother but she needs to talk to *him* and *he* needs to be the one who tells her what's going on, not me. I'm not giving him the easy way out. I'm sure as hell not going to give him any extra ammunition to push me away, either.

"Then I don't know what else to say to you, Makenna." There's silence between us now and I don't want to be on the phone anymore. I've always liked Makenna and she's always been kind, sweet and welcoming to me, but I can't do this. "Look, I'm sorry, Makenna but I have to go. Work and all that, OK?"

"OK, sure Jules, I understand." She doesn't but she wants to. If only her big brother trusted her enough to tell her the truth. "I'll see you when you get home."

"Kenna." I say, trying not to sound as angry as I am. This isn't her fault and the position she's in obviously sucks. I'm mad at her brother for putting us *both* in this position. I'm also mad with her for meddling, even though she's being very sweet about it.

"I just want you to know that we love you Jules. No matter what happens between you and grumpy pants, you're always welcome out here. Always." She sounds so sure but I won't be going out there but I'm not sure what to say to her to make her understand. I love Kenna, Brady and Caleb, but if Logan can't come clean, then I won't be visiting his family's business to see his siblings. Talk about awkward, not to mention it will hurt way too much. I couldn't see him, knowing he wasn't mine anymore.

"I love you too Kenna, but I think that might end up being a little awkward, don't you?" I ask her.

"Only if we let it –" I can't let her finish, it just doesn't seem fair.

"It would be and you know it Kenna. You can't fix everything for your brothers you know that, right? At some point they have to make their own choices and you have to let them sweetheart." I sigh into the phone. "I love you Kenna, but I have to go, I've got a meeting to get to."

"I love you Jules. I'll talk to you soon." It's sounds more like a question than a statement.

"Good-bye Kenna." That goodbye sounds so *very* final, so I hang up before either of us can say too much. Before I can say or do anything stupid. Like promise to always be there for her and the guys.

That's a promise I can't make.

I open the mini bar and take out the tiny bottle of whiskey but I can't open it. Logan and I used to have a glass most nights after work to relax. I put it right back in the fridge. I pick up the room phone to order a bottle of vodka, and some soft drinks from room service. I don't care what flavour, just as long as I can mix the vodka with them.

I'm grateful that I'm alone in the room. I couldn't stand sharing with anyone else, especially with how drunk I am right now. Drunk, crying into my vodka and missing Logan.

I've tried to understand how Logan feels about telling his family the truth about our relationship but I can't. I get that his family is a traditional Italian one and he's afraid of how they'll behave but I didn't even have to think about telling my parents about us. He's met them and was introduced and accepted as my boyfriend. My parents didn't blink.

I feel like I said goodbye a week ago and now I'm mourning our relationship.

Chapter Three
LOGAN

Sitting on my couch drinking whiskey and staring at the TV, my thoughts keep wandering back to my conversation with Kenna. I can't shake the feeling that she suspects the truth and the only person I want to talk about it is Jules, but my calls and messages remain unanswered. I wonder how long that will last? Do I have to wait until next week when his business trip is over before I get the chance to talk to him again?

My phone vibrates across the coffee table as a message comes through and even though I'm hoping it's Jules, I have a feeling it's going to be Kenna. I want to pick it up and look but I don't want to feel the disappointment when it's not Jules. So, instead of picking it up, I stand up and walk to the kitchen to get food. Standing there for way longer than I should, just staring at in my fridge. I eventually decide to order a pizza, but to do that I need my stupid phone. I sink back onto the couch and bravely pick up the stupid thing like it's on fire.

Makenna: *Please come up and join us for dinner? Kenna xx*

Not Jules.

Me: *Not tonight Kenna xx*

Then I pull up the app I use to order pizza and place 'my usual'. I realise too late that my usual order takes into account that a certain other person is usually here to eat with me and I groan. Guess I'll be eating reheated pizza tomorrow night as well. That is, unless I can palm it off onto Caleb but that would mean I'd have to speak to him and I really don't feel like seeing anyone. Least of all a sibling.

My phone chimes with another message and even though I don't want to see who it is, I run a business and I know I need to at least look.

Makenna: *We're here for you Logan.*

I think about answering her, but I don't know what to say, when another one comes through.

Makenna: *For food or to talk. I love you no matter what*

I read both messages a couple of times, still at a loss as to what I should reply with, when there's a knock on my door. I hang my head to my chest, hoping like hell Kenna hasn't decided she needs to come *here* to convince me to let her feed me. I swear she treats me like I'm the youngest sibling sometimes and not the oldest!

Opening the door I'm ready to tell Kenna to leave me alone but the words die on my lips when I'm looking at the young kid who delivers pizza, smiling at me.

"Good evening, Mr Drake, here's the pizzas you ordered. I hope you and Mr Bishop enjoy your pizzas tonight."

"Thanks Benji." I say, holding back from sighing, because even the pizza delivery kid assumes Jules is here tonight.

"No worries Mr Drake. You guys have a great night." He says, smiling and waving as he turns back to his car. I close the door behind him and I can feel the sadness creeping into my very core.

I put what would have been Jules' pizza straight in the fridge without even looking at it, pour myself another whiskey, larger than the last one and put myself back on the couch to stare at the TV, I hope no-one asks me what I watched tonight, because I'll never be able to tell them!

After half a pizza and more whiskey than I usually have on a weeknight or weekend for that matter, I take my sorry self to bed and lie there staring at the ceiling. Thinking.

All I can think about is the fact that I'm lying in my bed and Jules isn't here with me. I know there's no-one to blame but myself. I want to forget what was said, I didn't mean that he was worth less to me than my family. My siblings. I'm not sure I can ever unpack the baggage and tell them about me. What does that make me? Am I someone that can't talk about his feelings and the person that he loves, without feeling like he's being judged?

I can tell Jules I miss him, and he can miss me too, but knowing that won't change a damned thing if we can't be honest about our relationship. If I can't be honest about our relationship. I need to first be honest with myself, then perhaps I can be honest with my family. That's my last thought as I drifted off to sleep. Julian Bishop. Love of my life.

"OHHHH LOGAN. I MISSED you so much, kiss me again Sweets." Jules murmurs against my lips.

"God I missed you too, Love." I mumble against his luscious, kissable lips. "I need you more than you'll ever know Jules."

Our kiss is hot. Desperate. I need him so much it hurts. I deepen the kiss, while running my hands over his back, arms, shoulders and any other part of him I can reach. I grab hold of his hips, pulling them into mine, grinding my cock into his.

"I need you Logan."

"I need you too, Jules." I groan.

"What if I'm someone you can't talk about? What am I to you Logan?" He asks, desperation and confusion in his voice.

"You're everything Jules." I say, trying to convey exactly how I feel about him.

"No, I'm not. You know it and I know it. You can't even tell your family about me. About *you*." He says, taking a step away from me.

"That's not true. You're everything to me. I would walk through fire for you Jules, don't you know that?" I'm not above begging him to come back to me. I need him. I want to touch him, to kiss him.

"You'd walk through fire for me but you can't tell your family the truth about us? To them, it's just a friendship and I can't continue like that anymore Logan." He's further away from me now and getting further away with every breath.

"I'll tell them, I swear to you, I just need more time." I beg.

"No more time Logan." He says with a shake of his head and his eyes fill with tears. "I can't do it. You've had more than enough time."

"Don't leave me Jules. I love you." I beg.

"I know you do and I love you too Sweets but I can't live like this anymore." He says it quietly but I can see the determination on his face. He's made his decision but that doesn't mean I have to like it.

"I need more time." I beg again.

"No! No more time Logan, your time to explain to your family about who I am is gone. I have to go." He says, turning away from me, his head down as he walks away from me.

"Don't go! Jules! *Don't. Leave. Me*!" I yell at the top of my lungs but I'm too late, he disappears into the distance.

I wake up, sitting upright in bed, still screaming his name and drenched in sweat. I run my hand over the scruff that's grown over my jaw the last week. I haven't really felt the need to clean myself up with Jules not here. I haven't really felt the need to do too much at all while Jules hasn't been around, except drink whiskey and eat enough food to survive, to keep Kenna off my back.

I fall back onto my pillow and cover my eyes with my arm. That dream, or should I say nightmare, felt so fucking real I'm still trying to slow my heartbeat down. Finally, as I start to calm down, the alarm on my phone goes off. Out in the living room. Drunk me managed to stumble to bed and strip off, but that's about all. If I don't get up now, the fucking thing will just keep making noise. Noise that I don't want to hear. Groaning, I put my feet on the floor and wander out to find my phone.

"It's about time you came out to turn off this annoying thing! Ohhhh, Jesus fucking Christ bro, can you cover yourself up man?" My hands instantly reach down to cover up my dick when I hear my brother's voice, and then it registers that he's in *my* fucking house and that makes it *his* problem that he's looking at me in all my naked glory.

"Well, that's what you get for letting yourself into *my* house, *bro*." I grab my phone off the coffee table where I left it without worrying about covering myself up again. I press the dismiss button on my phone and that's when I realise it's Saturday and I didn't set a fucking alarm for this morning. "What are you doing here Caleb?" I ask, growling at my brother but it actually hurts my head to do it, so I stop. "And why the fuck did you set an alarm on my phone?" I ask, making my way back to my room to pull on a pair of jeans to cover up. I'll cover up my arse, because let's face it, I wouldn't want to see him naked either, but that's all the concession he gets for being in my house uninvited this morning.

"To wake you up idiot." He says, like he can't believe I even have to ask, when I walk back into the living room.

"How long have you been here Caleb?" I ask, suddenly realising he might have heard me begging Jules to stay.

"Long enough, Logan, long enough." What the fuck does that mean, long enough? Whatever, I'm going to choose not to ask anything else because I don't have it in me for an argument. I'm not explaining myself to my little brother this morning. The whiskey that I drank last night is making me pay for my efforts this morning and that nightmare about Jules leaving, makes me shudder. Now I also have to put up with my brother. Can this day get any better?

"Good morning my favourite brothers!" Why did I have to ask if my day could get any worse? I should have known the universe would take it as a challenge.

"Good morning Kenna!" Caleb yells out from my couch, as our sister strolls in my door without knocking.

"There's nothing good about this morning." I mumble to myself as I drag my sorry arse over to make a coffee.

"Did you say something big brother?" Caleb asks loudly. He *really* needs to tone it down this morning before I kill him.

"No, I didn't say a word." I reply, my voice still rough from sleep and too much whiskey. "Was there a meeting I didn't know about this morning?" I ask, dragging through my memory, trying to remember my calendar. After a minute or two of thinking while pouring a coffee, I'm pretty certain we didn't have anything scheduled. So, I turn to look at my siblings only to find them staring at me like I've grown an extra head or something. They make me *so* self-conscious that I run the hand not holding my coffee mug over my face and neck, then through my hair, just to check that there's nothing unusual going on. I'm met with more silence and staring. "What?"

"Why are you only half dressed?" Kenna asks.

"Be grateful you weren't here a couple of minutes earlier, you would have seen your older brother in all his glory. My eyes may never recover!" Caleb tells her, closing and rubbing his eyes.

"What do you mean?" Kenna asks and then it hits her. "Ohhh no! Really? You saw him naked? Dude, I am *so* glad I missed that display."

"I wish I had, but unfortunately the sight is now burnt into my brain!" Caleb sighs with disgust.

"Shut up, both of you." I say a little too loudly and I cringe. "What do you two care what I look like? You know what Caleb, that's what you get when you enter my house uninvited and just wait for me to wake up!"

"We're worried about you Logan." Kenna says quietly.

"You look like shit bro." Ahh, I can always count on my little brother to get straight to the point.

"Don't hold back on my account, Caleb." I grumble as I shuffle over to an armchair, drop my body into it and take a big gulp of the delicious hot black liquid. When I look up, they're both just staring at me, genuinely looking shocked. "What? Your big brother isn't allowed to go on a bender every now and then? Come on guys, I haven't always been responsible for the business and the family. I was once a young man who could and *did* party. Hard. And before you say anything Kenna, I'm also allowed to decide I don't want to shave anymore and no, I won't let anything get in the way of running the business." I look at each of my siblings, one at a time, making eye contact with them and letting them know I mean business. "Ok, good. Now what the hell are you two doing here so early on the weekend? I'm allowed some down time you know?"

"Well, I came by earlier to check in on you but there wasn't any movement in here, so I left you alone, but when I saw Caleb's car sitting outside, I figured you were up."

"Thanks for checking in on me Kenna, but I'm OK. Honestly, I'm fine. I don't need a babysitter and I don't need you two checking in on me all day every day. No-one died." I say, knowing it will hit a nerve and they'll both shy away from the conversation. It makes me a bastard, I know that, but I really don't want to talk to them about this right now. If ever.

I know I have to talk to them about it one day, and soon but today will not be that day.

"Fine. If that's how you want it, I'm going out for the day with Brady, if you need us call my phone." Kenna looks at me, hard, staring into my eyes like she's trying to see into my very soul. It's kind of fucking scary but I don't flinch from her gaze because I know if I show any sign of weakness she'll stay and that's the last thing I want right now. "Everything is under control, no-one should need your help today and by the looks of you, that's a good thing." She huffs and starts to head towards the door to leave. "See you later Caleb, behave yourself."

"Always sis." Caleb yells back. Geezus I wish he'd lower his fucking voice today.

"Love you Makenna." I tell her, making her hesitate as her hand reaches out for the door handle.

"I love you too Logan, no matter what." She says, looking back over her shoulder at me with a sad smile. "I love you too Caleb, but you still need to behave." Kenna doesn't give him a chance to reply and yet he yells out a response to her anyway.

"Love you Makennnnnnna!"

"Ohhhh can you shut the hell up Caleb?" I growl at him and he laughs hysterically. I knew it! The bastard was being loud on purpose. "What is it that you want Caleb?

"I need your help at Vines for a few hours."

"Don't we have staff for that?" I ask grumpily. Again, I know I'm being a bastard, but I can't help myself.

"Yeah, we do you grumpy bastard but they're not as much fun to work with as you are." He smirks at me.

"Fine but you can wait until I've had a shower and some pain killers." I tell him, as I stand up and take my mug to the sink, rinse it and put it in the dishwasher. I smile to myself because rinsing my dishes before putting them in the dishwasher has become a habit because Jules hates it if I don't do it. The memory hits me hard and I groan quietly, leaning against the bench to hold myself up.

"Are you OK Logan?" Caleb asks quietly, all his joking and light-heartedness has disappeared concern replacing them.

"Yeah, just feeling a bit queasy. Learn from your big brother Cal, don't drink copious amounts of whiskey to drown out things you don't want to think about. In fact, never drink to drown out your thoughts."

"You know you can talk to me Logan, I'm not a little kid that needs protection anymore."

"Yeah I know, man." I tell him as I walk by him, slapping him on the shoulder in some long ago learned manly way that is supposed to convey love and support somehow. "I'm gonna go have that shower now."

"I'll be here when you get out." I nod his way, then regret the sudden movement and head to the bathroom. A long hot shower can't come at me fast enough this morning and I'm going to enjoy the endless stream of hot water today more than any day since I had it installed.

"Look forward to it Cal." I mumble, not waiting for him to answer me again.

I close and lock the bathroom door behind me. When I look up into the mirror over the sink I see a sorry excuse for myself reflected back at me. I don't think I've ever grown facial hair longer than a twelve o'clock shadow, but there's always a first time for everything and now is that time apparently. I grab two pain killers from the cabinet and swallow them down without water. I chuckle at the memory of Jules seeing me do that for the first time. He was absolutely horrified that any dignified human being would take any kind of tablet without drinking water with it. I would have agreed with him, except it was more fun to rile him up not taking them with water after that and I just got used to doing it.

Jules. I need to stop thinking about him, but I can't, the memories follow me constantly and the pain that follows the joy is immense.

I step into the shower stall and turn the hot water on as hot as I can stand it. I don't know what I'm hoping it will do for me. Am I hoping it burns off the memories that hurt so much I can barely breathe afterwards or fix the ache in my head and neck. Who knows?

I don't think it can fix the ache in my heart and that's what I really want.

I don't know how long I stay under the warmth of the water, I know it's longer than I should. I also know, I don't care. I was half expecting Caleb to come banging on the door to hurry me up, but he hasn't, so maybe it hasn't been so long after all.

I turn off the water, step out and dry myself with the towels that Jules picked out. That's when I realise that everything I see around here is going to have a memory of Jules attached to it. I don't know if I can bring myself to get rid of everything that he's had a hand in, but I decide I'm going to have to get rid of some of the everyday things otherwise I'm going to drive myself insane with the memories.

I walk from the bathroom into my room to get dressed. Jeans with a t-shirt and socks with runners on my feet. If my brother wants anything more today, then he's asking the wrong person for help.

"Come on then, let's get over to Vines and get done whatever you need done. I've got other stuff to do today that doesn't involve you." I grumble at him as I walk by him to the door ready to leave. "If you want my help little brother you better move it or I'm going back to bed."

"Alone?" He asks from right behind me and I jump because I didn't hear him move.

"Of course alone! Who the hell else do you think is here?" It's not like I've had a parade of women staying here since I moved into the house I built on the Drake Wines property. The only one who has stayed here regularly is Jules and well, that isn't happening tonight or any night soon I imagine.

"Just thought Jules would be over, that's all."

"No." I say sharply. Sharper than Caleb deserves. "He won't be around much anymore." I say brusquely, trying to move off the subject.

"Well, that's a shame, I really like Julian."

"Me too." I mumble to myself and then a little louder I say to Caleb, "Yes, most people do like him. Come on move it or I'm seriously going back to bed."

We get to the tastings room at Vines and get to work. The physical labour and movement helps me to stop thinking about Jules, I just move, no thinking involved really. It also clears the alcohol fog in my head so that when we sit down to eat the lunch that Leila brings out for us, I can't help but see the sparks between her and my little brother. They both seem to be ignoring it so I'm happy, for now, to let it be. I've got enough of my own relationship dramas but I might have a quiet word to Caleb about the dangers of getting involved with someone we employ before he decides to act on what appears to be some weird but innocent flirtations for now.

"So, are we going to talk about the dream that woke you up, that caused you to scream out Jules' name this morning?" Caleb asks, bringing me out of my thoughts.

"Are we going to talk about what's going on between you and Leila?" I fire back at him.

He scowls at me. "There's nothing to talk about."

"That's what I thought. Keep it that way, we can't afford to lose Leila."

"Geez thanks for the overwhelming belief in me big brother." His voice is dripping with sarcasm but I don't have it in me to fight with him today.

"If it makes you feel any better, we don't want to lose you either." I tease him with a grin.

"Nice to know." He grumbles, barely looking up from his food.

That's how we spend the rest of our lunch together. In silence. Then we part ways, with him heading to one of the cottages on the property and me back to my house.

The house I built with every intention of Jules and I making it our home. God damn it! I need more whiskey and more sleep, I can feel my head starting to pound at my temples and the only thing I want is my bed and some peace and quiet.

Why is it I never seem to get what I want?

Chapter Four
JULES

Part of me is tempted to call Logan after I spoke to Kenna on Friday, but I just can't bring myself to tap the call button on my screen. Instead I sit on the edge of the bed in my hotel room and stare at the picture looking back at me, wondering if I'll ever be someone that he can talk about or whether I'll always be his secret lover.

I'm even more convinced that Makenna knows what's going on, but wants Logan to say something. Why? I don't know. If she wants to know what's going on, why can't *she* ask *him*? Maybe that's just me wanting someone to say *something*, to get this whole thing out in the open?

Instead I'm sitting here, in a fluffy white robe that is a poor substitute for a set of strong, tattooed arms, on the edge of my bed in a hotel room. There's so much baggage that I don't even know how we can possibly unpack it anymore. I know he said he loves me and I don't doubt that for one second, but I don't know if I can keep doing this. I keep falling for him, over and over again. I give him time to get everything sorted and to tell those that mean the most to him about us, but he never takes that step.

What scares me the most is, I don't know who I am *without* Logan Drake.

It breaks my heart to think that leaving Logan also means that I leave Makenna, Brady and Caleb, because they've become like family to me, but I can't see them anymore. It will break my heart every time I see them and he's not with me *or* if I see them and he's *with* them, it will break me even more. If I had to watch him with someone else it would kill me. Which means I have to walk away from all the Drakes and those who are connected to them. Which hurts like hell, but I won't be able to stop myself from asking how he is.

"Argghhhh!!" I scream out in frustration as I fling myself back on to the bed, staring at the ceiling.

"Everything OK Jules?"

"Holy crap!" I sit upright, resting my hand over my heart. "Fuck me Gavin! How long have you been standing there?"

"No thanks, you're not my type. Also, I'm not sure my wife would forgive me." He says with a smirk, until he sees that I'm not smiling. "I just got back." He says quietly.

"What are you doing in my room?" I can't remember giving him permission or a key to get in here, then again my mind hasn't been completely focused this week.

"We're sharing a room. Remember?" He gives me a weird look as he walks by me to get to the other bed in the room and sits down on it.

How the hell did I forget that the hotel overbooked themselves, and asked us to share a room for the last week of our stay. My brain just isn't functioning correctly the last week or so.

"Yes, of course!" I stop speaking, because I have no damned clue what to say next and we both know it.

"Are you sure you're OK Julian?" When I don't answer him, he continues. "You know, you can always talk to me, no matter what."

"Thanks." I don't know what else to say to the man. We're friends at work, but we've never really been social outside of that. "Why did you come back so early?"

He shrugs his shoulders. "I figured you could do with a friend."

"You didn't need to cut your night short for me Gavin, I can look after myself."

"We're all capable of looking after ourselves Julian." I raise an eyebrow at him because we know plenty of people that we work with that aren't capable of any such thing and he knows it. He laughs at me but continues speaking. "You're right, we know a few useless people that can't, but you *can*. That doesn't mean you should *have* to though." He sighs and when I don't say anything, he keeps talking. "Look, I kind of know what you're going through." This one sentence makes me snort, which earns *me* a raised eyebrow this time. "Just because I'm straight doesn't mean I don't get it Julian." The sadness in his eyes makes me regret disrespecting his feelings.

"You're right, I'm sorry." He nods at my apology.

"You only know Jilly and I together. Married with kids. Before all the domestic bliss I wasn't a good guy."

"I find that hard to believe." I interrupt him with another snort.

"Shut up and let me finish would you?" I nod and wave my hand for him to keep going. "I was a bit of douchebag back in the day and I treated girls, women like they were a simple means to an end. Jilly was no different." He snorts derisively and shakes his head. "That's not true actually. She was *always* different and I think I knew that from the day we met. I treated her worse than any other woman I'd ever been with. To this day I'm not sure why she hung on for as long as she did before she booted my arrogant arse to the curb." He shakes his head in disbelief.

"She stayed because she loved you and could see the man you had the potential to be Gavin." I tell him honestly.

"I don't know how but you're right, she did. Even when I wouldn't tell people we were dating and we'd agreed, between the two of us that we were exclusive. I still had numbers in my phone and other women, not exactly throwing themselves at me but they had expectations, if you know what I mean. I had definitely been free with certain affections prior to meeting Jilly." I raise an eyebrow at *him* this time and he chuckles dryly. "Yeah OK, I'll admit I was what people like to call a manwhore. I was away from home for the first time and at University with freedoms I'd never had before. Then I met Jilly and I knew everything had changed. I just couldn't admit it to myself and I didn't think it was possible for her to feel the same way about me, so I made it easy for her to walk away. Only she didn't, not until I screwed up so badly that she just couldn't see a way to make me see that I was worth it."

"You mean, she forgave you for whatever it was but she left because of *you*?"

He nods. "I was caught in another girls room and it looked like we were up to no good, at least that's what she wanted everyone, especially Jilly, to believe. The truth is we were studying. Jilly believed me, even when most people didn't. She didn't dump my sorry arse without a backwards glance because of a rumoured infidelity. No she dumped me because my first course of action when she asked me what happened was to tell her that if she believed what everyone else was saying then she could go to hell and that I might as well have had sex with the other girl. I'm sure Jilly could recite the exact words I spewed at her that day but effectively I said I'd wished I'd slept with her so that at least when she left me for a rumour she could feel justified and I'd feel better about it. Pretty sure I also reminded her what I was and that she knew what she was getting into when she agreed to be my girlfriend. So, basically I told her it was her own fault."

"Jesus Gavin!" I close my eyes and shake my head. I can't connect the Gavin I know now to the picture he's painting of the younger version of him. "You idiot! How did you get her back?"

"By pure accident." He laughs but it has no humour in it. "About six months later we ran into each other completely by chance. In the weeks after she walked away, I tried to accidently bump into her around campus but I never found her. In retrospect I think she was just as determined to *not* 'bump' into me. School was pretty much done for me and I was feeling pretty sorry for myself because I couldn't find Jilly anywhere. I knew we'd both graduate and go our separate ways and I had missed without a doubt, the chance to be with the love of my life." He takes a deep breath and then continues, a small smile spreading across his lips as he remembers their chance meeting. "I was grabbing a coffee, taking some time to myself before meeting up with some friends. I'd ditched all my old group and hadn't been on a date or anything else in the time since Jilly and I had first gotten together. I could have easily blamed the crowd I'd been hanging out with for being bad influences but I had to take responsibility for my own behaviour, so I did. I picked up the coffee that I'd ordered and sat in a seat at a table for two near the window when someone slipped into the seat opposite me without asking or waiting for an invitation. I knew it was a female because of the floral and vanilla scent that followed her and the flowy dress that floated under the table as she sat down. I took a deep breath before looking up to tell the woman that I wasn't interested, only to look into the eyes that haunted my dreams. We hung out that day at the coffee shop, buying a second and maybe even a third cup and some snacks to go with them. I called my friend in front of her to let him know that I'd catch up with him later or the next day. We talked about everything and nothing."

"So, she forgave you?"

"She did, but she'd already done that months prior. It wasn't about forgiveness for her, it was more about me making a choice. I was young and stupid, it took her walking away for me to realise what I was missing."

"We all do stupid shit when we're young Gavin, but I'm glad it worked out well for you guys."

"Yeah we do, but sometimes we do stupid things as adults too. I think it can work out for you guys too, Julian."

I let out a dry laugh of my own at his statement. "We do and like Jilly, I've forgiven him, multiple times unfortunately, the rest is up to him. I can't keep putting myself in second place any more Gavin. It hurts to leave, because I'm not just walking away from him, I'm walking away from his family as well, but I can't live that way anymore. He hasn't accepted himself, so how can he accept me? Or *us*?"

"Maybe he needs the time apart to realise what he's missing Julian?" Gavin says quietly.

"I know he loves me Gavin. I know he's hurting as much as I am, I have no doubt about that. He is, was, my future, I couldn't see anyone else in it. I still can't if I'm being honest, and I truly hope he can find himself somewhere along the way, but I've tried for years and I can't do it anymore. There has to be a line drawn somewhere, doesn't there?" I ask hopefully.

"Perhaps you're right." He replies sadly. "It took for Jilly to draw that line and walk away, for me to wake up and realise what I'd done. Maybe you need to give Logan that time as well? Men can be pretty stupid when it comes to love, Julian." His name on Gavin's lips almost kills me. I managed to get through this entire conversation *not* saying it and hearing it actually physically hurts. Making me wince.

"He's had plenty of time." I say firmly, hoping to convince Gavin as well as myself that this is for the best.

"You know, you don't have to cut everyone off. You can still have a relationship with his siblings. Surely they want that too if you're as close as you say you are?"

"I could and I would love to, but it would hurt too much to see them. I wouldn't want them to have to censor themselves and what they talk about, but I also wouldn't want to hear about him. I don't want to know when he moves on and I'm nothing but a memory." I shake my head vigorously. "No,

I need a clean break. No Drakes, otherwise, I'll be tempted to ask about him and they'll want to talk about him because they're all close. They rarely go a day without seeing or talking to each other. Their lives are intertwined and it would be hell for all of us. Nope, I can't do it to them or myself."

"Fair enough." He nods sombrely at me. "Just promise me that you'll keep the possibilities open, OK? You never know what the future will bring, and I think we both know that you two love each other enough for this to work out."

"Maybe." Is all I manage in response, because I can't trust myself to speak.

"Relationships don't come without their obstacles Julian. No-one is perfect, not even you." He says with a low chuckle and I roll my eyes at his joke. People at work call me a perfectionist, it isn't untrue but still, not fair right now. "I know this is a big obstacle and I'm not telling you that you should compromise on this one, or that you shouldn't look after yourself and your own feelings. I'm just saying, don't close the door, leave it open just a little because I think you'll regret it if you slam that door closed without looking back."

"Enough with the door metaphor, I get it." I sigh. " I promise I'll give it time, but I'm not waiting forever. I have to live my life otherwise, well I guess I turn into an old spinster."

"You. An old spinster? I doubt that very much Julian, very much indeed." He laughs, this time it's filled with humour. "I haven't seen too many people who love each other the way you two do. I hope it works out, for both of your sakes."

"Thanks." I say quietly.

"Right, well I'm gonna go have a shower. Then I'm going to message my beautiful wife." He gathers all of his things that he needs to take to the bathroom before adding, "How about we get an early start tomorrow and hopefully we can be done with the job by the end of the day and get home early?"

"Yeah, sure." I say, I can hear the lack of enthusiasm about actually getting a job done early, where usually I'm the one pushing everyone to work harder and faster so that we can get home. This time I have no good reason to get home. I have no-one to get home to.

Gavin doesn't say another word about it, he simply disappears into the bathroom, closing the door behind him. I throw myself back onto the mattress and stare at the ceiling for a few minutes, before I grab my pyjamas because I'm sharing a room with another *guy*, how did I forget that? So, I need to actually wear something to bed, because he's not my lover and he'd probably not be interested in seeing my naked butt hanging out of the bed in the morning. Mainly because he's married. To a woman, making him not gay.

I drop the robe after pulling up my pants and throw on a t-shirt to cover up the top half of me. I crawl into the bed that feels big and lonely. Exhausted from the day and the two emotional conversations, I decide that Gavin's right. If we get an early start tomorrow, maybe we can head home early and everyone will be happy. Well, everyone but me, but that's OK.

I close my eyes and fall asleep before Gavin finishes his shower. At least I don't hear him finish and go to bed. I'm too busy dreaming about the sexiest pair of grey green eyes staring right into my soul and taking my heart with them. I am *so* screwed.

Chapter Five
LOGAN

When I get back to my place, I breathe a sigh of relief because I'm finally alone in my misery again. I grab a couple more pain killers and a drink of water, before collapsing back onto my bed. Breathing in and out slowly, with my arm crossed over my eyes in the dark room, taking the time to just relax. I also have time to think. I don't want to think because every time I do, I think about him. About *us* and I have to admit that to myself, I miss *us*.

I want more whiskey to drown it all out, but I know I can't. Well, not can't, I *shouldn't, that's* for sure, because if I know my siblings as well as I think I do, one of them will be here shortly to check in on me. Seeing as I was just with Caleb, I'm going with Makenna just happening to drop on in. At that thought, I push out a rough grunt that borders on a laugh. A laugh that's mocking me because I don't feel the slightest bit amused at my current situation!

Fuck! It's just hit me just how badly I've screwed up. I knew I did all those days ago when he walked out, but now?

I miss everything about Jules, about us together. I made a promise the day he left, a promise to myself and to Jules and I don't intend on forgetting it or going back on it. Before I actually make some progress on that promise though, I need to get rid of this throbbing headache. My head isn't the only thing throbbing though, get your dirty mind out of the gutter, I meant my heart. Although my dick is throbbing too because I'm thinking about Jules. It always does. I'm always ready for him, in every damned way.

"Hey, Logan. Are you home?" I hear Brady's voice yell out and I groan. "Dude, are you OK?" He asks the one question I don't have an answer for.

"Mmmmmm." I ground out, not moving from my position on the bed for a minute. When I drag my arm from my face and crack open an eye, I see the shape of a person standing in the doorway.

"Come on, hopefully you've slept off your hangover because I'm here to drag you up to the house for dinner." His announcement makes me groan louder.

"But I don't *want* to join you guys for dinner Brady." I know how I sound. I can hear the whine in my voice and as much as I hate it, I hate the idea of eating a meal with my sister and brother in law even more. Don't get me wrong, I love them both dearly and Brady is more like a brother than an in law but still. That doesn't mean I feel like being around other people.

"I know you don't, bro, but if I don't return to that house with you in tow, my wife isn't going to be happy and well, we can do this the easy way or the hard way. You know your sister, she'll come down here and get you up there one way or another. I offered to come and get you because I figured I would be, let's say, more gentle with you."

"Brady." Is all I manage to get out before he cuts me off.

"You know, you didn't help yourself this morning. When she saw the state you were in after drinking yourself into oblivion again, she decided that you were coming for dinner whether you liked it or not. You're better off just doing what she wants, you know that better than anyone. You don't want her to come down here and see you asleep late in the afternoon."

"Urghhh." I grunt in agreement, not really able to form the words yet.

"Your behaviour the past week and a bit haven't helped either." He's not wrong.

"Fine. Just give me a few seconds to wake up before you expect me to go up to the house, OK?" I ask him just as his phone beeps with a message. I can tell by the grin that spreads across his face that it's my sister. Damn, they're so in love, it almost fucking hurts. I'm happy for them, obviously, but that kind of love hurts me right now.

"Speaking of my gorgeous wife, that was a message from Kenna. She said, and I quote, *'tell that grumpy arsehole to move his butt before I come down there and drag him up here myself'.*" He throws his head back and laughs. A genuinely happy laugh.

"Tell her I'll be there, I just need a few minutes."

"Seconds or minutes?"

"What?" I ask him confused.

"Well, the first time you said you needed a few seconds but just now you said you needed a few minutes. Make up your mind and I'll tell her your answer." The arsehole says, smiling broadly.

"Minutes. I need a couple of minutes Brady." I actually think I need more like a couple of hours, or even days, to prepare myself for this dinner. I don't know if I can ever be totally prepared for this meal with my sister. "Just let me go to the bathroom and clean up a bit, OK?"

"Sure, I'll go wait on the couch but if you take too long, I'm coming back in here to drag your sorry arse up to the house, OK?"

"Got it." He nods his head as he wanders out of my room and I move my 'sorry arse' into the bathroom. I stand at the vanity, the shock of everything that's happened hits me again. Everything here reminds me of Jules and it's driving me to the brink of insanity. Ignoring all of it, I use the toilet, wash my hands, and splash cold water on my face to wake myself up. I look in the mirror again, and I find the same man staring back at me as I did this morning. Sad and miserable with dark circles under his eyes, proving how little sleep he's gotten since his life got turned upside down.

"You ready yet Logan?" Brady yells out, *way* louder than necessary, because obviously I've taken longer than I should have.

I sigh, deciding I might as well get this shitshow over with.

"Yeah, I'm coming." I mumble as I walk out of my bedroom and into the living room only to hear Brady mumble, "That's what she said." I can't help rolling my eyes at his juvenile behaviour. I know he's not that much younger than me and everyone's allowed to have some fun but damn if he and Caleb aren't on the same maturity level some days. "That's my sister you're referring to douchebag, so cut it the fuck out."

"That's *not* what she says." He retorts as he stands up, so I punch him on the arm, he frowns at me. "What the fuck man? What was that for?"

"Don't talk about Makenna like that. If she heard you, you'd be hurting more than that right now and you know it idiot." I warn him with a raised eyebrow.

"Yeah, maybe, but Kenna has a sense of fucking humour unlike *you* at the moment." He grumbles while rubbing his arm.

"Stop being a baby, I didn't hit you that hard." I say to him with another roll of my eyes, while slapping him on the back of his shoulder and pushing him towards the door.

"Still hurt though." He mumbles as I lock my door. I laugh for the first time in a week. "Glad my pain makes you laugh arsehole." Brady grumbles, making me laugh again.

"Thanks for the first laugh I've had in a while bro." I say, wrapping an arm around his shoulder, as we walk towards the house he shares with my sister.

"Well, when you put it like that, I guess you're welcome." A smile is back on his face, as he jams his hands in his pockets.

For the first time in what feels like forever I'm actually almost happy. That is until we walk in the front door of the main house and I see not just my sister in the kitchen waiting for me but our little brother as well.

"Sorry man, but I was just in charge of getting you here." Brady says quietly, ducking out from under my arm, to walk over to kiss his wife because god forbid they're not joined at the lips or hips.

"Thank you for joining us this evening, Logan." Makenna says with a smile as Brady wraps his body around her from behind. Can't they keep their hands off each other? I really am a douchebag, I should just let them be happy, they are still technically newlyweds after all. Just because I'm a miserable bastard doesn't mean everyone else should be or that I should make them suffer alongside me.

"Like I had a choice Makenna." I say with a scowl directed her way.

"Ohhhh you got full named Kenna, you're in trouble." Caleb teases, so I send a look that could kill his way for good measure but the prick just laughs at me. "You think you're scary? I've seen you angry before Logan, this isn't it." He says with a snort of laughter and Brady laughs with him. Who needs enemies when you've got brothers like these two?

"Whatever. What's for dinner Makenna?" I ask, turning my attention away from my annoying little brothers.

"You've had a choice for well over a week now Logan. You chose to stay in your cave and I decided to drag you away from the whiskey bottle, dark house and pizza. You need a real meal, with company, outside of your place and without the whiskey."

"A real meal? Who the hell's cooking tonight then? Have you got Leila hidden back there somewhere?" I ask, teasing my little sister, because we all know she's not as talented in the kitchen as she'd like to think she is.

"Hey, that's enough Logan. Just because you're grumpier than your normal grumpy self, that doesn't mean you get to take it out on Makenna." Brady jumps to my sister's defence, proving why he was welcomed with open arms into the family. He defends her every single time.

"Hey, you didn't defend me when he was picking on me!" Caleb scowls at Brady.

"You can look after yourself Caleb." Brady glares at him and before Caleb can come back at him Makenna spins in his arms to pin him with a look that would kill a lesser man.

"I can look after myself too Brady Harris. I've been doing it against these two for longer than we've known each other." She glares at him.

"I know you can baby but when I'm around, you'll never have to." He reassures her and then kisses her. It's a kiss that as her brothers we *never* should have to witness.

"Alright, that's enough, if we're here to argue and fight, I'm heading back to the quiet of my place." I turn around to head towards the door. Before I can get more than half a step away, Makenna is by my side, her hand on my arm.

"You're not going anywhere and you're not using our normal behaviour to get away either." Then quieter, so that just the two of us can hear it, she says, "Please Logan. Let us take care of you for a change." How can I refuse her?

"Sure." I say quietly to her, then I turn around and head towards the table to sit down. "Fine, I'll stay but you need to let me have at least one damned glass of whiskey to get through this night Kenna." This earns me a laugh as she grabs a glass and Brady pours me a drink of whiskey over ice and brings it over.

"Here you go Sunshine, enjoy it because it's your only one while you're here tonight. You're not getting blind drunk again tonight, not here anyway, because I don't feel like carrying your arse home, nor do I feel like dragging you into a spare bedroom."

"I don't want you carrying or dragging me anywhere either but thanks for the offer Brady."

Just like that, the evening carries on as if it were any other. Except for the fact that Makenna dishes up all my favourites and Caleb doesn't make one complaint about how he's always the forgotten one.

I'm surprised when a nice juicy steak with prawns in a creamy garlic butter sauce poured over the top, with garlic rosemary potatoes and a salad on the side is placed in front of me. I'm even more surprised when Caleb thanks Kenna for dinner and then just tucks in, never offering up a complaint, because I know for a fact that he doesn't enjoy mixing his seafood with his steak. I don't ask any questions though, I don't care to know why he's so agreeable tonight. Instead, I eat my meal while listening to the conversation going on around me, adding a few words here and there, but pretty much keeping quiet. When we're finished, I go to help clear off the table, I get told to sit back down, while Caleb and Brady take care of them. That's when the first niggle of warning happens but I don't listen to it because I'm an idiot. I always listen to that voice in business and I usually do in these situations as well. This just proves that I'm off my game.

"Thanks for dinner Makenna." I say, because I can't stand the quiet in the room any longer or the fact that she's just sitting there looking at me. Waiting. For what I have no fucking idea.

"You're welcome Logan. Thank you for finally agreeing to join us." She says with a smirk and I decide it's just not worth bringing up the fact that really, I had no damned choice.

The next not so subtle hint that something is about to hit me comes in the form of dessert. I should have known something big was coming when Caleb and Brady walked out of the kitchen with four rather large slices of my favourite, lemon meringue pie. Still, I didn't put all the puzzle pieces together because I enjoyed my dessert without complaint.

My final hint hit more like a sledgehammer when Makenna put her spoon down, took a drink of her wine and took a deep breath before speaking in a passionate and intense voice.

"Logan, we need to talk."

"No, no we don't." I argue.

God fucking damn it! I should have known better than to believe that my family were all sitting here, for no real reason, no special occasion but for an impromptu meal, that this wasn't going to end well. For me at least.

I take a deep breath, before slowly releasing it, then I say. "Makenna, whatever it is you *think* we need to talk about, we really don't. I know I haven't been myself recently, but I'm back on track. No more pass out drunken nights, I promise and I haven't let anything slip at work. You know I would never let you guys down. So, therefore, there's nothing to talk about little sis, we're all good." I smile, well I hope it's more of a smile than the grimace that it feels like. I'm trying to convince them and quite possibly myself, that everything is fine. Everything *is* fine, but I can see, as I look around the faces at the table, that none of them believe me.

Fuck it! I screwed up again.

Chapter Six
LOGAN

"**E**verything is *not good* Logan." Makenna says sternly.

"Everything is perfectly *fine*, Makenna." I reply just as sternly, but then I soften because I know she's coming from a place of love. "I promise you, I'm OK. We all lose friendships Kenna. We all lose people from our lives, we understand that better than most." I say quietly, almost tripping over classing what Jules and I had as friendship. It was so much more than that, I think to myself, closing my eyes to swallow the pain.

My eyes spring open when I feel the light touch of Kenna's hand on mine. I didn't even notice her move to sit next to me. "Logan, we both know that's not the case." She looks around the table at our brother and her husband. "In fact, everyone sitting at this table knows that's not the truth. You're hurting Logan, and I don't like seeing you in so much pain." I look to the others and they're both nodding their agreement.

"I'm not in pain, Makenna." I grimace inwardly as I say the words, until I hear a snort from either end of the dining table, I suspect my pain is written all over my face as I let out a growl that sounds like a wounded animal.

"You are Logan and we just want to help you." Caleb says from on my other side. I don't know when he moved to sit there either.

"You don't need to help me. No." I hold up my hand to stop anyone from talking. "Let me rephrase. There isn't anything you guys can help me with, this is something I have to deal with on my own. I'm the one who has to learn to live without my friend." I swallow deeply, almost choking it out. "My best friend."

"Are you sure that's all you've lost, Logan?" Makenna asks me in a whisper that's barely loud enough for me to hear.

"No." I return, just as quietly, hoping that she doesn't hear me because my emotions are threatening to come to the surface and bubble over. Sensing my looming emotional breakdown, Kenna launches herself out of her chair and envelops me in a tight hug. She's always been able to tell when my emotions get the better of me, no matter how rare they are, especially in the last few years.

"You don't always have to be the strong one Lo, you're allowed to lean on us you know. It goes both ways." She murmurs in my ear and I can't help squeezing her tight in a hug of my own.

"I love him, Kenna." Her sharp intake of breath makes me try to pull away and quickly decide how to cover my tracks. " I mean, you know."

Kenna leans slightly out of our embrace, grips my face in her hands and says, "Don't you dare Logan Patrick Drake. Don't you dare take that back."

"You're shocked." I state plainly.

"My shock is at you finally admitting it, not because of what you said Logan."

"What did he say?" Caleb asks.

I look at Kenna, needing any kind of reassurance that I can find, then not taking her eyes off mine she says, "Tell them, I think you're going to be surprised."

"Jules isn't just my best friend, he's my lover and more than that, I'm in love with him." Caleb and Brady move from their chairs, enveloping Kenna and myself in a massive group bear hug.

"Thank fuck for that." Brady mutters.

"We know, but it's so damned nice to hear you say it. That's awesome dude, congratulations." Caleb says.

"That's it? That's all you've got to say? We know and congratulations. Seriously?" My disbelief obvious.

Caleb looks at me, confused. "What else did you want us to say? We've known for years that you and Jules were together." He says it in such an offhanded way that it makes me angry and I know my anger isn't directed at the right person, he's just the one on the receiving end of it.

"Then why the *fuck* haven't you ever *said* anything?" I ask, frustrated as hell that my family decided to just let me go on believing they didn't know Jules and I were together.

"I didn't think I had to. I never had to say anything to Brady and Kenna." He looks at our sister and brother in law, his confusion is evident by the look on his face. "They were just together. Same as you and Jules. We all just accepted it."

"You mean you three knew about us, and you've just recently picked up on it, right?" I ask, gasping to pull some oxygen into my lungs.

"Geezus Logan, you never had to 'come out ' or make an announcement. Ever. The only thing you had to do was bring a guy home and introduce him as your boyfriend. Do you think we're stupid?" Kenna asks me while shaking her head. "Did you think that we wouldn't love you anymore because of who you love?" The hurt lacing her voice almost kills me.

"I guess. I don't know, Kenna." I tell her, shaking my head confused.

"Geez, thanks for the vote of confidence Logan. It's nice to hear you think so much of us, your *family*. You know, the people who love you *unconditionally* and forever." Kenna huffs, crossing her arms over her chest.

She moves away from where I'm sitting and Brady wraps her in his arms, kissing the top of her head before he says, "Give him a break baby. He thinks he's been in the closet all his life. It's not his fault he's behind the eight ball with this one. He thinks it's a revelation, when we've known for years." This just causes my sister to huff again, the scowl on her face deepening.

"Mum and Dad were always expecting you to tell them you were together every time he came to the house for dinner, but he was always with you as a friend. Then, when dinner was over, you guys would leave together, and they hoped that the next one would be the one where you told them." Caleb tells me.

"You mean they knew?" I ask, shocked? I wish they were still here so that we could talk things through.

"Oh big brother, did you really think you hid yourself from us?" Caleb laughs with only a small amount humour. "Let me tell you, you didn't. You and Kenna liked a *lot* of the same rock stars and celebrities growing up. You tried to hide it and call it hero worship, or some kind of bullshit like that, but we all knew the truth Lo. We thought you knew that too." Cal laughs again, but it's laced with sadness now too.

"Why didn't one of you or our parents *say* something? I would have welcomed, no I would have *loved* to have had that conversation with Mum and Dad while they were still here. Geezus, I would have loved to have had this conversation long before now with *you* guys as well." I sigh, rubbing my hands down my face, muttering, "Could have saved me from some heartache if we had."

"No, you don't get to blame us for your mistakes Logan. You did this, *you* imploded your relationship with Jules, not us. We welcomed that man with open arms." Kenna yells at me, and I can't say I don't deserve her anger. She's one hundred percent right, and I know it.

Before I can respond, Caleb adds in his two cents worth, Brady not too far behind him. "Never thought it was a secret bro. I didn't have to announce I was straight. Did you Braids?"

"Nope. Just bought my girl home, introduced her as my girlfriend and that was that." He answers with a shrug.

"Kenna? Did you have to announce that you were straight?" Caleb asks her.

Kenna's doesn't answer right away. It's not like her to be so quiet, and not have an answer or opinion on something. Especially something as personal as this. "No I didn't." She says quietly.

"Hey, are you ok baby?" Brady asks her, holding her close. She shakes her head, but doesn't speak.

"What's the matter Kenna?" I ask her, expecting her to tell me how mad she is at me, but her answer hurts more than her being mad ever could.

"Nothing. It doesn't matter."

"Baby. Just tell him, get it all off your chest. Now is the time to let it all out." Brady advises her and I hate that I've caused my beautiful sister to think that she can't talk to me honestly. I flinch at the thought, because isn't that exactly what I've been doing, holding back part of myself from them?

"Brady's right Kenna, get it all out here and now. What do you need to tell me?" I ask, not really sure I want to hear it.

"I hate that you've tortured yourself over this for so long Logan, and I'm just so mad with you." She cries, her pain is so damned obvious to me that it slices me like a damned knife to my heart.

"Mad?" I cringe, knowing that I'm in for an earful from my sister and I know that everything she says, she's going to be right about too. That hurts more than she'll ever know.

"Yeah. Raging fucking mad actually." Her entire body is vibrating with anger and Brady is still standing behind his wife, gripping onto her shoulders, trying to calm her down or keep her grounded, I'm not sure. "In fact, for the first time in our lives I think I actually hate you right now." I open my mouth to speak but Kenna rushes on. "How many people have you hurt with this? Hmm? Shall we count them? Mum, Dad, me, Brady, Caleb and last but not least Julian. How dare you do this to him? I can only imagine how hurt he is right now. You better fix this and if he doesn't let you, it's your own stupid fault." Her face is red and her cheeks wet from her tears of frustration, she turns and buries her face in Brady's chest.

"She's right Logan." Caleb says quietly. "I respect and admire you for everything else you've done in your life brother, but this, you've caused so much pain that could have been avoided. Now me, I don't care. I've never needed you to make an announcement one way or the other, but to treat us like we're stupid and didn't know why Julian was staying at your place so often? Yeah that's hard to take man." He gets up from his chair, walks over to Kenna and Brady, bringing them both into a tight hug.

Our family has always been big on hugs, and when our parent's died, I didn't want that to change, so I made sure to hug my siblings as much as possible. The fact that I'm currently on the outside of a hug looking in, really hits me hard.

"I'm sorry." I say quietly, but I know they all heard me because they break apart to look at me not saying a thing. "I'm sorry OK?" My voice cracks on the OK, and I look away to gather myself. I don't want them to see me breakdown.

"Still trying to be strong for everyone else hey?" Makenna asks, seconds before she throws her arms around me, pulling me out of my chair and gathering me up in her arms, holding me tightly.

"I screwed up Kenna and I don't think I can get him back." A sob that I can't hold in, escapes me.

"Oh you can Logan, he loves you."

"What if that's not enough Kenna? What if he can't forgive me?"

"I have to believe he will Logan, because I see how much you love each other, and I want to see you *both* happy. Together." Her kind words hit my soul and I break. I let out a loud sob before I even realise that I'm actually crying. Sobbing on my little sister's shoulders and holding on so tight to her that I could almost break her, but when I make to move away from her, she holds me tighter. "No. You don't get out of this embrace until I tell you, you can. Logan you have to stop thinking that we're not capable or willing to support *you*. You've taken on so damned much since Mum and Dad died, but you don't have to do everything alone. We're a team you idiot. The four of us are. Well, the five of us once you win Julian back and then six when Caleb finds the love of his life too."

That declaration causes Caleb to snort, and we all let out a small laugh. Makenna still hasn't let me go, and within seconds we're engulfed by more arms.

"Group hug!" Brady yells out. "We love you brother and you never have to deal with things on your own. Ever."

"What he said." Caleb chimes in. "Seriously though Logan, you're not alone. I'm not a kid anymore, you don't need to protect me from the big bad world anymore. Like Kenna said, I know you took the weight of the world and our family on your shoulders when Mum and Dad died, but you don't have to do that anymore. We're all here for you brother, always."

"Thanks guys, but I still feel the need to be the head of the family and look after you all. It's what Dad would have wanted, what he would have expected. I need to be the man he expected me to be."

"That may be so, but that doesn't mean we can't realign those expectations Logan and even out that weight you carry. He would still be proud of the man you've become Logan. You *are* the man he expected you to be, but you're allowed to make improvements along the way." Makenna announces. "How about we make a deal right here and now, tonight? None of us and I mean *none* of us takes on the weight of this family on our own. We talk things through and make decisions together. Well, you know, not personal ones but ones that concern the family, as a whole."

"No-one takes on all of the responsibility, but that doesn't mean we're taking anything away from you Logan, it just means sharing the fucking load you stubborn bastard." Caleb says.

We all take a step back from the comfort of the embrace and look at one another.

"I'm with these two. You've been carrying this on your own for far too long Logan." Brady says.

Now I have three faces all looking at me expectantly, waiting for me to agree, but probably expecting me to fight them tooth and nail.

"OK." I say simply. I'm done fighting and I'm done taking on everything, for everyone, but seeing the shocked joy on their faces is definitely worth it.

"Really? It's that easy?" Kenna asks.

"Yeah." I say with a shrug of my shoulders. "Maybe you got me in a moment of weakness Kenna, but I'm tired. Exhausted in fact. Losing Jules, talking this out with you guys, and this hangover still trying to kick my arse, I'm done in sweetness." This admission causes Kenna to give me another bone crushing hug. I honestly didn't know my sister had that in her.

"So, we fixed the emotional exhaustion. We can fix the hangover and the lack of sleep easily enough." She pauses and Brady groans behind me like he knows what she's about to say and he doesn't approve. Caleb just shakes his head and I swear I hear him mutter, 'it's your funeral sis.' "Now we just have to fix you and Julian."

"No. No this is my mess to clean up Makenna. This isn't a group project, ok? Promise me Makenna. Seriously, look me in the eyes and *promise* me that you'll leave this alone. Please?" I'm not above begging her. Nor am I above demanding that she mind her own damned business. We might have had a bit of a lovefest here tonight, but I'm still the same grumpy bastard I've always been.

"*Are* you going to do something about it? You're not going to let him just walk away? You're going to fight for him, aren't you?"

"Yes Makenna, I'm going to work extremely hard to fix this."

"Promise?" She demands.

"I swear to you that I will do everything I can, in my own way and my own time, to sort things out with Jules." She stares me down until I say what she's waiting for. "Promise."

"Yes!" She squeals and jumps up and down with unbridled joy.

I can't let her down. I never have before.

I have to work out a way to get Jules to talk to me *and* take me back. Not just because I promised Makenna, but because I don't want to live without him in my life.

I need him. Now I just have to prove it to *him*.

Chapter Seven
JULES

Gavin had a breakthrough early Monday morning. Which means after finalising a few things over the next couple of days we end up heading home a few days earlier than expected. Any other trip, and I would have welcomed this kind of turn of events, because I would have had a few extra days with Logan. As it stands, I blame Gavin for my current predicament, because if he hadn't found the problem and had a solution for it in record time, I wouldn't be standing here talking to Makenna Drake. I wasn't supposed to be home for another couple of days, and right now, I'm wishing I was still out of town. The last thing I wanted to do was to run into Kenna on the footpath in front of my favourite bookstore, and I sure as hell didn't want to have *this* conversation, *ever*. Unless, of course, she chooses to not talk about her oldest brother.

"Look, Kenna, I don't know what you think is going on, but I can be almost one hundred percent positive it's *not* what you think."

"You and Logan both think we're all stupid *and* blind! I know *exactly* what's going on Julian. Don't you dare ever talk to me like that again." She warns me.

"Talk to you like what?" I ask, surprised by her outburst, not to mention I know for a fact that she has no idea what's going because Logan hasn't told a soul about us.

"He told me Jules. He told us." She says quietly. I can't help the shock that I know must be all over my face. I can't speak, but I don't need to because Kenna does. "I made Brady go and get him after one too many refusals from him to join us for dinner in favour of getting himself blind drunk so that he didn't have to think. He told us that he loves you Jules, that it's killing him not having you around. But I have to tell you something

49

Jules, he didn't have to tell us. Neither of you had to *tell* us anything. We knew. We all knew."

"You knew?" I ask, knowing my jaw must be almost grazing the concrete. "How? Who? Who do you mean when you say, 'all of us'?"

Kenna shakes her head and laughs dryly. "Come on, let's go sit down." I nod dumbly and follow her to an empty table and chairs. I drop myself into a chair and put the takeaway coffee that I'd forgotten I was actually carrying, down onto the table. "I can't believe you both have to ask the same stupid question. How could we *not* know? I think that's the question you should both be asking. Before you say anything, no it isn't *obvious* that either of you are gay, it's just obvious that you're in love with each other. All of us could see that and yes, I do mean my parents saw it too." I can't speak, my thoughts are a jumbled mess of questions that I can't put into words. I can't believe what she's telling me after all these years of thinking our relationship wasn't common knowledge that it really kind of was. "You were the only person he ever brought to the house. The only person invited to family dinners on Sunday's. The only one who stayed at the house. *You* were at his house more often than any of us and you guys had friends over a lot for dinners. How could you *not* think that we at least *suspected* what was going on between the two of you?" She asks with more kindness, than anger in her voice.

"The simple answer is, we thought we were clever and had it all under wraps." I say with a shrug of my shoulders, still not really being able to put my thoughts into any kind of order. "If you knew, why didn't you *say* something Kenna? You know Logan, you had to know that he wouldn't speak up because he didn't know how."

"Why would I? It's not like I ever had to say, '*hey everyone, I'm straight and this is my boyfriend Brady.*' So, explain to me *why* you two couldn't have just walked into Sunday dinner and said, '*hey, this is Jules, my boyfriend.*' I mean, I asked Logan the same question, but I'd love to hear your reasoning as well." She says, sounding exceptionally pissed and crossing her arms over her chest. Surely if either of us have the right to be pissed, it should be *me* right?

"I don't know." I say with a shrug of my shoulders. "I guess because it's just different for us. " Even I know it's a pathetic excuse, but it wasn't my choice not to tell the Drake's about our relationship, I can't give her the answer she wants, that she seems to need.

"By 'us' I'm going to assume you mean because you're gay and not because you're so special to the world." She asks full of attitude and I'm taken aback by just how angry she seems to be about the whole thing.

"I can't give you an answer for that either Kenna, and I don't know why you're so damned angry with me either. Your brother made his choices and even though I wasn't happy with them, I understood them. To a degree anyway."

"Then what happened? If you waited for all these years, why did you suddenly decide to walk away?"

Damn, how do I explain this to Kenna? How do I explain it when what I really want is for Logan to be explaining this to her, not me. Does she really want to know that I'm out to all my family and friends? That we could be a couple when we were with my family, even though we weren't around her family? Won't that just hurt her even more? So many questions, and I'm not sure how to answer them. I watched Kenna and Brady get married from the sidelines, that hurt so deeply that I don't think I ever truly got over it. In the end, I decide to go with honesty.

"I didn't want to be his dirty little secret anymore Kenna." I say, my voice barely above a whisper. "You're not wrong, I love your brother, with every part of me, but I just couldn't do it anymore Kenna. Watching from the sidelines, never being able to be with him when it mattered." My voice is rough with emotion. "He wasn't ready but that's the problem isn't it? How long am I supposed to wait until he *is* ready to admit who he really is? We're not in the 1950's anymore Kenna, we don't need to hide behind half-truths."

"Oh Jules, I'm so sorry you felt like his dirty secret." Kenna says gently, reaching across the table to rest her hand on mine. "You were never that to the rest of us, you've always been a part of our family and I doubt you were ever that to Logan either. He loves you. He's a wreck without you Jules. He misses you desperately."

"I miss him too."

"Then come back. Come and talk to him." Kenna begs me, her voice and face reflecting my own emotions.

"I can't Kenna." I whisper, breaking my own heart along with hers.

"Why?" Her voice a quiet whisper as well.

"Because he doesn't want me to." I look down at our hands, pulling mine out from under hers, I need to leave. I can't look at her and see my own pain reflected in her eyes anymore. "I have to go Kenna. Take care of yourself. Take care of Logan too, he's going to need it." I get up to leave and as I walk away, I've never felt so alone. Or, so absolutely miserable in all my life.

"But he does Jules." Kenna calls out to me as I walk away.

"No, he doesn't Kenna. He doesn't answer when I call or message anymore. Goodbye lovely." I say loud enough for her to hear me but without turning to look at her. I can't bear to see the hurt on her face anymore. I love Makenna, Brady and Caleb as if they're my own family but I can't do this anymore. Seeing any of them makes me think of Logan and the pain is just too much.

"I love you Jules. Logan loves you too." Kenna yells out.

"I love you and Logan too Kenna." I whisper but she can't hear me. I keep walking, I can feel the tears running down my face but I don't wipe them away. I don't want to, I need to let them fall. I need to let the pain out so that I can move on because that's what I need to do. I tried to call and message him earlier today but he didn't answer any of them. Logan and I are done and I need to come to terms with that.

I realise now after running into Kenna that I can't see any of them anymore either, and the pain is excruciating, making the tears fall faster than they had been. I pick up my pace in an effort to reach my apartment building, bypassing other residents without so much as acknowledging their existence, I make it into the sanctuary of my apartment. After locking the door behind me, I drop the bags in my hands to the floor, my keys and phone follow close behind. I walk over to my couch, sinking numbly into the cushions and that's when the misery hits me full force, making me a complete, blubbering mess.

I'm not sure how long I sit there staring blankly at the wall, letting the tears fall but it's dark now when it wasn't when I got home. All I know is that I needed to let them fall to let everything out, because I need to let it go to move on. I realise how heartless I sound because we were 'together' for years and it's only been a couple of weeks since I walked away. Still, I need to do this for my own sanity. I invested a lot of myself into our relationship but Logan wasn't invested in the same way. I'm not rushing out to find someone else, trust me, I don't need someone to fill the void. I've loved Logan Drake from almost the first time we met and he won't be easy to forget.

My phone vibrates across the floor, as The Great Escape by PINK! blares from its speakers. The same tune has been singing from the floor since just before the sky started to go dark. I know who it is and I don't want to answer it. He's only calling me back because Kenna told him we ran into one another.

Moving off the couch, I collect my keys, phone and the bags of food that I bought before I ran into Kenna. I dump them all on the kitchen bench, then I start putting the food away to distract me from my phone. Which starts skittering across the bench and PINK! sings about love again, I pick it up and fight the urge to throw it against the wall. Instead, I put it on silent and finish putting the food that looked so inviting not so long ago, away. The thought of eating anything makes me feel sick.

Without looking at the time, I take myself to the bathroom, strip off and step under the heated water to soak for a few minutes. When I'm finished washing myself I turn it all off, get dried, then without picking up my discarded clothes, or checking my phone, I turn off all the lights and take myself to bed. With any luck I can fall asleep and forget the pain for a while.

Chapter Eight
LOGAN

The morning after admitting the truth about my relationship to my family, I wake up before my alarm. I lie there thinking about all the time and energy I've wasted worrying about what they would say, instead of enjoying my life with Jules. The realisation that in worrying about what others *might* think, I've hurt the one person that matters the most to me, hurts my heart. I made Jules feel like *he* didn't matter to me and I did it for years, expecting him to be OK with it. When he finally couldn't take it anymore after trying to get me to understand, he left. I can't say I blame him.

I was grateful every day that Julian was with me and not someone else, but I never told him that. I never showed him how much he means to me. Not in the way that mattered the most, and I've never regretted something so much in my entire life. I'll carry that regret and guilt for the rest of my life.

Now, all I have to do is work out how to get the love of my life to believe that he means the world to me and get him to take me back. I won't give up on us being together, I will prove to him that he means everything to me and that from now on, no matter how dark or hard things get, I won't give up.

My alarm rings out from my phone, but it only lasts for a second before I've dismissed it. Throwing the covers off, I swing my legs over the edge off the bed and head to the bathroom. The sight of the few things of Julian's still scattered over the counter cause my heart to ache but this morning there's a difference. This morning I'm determined to find a way to get him back. I won't accept anything else, I need him in my life.

After showering, I dry myself off and get dressed in the dark blue, tight jeans Julian loves me in and his favourite, dark grey button down shirt. I smile as I lace up my boots and grab my keys. I'm pulling out the big guns to get him to take me back. It's not until I'm heading to my car and see Makenna walking towards me dressed in her work clothes that I realise that I'm supposed to be going to the office this morning. Too bad, this means more to me than business.

"Good morning Makenna." A smile spreading across my face as I speak.

"Good morning Logan." She says, returning my smile. "You look a lot happier this morning and can I assume by your attire that you're not planning on heading to the office this morning?" She looks me up and down, taking in the way I'm dressed with a twinkle in her eyes, her smile growing bigger, like she can take an educated guess as to where I am actually headed.

"No, I've decided to take a day off, if that's OK? I know it's short notice, but I have somewhere I need to be." I smile at my sister, as she smiles broadly back at me. "And I'm sure everyone will be happy to have a day off from my grumpiness." I know I've been a grumpy bastard, worse than usual, but I think that will be in the past if today goes to plan.

"I'd love to tell you to go for it, but I can't Logan." She says with a sad frown.

"Why not? It's not like I ever take time off Makenna, I'm always around here, this place has taken top priority in my life."

"I know Logan, but today is different." I interrupt her.

"The winery has cost me a lot Makenna. Aren't you the one who told me last night that I had to go for it and make amends with Jules? What happened to that Makenna? Where's my sister who begged me to take the time to be happy?" My anger clear in the tone of my voice, and if the wince that pains her face is anything to go by, it's definitely unmistakable.

"I know what I said last night Logan, and I still mean every word this morning. If I could change the two meetings I need you in today, I would but I need you this morning and I can't step in for the one you have this afternoon. I'm sorry Logan." I can see the regret on her face and while I know she's right and I can't skip out of these meetings, I'm angry that once again my life has to be put on hold for Drake Wines.

"But I have plans Makenna." I growl, frowning at her. I know I'm behaving like an arsehole and while I see her face soften, her voice takes on a hard edge to it when she replies.

"I know you do and any other day I wouldn't stand in your way." When she puts her hands on her hips and scowls at me, I know she's about to unleash some harsh words on me. "I'm sorry our little family business is too much *hassle* for you right now."

"That's not what I said Kenna." I say, trying to placate her but I don't get too far.

"Isn't it though?" Obviously, that wasn't a question she wanted an answer to because she keeps talking without giving me the chance to speak. "I know you have more pressing personal matters that you need to attend Logan but this *business* pays all of our bills, not just yours. While I understand that your relationship with Jules is very important, so is keeping the rest of us afloat."

"I know that Kenna and I didn't mean that I wouldn't go to the meetings, I just meant." She doesn't let me finish again and if she doesn't stop interrupting me I'm going to lose my fucking patience.

"I *know* what you meant Logan Drake but you're coming with me, we're going to the tasting room and we're having this damned meeting that I've worked *my* arse off to organise. The one *you* told me was a good idea and you were totally on board with. *Then,* after lunch, you're going to the meeting with your clients to finish the contract that you've been working *your* arse off for. After that, feel free to go get Julian back because we're all over watching you grumbling around the place. We *can* deal with stuff around here without you Logan." She says angrily. I didn't mean to upset her and that makes me fumble around for the right words to say, and that's pretty rare for me, but she beats me to it once again, raising her hand to stop me from saying anything so that she can speak. "I know you didn't mean to offend me, but the truth is, you don't have to eat, sleep and breathe this place Logan. You're allowed to have a life outside of this and us. We're all adults now, you don't have to father us."

"I got that message loud and clear last night Makenna." This time it's my turn to hold my hand to stop *her* from speaking before I can finish what I want to say. "I took my responsibilities about taking over Drake Wines and the family seriously when our parents died, probably a little too seriously." She snorts and it's a like we're kids again for a second and I smile. "The thing is though, you and Caleb were right last night, we're all adults and we've got our parts to play around here. We all deserve to be happy and I'm going to get my happy back, if he'll have me." I feel my smile spread across my face as I think about seeing Jules again but then it slips a little at the thought that maybe what I say won't be enough for him to forgive me.

"Come on then, let's get this meeting started so that you can sort everything else out." Without another word, or looking back to see if I'm following her, Makenna marches her way from my place to Vines and the tasting room. Knowing that although my sister could and most definitely would take the reins in this meeting, I also know that she might say she's put the work into getting us here, I've worked just as hard. We're in this thing together. I can't and I won't let her shoulder the responsibility of Drake Wines on her own, no matter what else is going on with me. So, without a second thought I pocket my keys and catch up to her just as she reaches for the door to Vines.

"Allow me." I say, reaching for the door and opening it for her. I might be a grumpy bastard, but my parents raised me to be a gentleman and would kick my arse if I let Makenna down in any way.

"Thank you." She sends what anyone else would see as a smile, but I see it for what it is, a grimace, and nods her head before walking in the door.

"You're welcome." I respond with a smile plastered across my face.

"Don't do that Logan, it looks weird and we all know you're never *that* happy." She retorts over her shoulder as she makes her way through the bistro, towards the kitchen to check in with Leila without waiting for me.

"Thank you handsome." A warm hand pats my chest and I look down to see Martha, one of a group of grandma's that frequent the bistro and are a little too familiar with Caleb and myself, if you know what I mean? "For holding the door open for me. You know, you're parents would be proud of the man you've become Logan Drake."

"Thank you Martha." I say, looking behind her.

"The others aren't here yet, you can step away from the door now." Martha says with a chuckle. "I think your sister is waiting for you handsome." Another low chuckle escapes her as she nods her head towards the kitchen entrance where Makenna stands, hands on hips and an impatient frown on her face.

"I think you're right Martha, sorry I can't stay and chat, but I think my sister might kick my butt if I don't move it to the meeting we've got scheduled in about ten minutes." I give her what I hope is one of my best smiles and start to walk to where Kenna is waiting not so patiently for me.

"Be happy Logan, your parents would want that for you, no matter what that happiness looks like." Martha lightly touches my arm and gives me a warm smile, before heading to her table. Yeah that's right, these ladies are here so often they have their own table. A quick scan of the room tells me that Caleb isn't in here today, which is very unusual considering her prefers working in here than the office we gave him. I have a sneaky suspicion I know *why* he likes it in here more. Not to mention, Martha and her cohorts give him a pretty hard time if they're in here the same time as he is, and that just really does give me a happiness you can't imagine.

"Logan?!" I look up to find Makenna still looking at me like she's ready to stab me, so I say goodbye to Martha and make my way towards where my sister and Leila are standing.

"Good morning Logan." Leila says with a warm smile.

"Good morning Leila. Thanks again for providing morning tea for us." I say, not really knowing what I'm supposed to say because obviously I missed anything that Makenna already said.

"Of course, it's part of the job, Logan." Leila responds with a genuine, warm smile and I feel myself relax a little, until Kenna speaks again.

"So, we'll see you in about a half an hour right Leila?" Makenna asks, making Leila swing her attention back to her.

"Absolutely Makenna. Is there anything specific you'd like us to bring in?"

"No, just bring a tray of assorted baked goods, sweet and savoury, that should keep them happy, and if you can take coffee orders as well, that would be perfect."

"You've got it. Good luck."

"Thanks Leila but Makenna and I don't need luck, we work hard, so I have every confidence that my sister can pull this off without a hitch." I smile broadly switching between the two of them and Leila looks like she's struggling to not laugh, my sister, she doesn't hold back.

"Please don't do that anymore this morning." She says, waving her hand around in crazy circles and up and down in my general direction. "You're scaring me and I don't want you to scare my potential clients this morning. Just be your normal grumpy self please, OK?"

"You told me to get over myself and be nice. This is me being nice, you can't have it both ways Makenna." I say in a huff, I'm so fucking frustrated right now she should be happy that I'm even trying to fucking smile honestly.

"No, I told you to be normal, not whatever this is." Makenna says in a huff. Leila laughs as she walks away from us.

"Well, that wasn't embarrassing at all, thanks Kenna."

"Just be your fine, grumpy self and we'll be great."

"Really, be my grumpy self and we'll be great?" I ask, feeling reasonably grumpy now. Not that I was feeling overly happy previously, but I was filled with hope thinking about going to see Jules. My thoughts stray to how our conversation might go and just like that, I'm back to grumpy arsehole me that Kenna seems to want.

"There you are." She says while smacking my cheek. "This is the Logan Drake I need this morning. The intimidating arsehole who just has to sit in a room to make weaker men piss their pants."

"Well, isn't that fucking charming?" I mumble to myself, but I know she heard me, because she chuckles quietly. "Nice to know that's all I'm useful for. I mean, it's not like I have a business degree or worked my arse off to learn the family business *and* the wine business from head to toe. What a waste of time and energy, when I could have just been used as a grumpy arsehole heavy to coerce other businessmen and women into doing shit they're really not sure about with my not so easy charm."

"Oh shut it you grumpy arsehole, you know what I mean." She whacks me on the arm, and I flinch like she's hurt me, causing her to roll her eyes, because she knows she hasn't.

"Don't make me smile Makenna Harris, I'm doing my best to stay a grumpy arsehole over here just for you." Before she can respond the door to the tasting room swings open and our personal assistant, Margot, enters the room with half a dozen business people following right behind her.

"Good morning ladies and gentlemen." Makenna says, switching from ball-busting sister to perfect businesswoman so fast it makes my head spin! "Logan and I are so happy you could make it out here today. Let's get down to business, then we can enjoy the delicious morning tea provided by Vines next door. They also provide snacks and small meals when we have events here in the tasting room." She smiles around the room, there's a round of humming and good mornings, then we get down to the reason they're here. Drake Wines.

Chapter Nine
LOGAN

With the meeting over, and a new deal signed, Margot leads the group of well fed, satisfied new clients out of the tasting room and back to their cars.

"Well, that went well." I say, turning to look at Makenna.

"Yeah, it really did."

"You sound surprised, but you worked hard on this deal, Makenna. I'm proud of you, I'm also not surprised at all that you managed to pull it off." She sounds tired and I swear she's surprised that this went off without a hitch.

"It was genius of Leila to suggest sending some food in for them to sample." Makenna says, deflecting my praise.

"Wasn't that your idea?" I'm pretty sure she mentioned it about a week ago and decided to ask Leila if it was possible.

"Well, yes, but I left what to serve completely up to Leila. I mean she knows what people are enjoying in the bistro, so ..." She doesn't finish the sentence, just shrugs.

"That may be true, but we both have a pretty good knowledge of what she's serving in here every day Makenna." I scowl at her when she looks up at me. "*You* pulled this deal off Makenna Harris, not Leila and not me. Take the credit you deserve. I'm not saying Leila doesn't bake everything with perfection, nor am I saying that she didn't make the right choices in what to put out for us, but *you* made this deal came to fruition, and you should be proud as hell." What the hell is going on with my tough as nails, strong sister?

"I guess you're right. I just need time to let it sink in that everything worked out. I thought they were going to fight a little harder than they did today, and I figure it wasn't me that helped them to see the potential of the deal, but Leila's food. I mean that always wins me over." She smiles a genuine smile for the first time today.

"Hey, is everything OK?" I ask. I know I've been caught up with my own shit lately, but that doesn't mean I don't care about my family. "Why don't we go have some lunch and chat?" I suggest, feeling like a complete arsehole for not noticing my sister has something going on with her.

"I'd love to but I can't."

"Oh, OK." I guess I deserve that brush off.

"No, I mean I really can't Logan. I have an appointment in town. I scheduled it for after this meeting because I have nothing else important to do this afternoon." Placing her hand gently on my arm she says, "I'm not brushing you off. If I could postpone it I would, but I really can't."

"That's OK, no problem." I say, brushing off the hint of hurt I'm feeling.

'If I didn't have this appointment, I would sit with you and plot how you're going to get him back Logan, I promise." Kenna steps forward and wraps her arms around my waist, holding me close and my arms wrap around her automatically. What can I say, we've always been a hugging kind of family. "He loves you Logan, just make sure you say the right thing, and I *know* without a doubt in my mind, he'll forgive you." She says quietly in my ear.

"I hope you're right Kenna." I reply just as quietly. When we step out of the embrace, Kenna's smile is hopeful but also a little sad. "But that wasn't why I wanted to have lunch with you Makenna. I want to talk to you, see what's going on with *you*. I know I've been stuck in my own drama the past few weeks and I can see I've missed out on a few things with you and Caleb."

"You know that's not true Logan, you've always been there for us. I just don't want to jinx it by telling you what's going on but I promise when we know, you'll know. OK?"

"Just know Kenna, that no matter what I have going on in *my* life, I've always got time for you and Brady."

"Trust me, we know that. Brady may not always *want* that attention but we both know that you have our backs, no matter what. Trust me, when we have something to tell you, you'll know."

"I'll always trust you Makenna, with my life." I smile, giving her another quick hug.

"Which is why I would do anything to help you and Jules find your way back to one another. It's just unfortunate that I have other plans today." She says as she pulls out of my embrace, placing her hand on my cheek her eyes soften when she tells me, "He loves you Logan, I know he does. He'll forgive you. You just have to make sure you give him a reason to."

"From your lips to Julian's ears Kenna." She reaches up, leaving a kiss on my cheek. "I really hope you're right this time, I don't think I can live without him."

"I know I'm right Logan, go get your man back. Well, after your meeting this afternoon, but we're more than capable of keeping things working around here while you're gone after that." She kisses me on the other cheek and smacks me on the shoulder. "I love you Logan."

"I love you too Kenna." I choke on the words because they mean everything to me. It's done my heart good to hear them too.

"Get out of here." She pushes me towards the door. "Go on, get yourself some lunch, then go get your other meeting over with."

"I'm going." I tell her, but as I reach for the door handle and open it, I turn back to her. "Good luck at your appointment Kenna."

"Thanks Logan." She says, checking the time on her phone. "Speaking of, I better get out of here if I'm going to make it on time. I'll see you when I get back." She pauses at the door, then turns back to me. "No, I hope I don't see you until tomorrow or the next day." She throws me a wink as she walks out the door, leaving me alone in the tasting room.

I'm startled out of staring blankly at Makenna's retreating form by Sara, Leila's right hand woman, walking in the door that joins the tasting room to the rear of Vines dining room.

"Oh, sorry Mr Drake I didn't realise anyone was still in here. I was just going to clear up the mess and give the place a clean, but that can wait until you're finished in here." She says as she starts to back out of the room.

"No Sara, it's fine I was just about to come into Vines and get some lunch." I smile at her, trying to be less of the grumpy bastard I'm apparently known for. "Logan, not Mr Drake, please Sara."

"If you're sure, Logan." She asks, trying out my name.

"Absolutely, Mr Drake was my Dad and well, he's not here anymore. Even then, most of the people who worked for him called him Jack."

"OK Logan, why don't you let me do my job and clean up in here, and you can go get some lunch. The brisket pie is pretty popular today, so if you want one you better get in quick." I'm just about to ask about the pastries of the day, they're Leila's specialty when Sara continues, "and I recommend the individual lemon meringue pies that Leila made this morning. They're going pretty quickly too. I think your brother has had two already today, so you might want to get in there before they're all gone. You know Leila, she doesn't make huge batches of anything." She shakes her head. "I keep telling her she needs to make a few more, but she likes to keep people guessing and coming back for more. Less is more is her motto, so she tells me."

"Thanks for the heads up." She doesn't need to tell me twice. I head through the door Sara's holding open for me, thanking her as I pass through into Vines. The smell and the sound of the busy bistro is music to my ears. Seeing my little brother sitting at 'his' table and working away on his laptop is even better. I put my order in at the counter, then walk over to where Caleb is seated. "Hey Cal, mind if I join you?" I watch my brother jump in surprise and closes the window on his screen. I want to ask him what he was working on, but I get the feeling he's not ready to share, so I'll wait until he is.

"Yeah of course you can sit with me. Are you having lunch on your own?" His words are spoken in a bit of a nervous rush, but I don't say anything. I'm not in the mood to start an argument with my little brother.

"Yeah, Kenna and I just had a meeting in the tasting room, but she had to go into town for an appointment. I've got another meeting shortly, but I wanted some food, so here I am." He nods his head and closes his laptop.

"Have you ordered?" I nod my head in answer, but he doesn't notice because he's already moving on. 'You need to try to the brisket pie, Leila really outdid herself with that one and the lemon meringue pies, man I've never tasted anything more delicious. Don't tell Leila because she thinks her chocolate cake is my favourite and it totally is, but if she's got anything lemon meringue on the desserts list, I *always* get one. Ohh and I think the pie was Sara's little test run, but I like giving her a bit of grief, so I always give credit to Leila." I can't help laughing at him, he takes joy in things that

I would never think of. He surprises me every day, while also reminding me to enjoy the simple things in life.

"Yeah, Sara suggested those exact two dishes to me when she came into the tasting room to clear up the dishes." I say with the first genuine smile I've had in quite a while.

"Damn. Maybe that means she had more to do with both of them than I thought." His thoughts are interrupted by Georgie placing his lunch down in front of him. "Thanks Georgie."

"No problems Caleb." She says with a genuine, warm smile. "Yours will be over soon Mr Drake." She says turning to me, wiping the smile clean off my face. How come they feel comfortable calling Caleb by his first name and not me? Is it because he's closer to their age, or perhaps because he's in here every day? I'm in here most days too though.

I wait until she's out of hearing distance and I ask Caleb, "How come people around here call *you* by your first name but I'm *Mr Drake?*" I ask, knowing I sound like a petulant child. I can also admit that I may be feeling slightly more on edge since Jules walked out of my life a few weeks ago. It made me reassess quite a few things.

He gives me a, 'are you serious?' look and must see something in my face that gives him the answer, because for a second he looks shocked, but he covers it quickly. "The answer is simple Mr Drake." I scowl at him, ready to rip into him, but his loud laugh startles me into silence. "That right there is why Logan. To Makenna, Brady, and I, you're just Logan. You're our brother and a pain in the arse, but we're also used to your grumpiness being a cover for how much you care for people. Your employees are exactly that. Take it as a compliment boss man." He says with a shrug and small grin.

"What's that supposed to mean? You're their boss too, especially here in Vines." A sudden realisation hits me and I feel terrible. "Do I intimidate people Caleb?"

Caleb laughs loudly, too loud for the space we're in. "Oh my god Logan are you serious? Yes, you're intimidating as fuck brother. At least to those who don't know you so well."

"But I'm in here every other day, not as often as *you,* but still at least a few times a week, and I'm courteous and nice to everyone. It's not like I don't have any social skills Cal." I feel like I'm scowling again and I try not to because I don't want to look like I'm mad. I'm not really mad as such, I *am* disappointed though.

"Ahhh yes but unlike *some*, you don't hold conversations with the staff, and you don't share your life with them. Damn Logan you barely share your personal stuff with us and we're family."

"I call bullshit Caleb. I know that Leila worked hard to get to where she is and that she's helping to put her brother through school and her mum isn't well." I pause as Georgie places my lunch on the table in front of me. "I know Georgie here is working to pay her way through school." I say, nodding towards Georgia with a smile.

"I've finished now Mr Drake." She smiles and starts to walk away.

"Georgie." She turns back our way. "Call me Logan, please. Mr Drake is our father, not me."

"No worries Mr Dra ... Logan." She smiles and walks away.

"See, I can be as friendly as you." I say a smile spreading across my face as I relax.

"Sure you can Lo, except she took that as a directive, not a suggestion." He says with a smirk. "You *told* her what to do, you didn't *ask* her to change the way she addresses you."

"God damn it Caleb, I just can't fucking win no matter what I do. At least that's how it feels lately anyway." I mumble but I know Caleb heard me. I cut into my pie and shove a piece in my mouth, filling it so I can't speak again. Caleb takes the hint and does the same, but I can tell he wants to say something. "What is it Caleb? Whatever it is just spit it out." I demand. I guess this is why people find me intimidating?

"No, it can wait Logan. Let's just enjoy our lunch." I raise an eyebrow at him in question, but he says, "Honestly, it can wait. Enjoy the food." We both sit there in companionable silence while stuffing our faces with the most delicious meat I've ever had!

"My god that was delicious!" I announce without reservation, while placing my fork down on my plate. "Leila is a fucking genius."

"Well, thanks Logan but this one is Sara's dish." Leila laughs. I'm not sure where she appeared from but she's standing pretty close to Caleb's chair and he doesn't seem to mind one bit. I make a mental note to ask him about their 'friendship' after I've sorted everything out with Jules. Right now, they're not doing anything inappropriate so I'm not going to question them.

"Remind me to thank Sara then, that pie was amazing!" I repeat this time rubbing my hand over my stomach in satisfaction.

"I'm sure she'll love hearing the boss man loved her food." Leila laughs, leaning on the back of Caleb's chair like they're comfortable with each other's company. Interesting. "Did you leave room for something sweet, or should I give that to someone else?"

"Don't you dare." I growl at her as Caleb says, "You wouldn't dare!" The only thing our outburst does is cause Leila to laugh louder and motion behind her to someone. That someone is Sara and she's got two lemon meringue pies with a couple of coffees balancing on a tray. I know I feel full, but I can't help the saliva build up in my mouth just thinking about that pie. It's one of Leila's specialties and I always make sure to grab one when she makes it. Don't tell Jules, but Leila's is better than his. Pie that is.

"Thanks Sara." I say as she places a pie in front of both of us, along with our coffees. "Leila tells me that the brisket pie was your creation." She nods in answer. "Well, I have to say it was a stroke of brilliance. Are you going to keep that one on the menu, or will you be rotating that as well?" I ask, hoping either one of them will answer me with its staying permanently.

"Thank you Mr Drake" Sara starts.

"Logan, please call me Logan." I feel like I'm begging now.

"Ummm Logan, I think it might go on rotation, but I'm sure if you give me some notice, I can make sure we have one or two available whenever you want." She smiles at me. "If I can convince the boss that is." She winks at me. "Talking about the boss, I best get back to the kitchen. Do you guys need anything else?" She asks Caleb and Leila, who both shake their heads no.

"I better get back to it too, enjoy your food." Leila says, turning to face Caleb with a smile on her face, "I'll see you later."

"See you later." Caleb returns her smile and I concentrate on putting some sugar in my damned coffee because I don't want to have that conversation with him right now. This isn't the time or the place.

"We're friends." Caleb says.

Without looking up, I say, "I never said you weren't."

"When are you going to see Jules?"

"I planned on going first thing this morning but then Makenna re-minded me of the meeting we just had and another one I have after lunch. So, I won't be going until later this afternoon. Not what I'd planned but I have to live with it I guess." I say with a shrug.

"He loves you Logan, he'll take you back." Caleb says quietly, taking a big bite of his pie.

"I wish I had your confidence Caleb, I really do, but I know how much I've hurt him." I sigh. "I don't know if he *should* forgive me if I'm being honest. I don't know if I could forgive him if the tables were turned."

His head shoots up from staring at the crumbs left on his plate. "That's not true Logan. You two are meant for each other and I won't, I can't believe that you two can't work this out. He wanted you to admit to your family who you are, right?" He asks me, I shrug a shoulder, but nod my head in agreement at the same time.

"Yes."

"You did that. Now you have to explain to him how much he means to you." He makes it sound so damned simple, but I have a feeling, it's not going to be quite that easy.

Quiet settles between the two of us as I think about what he's said. I hope he's right, I truly do.

"Thanks for letting me crash your lunch Caleb, but I have to get to this other meeting." I say, checking the time on my phone, while Caleb scrapes the plate for crumbs.

"Any time brother, you know that."

Standing up, I throw some cash onto the table and Caleb snorts a laugh at me. "You know that's going to piss Leila off, right?"

"Well, we're running a business, we need to pay for what we eat." I pause for a second and look at him with a scowl. "I hope you pay for your meals Caleb?"

"Of course I do." He scoffs, but I get the feeling that somehow he pays in a different way to what I do. "Tell Leila her pie was delicious, as usual."

"Will do." I turn to walk away, until I feel a hand on my arm. I stop, knowing that Caleb's standing next to me. "I don't think you're going to need it, but good luck talking to Jules later. I have faith that it's all going to work out for you guys."

I rest my hand on his. "Thanks Cal, I need as much luck as I can get." I walk out of Vines, heading straight to my office. As soon as I can get this meeting over and done with, the sooner I can make my way to see Jules and try to work this shit out.

Chapter Ten
LOGAN

Clicking the button on my screen to end the video conference call, I let out a sigh of relief, because that's the second successful meeting for the day done. I look up as the door to my office opens and Margot walks in.

"Hey Logan, I got the paperwork ready, you just have to sign it, then I can scan it and email it over to the group for them to sign too."

"Thanks Margot." I say, picking up a pen and signing where she's put little sticky notes indicating where it's required. With those done, I smile at her as I hand them back.

"I'll get those done now so that the deal can be all wrapped up sooner rather than later."

"Thanks again, Margot." She smiles at me and turns to leave. Margot is technically Makenna's personal assistant but we kind of share her. She mostly works for my sister, but on the odd occasion she does a few things for me too. She's an absolute godsend and I'm sure we don't pay her nearly enough to put up with *me*, but we definitely don't pay her enough to put up with the both of us.

The door closes behind Margot and silence fills my office. I take a deep breath, rub my hands over my face, the stubble on my cheeks and jaw scratching my hands. I can't help wondering if Jules will like it or will he prefer the clean shaven, businessman version he's used to? Taking another deep breath, I decide it's well beyond time to find out.

Placing my hands on the desk, I push myself to my feet and take another god damned deep breath. I feel like I can't catch my breath, even though I need to go and speak to Jules, I can't be sure he'll give me the chance to explain, and I need him to, very much.

Without giving myself the chance to think about it for another second, I snatch my keys off my desk, where I threw them earlier and walk out the door, locking it behind me. When I reach my car, I see my reflection in the window, I hesitate for a few seconds. Should I go have a shower? Clean up a bit? Put on some clean clothes after working all day in them?

Fuck! I can't remember the last time I second guessed myself when going to see Jules, or ever in anything. I never hesitate in business and I haven't with Jules. Well I think he might disagree because I wasn't honest about our relationship with my family. I'd like to disagree with him, but I guess to a degree he's absolutely right. I'm a true, unadulterated jerk.

I shake my head to clear it of any negative thoughts, I need everything to focus on Jules and getting him back to me. With a brand new determination, I get in my car, crank over the engine, only to be figuratively brought to my knees by the song on the fucking radio. I really can't catch a fucking break today, seriously. So, with Pink! blaring out of my speakers, reminding me even more of better times and how much of a jerk I've really been, as I pull out of my driveway. Then my phone vibrates in my pocket with a call. I debate grabbing it out of my pocket, but decide that maybe Jules has answered one of my texts or he could even be calling me back, but when I look at the screen, it's Kenna's name displayed so I put it in the cup holder, then drive out of the long driveway of Drake Wines.

I shake my head, frustrated with myself because I should have known who was calling by the song that was coming out of my phone. I just wanted it to be Jules so badly that I blanked on the fact that everyone has their own ringtone.

I'm almost off the property when I see Makenna's car pulling in the gate and towards me up the driveway. As we drive closer I can see her waving wildly at me, I wave back but keep driving. As I reach the front gate, my phone starts ringing again, when I look down briefly as I pull up to stop to check the road, I see Makenna's name on the screen again. She knows that I'm going to see Jules and I don't have the time, nor the inclination honestly, to answer her to just shoot the breeze with her while I drive. So, instead of answering I pull out onto the road and head towards town. I haven't driven for more than a few minutes when my phone starts ringing again, so I pull over to answer it and connect it to Bluetooth so that I can keep driving.

"Hello Makenna, is the place burning down or is someone in trouble?" I chuckle as I answer her call.

"Of course not!"

"Why are you blowing up my phone then?" I ask, smiling even though she can't see me.

"Are you on your way to speak to Jules?" She asks, sounding concerned, which confuses me because she knew that I planned on going to see him today.

"You already knew that Kenna." I confirm, sighing.

"I know, I know. It's just that." She hesitates and even though I want to know what she's thinking, I know better than to push her for an answer before she's ready to speak. "Just, be careful OK? And I don't just mean with Julian, I mean with yourself as well, OK?"

"Sure Kenna. It's not like I plan on barrelling in like a bull in a china shop you know?" I scoff down the line at her. "I know how to talk to Jules Kenna, I've been doing it for years."

"Yeah, I know, and you've been hurting the both of you for years Logan." She sighs. "All I'm asking is that you listen to Jules as well as have your say, OK?"

"Of course I will." Damn what does my sister think of me that she thinks that I wouldn't give the man I love the chance to tell me how he feels about all of this? Do I really come across as such an arsehole?

"I'd wish you good luck big brother, but I truly don't think you're going to need it." I can hear the smile in her voice and it's such a change from her lecture not even a minute ago that I almost feel dizzy.

"I hope you're right, and while I don't normally believe in luck, today I'll take as much luck as I can get."

"I love you Logan, remember that." She says and I feel a strange sense of foreboding with her words, even though she says them with kindness in her voice.

"I love you too, Kenna." Before I can ask her any questions she's hung up and I'm left to ponder what she means as I drive into town. I find that I'm grateful that she gave me something else to think about while I'm driving because before I know it I'm pulling up to Jules' building and parking my car. I look up at the building and when I see his windows are dark,

I wonder if I should have called first to make sure he's home. Shaking my head to get rid of the doubts that are suddenly crowding in, I pull the keys out of the ignition and get out of my car, making myself walk up the path that leads to the lobby of the building. Luckily, either Julian hasn't gotten around to telling his neighbours or the building manager that we've broken up, because a neighbour lets me in with a smile, and the manager greets me like an old friend, as usual. One step closer.

When I reach his door, I raise my hand to knock but hesitate. I still have the key he gave me when he moved in here, but I don't think I should use it, even though he didn't ask for it back the day he left me.

The memory of that day hurts so much that I can feel the stabbing pain in my heart.

I knock on the door and wait. And wait some more.

Just as I start to think that maybe Jules isn't home, I hear some rustling from behind the door.

"Jules?" The noise stops and I hold my breath. "Julian. Are you home?" I ask, trying to breathe quietly so that I can hear the evidence of him moving around behind the door, trying to ignore me.

I pull my phone out of my pocket and pull his name up on the screen. His gorgeous face fills the screen and my heart sinks. What if he *is* inside and he doesn't want to see me? I've come this far, I'm not backing down now, I *need* to speak to him, and I need him to talk to *me*. Pressing my thumb onto the green dial button in the screen, I wait. After a few seconds I can hear Pink! singing the tune that Jules has used as my ringtone for at least a year, through the closed door between us. Which means, Julian either left his phone at home, or he's ignoring me. I know this man pretty well, and I doubt he left his phone anywhere, so I guess it's the latter. Now I need to decide whether I'm going to let him get away with it, or whether I'm going to push him further. In the back on my mind I hear Kenna asking me to take it slow, to not push him too far, too fast, but I can't pull back now.

"Julian John Bishop. I know you're in there." I growl in frustration, before taking another fucking deep breath to calm down. "God damn it, I just want to talk to you. Jules please, can we talk?" I beg through the door, as I rest one hand on the frame, my body against door itself, my other hand flat against it. "Please." I close my eyes and rest my forehead on his door, because I'm suddenly so fucking exhausted. I hear one of his neighbours get off the elevator and I brace myself for the questions.

"Is everything OK Logan?" He asks and I sigh.

"Everything is fine, thanks for asking. I forgot my key and I'm just waiting for Julian to open the door for me. I must have caught him the shower." I explain without raising my head or opening my eyes.

"If you're sure." I know he's hesitant to move along and I don't know whether to be pissed off or happy that Julian has someone looking out for him.

"I am. Thank you, Ben." I say, trying my hardest to keep my voice as neutral as possible, but I don't think I succeed too well when he grunts but doesn't move away. It's like we're both waiting to see if Jules is going to open this god dammed door.

After a minute of silence in the hallway, the door suddenly opens and I almost lose my balance.

"It's fine Ben, really. A simple misunderstanding." Jules smiles at Ben and I feel my chest constrict as Ben smiles back. They seem to exchange an understanding without saying anything. It's only been a few weeks, has he moved on with Ben? "I'll talk to you later."

"If you're sure? Call me if you need anything." Ben asks, looking me up and down, then turning his attention back to Jules.

Jules smiles broadly at him and says, "Of course I'm sure." Ben seems to need no other assurance than a smile from Jules, before he's gone.

I haven't moved from leaning against the doorframe, only now, my arms are crossed over my chest. I never once bothered to look behind me to face Ben, my sole focus has been on Julian.

"Can we talk, please?" I ask him, gently.

"Sure, why not?" He answers, before turning his back to me and walking back into his apartment without waiting to see if I'll follow him or inviting me in. This isn't my Jules, but I guess I don't know if he *is* still *my* Jules yet.

I follow him inside, closing the door behind me and that's when I realise he doesn't have any lights on in the place. "Can we turn on a light?" I ask.

"Why? What is it you need to see Logan?" He asks, sounding exhausted.

"You." I answer simply. I want to see *him*. *I need* to see his handsome face so that I can see if he believes what I need to tell him. I need to see his reaction to my words, to my feelings.

"What if I don't want to be seen?" He asks.

"Don't be so dramatic Julian. I've missed you and I want to see your gorgeous face. Please." Damn it I'm begging him again, but I know I'll keep begging for as long as I need to if it will make him understand.

Without warning, the room lights up and I close my eyes against the sudden onslaught for a second. "Thanks for the warning Love." I say with a chuckle.

"Don't." Jules says with a quiet groan, closing his eyes and looking down at the floor.

"Don't what?" I ask, genuinely confused as to what I've done already.

"Don't speak to me like that, like before. Don't call me that." He answers, still looking anywhere but at me.

"Don't what? Call you Love?"

"Yes." His voice is low rasp now, full of the emotion he's trying to hold in.

"I would but that's what you are to me."

"Stop! Just tell me what you came to say and then leave. I can't do this with you Logan."

Leave? Not until I get him to listen to what I have to say and really hear me.

"You want me to leave?"

"I want you to say whatever it is you've decided you need to say and then yes, I want you to leave. It's late Logan, and I've had a hell of a day. All I want is to be left alone so that I can go to bed."

"Alone?" I ask, before I can stop myself.

Finally he looks at me and I can see the sadness all over his face. "How dare you! Yes alone, who do you think I am? You think I could move on from a relationship, no matter how secret it was, that lasted as long as ours did, so easily? Or is that what you want me to tell you, that you're too late? Would that make you happy? Would that make it easier for you to move forward with your life? God damn it Logan! I thought I could hear you out but I don't know if I have the energy." He closes his eyes and he's taking deep breaths like he can't quite get enough oxygen into his lungs.

I take a few large steps towards him, and that's when I notice his puffy eyes and when he opens them, they're red and bloodshot. "What happened? Who did this to you? Jules, Love please tell me."

"Don't, Logan. Nothing and no-one. Please, I beg you, just say what you came to say and then leave." He begs me. I hate seeing him like this, and I can't help blaming myself for it. "It's late, too late." He mumbles.

"Do you mean it's too late for us because I'm here to tell you that you mean everything to me Jules. I love you with everything in me and I need you. Julian, Love, please? Give me another chance?" I plead with him.

"Another chance to what Logan? Break my heart again? No thanks." He draws in a shuddering sigh and I know he's on the verge of his emotions spilling over. I also know that he doesn't want that to happen. "What do you want me to give you another chance to do, hmmm? To not tell people about the truth of our relationship? I just don't think I can do it Logan. Not again."

"Who made you cry, Love?" I ask gently. I know now that's what he was doing when I knocked on the door and why he didn't want to let me in. "Tell me and I'll never let them hurt you again. You're mine to protect."

"You want to know whose arse you have to kick? Really?" He asks me with a laugh that doesn't come close to being amused.

"Yes, Love."

"Yours. You did this to me. Are you happy now? I saw Makenna earlier and we had a talk. Before you go blaming her, this has nothing to do with what Makenna said to me, but more about what I realised I was losing by losing you, us. *You* did this to me Logan. I'm broken and I don't know if I'll ever feel whole again. I didn't just lose you, you know that right? I lost Makenna, Brady and Caleb as well. I lost the love of my life and along with him, his family that had become mine."

"You didn't lose anyone Love, not me and not my family. *Our family.* They love you Jules and they would never let you walk away, they would never leave you." I reach out to take his face in my hands and he starts under my touch as though he didn't realise I was close to enough to touch him. I wipe the tears that have fallen off his cheeks and he trembles under my touch. "I love you Jules. You didn't lose me, I'm yours always. Forever Love. I'm an idiot and I should have had a conversation with them years ago about who you were. About what we meant to each other. Please believe how sorry I am that I didn't. It had nothing to do with you, or how much you meant, you *mean* to me, and everything to do with me being an idiot. As it turns out I didn't have to say a damned thing, they all already knew! Which makes me an ever bigger douchebag for not telling them sooner." I say with a dry laugh.

"Logan." My name is little more than a hoarse whisper.

"I don't know what Makenna said to you today but I'll kick her arse if she hurt you Jules. I swear to god I will! You come first for me, always. You always have, I didn't show you but I should have and for that I am painfully sorry."

"Logan." He rasps out again, around tears. I don't want to hurt him any more than I already have.

"Don't say anything. You don't have to forgive me tonight. I want you to take some time, a few days, to think about what I've said tonight. I want you to know that things will change. Call me when you're ready, but if you take too long Julian Bishop, I *will* be back, and I won't take no for answer next time." I warn him, then I cradle his head in my hands and look into his eyes as a warning for what I plan. When he doesn't make a move to get out of my embrace, I lean in and kiss him. It's a soft, gentle kiss at first, but when he opens up to let me in, I can't help making it a more passionate, deeper kiss. I love this man and I want him to feel it.

My hand that was holding one side of his face, slowly slides down his neck, my fingers dancing over his collarbone, over his pec and down his body until it rests on his hip. I use my grip to pull his body closer into mine. When he doesn't resist me I sigh in relief, but I know I have to pull back. I'm not taking him to bed tonight, as much as I want to, I won't. He needs to think and I need to step back.

Pulling away is the hardest thing I've ever done in my life, but I know I need to, for both of us. Still holding him close, I rest my forehead on his, my eyes closed, both of our chests rising and falling in time with our heavy breathing.

"Damn it Logan." I couldn't agree with his assessment more, but I don't want him to say more. I want him to think about what I've said and that hot as fuck kiss, before he gives me any kind of answer. So, I drop my hands from his body and take two steps away from him, it's not enough distance but it's going to have to do. "What the hell do you want from me Logan?" He sounds so desperate.

"Everything Julian, just everything." I grin and turn to walk towards the door. "Remember, I love you Jules, but you have two, three days max, before I come back for my answer. Don't forget, I've still got a key. Next time, I won't wait for you to let me in." I warn him as I reach for the door handle, and walk out of his apartment without giving him a chance to speak.

Holy fuck! If I thought pulling away from kissing Jules was difficult, walking out the door of his building, getting in my car and driving away from him almost broke me. I almost turn around to go back to him a million times before I drive through the front gates of Drake Wines and pull into my garage.

Before I even get out of the car, my phone chimes with a message and without looking I know it's Kenna. How do I know? Because Jules gave everyone their own message tones so that I could tell who it was who without looking. I pick up my phone and walk into the house, I don't turn on any lights, I just walk straight through to my bedroom and collapse on the bed. I have to answer Kenna, because if I don't, I know she'll show up at my door. With Brady close behind her no doubt because it's dark outside.

Makenna: *How did it go? xx*

Me: *I'll talk to you in the morning, I promise xx*

Makenna: *Do you need anything? xx*

Me: *No I'm good. Love you xx*

Then I turn off my phone, strip out of my clothes and crawl into bed. Just to punish myself, I lie on the side that Jules normally lies on just so that I can smell his scent that's left on the sheets. I fall asleep thinking he's here, but knowing that he's really not.

Chapter Eleven
JULES

I swear it takes me a full minute to come back down to Earth after the door closes behind Logan's retreating form. When I do, I can't even process what the hell just happened. So, instead of trying to, I take myself to the bathroom, strip off my clothes and step into a steaming hot shower.

The shower is where I normally take the time to think and destress for the day, but today, well it's been a hell of a day. From running into Makenna, then Logan showing up here, and begging me to give him another chance, I just can't think.

Do I give him another chance? Do I believe him when he says things will change, that things *have* changed? I know that Makenna and the others know the true nature of our relationship, but I also understand that's not because Logan told them. They already *knew*. I'm still trying to work out how the hell *that* happened, because we were always so careful to *not* touch each other like a romantic couple would. Maybe that's what gave us away in the end? Does it matter how they know? Isn't it just enough that they know *now*, and that Logan didn't deny it when they asked him?

It shouldn't make any difference, and yet I feel like it does, to me.

I wanted *him* to be the one who explained everything to them. I needed for *him* to have to think about us and tell them the truth.

I turn the shower off and step out to grab a towel. There's no point staying in there, I can't sort any of this out in the shower despite my best efforts. Not to mention I'm tired. Fucking exhausted to tell the truth. My emotions are all over the place.

After drying myself I stand there for a second just thinking. I shake my head and hang up the towel. Before I met Logan, I would have left it on the floor or over the edge of the tub, but it annoys the shit out of him, so I hang it back up. I chuckle thinking about the amount of times I've left wet towels on the floor just to get a rise out of him. It works every single time.

I remember I left my phone on the floor in the living room, so I walk in there to grab it. I haven't looked at it since Logan called wanting to be let into my apartment, so I figure I should at least check it to see if anyone else has tried to contact me. I see it in front of me and head straight for it without looking around. The dim light is still on from when Logan was here.

"What the fuck is wrong with you two, and why am I the lucky one to see you both naked in the same week?" I jump at the voice, because I wasn't expecting anyone else to be in *my* apartment.

"What the hell are you doing in here Caleb?" I yell, while covering up my junk. I might like men, but that doesn't mean I want another guy to see what I'm packing, especially not my boyfriend's brother. Boyfriend, is he still that? "How the fuck did you get in here anyway?" I ask.

"I used the key." He says with a shrug.

"What key?" I know I didn't give Caleb Drake a key to my damned apartment. "And what do you mean you saw *both* of us naked this week?"

"Logan's key." He says with a roll of his eyes like I'm the one who's out of line here.

"You mean you stole Logan's key to my apartment?" I ask, putting my hands on my hips, only to realise that leaves me vulnerable again. Dropping my hands back to my groin, I try to give Caleb a death stare, but I don't think I'm too menacing when I'm naked.

"No, I mean I *'borrowed'* Logan's key to come over and make sure you were doing OK, but now that I've seen you, I think I know why my brother is so in love." He wiggles his eyebrows while looking down where my hands cover me.

"God damn it Caleb, why are you here?" Irritated beyond belief now, not to mention cold.

"Well, I was hoping we could have a chat, if that's OK?" I sigh, trying to bring my irritation back under control.

"Sure, why the hell not? Do you mind if I go put some clothes on before we start this 'chat'?" I ask.

"Well, I'd rather you were wearing clothes too but hey, this is your house, so whatever makes you comfortable." He says with a shrug of his shoulders, like he doesn't care either way.

"I'll be back in a minute." I reply, turning my back to him and walking back towards my bedroom.

"Nice arse there Bishop, I'm really starting to appreciate my brother's attraction to you man." My steps falter but I don't dignify his comment with a response. What the hell would I say to that anyway? Should I have curtsied and said, 'thank you kind sir'? I throw on the first pieces of clothing I find, which just happen to be workout shorts and a hoodie. As I pull the hoodie over my head I realise it's one that Logan left behind, because it smells like him, I hesitate for just a second and then decide, screw it, I want to get Caleb out of here as soon I possibly can without being rude.

I walk back out to the living room, drop into my armchair, and look at Logan's little brother. "What is it you've got to talk to me about Caleb? Just so you know, I still want to know how you got up here." I say, pointing my finger at him.

"OK, well to answer the question that's burning your soul, I got up here because the owner recognised me as Logan's brother. Also, I might have said you were expecting me." He says, a smirk spreading across his face. I can see why women fall all over themselves to be with him, he's an attractive guy and he certainly has enough charm in his little finger to keep a small country in electricity for a year. I can't wait to see this kid get knocked on his arse by the woman of his dreams!

"OK, that answers one question and the stolen key answers the other part of it." I sigh. "I can guess what you want to talk about, but I'm still not sure what you think you're going to achieve Caleb. I've already spoken to your sister today and Logan just left here not that long ago pleading his case. What is it that you think I need to hear that they haven't said already?"

"Probably nothing, but that doesn't mean what I think doesn't count, does it?" He shrugs again, but the smirk is wiped off his face. Logan and Makenna still treat him like a kid, and I can see how hard he's trying to get them to take him more seriously. In fact, I keep telling Logan he needs to let Cal grow up, but he doesn't think there's anything wrong, stubborn grumpy arse that he is. With that in mind, I can't tell him to mind his own business, because in his own way, he's just trying to look out for his big brother.

"OK Caleb let's hear it then. Tell me everything I've done wrong." I say, waving my hand for him to continue.

"What do you mean? What did you do wrong?" He asks, giving me this adorable, confused scowl. Yeah I can see why he's popular with the ladies for sure.

"Well, isn't that what you're here for? To tell me how I've done your brother wrong for forcing his hand?"

The creases in his forehead deepen as his confusion increases. "No, actually. I'm here to see if you're OK and to tell you my brother is a dick, no pun intended, and you did the right thing." Another shrug of his shoulders, but I can't speak because I'm shocked beyond belief. "You were right to force his hand Jules. The fact that we all knew, including our parents, the true extent of your relationship doesn't matter. It just doesn't count. He should have had the balls to tell us. His love for you should have been enough to confront the truth with us. I can't believe it took for you to walk away for him to tell us the truth!"

"You know Makenna said the same thing, about you guys all knowing we were a couple rather than just friends, but I don't understand how? Logan was always so careful not to be obvious about things in front of you guys. No touching and that kind of stuff." I say, amazed that they still knew.

"I think it's funny, hilarious actually, that you both think that. Logan said the same thing the other night, *'but we hid it so well.'* I'm sorry to burst your bubble but you didn't hide it at all. You think just because you didn't touch, hug or kiss that you could hide how you guys felt? You could be on the other side of the room from each other, and catch each other's eye, the same look on both of your faces told the story. You guys have always communicated without saying a damned word. One look, and you knew what he was thinking." He chuckles. "Do you really think we didn't know what you were doing when you guys snuck off for a few minutes? You might have left the room separately, but we always knew you were together. The fact that you came back with your hair not quite as neat as when you left was a pretty big giveaway too, but hey, what would I know, I'm just the kid brother right?"

"That's not true Caleb, well OK, it's technically true, but that doesn't mean your opinion doesn't count." I counter, but I can't get over the fact that they *knew* and didn't say anything. "If you all knew, your parents included, why didn't one of you say something? I don't understand why no-one spoke up. Why did this all have to be such a secret? Your parents didn't talk to Logan, which to a degree I kind of understand, but you and Kenna? Brady? I'm trying to understand Caleb, truly I am, but I just don't. I don't understand why Logan felt like he couldn't tell his family the truth. About himself, not just us, and I really don't understand why none of you said anything when you knew, considering you knew how he felt. Maybe it's just because I've always been so open with my family, and it's never been an issue for me, I don't know." I close my eyes because I'm frustrated, irritated and plain old pissed off.

"It's not an excuse, I'm not trying to excuse the way things have played out for you guys Jules but I want to try to explain because I doubt, no matter what Logan said when he was here earlier, he never explained anything except that he loves and misses you. The truth is though, our parents were very traditional, so I can understand why Logan was hesitant to tell them about his love life. The other side to that coin is, our parents were intent on not invading his privacy and that's why they never asked any questions. It's also why they didn't want us to ask him about it either. It wasn't any of our business, they told us." Caleb sighs and takes a deep breath. "I guess, being so much younger than Logan, I just let it slide. I always knew he liked guys and it never bothered me for a second. He was just my big brother, Logan. I was happy when he found you because you make him happy. I think you make each other happy and that's the aim, isn't it? The fact is Makenna and Brady never had to announce that they're straight. Makenna never walked into the house and said this is Brady my boyfriend and we're straight. I've never had to tell anyone I'm straight and I guess it just never occurred to any of us that Logan had to announce that he wasn't. We all just accepted that you two were together, even our parents and while I can understand that Logan has regrets now that he can't tell our parents about you and him, I think that's the only thing he regrets. Well, and hurting you."

"I was his secret. For years." I say quietly.

"And I'm sorry that you felt like you were his dirty little secret." I look at him, shocked. "Yeah, I know you *think* there are plenty of secrets in this family, but honestly, there really aren't too many I'm afraid to say. Makenna and I spoke earlier, I know what you spoke about, but that's not why I'm here. I'm here because I've seen how much pain my brother has been in since you left, and I don't want him to live that way anymore. I don't want either of you to live like that Jules, because I can see the same pain all over your face, that I see on Logan's too. You two were meant for each other, and I don't want to see you guys walk away from that because of a simple family misunderstanding. Perhaps it's not that simple to you, but it should be. We love you Jules, you're already part of the Drake family. You're already my big brother, so I guess what I'm saying is, don't walk away from Logan, and don't walk away from us. Please?"

I can't say I've ever seen Caleb look so hopeful. He's normally the guy who makes everyone else feel better about any given situation. He's always so happy, like he doesn't have a care in the world, but I can see that he cares about this. About his brother. About me.

"I promise to think about everything you've said." I say, hoping that is enough for him tonight. "I also promise to think about what Kenna told me as well. It wasn't too far from what you just said."

"And Logan? What about what he said tonight?" He asks, his voice full of concern.

"I will think about everything that *everyone* has said today, I promise." I sigh, damn I'm sick of sighing. "I love him Caleb, I don't doubt that for a second and I know he loves me too, what I have to decide is, if things have changed enough for me. I can't, and I won't, settle for being in the background again, not even for Logan."

"Fair enough." He gets to his feet and I follow his lead. He comes close to me and pulls me into a warm hug that I didn't know I needed today. I'm not going to lie, it feels damned good, different to the embrace Logan gave me for obvious reasons, but warm and loving all the same. "Just remember we *all* love you Julian, all of us and we want you in our family. You're already a part of our family and you have been for years dude." He plants a sloppy kiss on my cheek, pats me hard on the shoulder and starts for the door.

"That's it? You're just leaving now?" I ask, dumbfounded but not sure why.

"Well, I could stay the night if you really want, but one, I don't swing that way and two, I think Logan might just take a swing at me if I did." He snorts with laughter.

"Logan would never take a swing at you Caleb, you're his brother and he would never hit you. Ever." I protest.

"Ohhh don't get me wrong, I know my brother loves me and he would do just about anything for me, but if he thought for one second that I stayed the night here, innocent or not, I'm sure I would end up with a black eye." He gives me another snort of laughter before speaking again. "You don't have to look so shocked Jules, he's loves you. He's *in love with you* and it would kill him to think that you've been with someone else, even his little brother. Even though he knows that logically, neither of us would do that to him." He gets this mischievous look on his face and I don't want to ask what he's thinking, but I don't need to, because he tells me anyway. "Now I feel like I want to stay the night, just to see his reaction."

"No. No, no, no, NO!" I say pushing him out the door he's already opened. "I won't cause any kind of trouble within your family Caleb, and even though I don't think Logan would react that way, I'm not going to test it. What I need, is for you to leave and let me think. I promise to not leave your brother hanging for too long, not that he'll let me anyway, he's already made it abundantly clear that if he hasn't heard from me within the next two days, he'll be back here demanding answers."

"Wow, who knew Logan could be so demanding and kinda hot?" Caleb says, surprise written all over his face.

"I knew Caleb, I knew, and I believe without a doubt that he will bring his grumpy demanding, gorgeous self here if he thinks I've taken too long to think. Make no mistake, I love your brother, but I have to decide whether I can trust myself to return to our relationship. I need things to change Caleb, and I need things to change now."

"Of course you do. Now go get some sleep, I'm sure things will be clearer in the morning after a good night's sleep. Goodnight Julian."

"Goodnight Caleb." He waves and then he's gone. I close and lock my door, resting my back against it hoping like hell I don't get another visit from any more Drake's tonight, because if Logan comes back, I won't be able to say no to him. I've never been able to say no to him and that's why it broke my heart to walk away two weeks ago and why it broke me again to let him walk away today, but it needed to be done.

Caleb's right, I need to get some rest. I push off the door and walk back through the living room towards my bedroom. That's when I notice my phone sitting on the coffee table and realise I never did get around to checking it earlier when I discovered Caleb sitting on my couch.

Picking it up I look at the screen and the only notification on it is a text message from Logan. With my finger hovering over the screen, I can't decide whether to open it or not. In the end, I choose to look at it, but I wait until I reach my bedroom and I'm sitting comfortably on my bed, to open it.

Logan: *I love you Julian Bishop and I always will, I promise xx*

I look at the time stamp and realise that he must have been sitting in his car before he left here earlier. Knowing that he didn't just leave here without giving me a second thought makes my heart beat faster. I want to answer him. I know I should answer him, because I can almost imagine him waiting for my reply, but I can't. My heart and my mind are fighting each other, and I need to have both of them on board before I speak to Logan.

Going to bed without answering him seems like a cruel and unusual punishment, but it's exactly what I do. I don't sleep well though, and I accept that as my punishment.

After waking up the next morning and staring at the ceiling for a good five minutes or more, I decide I know exactly what I have to do. I get up, shower to wake up properly, get dressed and head over to Drake Wines.

As I pull in past the gates that announce I've arrived at Drake Wines, I'm hoping against hope that Logan hasn't changed his routine and I know exactly where he is at this time of day. I head straight for Vines, the bistro on the property. Parking my car, I don't dare look around to see if I can see his car here, because it's more than likely that he walked here, even from his house or office.

I get out of the car without giving myself a chance to think about what I'm about to do. If I give myself time to think, I'll talk myself out of it and I want to do this.

Pushing open the door to Vines, I take a deep breath and walk inside like I have at least a thousand times before. Like I belong here. I hear Caleb, before I see him, because the only person I see in the room is Logan. His broad back to me, in his perfectly cut suit, and I know without a doubt he's got one of his vests on underneath that suit jacket and my mouth starts to water. I love the vision of Logan Drake in a 3 piece fucking suit. There is nothing and I mean *nothing* sexier.

"Logan. Logan I think you're gonna want to turn around bro." Caleb smiles broadly at me, when I nod my head at him. He knows what I mean, and I'm glad.

"Caleb, what is it now?" The low rumble of his voice sets all the little hairs on my body on edge, and sends my heart racing. God damn I hope I'm doing the right thing today. He sounds angry as Caleb keeps tugging on the sleeve of his jacket. "What Caleb?" He growls, if we weren't in a public place I'd grab him by the lapels of his jacket and kiss the life out of him, but we *are* in a public place, so I stand my ground waiting for him to turn completely around to see me.

"Turn around idiot." Caleb says urgently. I can feel the frustration pouring off Logan in waves, and I really start to wonder if I should have just waited until tonight when I knew he would be at home, but I couldn't, I needed to see him now.

"Fine, what is it that I need to see so damned desperately Caleb?" He asks, as he turns sharply to face my direction. "Julian?" He sounds surprised.

"I hope it's OK that I'm here? I mean I can come back later, if you're busy."

"He's not busy and of course it's OK you're here, you're family." Caleb says, as he pushes his brother towards me.

"Julian?" He asks again. "What are you doing here?"

"I came to talk to you. Is now a good time?" He hasn't taken his eyes off me, it's almost like he's scared if he does, I might disappear, and I hate that I've done this to him.

"Of course it's a good time, right Logan?" Caleb asks, jabbing him in the ribs.

"What? Oh yes, of course now is a good time. Do you want to sit? Go to the tasting room? Go home?" He asks all at once. Home. He doesn't invite me to his house, he invites me home. "Or we can stay right here, whatever you're comfortable with."

"Right now, I just want to talk to you."

"Here it is then. Tell me whatever you need to Julian." The hope in his eyes is so hypnotising, and everyone else around us disappears, including Caleb.

"I love you Logan Drake." I hear a round of gasps all around us, but all I see is Logan.

"But?" He asks, the hesitation written all over his face.

Before I can answer him, I'm swamped in a hug and kisses land all over my face. My eyes never leave Logan's, but I know who it is without looking and I didn't even see her in the room when I came in.

"Makenna get off him, let the damn man speak would you?" Caleb says, as I feel Makenna getting dragged away. I think he may have needed the help of Brady as well, but I don't know for sure, because my eyes still haven't strayed from Logan's.

"Nothing." I say. "No if's, buts or maybe's. I promise."

The smile that spreads across his handsome face is hesitant, but no less brilliant.

"Really?" I nod my head, yes. I don't think I can speak again yet.

"OK." He nods, still not breaking eye contact with me. Not quite the response I was hoping for, but I'll take it for now. He's never been one for public displays of affection, but I thought that was because we were a secret, maybe that's just the way he is.

"OK." I repeat back to him, not sure what else to say. What else is there to say?

Chapter Twelve
LOGAN

He's here, in Vines and did he just say he *loves* me? And was my response seriously OK?

It was and while I can hear Makenna, Brady and Caleb all arguing about something, and I know that we're standing in the middle of our busy family bistro, the rest of the world has faded into the distance, and all I can see is Julian. This is why I notice the exact moment I've taken too long to give him a real reply, because his expression shows how rejected he feels right now. He nods slightly and turns to leave.

"No!" That one word booms around the building, too loud for the space, and I notice then that everyone has stopped moving and talking, but I don't fucking care. "Don't go. Please."

He's already got his back to me and I see his shoulders sag. I don't know whether it's with regret, sadness or resignation. He thinks he knows what I'm going to say, but I don't even know yet. Me, the guy who always has the right words and can talk hard-nosed business men into deals that aren't necessarily in their best interest.

"Why?"

"Why what?" I ask, confused.

He sighs, I watch his shoulders rise and fall as he does, because he still hasn't turned around to look at me yet. "Why should I stay Logan? I just told you I love you and your response was, 'OK.'"

"You surprised me." I say, trying to defend myself.

"No, I did what I know you hate. I spoke about us in public, I get it. I'll just be leaving now." He says, his head hanging down. I hate seeing him like this.

"Don't you dare walk away from me now." I roar, knowing I look and sound like a crazy man, but I can't find it in me to care too much about the public spectacle I'm making of myself. The man I love will not walk away from me again. "I will *not* watch you walk away from me again Julian Bishop. You are the love of my life and I will not let you leave me again."

"Well, that's a little bit possessive Neanderthal of you don't you think Drake?" I can hear the laughter in his voice, and as he turns to look at me, I can see the amusement lighting his beautiful ice blue eyes.

"You like it when I get growly and possessive and you know it." I say back to him in challenge.

"You better believe I do." His voice a deep, sexy rumble, and I know what that means. Man, do I know what that means.

"Come here." I demand.

"Why don't you come here?" He challenges me.

"Because, you know you want to come to me." I tell him, my voice leaving no room for argument. Until I soften my features and say quietly, my voice hoarse with emotions. "And because I *need* you to come back to me." Without another word he takes two strides towards me and without even realising it, I take a step to meet him in the middle. My hands reach for his face, holding his cheeks and slowly pulling him towards me, giving him time to pull away if that's what he wants to do. When he doesn't pull away from me, I take that as a signal to move forward and I bring his lips to mine. I'm not sure which one of us sighs, it could be both of us, all I know is I've come home, and I feel like this is where I belong. With Julian's lips on mine and his body up against mine. Julian sighs again and that gives me access to his mouth and I take full advantage with my tongue tangling with his. God I've missed this. I've missed *him!* It's only been a few weeks at most and yet it feels like a lifetime since I've touched him like this.

"Ahem." Someone coughing enters my head, but I ignore them. "Ahhh guys. You might want to stop unless you want to give our customers a show that is." Caleb says with a chuckle.

"Ahh yeah, look I don't want to break up this reunion at all, but you really should take this home Logan." Makenna chimes in. Breaking our kiss, I rest my forehead on Jules' because I can't stand the thought of completely pulling away from him now that I have him back in my arms.

"They're probably not wrong Logan, especially knowing how much you just love public displays of affection." Jules says quietly, not looking me in the eyes.

"That ends now. I don't care who sees me loving you. Well, you know, I mean showing you affection not full on naked displays or anything. That's for me, *only* for me." He attempts to throw his head back in laughter, but he doesn't get too far because my hand is still cupped around the back his head, holding him to me. "Promise me Julian."

"Promise you what, Logan?" He asks, and while I can see the mischief in his eyes, I can also see that he's not as certain about where he stands with me.

"That you're mine and I'm yours. Always." I stare deep into his eyes, searching for the truth when he doesn't answer me right away. I'm more than happy with what I find in his eyes, but I'd love to hear him say it as well.

"I'm not going anywhere Sweets." He declares, resting his cheek on my shoulder and pulling me into a tight embrace like he's scared if he lets go I might disappear. I'm not leaving him for anything ever again if I can help it.

"Sweets." I hear Caleb snicker. "Dude, you *know* I love you, both of you, but really ... *Sweets*? I don't think anyone has ever accused Logan of being *sweet*." He laughs again and I hear his curse. "What was that for Makenna?" And I know without even looking that our sister has given him a clip over the ear, the likes of which only our mother did better when she was still with us. I wrap my arms around Jules' waist and pull him in closer. "Hey, *Sweets*, you need to take *Love* home and do whatever making up you're going to do there, because people are trying to eat here and you two are starting to get a bit sickening really."

"What he's *trying* to say is, you guys should get out of here and celebrate being in love." Makenna says while giving our little brother a scowl that could make most adults cower, but not our brother.

"Isn't that what I just said?"

"No."

"Hey guys, how about you both stop and just congratulate these two?" Brady, ever the voice of reason, which is scary really, says.

"You're right." Makenna says. Then in the blink of an eye Jules and I are swamped in a huge hug from my siblings.

"Ahh screw it." Then Brady joins in.

When we all separate, I say to Makenna, "I'm taking the rest of the day off."

"Of course you are!" She agrees. "Now get out of here you two before Logan changes his mind and decides he needs to do 'just one more thing' before he can leave." Then she's pushing us towards the door, and I have to untangle myself from Jules so that we can walk without tripping over. I don't let him move too far away from me though, because I take his hand in mine, then pull him into my side.

I can feel every set of eyes in Vines on us and I couldn't give two shits about any of them. Then, just as I reach for the door to open it and leave, All of Me by John Legend starts playing and I hear Kenna say, "Nice one."

"Thanks Caleb." I say over my shoulder without actually looking back and walk out the door with Julian beside me. "So, are you coming to my place, or do you need more time to think?"

"You're giving me the option? What happened to the growly, demanding Neanderthal in Vines just now?"

I stop walking, causing Jules to stop suddenly, because I've still got his hand in mine. He raises his eyebrow at me, slightly questioning what I'm doing.

"You always have a choice Julian, you know that, right? I might be a bossy bastard, but I never want you to feel pushed into anything. You always have the right to say no, Love."

He steps in close to me, and rests his hand on my chest. "I know Sweets, have no fear, if I didn't want to be here I wouldn't be, but I love you, you grumpy, bossy bastard and I don't want to be anywhere else but here with you, always." He says smiling.

"So you're coming home then?" I ask him hopefully.

"Yes Logan, I'm coming home with you." It's not quite what I meant, but that can wait until later, right now all I can think about is how to get Jules home as quickly as possible. "We can take my car, it's just here." I don't let him finish, can we walk faster? I don't know but that's what I want.

"Leave your car here, no-one is going to touch it. Walk with me?" I ask and he smiles back at me. He's just so fucking handsome I can't wait to have him all to myself.

"Let's walk then Logan." He says with a smile, and pulls away from me, loosening his grip on my hand, but I don't let him. Instead, I tighten my hold and pull him into my side. When I've got him secured there, I drop his hand, but I wrap that arm around his waist, resting my hand on his hip. I feel his arm around my back and his hand rests on my hip too. I can't explain how happy his touch makes me. I need him to understand that there's no more hiding for us. He thinks I don't like public displays of affection, but he couldn't be more wrong, I've longed to show the world that this man belongs to me.

"Oh hey, Mr Drake." One of my guys from the Winery starts, but I don't let him finish.

"I'm off for the rest of the day Gary, if it's urgent you'll need to talk to Makenna, I'm sure she can help you out. If not, it's going to have to wait until tomorrow."

He looks between Jules and myself and smiles. "Sure Mr Drake, you enjoy your day. Nice to see you again Julian." He says with a nod in Jules' direction, then walks away .

"Damn it, even you get called by your first name around here." I grumble, and Jules laughs.

"Well, you give off the aura of a boss and I'm just the boss' friend, therefore I'm on a more level playing field."

"You're more than the boss' friend Julian."

"What am I then?"

"You're the boss' boyfriend. His lover. His world." I say as we reach the front of my house.

"That sounds good, Logan."

"No, that sounds like not enough, but it's perfect for right now." I correct him, and then I kiss him until he's breathless and I feel a little dizzy myself.

With his eyes still shut, he asks, "What does that mean, 'right now'?"

"That means, that for right now Mr Bishop, I can be content with you being my *boyfriend,* but one day, and it better be soon, you're going to be my husband."

I watch as the shock rolls over his gorgeous face. "Are you for real? Are you proposing to me right now?"

"Oh I'm for real Julian but believe me when I say, you'll know when I'm fucking proposing to you Love. You won't be questioning me, but you will be agreeing to marry me."

"Oh I will, will I?"

"One day soon you will, yes."

While we've been talking, I've managed to push open the door and walk him backwards into the house. I slam the door closed and lock it. There's no fucking way I want Caleb or anyone else just walking in here like they live here when all I plan to do is make up with Jules all day long. Possibly all night too.

"Well, OK then I guess."

"I'm so glad you agree with me. That's one less thing I have to worry about."

"You were worried?" He asks, running his hands up and down my arms, then his hands disappear under my suit jacket. I can feel the heat of his touch on my shoulders as he pushes the jacket off my body. I know I should let it fall to the floor, but I just can't do it. I catch it by the collar and throw it over the back of the couch.

"Yes." I answer simply.

"God Logan, wearing a vest should be illegal. You're so sexy in this damned thing." I watch as his hands roam over my chest, playing with the buttons on my vest. "You're always so well put together. Crisp business shirt, tailored pants and suit jacket, then there's these fucking vests. I can't resist you when you're wearing one, you know that right Sweets?"

"I know it for sure now Love, and I promise that when I wear them, I'm only wearing it to drive you insane." I say with a smirk and he groans.

"You're such a tease."

"It's not a tease when you can have what's underneath the vest any time you want, is it?" I ask seriously.

"Any time I want huh? So, if I walk into your office in the middle of the day, and you're looking all hot, sexy businessman in your vest, with your shirt sleeves rolled up to your elbows, you're saying I can just jump you right there and then, because I can have you any time I want?"

I groan at the visual he just created in my mind. "Damn it, please tell me that's likely to happen Love, and I will promise that if I'm not on a call, voice or video, that you can have your wicked way with me there and then."

"I promise." He says, his voice a rough murmur, almost like he's lost in the thought of it too.

I break my gaze away from him to look around us, and I realise that somehow without even trying, we've managed to find the bedroom.

"Naked, now." I growl.

"You first." He growls back at me. Without thinking about my next move, I toe off my shoes, undo my vest and shirt, taking them off together. As they drop to the floor I can't find a fuck to give about the mess we're leaving in our wake, because Jules is naked from the waist up as well.

"Julian." I rasp out.

"Logan."

Pants with belts clutter to the floor and I can't keep my distance for another second. When I get close enough to him to feel the heat of his body on mine, I wrap one hand around the side of his neck so that I can grip his jaw tightly, and pull his lips to mine, taking them in a searing kiss that feels like it could burn my soul deeply. This man is *mine* and I'm going to prove it to him.

Sex between us has always been raw, instinctual, and even though that's how we've started things tonight, all our built up need pushing us along, I'm going to prove to Jules that it's also about love and connection. Today I feel the need to prove to him that we're more than just desire, and if he lets me I know I'll love him for the rest of my life.

"I need you Jules." I whisper against his lips, but I know without a doubt he heard me because I hear his breath hitch before he speaks.

"Logan." My name drops off his lips as more of a sigh than an actual word.

"Tell me to stop, and I will, but I need you to know that I don't want to Love."

"Don't stop Sweets. God, please don't stop. I need you Logan." Those are the words I needed to hear.

"I need you too Love. Always you. Only you. Forever." I declare.

"Damn it Logan, I missed you. So. Damned. Much!"

"Let me love you." I say, dragging my lips along his jaw and down his neck. Licking and sucking on the skin that I can reach on his neck and shoulder. I turn his jaw so that his neck stretches to the side, giving me better access and a clear answer to my question but he's still not touching *me*. My other hand moves to his hip, pulling him in to my body and causing him to lose his balance slightly. His hands reach up to hold onto my shoulders to stop himself from falling. Just like I knew he would.

I slide my leg between his, being just a couple of inches taller than him gives me a slight advantage for my next move. My knee is at just the right height to be able to press up against his balls and he rolls his hips searching for more, his hands gripping on tightly to my biceps.

"Fuck Logan."

My hand drops from his neck down to his hip. Now both of my hands are pulling him closer to me. I'm rocking both of us slowly back and forth, our cocks pushing against each other, every time our hips collide, straining to get out of our boxer briefs. The thin fabric the only thing between us. I bring my hand around from his hip and squeeze it between our bodies. I rub up and down the imprint of his impressive cock outlined in his boxers and I want more, I want to hold his weight in my hand. I need to feel him twitch with my touch, and stroke him until he can't take anymore.

"Logan." My name is a hoarse whisper on his tongue. I know what else I'd like on his tongue, but that can wait until next time, this is all about him.

"What do you need Love? Tell me."

"You, me and everything in between, with nothing between us." His hands roam over my stomach, up my chest, over my shoulders and down arms, only to trace their path back to the waist of my boxers, which he pushes off my hips. They fall down my legs and I kick them to the side out of the way.

Following his lead, I push my hands past the band on his boxers and give his butt cheeks a tight squeeze, before pushing his boxers down his legs, until I'm on my knees helping him get rid of them completely.

"Get back up here." He demands.

"What if I want to stay down here all afternoon?" I say with a suggestive smile.

"No. Not yet. Logan, please." He looks down at me with desire and a desperation.

Without saying a word, I get off my knees, balancing on the balls of my feet. When I'm steady, I take his cock in my mouth and suck on the head, hard. His eyes squeeze shut, and he pulls the corner of his bottom lip into his mouth with his teeth. "Lo. Stop." I don't do as he asks, instead I take his entire length into my mouth, and roll his balls in my hand. "Fuck. Me. Logan!" I chuckle around his cock and then draw him further into the back of my throat and he groans. His chin is resting on his chest, which is rising and falling hard with every breath he takes. I draw my mouth back up to the head, run my tongue through his slit and then drop my mouth back down his cock to the base. "Argghhh."

I feel his legs give way slightly, and I drag my mouth off his cock, kissing my way up his body until I find his lips again. "You OK Love?" I ask in a whisper against his throat. He doesn't answer with words, just a groan that I feel vibrate on my lips that are resting on his Adam's apple.

"I need you, now." He grounds out between clenched teeth.

I gently push him away, "You can have me. On your hands and knees, now."

Without hesitating, Jules is on his hands and knees on the bed. The view takes my breath away and I can't look away from him as I open the bedside drawer to find a condom and some lube. Squirting some lube onto my fingers I play with him until he's loose and ready for me. His entire body is shaking as I roll the condom down my hard cock.

"Are you ready Love?" I ask, my voice barely above a whisper but I know that he heard me, because he drops his head to the mattress and groans his answer.

"Logan. Please. I need you." He says into the bed.

Slowly, I slide into his body, letting him adjust to me being there. I massage his back and shoulders as I slowly start to move inside him. The house is silent except for us, the sounds of skin slapping together, moans and groans echoing off the walls.

"Up." I command and he doesn't hesitate to pull himself up to his knees, bringing his back to my front and I wrap my arms around him to hold onto his pecs, keeping him pinned to me. He reaches behind his body to hold onto my hips as I start to move faster. "I'm not going to last very long this time Love."

"Me either, Lo." He rests his head on my shoulder and sighs. "You feel so good. I missed you."

"I missed you too." Our words are whispered into the room, the sun is shining through the sheer curtains on the window. "I'm going to come soon Jules." I tell him as I run a hand down his stomach and take his hard cock in my hand, my other hand, still on his chest, holding him to me. His hands release my hips and travel up to grip my neck. I take the hint and start to kiss and suck on his neck as he stretches to give me better access.

"I'm so close Logan." His whole body shudders. "So. Damned. Close."

"Me too Love." I say as I feel the tell-tale tingle in the base of my spine that says I'm on the brink. My movements start to become a little out of control and Jules is pushing back into me, meeting every push and pull of my body. I jerk him off, until he comes in my hand, and just as he cries out his release I feel mine. "I love you Julian." I say in grunts in his ear.

"I love you too Logan." He says, in a voice that's hoarse from exertion.

Leaving kisses down the back of his neck and between his shoulder blades, I pull out of his body and gently push against his back so that he lies down. I'll never tire of seeing this man in my bed. Our bed.

Kissing his forehead, I whisper, "I'll be back in a second." He hums in answer and I know he feels good. Leaving him there, I walk into the bathroom, get rid of the condom, and wash my hands, cleaning up the mess we both made. A smile creeps across my face as I remember Jules coming hard in my hand.

I walk back into the bedroom, I can't remember the last time I felt this happy.

"What's that goofy grin all about Logan?" Jules asks, his voice sleepy and his eyes half closed.

"Just happy my love." I answer him, sure that my grin looks even more stupid after his question. "Here, let me clean you up." He bats my hand away when I try to clean away the remnants of his orgasm with a warm wash cloth.

"Stop it Logan. I'm going to the bathroom, I was just waiting for you to get out of there." He grumbles, not looking at all like he plans on moving anywhere.

"Uhuh, looks like you're moving really fast there sloth." I laugh. "Come on, just let me." I don't get to finish, he growls and sits up, giving me a death glare.

"You couldn't just let me lie there for a minute could you? I was getting up, just not on your schedule. Give me the cloth, I'll take it back to the bathroom with me, arsehole." He's frowning but I can see the corners of his lips twitching with a smile.

I watch him walk away, then quickly fix up the covers on the bed and pull them back to lie there waiting for Jules to come back, one arm resting across my stomach the other across my eyes.

"Stop looking so sexy or it's going to be my turn to take you real damned quick Sweets." He sounds sleepy, satisfied, but tired.

"Come here Love, let me take care of you." I wiggle over to the other side of the bed so that he can lie next to me.

"I don't need you to take care of me Logan, I'm a big boy, I can take care of myself." He grumbles, even as he lies down next to me, his back to my front once again, and pulls the covers up.

We're silent for a few minutes, I can feel Jules relaxing and he's almost asleep. "I'm glad you're here Julian."

"I'm glad I'm here too Logan." He says quietly.

"Then stay." I say against his shoulder.

"I'm not going anywhere Sweets."

"That's not what I mean." I say, my lips still on his shoulder.

"Then what *do* you mean Logan?" Before I answer him, I slide an arm under his neck and put a hand on his chest, pulling him back into me. Then, I wrap my other arm around his waist to pull his back tightly against my front, happy that he didn't struggle and try to pull away, I finally answer.

"I mean don't leave."

"Yeah, I heard you Logan, but what exactly do you mean?" His body stiffens and I know he understands what I mean.

"Move in." I blurt out.

"Move in here?" he asks.

"Yes here, where else?" I ask more than a little pissed off.

"This is the afterglow talking Logan." Jules says with a nervous laugh, trying to pull away from me.

"No, it's not. I built this house for you, for us. It was always supposed to be *our* house Jules. Always. I never planned on living here without you." I assure him. "You had a say in everything that went into this place, didn't you ever stop to wonder why?"

"It's too soon, Logan." He says hesitantly.

"No, it's not Julian. We've been together for years and I know you feel like most of it wasn't real, but it was as real to me as this vineyard, the winery, and this house. The house I built for us."

"Logan, I can't." He says so quietly I almost miss it. Almost.

"Just think about it, OK? Do I want you to move in today? Hell yes, *but* I'm willing to give you some time to think about it and get used to the idea." I haven't moved my lips off his skin.

"How very generous of you." I don't need to see his face to know that his sarcasm filled sentence was also accompanied by a rolling of his eyes.

"Just think about it Jules, please." I won't stop until I get what I want, but I can give him a day or two to get used to the idea before I try again.

"Sure." That one word brings me hope.

"Now, get some sleep, because I'm not done with you yet and you're going to need some rest."

"Promises, promises, Mr Drake." I growl against his skin.

"You're the only one who can make calling me that sound sexy as fuck."

"I would hope so, because if anyone else turned you on by calling you Mr Drake, you'd be in a lot of trouble, mister."

I chuckle. I'm feeling lighter than I have in weeks, months, to be honest, perhaps years. "No-one turns me on like you do Mr Bishop. Sleep well Love." I say, dropping a few kisses over his neck and shoulders as I get comfy on my pillow.

"Sleep well, Sweets." He murmurs and then he's snoring lightly. He's always been able to fall asleep quicker than anyone I've ever known, but it doesn't take me long to follow behind him. I dream about the love of my life living with me in our house and a little girl with light brown, curly hair running around the backyard with a puppy chasing her, laughter echoing around the garden.

It's a sweet dream, made even sweeter because of the fact that the love of my life is sharing it with me.

Chapter Thirteen
JULES

I wake with the sun shining on my face and a naked, sexy as hell man wrapped around me, holding on tight like he's afraid if he lets go I might just disappear. I guess I can't blame him for that, I did walk away from him almost two weeks ago.

I smile as I remember his display of affection in Vines earlier. I never thought I would be on the receiving end of that kind of affection in public from Logan. As I lie there, my eyes shut to block out the sun, enjoying being wrapped up in his arms, another memory floods back, making me twitch a little and my eyes to fly open. Logan stirs slightly behind me and I freeze, not wanting to wake him up yet.

Did he really ask me to move in with him before? I swear that's the last thing I remember happening before we fell asleep! Was it just from the afterglow of the amazing make up sex? Not that sex isn't always amazing between us, surely he only asked because he was happy? *Was* he happy? *Is* he happy? Why am I thinking about this now? I should lie here and enjoy being back here, in Logan's arms.

"Stop thinking so hard, Love." His voice still husky and deep from sleep, rumbles though my ribcage.

"I thought you were asleep." I say, surprised not only by him speaking but also because he knew I was thinking. Perhaps starting to freak out a little.

"You're also thinking too hard, Love after I asked you to move in here, with me. I figured that would be what you're thinking about, now that you're awake." He chuckles. "I felt your entire body stiffen as you remembered me asking you."

"But how?" I start.

"How did I know you were awake *and* what you were thinking?"

"Yes!" I demand, doubting his ability to read my mind, while trying to turn around in his arms to face him and not getting too far with his arms of steel banded around me tightly. Which all earns me another low chuckle.

"We've been doing this for what? Six years, just over?" I nod in agreement because that's about all I can move. "Right. So you think I don't know you well enough by now then?"

"But." I stammer.

"But *you* think I wasn't taking any notice?" He lets out a long, loud sigh. "Turn around and look at me Love."

"I can't." I say quietly and he loosens his hold on me so that I can turn to face him. When I'm finally facing him, he reaches up and gently takes my jaw in his hand, forcing me to look him in the eyes.

"I noticed *everything* Julian John Bishop. Don't mistake my stupidity about not being honest with myself and the people around me, for not loving *you*. I will never forgive myself for making you doubt my love for you, ever. I will spend the rest of our lives making it up to you, I promise you that Jules."

"You don't have to Logan."

"I do Jules and I will. You will never again doubt my love for you Julian. I swear to you." His eyes are swinging between mine to see if I'm hearing and believing him.

"I never thought that you didn't love me Logan." I tell him, my voice barely above a whisper, as I reach up and caress his stubbly cheek.

"Just that I didn't love you enough." His voice just as quiet as mine now and I know it's statement as much as it is a question.

"No, not really." I try to reassure him.

"No, don't do that Jules. Don't make it out to be less than it is. That's not how this is going to work, not again. You need to be honest with me. You *need* to tell me when I'm being stupid and I'm making you feel like you're not enough because you *are* enough. In fact you're too good for a bastard like me but I'm keeping you anyway." His smile is so sweet, so gentle I can't help myself, I lean in leaving a light kiss on his lips.

"I don't think either one of is too good for the other Logan." I kiss him again. "I think together, we make sense."

"I do too." He mumbles against my lips. I feel the vibrations through my entire body, making it useless to resist kissing him, so I don't. I press my lips harder to his, his open on a moan and I take full advantage. My mouth crashes into his, our tongues tangling together, causing us both to moan loudly. Reaching up, I grip the back of his head, pulling him impossibly closer to me, pouring the overwhelming aching need pulsing through me from almost two weeks of not seeing him, into that one kiss. I need him to understand just how much I missed him. "I missed you too Jules." He says as he pulls back from my kiss, smiling against my lips.

"I'm glad because the next time you hide from me Logan Drake, I might just kill you." I scold him, trying to pull completely out of his embrace.

"I wasn't hiding from you Love, I never hide from you." He looks so sexy when he's deadly serious.

"Not me, *me* you idiot. I mean *me, everybody*." I roll my eyes at him.

"Don't be so dramatic Jules." He says with a raised eyebrow and a low chuckle.

"Me? Dramatic? I don't think so Sweets!" I push on his chest to get out of his embrace as he throws his head back and lets out a roar of laughter that makes my work easier. I roll backwards while moving to sit up and when my feet land on the floor I stand up.

"Come back here Julian." Logan demands, his laughter dying out as soon as he realises I've moved off the bed. I don't respond, I don't look back at him either and I hear the covers rustling around. That's my only warning that he's on the move as I walk my naked body to the bathroom. I can *feel* him walking behind me, but I don't turn around and he doesn't touch me. He doesn't hesitate though when I turn the shower on and step under the warm water. I am *so* glad we designed this shower not only to accommodate two grown men but to also have instant hot water.

His hands are on me instantly, roaming over my now wet body and it feels so damn good. Even if I *was* mad at him, which I'm not, I wouldn't be able to stay mad at him for long when he's touching me like this. The problem I have with that, is that I *know* he knows it as well and he definitely uses it to his advantage.

"What are you doing Logan?" I ask, already well aware of what he's doing, I honestly don't need clarification I just want to hear him say it.

"Nothing." He says, before leaving a kiss between my shoulder blades.

"I think we both know that's not true, Logan." I can feel a grin spread across his lips that are still firmly planted between my shoulder blades.

"What do *you* think I'm doing then Mr Bishop?" I struggle to concentrate on his question as his hands travel up my stomach, coming to rest on my pecs. Not to mention I can still feel that deep voice of his rumbling through my body because he's leaning his mouth against my back.

"Hmmmm?" Is all I manage to get out, I've completely lost all train of thought or where this conversation was going. He chuckles again, and I press my hands against the wall of the shower, hoping that will hold me up as one of his hands travels back down my chest, over my stomach and down to my balls. I groan as he starts to lightly roll them in his hand.

"What do you think I'm doing Love?" He asks again, as he sucks my earlobe into his mouth, then bites gently along the column of my neck. My thought processes are fried, and I can't think at *all,* as one hand plays and tweaks my nipples, while the other runs up and down my cock, stopping every other stroke to play with my balls. I'm in sensory fucking overload. "Do you know what I'm doing yet Love?" He growls in my ear.

"Driving me fucking insane." I mumble, not truly sure if I spoke the words out loud or not.

"I'm going to make you come."

"So. Close."

"I know and you're going to come in my hand, then I'm going to clean you up."

"Uhuh." I say, my head hanging between my arms pushing against the shower wall, that are barely holding me upright, my chin resting on my chest. "Fuck!"

"That's right Love, fuck my hand." My hips rock into his hand, not because he told me too but because I couldn't stop myself if I wanted to and do not want to. "Come for me Jules." He commands, his hot breath in my ear. I'm *so* close, then he bites the skin where my neck meets my shoulder and I'm done.

My knees buckle and Logan stops pulling on my nipple to wrap his arm around my waist, holding me up. Knowing that he's got me, I let go and do as he demands.

"Logan!" His name more like a groan than an actual word.

"That's it. Come for me Jules. Now!" That's all the encouragement I need to come in his hand.

Chapter Fourteen
LOGAN

I give Jules a couple of minutes to gather himself but he's still quite dazed after coming so hard in my hand, so I let him lean on the wall while I soap up his shoulders, back and legs. Then I rinse him clean, paying special attention to the crack between his butt cheeks. He starts to push back against my hand while groaning quietly at my touch, but I don't let him take it too far.

Stopping, I place my hands on his shoulders to turn him around.

"Logan." His eyes are mostly closed and I gently push him backwards so that his back is against the wall, giving him support to stand. I take the bottle of body wash off the shelf again and squeeze a generous amount into my hand. Jules takes the bottle out of my hand and places it back on the shelf without looking. He knocks the few other things on the shelf over but neither of us cares to fix them, as I start rubbing the soap all over his chest and stomach. He stops me, his hand gripping my wrist tightly, before I reach his already half-mast cock. "I can't go again. It's too soon."

"Do you have such little faith in me Love? I was just making sure every gorgeous inch of you is clean." I say to him, with fake outrage.

"Sure you were Logan, I believe you when thousands wouldn't Sweets but I can't go again, so let's not tempt fate shall we?" He teases me, a sparkle in his eyes when I look up into them.

"I'm sure you can Love but I'm not going to push you too hard on our first day back together." The grin on my face is too wide, I know I must look like a maniac.

"Don't look at me like that Logan Drake! I can see the mischief in your eyes and I'm telling you, I can't go again. Not so soon anyway." His smile is lazy, adorably sexy and I know that I've worn him out.

"I promise, no more fun." I can't help laughing at the way his eyes pop open and his jaw almost hits the floor in shock. "I haven't had my fill, not by a long shot Jules, I have close to two weeks to make up for, but I can pace myself. I can allow you some time to rest and recuperate." I grin at him.

"How very generous of you Logan." He says, sarcasm lacing his words, even as his hands rest on my shoulders to steady himself as I continue to run my hands up and down his chest, stomach and ribs.

"I know, I'm sweet like that, that's why you call me Sweets, right?"

"You keep telling yourself that, *Sweets*." He smirks, letting his eyes drift closed again. Before he knows what's going on, my hands that were resting on his hips, move to his backside and I leave a stinging smack on them both. His eyes fly wide open again and his jaw is slack with shock.

"Move that cute derrière out of the way so that I can quickly wash myself." He closes his mouth and raises an eyebrow at me. "Please Jules." Without a word he slides out the way, managing to rub most of his front over mine in the process.

"Your turn." He says as he reaches for the body wash.

"Not this time, we don't have the time." I say, shaking my head and taking the bottle off him.

"Why not?" His confusion is adorable!

"I promised to have dinner with Makenna and Brady. No doubt Caleb will be there as well." I tell him as I soap up my body, his eyes following every movement.

"I'm sure she'll forgive you if you don't show." He says, distractedly, making me grin in satisfaction.

"You mean if *we* don't show?" More confusion registers on his face. "If I go you go. You understand that she means that you're automatically invited as well, right?"

"I'm not so sure about that Logan." He says, turning away from me while soaping up his chest. Placing my hands on his shoulders, I try to turn him around but he doesn't budge.

"Jules." I say, quietly. "Julian Bishop, love of my life, please turn around and look at me." I feel the sigh that he lets out but slowly he turns around so that we're facing each other but he's not looking at me. I'm not used to this Julian, the one that seems so unsure of what he means to me and whether he belongs or not. So, I take his chin in my hand and bring his eyes up to meet mine. There will be no doubt left in his mind that he belongs with me, or with my family. "Jules, make no mistake, that where I go you go. If I'm invited, you're invited. Especially when it comes to my family and do you want to know why?"

"Cause Kenna would kill you?" He mumbles and I can't help throwing my head back a little to laugh loudly.

"You're not wrong there but mainly because I *want* you there. You *are* my family Love, I wouldn't want anyone else by my side and I'm sorry Julian. I'm so fucking sorry that I made you feel anything less than that. I'm so fucking sorry that I made you feel like you meant nothing to me because nothing could be further from the damned truth!" I grip him a tight hug, one that is probably squeezing the breath out of him, causing him to wrap his arms around my waist for balance. "Never again will you question how I feel about us or where you fit. You fit with me, wherever I am that's where you fit and wherever you are, that's where I fit. I love you Jules."

"I love you too Logan." I feel him relax in my arms and hear the sigh that escapes him. The stress he was feeling and the relief he's feeling now, obvious.

"I'm so sorry I ever made you doubt me Love. I know I have a lot to make up to you but I promise to keep trying for the rest of our lives, if you'll let me."

"No, you don't Logan. I have to take some of the responsibility as well. I could have told you years ago that I'd had enough. The truth is, I kinda liked having you all to myself in a way." He smirks at me and I can't resist kissing him. Before we get too carried away, I pull back from his lips and rest my forehead on his.

"I liked having you to myself too, Jules."

"It's just that in the end, I felt like I was a dirty secret. Something, well someone, you never wanted anyone else to know about and not because you didn't want to share me. It felt like I wasn't enough Logan. That I didn't mean enough to you, that you wouldn't have a conversation with your family, with *anyone*, about me, about us. The real us and that hurt." His hold tightens around me and I relish it because it means he's here with me. "I guess watching Makenna and Brady get married just drove home how far apart we really were."

I don't answer him straight away, I take the time to think about what he said and discover, to my horror, that he's right. I put that wedge between us.

"You're right Love. I put that distance between us and I'm sorry. So fucking sorry but I didn't see it before, honestly. I didn't do it on purpose, I promise you that." He raises an eyebrow at me, questioning whether I truly didn't see it and that makes me think. "You know, you're right. On some subconscious level I guess I *did* know what I was doing but I swear, if I'd realised sooner how it was affecting you, affecting our relationship, I would have put a stop to it sooner."

"OK." He says, stepping out of the shower and taking a towel off the rack to start drying himself.

"That's it, OK?" I ask, turning off the shower and reaching by him to get a towel of my own.

"Yup." He says, the 'p' making a popping sound and walking back into our bedroom. I finish drying myself off and join him, both of us pulling on clothes in silence.

"Are you sure it's that simple Jules?" I ask, making sure that it really is that simple. He stops when he has jeans on but is still holding his shirt in his hands and I take a minute to enjoy the view.

"Yes, it's really that simple Logan." He takes a step closer to me, resting a hand on my bare chest, right over my rapidly beating heart. "When I decided to come here earlier today, I had to make a choice. I had to decide whether you loved me enough and whether I loved *you* enough to move forward. To be open, honest with each other and our loved ones. I had to decide whether I believed in *you* enough to come back. I wouldn't be here, especially not in your bed, if I was even a little unsure of *us*, Logan."

"Are you?"

"What?" He doesn't look up from the drawer he's rummaging around in for what, I'm not sure.

"Sure. Are you sure of us, that you want to be here?" I ask, not sure if I'm going to like the answer, even though he *has* already told me he is but here I am giving him a chance to change his mind.

"I am one hundred percent sure." He answers me, sounding a little distracted by his search but confident. He stops rummaging and looks at me sharply, with a scowl. "Aren't you? I mean, you said when you came to my place last night that you wouldn't walk away. Was that just to make me feel better? To make yourself feel better about breaking up with me? And if that's the case, what the hell was this?" His voice hitches and I take two long strides towards him, then pull him into my arms.

"Julian, there have never been words that have meant more to me or that I have ever meant more in my life! *If* you forgive and *if* you take me back, you won't get another chance to walk away. This is it for you! *You're it for me Love.*" I move away from him, only to take his face in my hands. "*You* mean more to me than anything else and your happiness is everything to me."

"I don't plan on walking away again."

"You promise?"

"I promise Sweets. You're stuck with me." I feel his smile on his lips as I kiss the breath out of him and he holds onto my biceps to steady himself. We only stop when we hear my phone chime with a message from Makenna. "That sister of yours has impeccable timing!" Julian says, his lips a breath away from mine, curling up into a smile.

"Yes she does and we would be able to ignore my phone, not knowing or caring who it was, except that *you* decided to give everyone their own ringtones." I say, my own lips smiling against his.

"And message tones. I can't believe you kept them like that for so long." He says pulling out of my embrace and walking over to get my phone for me.

"Why wouldn't I leave them?" I ask, confused.

"Because and I quote, 'that's not what a phone is used for.'"

"That's a very poor impersonation of me, Julian!" Fake indignation lacing my voice, making him laugh.

"That was a perfect impression of you, *Logan.* I've had a long time to perfect it." Laughter still in his voice and I can't help the smile his happiness brings to my face. He's happy, relaxed and comfortable in this house, *our* house and it warms my soul. I can't help just staring at him, watching him move around the space as if it's home. "Are you OK Logan?"

"Hmmmm?"

"Are you going to check what your sister sent you or are you going to ignore her long enough that she comes here or sends Brady down to get us?"

"Get dressed." I command, making him raise an eyebrow at me. "Please Love. She might send Caleb down here and I don't need him to see you even half naked." Jules mumbles something to himself that I don't catch, just as I'm about to ask him to repeat himself, my phone chimes with another message.

Makenna: *You and Jules are excused from joining us for dinner*

Makenna: *I organised some food for you guys from Vines, you just have to let Leila know when you want it. Just don't leave it too late, please?*

Me: *Thank you Kenna. We were just about to leave to come to dinner though*

I don't even have to wait a minute for her reply.

Makenna: *No! You're both banned from the main house for at least the next few days. Get reacquainted. Dinner with us can wait.*

Me: *Thank you Kenna. I love you*

Makenna: *I love you too. Now go feed your man and tell him we love him too!* She tags at least a dozen hearts on the end of her message, making me smile.

"Is everything OK?"

"We are excused from family dinner." I smile at him but my smile disappears as I watch his shoulders sag in disappointment. "Hey, not because they don't want to see you, well maybe they don't." He stiffens in front of me. "What I mean to say is, Makenna wants us to get 'reacquainted', her word not mine and she's organised for Leila to deliver us some dinner. As long as we don't leave it too late to tell her what we want."

"That's kind of sweet."

"She said we're banned from the main house for the next couple of days. I've also been instructed to tell you, they love you. *She* loves you and can't wait to catch up with you."

The smile he gives me, makes my heart happy. "Let's call Leila then. Do you think she'll send Caleb?"

"Who knows. They'll probably come together." Jules snorts behind me as I press my phone to my ear waiting for Leila to pick up. When I look at him, he makes his face the perfect picture of innocence, making me realise what I said. "Ohhh really Jules? Ewwww!"

"Logan, is that you?" Leila's voice speaks in my ear, making me start.

"Huh? Oh yes, sorry Leila, Jules just said something to me as you answered the phone." This earns me a chuckle from her.

"Now worries Logan. I take it Makenna messaged you about dinner? We have it all set here and ready for you whenever you want it."

"We can come and get it now." I tell her, hoping that she'll take me up on the offer, which will mean no-one comes *here*.

"That's not necessary, we'll deliver it to you. In fact, we can deliver it now if that's OK with you?" She asks cheerfully.

"That would be great, thank you Leila."

"No problems, see you soon Logan." She's hung up before I can reply.

"They'll be here any minute." I tell Jules, looking up at him from my phone.

"Them? I thought it was just Leila."

"Where there's Leila." I start.

"There's Caleb." Jules finishes.

"She might have Sara with her." I say hopefully, knowing it's a lost cause. We look at each other and laugh.

"It's a possibility, sure." Jules says, as there's a knock on the door. "Guess we're about to find out."

Moving to the door, I'm ready to greet Leila when the door flies open, answering the question about who she brought with her to bring us dinner.

"Good evening Leila." I say smiling warmly at her. "Caleb." I greet my brother without amusement.

"Good evening brother and brother in law. Allow us to set up dinner for you."

"Caleb, we're just here to drop off the food, not dish it up for them. I'm sure between them, Logan and Julian can deal with that. I've seen some of the amazing meals that Julian cooks, he doesn't need us here." Leila blushes as Caleb barges his way into my house like he lives here. "I'm sorry Logan."

"Don't be. I've had a couple of decades to get used to his behaviour." I smile at her. "Here, let me take that from you." I take the box she's carrying out of her hands and walk towards the kitchen.

"Why don't you come in Leila?" Jules motions for her to follow us. She seems a little uncomfortable but she follows my brother into the kitchen. Which reminds me to have another talk to him about their *friendship* again.

Chapter Fifteen
JULES

The last thing I want is to see Caleb so soon after he was at my apartment. I walk into the kitchen behind Leila. I'm not sure who's feeling more uncomfortable at this point, Leila or myself.

"Thank you for organising this Leila." Logan says.

"You're more than welcome. Both of you." She says turning her smile my way.

"We appreciate it Leila." I smile at back at her. "Caleb." I say, not meeting his eyes, making him laugh.

"You're welcome brothers. Now, we're going to get out of here but it sure is nice to see you both with clothes on. Specially seeing as how I have Miss Phillip's with me." He says with a smirk and Leila gives him a confused look. "I'll explain later." I just manage to hear him say in her ear, as he rests his hand gently on her lower back, guiding her towards the door. I look up to see Logan scowling at the intimate touch.

"Why would we be naked when we knew *Leila* was coming by?" Logan asks, confused.

"No reason. None at all." Caleb says that smirk of his plastered on his face, Leila ignores them both and starts to explain what needs to be done to our meal.

"You may not have to heat them up. They were just pulled out of the oven, so they should still be warm enough to eat them, if you eat them now. No pressure though." Caleb presses a little harder into her back to move her towards the door faster and I'm not sure if it's for our benefit or his. "Caleb, stop pushing me out the door, I need to give them a few instructions."

"They can work it out for themselves Darlin.'" He smiles warmly at her and boy does she return that smile. I can see that Logan's about to say something but one look from me and he stops. "Can't you guys? Of course you can. By your own admission, Jules is a brilliant cook Leila, I'm sure he knows how to heat some food up."

"True. You're right. Have a good night guys, I hope you enjoy your dinner."

"Night." Caleb says, waving behind him as he closes the door behind them both. We watch as they slowly walk back to Vines. They're not holding hands but they're not far off it.

"They're adults Logan." I warn, before he can say anything.

"But." He starts but stops when I look at him with a raised eyebrow.

"I get it Sweets, I truly do. She's a valued employee *and* you actually like her." He's leaning back on the kitchen island, legs crossed at the ankles, and arms crossed over his chest, an adorable frown on his face. I walk over to join him and bump his hip with mine. "I think she'll make him happy Logan." I say quietly.

"I'm not worried about what she'll do for him. I'm more worried about how he'll treat her."

"Well now that's just plain rude!" I say, insulted for Caleb. "So, you're saying she's too good for your own *brother*? Am I getting that right, Logan?"

"No. I mean." He rubs a hand over his face, collecting his thoughts. "He has a reputation Jules."

"Wow! I mean, I thought *you* of all people wouldn't believe reputations and rumours Logan Drake. Of all the ridiculous things you could have said, that is the *most* insulting one you could have gone with." He opens his mouth to speak but I hold my hand up to stop, while moving away from him to start plating up dinner. "No wonder he won't make his move, you've got him so worried about what you and Makenna will say to him, that he's just staying in the friend zone."

"It's business Jules. She's an *employee* and he's an owner of that business she works for. It could end in disaster." I stop what I'm doing and look him dead in the eyes.

"For *them* you mean, right Logan? Please tell me that you're not more worried about the affect a failed relationship *might* have on the family business, than you would about how it might affect your brother *or* Leila!" He doesn't answer me right away, instead he presses his lips together as though he's trying to *not* speak. "*Logan Drake!*"

"That's not what I'm saying Jules." He starts saying but stops.

"That kind of sounds exactly like what you're saying." I sigh before continuing. "Look, I get it, I do. I know how hard you and Makenna have worked to make Drake Wines the success it is today. I know how hard Jack worked before you to get it up and running as well. I know it means everything to you to *keep* it running and being successful."

"But?"

"*But* there's more to life Logan and you of all people should get that. You should understand that what people see isn't necessarily who a person *is*." I take our plates of food to the table and Logan follows behind me with the cutlery. "You and I both know that sometimes perception isn't reality."

"Do you want a drink?" He asks as I sit down at the table.

"Yes please." I watch as he moves around the kitchen pouring our drinks. "Just because people call Caleb a playboy or manwhore or whatever other crass turn of phrase they want to use, that doesn't make him one. I mean, have you seen him bring someone home since he's moved back onto the Drake Wines property?"

"No, but that doesn't mean he hasn't been with anyone." Logan defends himself, as he places our drinks on the table and sits opposite me at the table.

"That's true but he also rarely goes into town to party with mates anymore either." I remind him. "I know he did a fair bit when he first got home but he's really settled in here. He's taking being here and working for the family business seriously Logan. I think you should have more faith in your brother. Everyone has to grow up at some point and just because in his past he may have played the field a little, doesn't mean he still is or would while he's with someone like Leila."

"You're right." I know I am but it's always nice to hear Logan admitting that I am. "It's just that, I want to protect them. The both of them. He's my little brother Jules and she's a beautiful, brilliant girl with a very bright future ahead of her."

"Maybe they can be good for each other Logan. You never know, it could be Leila that breaks Caleb's heart you know and not the other way round." He nods in agreement and we spend the first minutes of the meal in silence. I know he's thinking about what I said, so I leave him to it.

"When did you become so wise Jules?" Logan asks when we're almost finished eating.

"I'm not any wiser than you are Logan. I just know that we all have own issues to deal with in relationships." I shrug. "For now, you don't have anything to worry about with those two, because they're friends. If one of them decides to make a move on the other, then you can worry but until then, you're stressing yourself out over nothing. They're not doing anything inappropriate while they're at work or in Vines, therefore it's none of your business. Yet."

Logan doesn't say anything, he just nods and puts our dishes in the dishwasher. We talk about other things, catching up on everything we've missed in the last couple of weeks. While I know the subject has been dropped, I also know he's still thinking about the situation as we settle in on the couch with dessert to watch a movie.

Chapter Sixteen
LOGAN

Dinner is delicious. I expected nothing less coming from the kitchen of Vines with Leila at the helm. Which is the main reason I'm against Caleb trying a relationship with her. We need her to *want* to stay working for us and if he screws up, then we could lose her.

When we've finished dessert, Jules snuggles into my side and I drape my arm around his shoulders, pulling him impossibly closer. I know what he said is right and I won't, probably should never, step into any kind of budding relationship between my brother and one of my favourite employees but it doesn't stop me from worrying about the possible outcomes.

"Stop thinking Logan. It's out of your control and as much as I know you *hate* that, you can't change it. Certainly not tonight that's for sure. So, be with *me*. It is our first day back together after all." The smile he gives me relaxes me and warms my heart. With my free hand, I grip his chin, bringing his lips up to meet mine as I drop my head down to meet him in the middle. The kiss I intended to be quick but passionate, turns into a deep, all-consuming kind of kiss that sucks the breath out of your lungs. When we part, we're both panting, trying to suck in as much oxygen as we can.

"We're missing the movie." Julian whispers, his voice husky with need.

"You've seen it before." I remind him. "A million times if I had to guess."

"I know but I want to relax with you. It can't be all about sex Logan." He grumbles as he lays his head back on my chest to watch the movie. A movie I couldn't tell you the title of but I know we've watched it plenty of times and I could probably tell you the plot. "Stop thinking so hard about things that you have no power to change Logan. If they fall for each other, they fall for each other. If they don't, they don't. If they break up, they break up and then you deal with the fall out. If there is any."

"I know all of that Jules." My attitude coming through the tone of my voice.

"Then stop worrying about it so much, Sweets. He's a grown man and she's a grown woman." He stretches up to kiss me on the cheek. "And you're here with *your* man, so relax."

"I love you Jules." I tell him, returning the favour and kissing his cheek.

"I love you too, now let me watch my movie." He relaxes back onto my chest and the rest of the movie goes by without interruption. When it finishes and Jules doesn't move, I assume he's fallen asleep as per usual and I sit for a few minutes trying to work out how I'm going to get us to bed. "I'm not asleep Logan." He speaks up, making me jump slightly and he laughs.

"I didn't think you were." I protest, making him laugh even more.

"Yes you did! You were trying to work out how to get us both to bed." He says teasingly as he jabs me in the side with a finger, making my body twitch away from him. I've got ticklish sides and he knows it! "Just admit it Sweets, you'd already turned off the TV and were sitting here in the silence, contemplating what to do next."

"Well, in my defence, you do normally fall asleep. So, why didn't you move then?"

"I was enjoying just being here, in your arms, on your couch, with you." His voice almost a whisper, like he didn't want to say it out loud just in case he ruined it.

"It's *our* couch and you should feel at home here because that's what it is, your home. Before you start protesting, yes I mean it and yes, I'll wait. You take as much time as you need, just don't make me wait too long because I need you here with me every day."

"What if I said I wanted to live in town, in my apartment. Would you move?" I feel my body stiffen as I take a minute to think about my answer. Even though this is my family's property and my siblings live out here, I decide that yes, I could definitely move away to be with Jules. "You don't have to answer."

"Yes."

"What?" He sits upright to look at my face but he's too far away from me, so I reach out for him but he slaps my hands away. "Do you mean that?"

"That I would move into your apartment with you? Absolutely I would, if that's what you wanted."

"But Drake Wines and your siblings are here." He sounds shocked and I hate that he doesn't understand even now that I would move heaven and earth to be with him.

"You're right they are. I also built and decorated this house with the express purpose of living in it with my husband one day. With you, Love. That's the only thing I want, to live with you. To make a life with *you* and if that means moving into town and your apartment, then that's what it means." I take his face in my hands and stare into his eyes. "I don't care where we live Julian, as long as we're together, that's all that fucking matters to me. Kids, no kids. Dogs, no dogs. Cats, no cats. We can have a tank full of goldfish for all I fucking care. I just want to live my life with you."

He doesn't say a word, he gets to his feet and I'm worried I went too far with the kids and pets thing. That is until he reaches out for my hand, pulls me to my feet and leads me to the bedroom.

"On the bed." He says, dropping my hand and spinning around to face me, pointing to the bed. "Naked. Then bed." My fingers start moving of their own accord, removing my clothes without saying a word. Usually it's me taking charge in the bedroom but I'm kind of liking take charge Jules, he's hot as fuck, so I do as he commands. I strip out of my clothes as he watches and then I crawl onto the bed. I lie on my back, stretch out my arms, then place my hands behind my head and spread my legs. If he wants control, he can have complete control tonight.

"I have never wanted you more than I do tonight." His voice is like gravel.

"Then have me. I'm yours Love, I'm not going anywhere." He growls, low and long. I watch as his eyes become darker and his muscles tense with anticipation.

Without warning, he's on the bed, prowling towards my body and my cock starts to harden, wanting his attention. The movement does exactly that, his eyes leave mine to look down at my cock and it grows slightly longer and thicker. Before I realise it, he's between my thighs, staring at my cock and licking his lips.

"Wrap those gorgeous lips around my cock and suck it Love." I command, forgetting that I'm letting Jules take the control tonight. His eyes dart up to meet mine and he growls at me.

"You lie there and don't talk, just enjoy Sweets." Then, before I can even think of replying he wraps his lips around my cock and draws it into the warmth of his mouth.

"Fuck!" I breathe out. Jules doesn't speak, he sits back on his haunches, bends at the hips one hand resting on my hip, the other wrapped around the base of my cock and he slides his mouth up and down my length. Over and over and over again. I close my eyes and just enjoy the sensation. "That feels amazing." I groan. He sucks harder, his cheeks hollowing out as he sucks me harder and harder, and when his hand leaves my hip to play with my balls, I can't help myself. My hips jerk up off the bed and my hands reach out for him, landing on his head and twisting in his hair.

He stops all movement and growls, sending vibrations from the head of my cock all the way down its length to my balls, and then my legs. I'm grateful to be lying down because otherwise I think I might have fallen down. He looks up at me, his mouth still wrapped around the head of my cock, his tongue playing with the slit in it but the look tells me, to move my hands back to where they were.

"But I need to touch you." He growls his disapproval again and I make a show of putting my hands back behind my head. The second I do, his mouth is around my cock, sliding over it again and again, my senses immediately overloaded.

Up down. Up down. The rhythm is mesmerising and hypnotic all at once.

"Fuck Jules!" I mumble out, sure that I'm barely understandable. "Julian!" I cry out as he runs his finger through the crease of my cheeks and starts to play with my taint. "I'm going to come baby." My voice barely a whisper.

"Not until I'm inside you you're not." He declares.

"Then you better get a move on or you're going to miss it." He's got a bottle of lube and a condom in his hand, that I have no idea where they came from or when the hell he got them but I'm not complaining. He lubes up his covered hard cock and his finger. He pushes his finger into me, getting me ready for him, as he strokes his cock, making sure he's ready for me.

He puts my legs on his hips, spreading me wide and slowly, he enters my body.

"Fuck Logan!" He groans as I growl out a long drawn out yes! Then he's moving inside me and I can't think of anything else but him. My hands move again without thinking, I need to touch my cock, to feel some relief but Jules tells me no with a shake of his head, so I keep my hands where they are. "You don't get to touch me or yourself." He punches every word with a jerk of his hips and I know I'm not going to last much longer.

"Jules." Without warning, I come all over my stomach and Jules follows right behind me, with a roar. He collapses on top of me, we're both breathing heavily for a few minutes. Once our breathing returns to normal, Jules rolls off me and lies beside me. "Can I touch you now?" I ask and he chuckles.

"Yes Logan, you can." He's already slung an arm over my chest, and a leg over mine. I bring my hands down and lay one on his back, dragging it lightly up and down his back in a soothing motion. The other one rests on my chest, taking his hand in mine and twisting our fingers together. Then I bring it up to my mouth and kiss the back of his hand. "Did you mean it?"

"That I'd move in with *you,* if that's what you want? Hell yes and if I'd known what admitting that would turn you into, I would have told you years ago." I chuckle.

"I mean it Logan, would you?"

"Yes, I would. I honestly don't care where we live, just that we're together Love."

"OK."

"OK? Does that mean I'm moving in with you then?"

"No." He shakes his head against me. "It means I'm happy to know that you would if I wanted you to but I still need more time to think."

"Fair enough. I'm ready whenever you are. I'm not going anywhere." I chuckle. "Well, I am going to the bathroom to clean up but I'm sure you'll survive."

"I'll join you, I need to clean up a bit too."

We walk to the bathroom, clean each other up because what else would we do? Then I turn off the lights, pull the covers up over us both, then I pull his back to my front.

"Goodnight Jules, I love you." I say quietly in his ear.

"Sleep well Logan, I love you."

I fall asleep smiling and have one of the best sleeps I've have in weeks. When I wake up the next morning I don't want to get up and leave Jules in bed but I have a few things I need to get done before I can spend the rest of the weekend with Julian without feeling guilty.

So, I get dressed quietly after a quick shower and leave him sleeping in our bed.

Chapter Seventeen
JULES

I wake up alone, the space beside me in the bed is cold, so I know that Logan left me sleeping a while ago. I can't hear the shower running or any noise coming from the kitchen, so I'm assuming he's no longer in the house. I roll over onto my back and let out a sigh. I'm disappointed not to wake up next to him but I also know that's the chance I'm taking being with a man who *lives o*n the property where the family business he runs with his siblings is located. What else can I expect?

I also know and understand that Logan is a workaholic, who likes to keep control of every little thing and struggles to delegate *anything*!

It's also one of the many reasons I love him. His dedication to his family and his job makes my heart melt and my dick hard. Now there's movement under the sheets, so I decide that's my cue to head to the shower.

I don't bother to cover myself to get to the bathroom but I *do* poke my head out the bedroom door to make sure there aren't any visitors I don't know about. Don't tell me I don't learn from my mistakes. When I don't see anyone else in the house, I stroll to the bathroom, closing the door behind me but not locking it. Now you can tell me I should learn from my mistakes!

Under the cascading warm water, I smile as I relax after washing everything. I feel blissed out. I'm back with the love of my life and he wants forever. I rest my hands on the wall, drop my chin to my chest and let the warm water rain over my shoulders, it feels amazing.

"Did you miss me or my shower?" Logan's grumbly voice says behind me, making me jump.

"What the fuck is with you Drake men scaring the bejesus out of me while I'm naked?" I say loudly as I turn around to find the sexy as fuck oldest Drake man leaning against the doorframe, legs crossed at the ankle and arms folded over his chest.

"I'm sorry, I didn't meant to startle you." He says, a smirk on his face.

"Sure you didn't." I roll my eyes at him. "How long have you been standing there, watching me like a creepy old man?"

"Old man?" He growls, making me laugh.

"*That's* what you find offensive Logan, really?" I turn off the shower and step out of the cubicle reaching for a towel. "What? You're not going to help a guy out?" I ask him, as I reach in front of the rack.

"Nah, I'm too old, might pull a muscle you know? All that exertion isn't good for us *old men*." He answers seriously but I can see the twinkle in his eyes.

"Well, you *are* an old man." I say as I wrap the towel around my hips and push by him to walk back to the bedroom. "The oldest Drake by far." He lets me by but just when I think he's not going to react, his large hand lands on my butt cheek with a muted slap, thanks to the towel taking most of the brunt.

"I'll never be as old as you are Julian, so don't get too smug." Logan reminds me as I rub my butt cheek and keep walking. I don't need to watch him to know that he pushes off the doorframe and follows me.

I bend over to pick my clothes up off the floor and I hear a deep groan from behind me that makes me smile. "I'm going to have to go home today. I need a change of clothes." Logan grunts behind me.

"You know you've still got clothes here, right?" His words are more like grunts, than actual properly enunciated words.

"No, I don't Logan I took them all with me." I say quietly as I pull yesterday's clothes on.

"Not all of them." He mumbles, walking to the walk in closet that I convinced him to build in the master bedroom when we did the floorplan. When he walks out, he hands me a full set of clothes that I didn't realise I'd left behind.

"Wow. Thanks." I strip out of my dirty clothes and put on the clean ones. "I still have to go home today Logan. I can't stay here indefinitely, I have to go back to work and I have other things to do." I tell him, trying to be gentle. I know he's not going to like me leaving him here.

"I'll come with you." It's more a statement than a question, as he starts moving around the room gathering clothes and packing them in a duffel. I stand there dumbfounded, just watching him move.

"Logan, stop." I beg him but he just keeps moving, gathering and packing. "Logan! Stop!" I raise my voice and he stops to look at me, his underwear in his hand. "What are you doing?"

"Coming with you. If you don't want to stay here with me, then I'm coming to stay with you." Once again, it's a statement, one that brooks no argument. Except that's exactly what I do.

"Logan, no." I start, shaking my head. I don't want this. "You don't have to come with me. You need to be here and I need to go to work myself."

"You don't want me to stay at your place?" He looks so forlorn and confused. I can't stop myself from walking up to him, taking his hand in mine and using the other to make him look me in the eye.

"Logan, Sweets." I start. "I'm not saying you can't and I'm not saying I won't stay here but we're both busy men. My apartment is closer to work for me and living here is more convenient for you."

"I don't want to be apart from you any longer than I have to be. Now that I've got you back, I don't want to lose you. I want the world to know that you're here, you're mine." His voice starts off so quietly, then builds back up to his grumbly, possessive normal self.

"I didn't mean I was leaving *now*, Logan. I just meant that at some point today, I have to go home." I smile at him. "I appreciate the clean clothes though. I didn't realise that I'd left them behind."

"You did. I slept in your shirt for a couple of days." He admits with a shrug, flooring me. "Then I couldn't stand it anymore, so I collected everything I could find and I washed them all. But even that didn't take your scent away from them, so I folded them up and tucked them away in your drawers. Your side of the closet is still empty. Well apart from the few things I found."

"I ... Wow!" I stand there, just looking at the man in front of me. "I didn't know."

"Well, I assumed you didn't realise you'd left anything behind, otherwise you would have been back to collect them or you would have asked Kenna to send them to you."

"She wouldn't have sent them, she would have dropped them at my place and lectured me. As it is, she managed to run into me and did it anyway." I laugh, taking his underwear out of his hands and dropping them onto the bed. "Come on, you can make me coffee and something to eat. You owe me at least that much this morning." I say with a smile, leading out of the bedroom and into the kitchen.

"Good morning lovebirds."

"What the fuck do you want Caleb?" Logan growls at his brother.

"We really need to find a new way to lock a door to keep him out of the house!" I mumble under my breath.

"I just wanted to check up on my brothers, make sure everything was OK?" He says with a smile. "*And* Leila asked me to bring you both over some breakfast. Actually, she wanted to bring it herself but they got a little busy, so I offered to do it. I mean, you never know what she might have walked in on around here." Another smirk spreads across his face.

"Well, I'm assuming that Leila wouldn't have just let herself in the fucking door, she would have knocked and waited for a response, like a *normal* person would have."

"Are you calling me *not* normal, Logan?" He asks, putting his hand on his chest and acting like he's shocked. "Well, I never! I'm just grateful you're both covered up this time." Before either of us can speak, he's up off the couch and walking towards the door. "Enjoy breakfast boys and don't forget to thank Leila for her efforts and thoughtfulness." With a slamming of the door he's gone again.

"That boy needs to learn some manners. Now I get why Brady got so annoyed with us just walking into their house without knocking. It's annoying as hell!" Logan grumbles. "Remind me to apologise to them the next time we see them would you?"

"No problems. I think Caleb needs to learn a lesson or two about privacy!" I say as I look through the goodies that Leila sent over. "He's right about one thing though, we do need to stop by Vines and thank Leila for going to the effort of sending this over for us."

Logan grunts out his agreement as we sit down to eat. It's comfortable silence for a few minutes, we've never needed to be constantly talking or making noise. In fact, we've sat in the house just doing whatever together in silence so many times, that this feel normal.

"Jules." I look up from my breakfast and reach for my coffee.

"Yes, Logan." He's scowling, while staring into his coffee. "What did Caleb mean when he said, it was nice to see *both* of us in clothes? When did my little brother see you naked?"

"Oh that? He came to my apartment the other night after you did." I say with a chuckle.

"OK, but how did he see you *naked?*" He asks again, head snapping up to look me in the eyes. "Did you open the door naked? Did you think it would be me back again?"

"No, actually I walked out of my bathroom into the living room to grab my phone and Caleb was sitting on my couch." I laugh at the memory because even though I wasn't impressed at the time, now I can see the funny side. "He scared the ever loving fuck out of me."

"He was *inside* your apartment without your invitation?"

"Yes." I say, nodding my head, still laughing. "I guess I truly am part of the family hey?"

"How. The. Fuck. Did. He. Get. In. If. You. Didn't. Invite. Him. In?" Logan enunciates every word very clearly and slowly.

"He had a key." I say shrugging my shoulders. "Said he had your key."

"*I* had my key in my pocket that night Jules." He explains.

"You didn't use it?"

"No. I wanted you to *invite* me in. I wanted you to *want* me there."

"Oh."

"Yes. Oh." He reaches over the table, taking my hand in his. "Did you give him a key?"

"No." I shake my head. "He said he used your key."

"That little bastard! He didn't mean that I *gave* him a key Jules, he meant that he went and got a copy cut *from* my key. Which means that at some point he managed to steal *my* key so that he could get it done!"

"Logan, it doesn't matter Sweets."

"It does if he saw you naked!"

"No, it doesn't! Look, I'm not saying that I'm glad he saw me naked because I'm not."

"Good because I'm the only who gets to see you naked."

"Wow! OK then Mr Neanderthal!" I laugh at him. "Maybe it will teach him a lesson."

"I walked out here a few days ago and he saw me naked then too, so I don't think he's really learnt a thing." Logan grumbles and I can't help laughing again.

"If it makes you feel any better, he did compliment your taste in men!" I grin at him.

"How?" I'll be damned if he doesn't look adorable and fuckable when his forehead and the bridge of his nose crinkles as he frowns. "In what way Jules?" The way he growls should be illegal, honestly!

"He said I had a great arse!" I laugh uncontrollably as Logan closes his eyes, mumbling to himself and I'm kind of worried for Caleb's safety right now.

"I'm going to fucking kill him. *Kill* him I swear! Makenna won't mind being one brother down, will she?"

"I'm sure she'll be fine with it." I choke out around my laughter. "I mean she has me now, so she won't miss Caleb."

"Damn straight, she's got you now." Then he's on my side of the table kissing the breath out of me.

Chapter Eighteen
LOGAN

I swear to all that is holy, I am going to kill my little brother. He's going to meet his maker and join our parents sooner than he expected!

Just after we finished breakfast and I found out that Caleb let himself into my boyfriend's home, Gavin called to check in with Jules. I left him to his call and made one of my own.

"Logan! I thought you'd be busy for the rest of the day with Jules." My brother sounds so fucking chirpy and happy on his end of the call.

"I am but I've got something to say to you first. Meet between your place and mine, now." I hang up without giving him a chance to respond.

I look over and Jules who's still talking on the phone and get his attention. "I'll be back in five minutes." I whisper to him, while holding up five fingers.

"Hold on a second Gavin." He says into the phone and then holds it away from his ear. "What was that Sweets?" He smiles at me.

"I'll be back in five minutes. I'm just going to take care of something." I tell him, pointing towards the door that I'm about leave through.

"Sure Sweets." He says with a smile. "Don't kill him OK?"

"What?" I stop with my hand on the door handle about to open the door.

"Caleb. Don't kill him, OK? I kind of like your brother and I'll miss him if you kill him. I think you would too if you're being honest with yourself." He smiles at me and then goes back to talking to Gavin.

After a minute of standing there watching him, I shake my head to clear it and walk out the door to meet my brother.

He's got his back to me and I'm surprised he's already standing there waiting for me. He's rarely early for anything. When I get a few steps away, he turns to face me, a huge smile on his face.

"At a guess, by the look on your face, you just found out that I saw Jules naked this week." The smirk spreads across his face, he's also holding out a hand to stop me talking. That raised hand also means that I can't get any closer to him either. Smart move! "Now, before you say anything, let me explain. Yes, I copied your key to Julian's apartment *but* I only did it in case of emergencies. I'd never used it before this weekend and it was certainly not my intention to see the man naked. That being said, nice one bro, I can see why you're head over heels for him!"

Until that last line, he almost saved his life.

"Caleb." His name is more of a growl than an actual word and I know he understands how I angry I am by the way his eyes widen and the smirk is wiped off his face.

"Honest. I'd never done it before and I swear I'll never do it again. I just wanted to check in on him and make sure he was OK." He looks down at the ground between us and runs the toe of his shoe through the dirt. "I was worried about him OK, Logan? He's my brother too and I knew that walking away from you would have almost killed him. I also knew that you were going to see him and well, I didn't know how that would go. Then you left so soon after you arrived that I felt like I needed to check on him."

"You could have knocked on the door Caleb."

"You're right, I *could* have but I had a feeling he wouldn't let me in." He's not wrong there. "I think he'd probably seen enough Drakes for the day but I needed to see for myself how he was. For the record he wasn't good." He says after a pause.

"I didn't mean to hurt him."

"I know you didn't. We all know you didn't, including Jules but you did and I expect you to be making that up to him for the rest of your lives. If you don't, I'm going to have to kick your arse for you." I laugh at his threat.

"You wish Cal."

"I've been working out Lo, you might be surprised with what I can do these days." He says quietly. I look closely at my little brother and realise that he's right, he has been working out and I've been so caught up in my own shit, I hadn't even noticed.

"Good for you Cal."

"Thank you." He says with another easy smile. I envy the easy way he has about him, he's so relaxed most of the time. There are very few times in recent years that I've seen him stressed out or worried about anything. "Now, can I get back to work or is there something else you'd like to say?"

"You need to start respecting other people's privacy and personal space, Caleb. Do you understand what I mean?"

"Yes sir!" He says, saluting me. "No more using spare keys to enter properties without prior permissions and I promise to knock on doors as well. I don't guarantee that I'll wait for the invitation to enter but I promise to at least give you a warning before I do."

"Then you enter at your own risk." I say, smiling back at him. "Our house and the main house."

"Gotcha." He says, nodding. "Anything else? I've got to get back."

"No, that's it. Just promise, no more entering homes without invitation Caleb."

"You got it, Logan." He says smiling as he turns to walk back to Vines. "He really does have a nice arse Logan, I approve." He says over his shoulder and I growl, his laughter trails behind him as he enters Vines in the distance.

"Is everything OK?" Jules asks from behind me, resting his hand on my shoulder. I reach up and rest my hand on his.

'Yeah, everything's fine."

"I see Caleb walked away alive and still laughing."

"Yeah, he did. I swear that kid could talk eskimo's into buying fresh ice!"

"He's not a kid anymore Logan but yeah, I think you're right. He's certainly got a way about him that makes people want to help him and do his bidding." He chuckles while we stand there watching the door to Vines where Caleb just disappeared into.

"How's Gavin?" I ask, turning to look at him.

"Ummm ... yeah good."

"But?"

"I'm going to have to go home Logan, I'm sorry." He wraps an arm around my waist, then seems to remember where we're standing and starts to move away. I rest my hand on his and put just enough pressure on it to keep it there, then I put my free arm around his waist and pull him closer to me. I hear his breath catch and I know I should have been doing this years ago. "I left all my work stuff at home, including my laptop and I need it."

"You could go get them and bring them back here. We could sit at the house and work together." I suggest, not wanting him to leave me so soon.

"I could but we'll distract each other and I need to concentrate."

"I can behave." I tell him, we both know that's not the problem.

"I know you can Sweets but I don't have that kind of self-control."

"Yes you do." I say, leaning to kiss him lightly, making him gasp.

"Let me go home and get some work done. I promise I'll be back in time to get a late lunch with you and then we can work together this after-noon." His voice a husky whisper.

"Why not this morning?" I push.

"Because I have some phone calls to make and I need to concentrate."

"Do I distract you?" I ask, kissing down his throat to his collarbone, making him groan.

"They're video calls, Logan. Group calls Logan."

"What if I promise to be good, Love?"

"God Logan, you're *always* good and you know it." He groans and grinds his cock against my leg. "You know we're still outside in the drive-way, right?"

"I do, Love and I don't give a fuck who sees us."

"You might care if you keep doing that." He warns as I kiss back up his throat and take his ear lobe into my mouth and suck. "Oh god!"

I step backwards, out of his embrace so that we're not touching any-where.

"You've got two hours, Love."

"What?" He asks, as he opens his eyes looking for me, wondering what the hell just happened.

"You've got two hours to get back to your place, have that conference call and then get back here. If you're not back in two hours, I'm coming to get you."

"I can't get there and back in two hours Logan!" He says, looking at his watch. Yeah the man still wears a watch on his wrist and it's the sexiest thing I've ever seen.

"Times a wasting then, Love." I tell him as I turn him around facing back towards the house. "You best get moving." I smack him on that perfect arse of his to get him moving.

"Ouch!" He grumbles and sends a dirty look my way.

"That didn't hurt and you know it. Now move!" I say, pointing towards the house but Jules turns and starts to walk towards Vines.

"I left my car over here last night, remember?" He says with a smile I want to remember forever. "I'll be back soon. Not in two hours Logan, I don't know how long the video meeting will go for but I *will* text you to let you know when I'm on my way, OK?"

"OK." I agree, knowing that he'll do his job and then come back to me. "Drive safely." His smile falters for a second, he knows that sentence isn't as innocent as it might sound to the casual observer.

"I promise."

"I love you Jules." I say loudly, as he gets further away from me and I watch as his step falters, making me feel guilty all over again for keeping our relationship under wraps for so long.

"I love you too, Logan." He turns away and makes his way to his car. I stand there, watching as his car disappears out of the Drake Wines front gate and make a promise to myself and Jules.

I will never again make him wonder how much I love him. He will never have to second guess what my feelings are, or whether or not I'm embarrassed about *us*.

I don't give a fuck what anyone else thinks. If they don't want to do business with us because of my love life, then we don't want to do business with them anyway. I just have to hope that Makenna and Caleb feel the same way.

Whatever they decide, I'm not hiding from the world any more. Jules means too much to me and I'm not going to ruin that in any way, ever again.

He's the love of my life.

Chapter Nineteen
JULES

I drive home from Drake Wines with a smile plastered on my face. Logan didn't hide from the world, he didn't shy away from affection or telling me he loved me as I left.

As I walk in the building, Ben, my neighbour catches up with me.

"Hi Julian, is everything OK with you and Logan?" He asks, as he reaches ahead of me and holds the door open. I nod my thanks to him and he smiles back at me.

"Yes." I smile warmly back at him.

"Oh." He frowns as we reach the elevator and I press the button. "It's just that things seemed a little tense the other night."

"Oh. Yeah they were but we've sorted things out." I smile at him as we step into the elevator together.

"Well, that's great."

"Are you sure?" I snort a laugh but when I look at Ben, I regret my laughter.

"Of course." The words are affirmative but he sounds miserable.

"You don't sound like it, Ben." I pause for a second as the car grinds to halt on our floor. "Is everything OK with you?"

"It sure is." He smiles at me as he steps out of the car, turning towards his apartment and I step out, then walk towards mine. "Julian?"

I pause with my keys in my hand, turning to look at Ben. "Yes Ben?"

"Just promise me that if you need anything, anything at all that you ask me, OK?"

"Thanks Ben, I'll keep that in mind." I smile at him again, hoping that will stop this weird conversation and I can escape inside my apartment. I've never thought of Ben as being creepy before but he's really starting to give me that vibe.

"I'm serious Julian. I'll always be there for you." Yeah, I'm done with this conversation now.

"Thanks Ben." I smile what I hope is a warm smile at him. "Logan is expecting me back at his house shortly, so I should go. Take care."

"Take care Julian."

Before he can say anything else, I quickly step into my apartment, closing the door swiftly behind me and locking it. A shiver runs through me as I think about how weird Ben just was and even though I was thinking of getting the building manager to organise a deadbolt for the door as a joke to keep Caleb out of my space, I think I might seriously ask them about one now.

I don't have time to think about any of that because my phones rings.

"Hey Gavin, how are you?"

"I'm good, are you OK? You sound a little weird."

"Yeah, just had a weird chat with my neighbour." I explain, still feeling strange about the whole encounter.

"You mean the guy who keeps tabs on who your visitors are?"

"He does that?" I ask, surprised.

"Oh yeah. Every damned time I show up he's peeking out his door or somehow just happens to be coming in the building or jumping in the elevator at the same time. That man is creepy! Jilly and I have commented on it plenty of times. I swear, if you go missing he's the first person we'll mention as a suspect."

"Well that's just great." I can't finish as a shiver runs down my spine.

"Yeah he's weird man. I'd stay as far away from him as I possibly could." I can hear the concern in his voice. "What did he do and have you told Logan?"

"He asked me about Logan actually. He saw him when he came here the other night to ask for forgiveness and I didn't let him in straight away."

"He didn't use his key?"

"No, he didn't." I smile as I realise that he let *me* choose whether he came in to my space or not.

"Wow! That's actually pretty cool of him." Gavin says, sounding more surprised than I think is necessary.

"He's a good guy, Gavin."

"I know he is Jules and I know you love him but I'm just looking out for you. You're my friend and I don't want you to get hurt. If you're happy, then I'm happy but I can tell you, if he screws it up again, I'll kick his fucking arse."

"I'll be sure to warn him." I laugh.

"Be sure to tell him about creepy Ben too. He'd want to know about it, Jules."

"Promise. Although I'm sure he's just being kind, not creepy." That earns me a snort of contempt from Gavin. "What? I'm sure he was just looking out for me, just like you are."

"Whatever you need to tell yourself to make it comfortable to still live there, dude. Just make me one more promise, OK?"

"What's that?' I roll my eyes, even though I know he can't see me.

"Tell the building manager as well. Maybe ask for an extra lock on the door. You can't be too careful my friend."

"Sure, I can do that and I swear I'll tell Logan all about it."

"Thank you."

"Do you feel better now? Can we get on with this meeting so that I can get back to Logan?"

"You're staying with him tonight?"

"Yeah. I stayed there last night too."

"So, he grovelled well then?"

"He told them Gavin and they don't care. In fact, they said they already knew."

"Wow! That's fantastic Jules, I'm happy for you. I know how much you love him. I know he loves you too, I can't imagine either one of you have been in top form the last few weeks." If only he knew, I think as he laughs.

"Alright, let's get to it."

"Turn on your camera so we can connect everyone else to the room and we can get started."

That's exactly what we do. I'm on that call with Gavin and the team from the last project for longer than I expected, so I send Logan a message just as we all start saying goodbye.

Me: *Meeting took longer than expected. Sorry I haven't left yet.*

A second later, as if he'd been sitting there waiting for me to call or message him, a message from him appears.

Logan: *No worries Love. Will you be leaving soon? xx*

I can't help the smile that spreads across my face when I see the two x's on my screen.

Me: *I need to pack up and grab some things but yeah. Maybe 20 minutes? xx*

Logan: *OK let me know when. I'm cooking your favourite.*

Me: *You've got a deal Sweets*

A ridiculously happy and content feeling settles over me. I know that the message was his way of making sure that I'm safe. After his parents accident all of the Drakes make sure to let someone else know when they're travelling and where they're expected. I know it's just one way that he shows that he cares about me and I'm more than happy to indulge him. Anything to ease his mind makes me happy.

"Hey, did you forget you were still on a video call with me?" I hear Gavin's voice call out from my laptop screen and I can't help laughing.

"I did, sorry Gavin."

"That's alright. I know that a certain wine maker trumps me every time." He pouts and bats his eyelashes at me.

"You idiot! Get off here and go talk to your wife. She might appreciate you batting your eyes at her."

"I think she'd appreciate me doing other things but the eyelashes might help my cause."

"I'll talk to you later Gavin. Tell Jilly I said hi."

"Will do. Tell Mr Drake hello from us too."

"I will." I smile. Our goodbyes ring out and I hang up just as I hear him telling Jilly that the dreamboat and I are back together.

I pack everything up, round up a few sets of clothes and look around the apartment to make sure I haven't left anything behind. When I'm satisfied that I haven't, I swing the handle of my duffel across my body, pick up my laptop bag and head out the door.

When I reach my car, I dump the bags in the back seat. I get in the driver's seat and lock the doors out of habit before I send Logan a message.

Me: *In the car, leaving in a couple of minutes.*

Again it takes less than a minute for Logan to respond.

Logan: *See you soon Love*

Within minutes I'm on my way back to Drake Wines and the love of my life. As my apartment building disappears in the rearview mirror, so do all thoughts of Ben and his weirdness.

All I can think about is getting back to Logan, nothing else matters in this moment.

Chapter Twenty
LOGAN

I took off from the office early today and headed home to get dinner organised. When Jules messaged to say that his meeting went longer than expected, I was a mixture of pleased and disappointed. Pleased that he let me know because that meant we were back on track. Disappointed because that meant I had less time with him.

Instead of hanging around the house waiting for him to return, I strolled up to Vines to get us some dessert. I could have made it but nothing I could make can compete with Leila's talents.

When I walk in the door, the first thing I notice is that Caleb isn't at his table. In fact, his table was completely void of any trace of him, which is highly unusual, even for mid-afternoon.

"Good afternoon Logan." I look from the table Caleb is usually sitting at, to the table full of, what we've lovingly labelled, the *Grandmas*. Martha, Betty, Edith and Beryl are trouble when they're all together but they're also our favourite customers.

"Good afternoon Martha, how are you today?" I smile at her.

"I'm doing well thank you." She returns my smile with a twinkle in her eyes that makes me feel a little apprehensive about continuing on the conversation.

"I'm glad to hear it." I say genuinely and begin to walk away.

"Sit with me for a few minutes, the others aren't here yet and I'd love the company." She indicates to the chair that I was leaning on the back of. I hesitate for a second but then I pull out the chair and sit down, deciding it can't hurt to spend a few minutes chatting to Martha, she's a customer after all.

"I can spare a few minutes to keep a beautiful lady company." I smile as I sit down next to her.

"Aren't you sweet?" She reaches out and rest her hand on mine. "I'm happy to hear you made up with Julian." She says, patting my hand gently. "Your parents would be very proud of you Logan." Before I can say anything, she keeps speaking. "All they ever wanted was for you and your siblings to be happy. No matter what that happiness looked like and you've got that in spades my dear."

"Thank you Martha, that means more than you could imagine." I say around the lump in my throat.

"You're welcome, now don't you keep Julian all to yourself, you make sure you bring him in here to see us old girls every now and then too, please."

"Will do." I promise with smile, giving her hand a gentle squeeze.

"Thank you."

"What's this now? You get here a little earlier than us and we walk in to find you sitting here with a handsome young man!" Edith says from just behind me, earning a very large eyeroll and huff from Martha.

"That's what happens when you're late because you can't work out how to put your granny undies on!" Martha throws back at her friend.

"You'd know." Beryl grumbles back. I swear, anyone who didn't know better, would think that these four ladies hated each other but truly, this is how they show they love one another.

"Good afternoon ladies." I say smiling at them all as I stand up and offer my chair to Betty, who smiles up at me.

"Thank you Logan, such a gentleman." She says quietly, as Beryl and Edith say hello to me. "Your Mumma would be so dang proud of the man you've become." She says while holding gently onto my arm as she gets comfortable in the chair I just vacated.

"Thank you Betty, you're too sweet." I say, smiling warmly at her. These four ladies were all friends of my Mums but honestly, I have a real soft spot for Betty. She's quieter than the other three but that doesn't mean she doesn't have fun or get loud with them, she's just a little more reserved, and I do mean a *little* bit! "Enjoy your afternoon ladies." As I turn to walk away, I hear Martha speak.

"He's getting dessert to share with the gorgeous Julian tonight. How sweet is that?"

"Ohh how adorable!" Edith exclaims.

"I wish my husband did that!" Betty grumbles.

"They're not married yet, Betty." Beryl says.

"They might as well be." Betty says. "They've been together for years. It's about time that Logan made an honest man out of Jules, don't you think?"

"One day soon, when they're ready I'm sure they will." Martha tells her friends. "That's none of our business. Now, let's talk about Caleb. I wonder where he is today."

I snort a quiet laugh as I leave them to gossip about my brother. I have to admit, I *am* tempted to hang around for a minute or two to hear what they have to say but then I decide, that's something I really don't want to hear. It's none of my business what they think about my brother or anything to do with him.

"Good afternoon Mr Drake, I mean Logan. What can I get for you today?" Georgie asks with an easy smile, even after the slight flinch as she changed my name.

"How are you today Georgie?"

"Really good Mr, sorry, Logan." This time she actually looks a little embarrassed by her slip.

"That's great. I need a dessert for tonight, what do you recommend? What has Leila dreamed up today?" I ask, rubbing my hands together and looking in the chilled case with enthusiasm.

"Is it for you and Jules?" She inquires with a smile.

"It is actually, how did you know?"

"I was here yesterday when he came in." She replies, not looking me in the eye and shrugging a shoulder.

"Oh." Is all I can think to say. Then I remember what Martha said as well and I can't help asking Georgie a question, even though I know I'm completely putting her on the spot and the question will no doubt make her uncomfortable. "So, everyone's talking about us then?"

"Well, yes. No!" I look at her with a raised eyebrow. "Well, yes but not in the way you think we are, they are."

"Oh?"

"We're all just so happy for you both Mr Drake, Logan." She hesitates for a few seconds, seems to have an internal conversation and seems to decide to tell me anyway. "I'll be honest, there have been some snide remarks but they get knocked down pretty quickly the majority of us are happy for you both. Happy that Jules makes *you* happy and that you've both found love. Jules is a great guy and you deserve all the happiness."

"Thank you Georgie." I know she doesn't realise it but she managed to say everything that I needed to hear. "He *does* make me happy, very happy."

"Well then, lets choose a delectable dessert for him." She says rubbing her hands together. "You know, Leila made this delicious chocolate cake today, four layers, filled with chocolate frosting and caramel in alternate layers and then covered in chocolate frosting. It's sinfully delicious, trust me I had a slice for breakfast, don't shame me! If you and Jules love chocolate, you'll love this cake."

"You've sold me! Can I get two slices boxed up and ready to go, please?"

"Absolutely! Give me a couple of minutes and you'll be ready to go." She takes the cake back to the bench to cut off the slices and box them up, while I peruse the case to see what else Leila has been up to.

"You know your money is no good here, right?"

"Yes, it is because you're running a business and so am I." I laugh as I turn to face the pastry chef extraordinaire herself.

"We are, yes but being that you *own* the business, I think a couple of slices of cake for free are a given." She puts her hand up to stop me from speaking, while also shaking her head. "Consider it my gift to you and Julian. I'm so happy you're back together Logan." She says quietly so that only the two of us can hear it.

"Thank you, me too!" I sigh. "Honestly? I didn't think I had a chance."

"I don't think there was ever any other option for either of you *but* I want you to take these slices of cake as my celebration for you both, please Logan, I insist." I can see the determination and sincerity on her face.

"Thank you Leila."

"It's my pleasure." She says as Georgie walks over and hands me the box.

"There you go, Logan. I hope you and Jules enjoy dessert." She says with a smile.

"Have a good night Logan." Leila reaches up and kisses me on the cheek. "Tell Jules I said hi and he owes me a visit."

"Will do. Thank you for the recommendation Georgie." We smile and wave at each other as I walk out of the shop. I only get stopped by the Grandmas again for a few seconds and say hello to a few other customers, before I reach the door. When I get outside, I let out a sigh of relief and walk home.

I smile all the way home. I have an amazing dessert and Jules will be home soon and we can relax, together.

Home. I know without a doubt, that wherever Jules is, that's my home.

I'm completely distracted as I open the door and walk through to the kitchen to put the cake in the fridge for later. So distracted that I almost drop the cake on the damned floor when Jules' voice speaks from the couch.

"Hey Sweets, I see you've been to Vines. What did you get?"

Chapter Twenty-one
JULES

"Holy fucking hell Julian!" Logan yells, causing me to laugh uproariously, while he stands at the kitchen bench with his hand on his heart and breathing deeply.

"I'm sorry." I say between breaths.

"Yeah, sounds like it too." He huffs at me, before finally managing to put the cake box in the fridge.

"Awwww you know I love you Sweets." I say, making my way over to him and pressing my front to his back, running my arms around him to rest my hands on his pecs.

"I know nothing of the sort." He sniffs, not moving away from me. I've seen this man cry twice in all the time I've known him. Once when his parents died and then when he found out Makenna had a miscarriage.

"Yes you do! I love you, Logan Jack Drake." I know it's not the first time I've said it since we got back together but it's probably the first time I've said it while we're not having sex. I feel him suck in a breath and his body stiffen ever so slightly.

"Move in with me then." It's my turn to stiffen. I try to walk away, to put some space between us so that we can talk this through but he suddenly reaches up and grasps my hands in his, pressing them in place on his chest.

"Logan. We've talked about this, it's too soon." I tell him, resting my chin on his shoulder and leaving a soft kiss on the side of his neck.

"It really isn't, Love. I know we broke up and it was one hundred percent my fault, I was an idiot." He takes my hands in his and removes them from his chest, turning to look at me, while still holding on tight to my hands. "But before all of that. Before you came to your senses and left me, before I came to my senses and asked for you to take me back." He swallows deeply, looks at our hands and then looks back at me. "Before all of that, we were together for six years. Six god damn years Jules, that has to count for something."

"Were we together though Logan?" It kills me to see the hurt on his face but I know I have to get it out of my system before we can continue to move forward. "Were we truly together, if no-one but us knew it?"

"Yes. Of course it counts! *We were together Julian.*" He closes his eyes and takes a *very* deep breath to calm himself down. I've seen him do this a thousand times before, it's his way of reigning in his emotions, always needing to be the strong and calm one in the room. "I loved you then and I love you now. We were in a relationship, Love and you know it."

"I do now but I often wondered what you thought was going on between us. I often felt like I was your - "

"I know, my dirty little secret." He finishes for me, releasing my hands and starts to walk away.

"Actually, I was going to say your good time guy and that's it. Nothing more and nothing less."

He stops in his tracks, his body frozen in place for maybe a minute, before spinning on his heels and coming towards me at such a pace, that I take a step or two backwards. He stops just shy of slamming into me and I brace my body for an impact but it doesn't come.

"You. Are. Not. A. Good. Time. Guy." He enunciates each word in an angry tone.

"Well, I was kind of hoping I was a good time Logan, otherwise I'm boring." I say with a smirk, trying to diffuse the situation and calm him down. It doesn't work. "That's *not* what I meant and you know it Julian." He growls and I feel a shiver start in my toes. I love it when he growls.

"Listen, we both know what the other one meant, OK? Let it go Logan." I bring my hand up and tap him lightly on the cheek. "We're all good now Sweets."

"Are we, really? Because you're the one who brings it up, not me. I don't know how many times I'm supposed to apologise for making you feel like you didn't mean anything to me Julian."

"You don't Logan." He raises an eyebrow at me and I know he doesn't believe me. "Honestly, I'm sorry. It was a joke and I guess it's too soon for jokes like that. I'm sorry." My phone chimes with a message from my back pocket and Logan's hand is suddenly covering my pocket so that I can't reach it.

"Don't answer it. Let's have dinner, no interruptions." He pleads.

"Let me just check who it is first and if I can deal with it quickly, I will, if not I'll put it away until after we've eaten. Deal?" He nods but doesn't say anything as he steps away from me, to start getting out plates and dishing up our meal.

"So, who is it? Does Gavin need you to do something else?" Logan asks as he puts the plates on the table. The table that I just now noticed was already set with glasses and cutlery. This man is something else!

"No, it's Ben actually." I say, surprised to see his name on my screen.

"Ben? Your neighbour Ben?" He asks, sounding as confused as I am.

"Yeah."

"Why?"

"Why, what?" I ask, looking him in the eyes.

"Why is he messaging you? I didn't even know you had each other numbers." He doesn't sound happy about it either.

"He watches my place for me when I go out of town, that's all, Logan." I explain simply.

He pauses as we both sit down at the table. "You mean he has a key to your place?"

"What? Oh no, god no! I wouldn't give him a key, I don't want his either, even though he's offered it a million times. I've almost run out of ways to say no thank you." I laugh, once again hoping to make light of the situation. "Logan! He doesn't have a key to my apartment and I don't have, nor do I want, a key to *his*. Has he offered me one? Yes. Have I taken it? No and I won't be."

"So, what did he want tonight then?"

"He was checking where I was because he noticed I hadn't come home."

"That's really kind of creepy that he knows when you're home and when you're not, Love."

"You have all that information too." Yeah OK, so I realise I shouldn't have pushed that particular button when he quirks an eyebrow at me.

"Are you comparing me, to your neighbour?" He asks with a frown. "I'm your *boyfriend,* I think that warrants me having a bit more information than your *neighbour,* Jules."

"You're absolutely right." I admit. "No doubt about it."

"What did you tell him?" He asks, nodding at my phone that's sitting on the table.

"I told him I was here with you." I look down at my phone as another message comes through.

"What's his reply Julian?"

"How do you know it's him?"

"Well, for one I saw his name on the screen and two, you look like you don't want to open that message." He's not wrong, I don't. "Open it Love."

I open it and read it, letting out a long sigh. Without waiting for him to ask, I hand the phone over to Logan so that he can read it too. There's no point hiding it and I didn't plan on it anyway.

Ben: *be careful OK that man is a little too possessive for my liking*

"Why that fucking little twat ..."

"Logan, don't. I'll talk to him when I go home and tell him to mind his own business."

"I'd like to have a chat with the little weasel."

"You might *want* to talk to him but you won't, do you hear me Logan? Do not give him any reason to cause problems for either one of us. Please Logan."

"Fine." He grumbles. "Let's eat dinner and forget about your nosy neighbour."

I don't answer Ben because Logan and Gavin are right, he's starting to give me the creeps and I haven't even told Logan about him popping up in various places.

I don't want to think about Ben tonight or for the rest of the weekend, while I stay out at Drake Wines either. I just want to enjoy dinner, dessert, a movie and bed with my man.

Chapter Twenty-two
LOGAN

Jules spends the next few weeks travelling between his place and mine. I stay at his apartment a few times but I don't think he's really comfortable there anymore. He hasn't said anything else but I get the feeling that creepy Ben, is getting creepier. He makes himself pretty scarce when I stay with Jules and I think that's why he wants me stay with him when he's not here at the winery.

One day, as I'm coming back to the apartment, find Ben closing Jules' door behind him. I'm not sure who was more surprised when the elevator doors opened and we saw each other as he stepped into the hallway.

"What are you doing?" I asked, my eyes zeroed in on the key in his hand but noticing that he looked everywhere but at *me* when he answered.

"I was just checking on something for Jules."

"On what? What were you checking on?" I asked then, staring him in the face.

"He asked me to go in and check if he left a notebook behind." He swallowed deeply as I stared him down. "Jules, he asked me to check if he left his notebook on the table."

"And did he?"

"What?"

"Did he leave the notebook on the table?"

"No, no he didn't." He answered, straightened up and closed the door behind him, getting ready to walk back to his place.

"So, let me get this straight. Jules called you, asked you to go into his apartment to check if he had left a notebook behind, is that what you're saying?"

"Yes." He nods. "Yup that's exactly what I'm saying."

"Even though he knew I would be here any minute, he called *you* to check for him? Doesn't that seem a bit odd to you, Ben?"

"I guess it does but I can't explain what Jules was thinking, Logan. He's your boyfriend after all, shouldn't you be the one that understands him?"

"Yes, he is *my* boyfriend and I *do* understand him, which is why I think this whole thing is strange."

'Well, I don't know what to say to you Logan, except I'll be on my way now, talk to you later." Then he was gone, disappearing behind the closed door of his own apartment. I knew that day, there and then, that I was going to have to talk to Jules about asking Ben for his key back and if he refused, we were going to be changing the fucking locks.

When Jules gets home a couple of hours later, that discussion is put on the backburner. Creepy Ben is the furthest thing from my mind when Julian walks through the door, drops all his work stuff on the floor and makes a bee line for me. The kiss he gives me is hot as fuck and I don't want to think about Ben. Ever again.

Sometime later, we're sprawled out on the living room floor, with the throw off the couch, flung over our naked and very sated bodies.

"Well, hello to you too Love." I say with a grin, pulling Jules in closer to me. It's the first chance I've had to speak more than his name and yes since he walked in the door!

"What can I say? I missed you." He mumbles, as he drapes one leg over mine and an arm over my chest, relaxing onto my body with a satisfied groan.

"I missed you too Jules." I say into the crown of his head as I wrap my arms around his upper body and pulling him in closer still.

"I really like having you here when I get home." Jules replies with a grin.

"I really like being here when you get home." I smile against his head. "It would be easier if we lived together."

"It would be easier if we lived at Drake Wines."

"In certain ways, yes but it's not necessary." I say, with my eyes closed, trying to be relaxed about this conversation. "I don't care where we live, as long we're together."

"Drake Wines is home." I don't know what to say to him, so I stay quiet. Yes, I would prefer to live in the house *we* built out at the vineyard but I also just want to be home when he gets home from work.

"Are you serious? You want to move in together?" I ask, trying not to get my hopes up.

"Deadly." Jules insists.

"OK." I feel my entire body go stiff as I hold my breath waiting for him to say more, to explain what he means. He rests his chin on my chest so that he can meet my eyes.

"Let's do it. Let's move in together." He says, not looking at me but I open my eyes slowly to watch him.

"Are you sure?" I'm too scared to move in case I spook him and he changes his mind.

"I am, yes."

"Don't Jules. Don't tell me what you think I want to hear and then change your mind at the last minute." I move to gently push him off me, instead he moves quickly to straddle my hips, resting his hands on my chest, effectively pinning me to the ground, even though we both know I could get up if I really wanted to. I don't want to for the record.

"I'm serious Logan. You're right, we've been together for years, why bother wasting anymore time?" He shrugs his shoulder, it is both the sexiest and most adorable thing at the same time, that I've ever seen. "I love you Logan Drake and I don't want to spend one more minute apart than we have to."

"OK." I say, gripping his hips in my hands. I'm sure I'm holding on too tightly but he doesn't complain. "I'll talk to Makenna, Brady and Caleb and let them know that I'll be moving in here. It's not like I have to give them notice or anything, so I think I can move in as soon as you're ready."

"You don't have to talk to them Logan."

"I know but it would be weird to just up and leave them, don't you think? I mean, I'm not asking for their permission or anything but I can't just *leave* and not say something." I say nodding, staring at his glorious chest. "Once I've spoken to them I can start moving some clothes and small stuff over. I'm sure Caleb will be able to give me a hand, Brady too."

"Hey Sweets, slow down." He chuckles, running his hands over my pecs and stomach, my cock hardening at his touch. "Before you go backtracking, thinking I've changed my mind or that you're moving too quickly, don't. Are you going to listen to me for a few minutes?" His smile is devastingly handsome.

"OK. Go ahead." I tell him, my hands gripping even tighter on to his hips because I feel like I'm not going to like what he has to say.

"Don't look so panicked Logan, I already said I'd move in with you." He laughs.

"I'm so glad my feelings amuse you." I grumble, close to dumping him on his arse on the cold floor.

"I don't want to live here." He smiles, and I frown, completely confused.

"You want to find somewhere else?" I ask, nodding. "Sure, we can do that. I mean, I'd rather move as far away from creepy Ben, as I can anyway. I don't think he's going to bring out the welcome wagon for me when I move in, so yes, let's find somewhere new."

"No." He says, a large smile on his face as he vigorously shakes his head no.

"No?"

"That's right, no. We don't need a new place, we already have one." His smile widens and his face lights up with excitement. I'm not going to lie, I love seeing him so happy.

"We do?"

"Yes Logan, we do." He smacks me on the cheek and my cock twitches under his arse, and he instinctively grinds down into my groin. "The house we built."

"Hmmmm?" I ask, losing the ability to listen as he grinds down harder onto my cock.

"The house at Drake Wines Logan. *Our* house." I tear my eyes away from watching his cock stiffen as he grinds away, making us both hot. "Did you hear me Sweets?"

"Did you just say you want to live out at the vineyard Julian?" I ask, trying to concentrate on what he's saying and not what he's doing to me.

"I did, yes."

"But I thought you didn't want that? That you weren't keen on living so close to my work and family?"

"I never said it was because of Makenna, Brady or Caleb. They're not the reason at all. The reason I didn't want to live there is because I didn't want you to become a workaholic but I think I've worked out a way of getting you home early."

"Are you promising me sex if I get home at a normal hour, is that what you're saying?" He laughs.

"I'm saying, I want to move out to Drake Wines and live on the property with you and your family. I think I can motivate you to come home if not early, then at a reasonable hour."

"If you're there, that's all the motivation I need to come home, Love."

"So, is that a yes? You want me to move in with you?"

"Hell yes! How soon can we get you packed and moved? Brady and Caleb just volunteered to help."

Julian laughs and his happiness is music to my ears.

"How about you give me the next week to sort out the lease here and a few other things and then we discuss the moving date?"

"Do we have to wait? I'll buy out your lease, Love, and I'll pay someone to pack." I tell him, only half joking.

"You're not buying out my lease Sweets. I heard the building manager talking a week or so ago about wanting to renovate each apartment as the leases come up and the tenants move out, maybe I can use that in my favour."

"OK, I guess I can wait, I've waited this long, what's another few weeks?"

"Exactly."

"As long you're one hundred percent sure this is what you want. If you have even the slightest doubt or concern, I want to know about it and we can put a stop to it all, at any time. OK?" I need him to know that I'm not forcing this on him, he always has a choice.

"No second thoughts, I want this, Logan. I want to spend every day and minute that we can together."

"Up." I demand and Jules lifts up onto his knees. I reach over and tear a condom off the strip that he got from the bedroom earlier and roll it down my hard cock. Before I can spread the lube over the condom, Jules lowers himself down. "Are you ready?"

"Yes!" He says, as I feel his hole stretch around me, making us both groan at the sensation.

"Jules." I breath out, as he lowers himself down to rest on my hips. "I love you ."

"I love you too, Logan."

Chapter Twenty-three
JULES

I can't breathe as I take his cock into my body, slowly, teasing us both, his 'I love you' comes out in a groan, mine is barely a breath.

I sit there, still for a few seconds, just enjoying the sensation of being full, until I can't stand it any longer and I have to move. I rest my hands on Logan's chest, using him as leverage as a start riding him.

"Open your eyes Julian." Logan demands and I didn't even realise that they'd fallen closed. "I want to see those gorgeous blue eyes of yours looking at me when you come."

My eyes spring open, meeting his bright green gaze. "I'm not going to last long."

"Me either, Jules." He grinds out between gritted teeth. "Just. Don't. stop!" I couldn't even if I wanted to. I need to keep moving, I need to feel him moving inside me. The sensation of the underside of my cock is rubbing against the ridges of his stomach with each movement, driving me insane. "Jules." My name is literally just a growl as his hands tighten on my hips. I know I'm going to have bruises there tomorrow and I don't care.

"Hmmmm." Is all I can manage.

"Fuck!" Logan roars as he empties his load into the condom and even though he's trying to hold me still on his cock, I keep moving for another minute, until I come all over his stomach. I slide my hands up rest on his shoulders and drop to lie on his chest. "You're making a mess there, Love."

"I don't care, that's what showers are for." I can feel his laughter rumble through his chest.

"You're absolutely right." He says as he pulls the throw that got discarded at some point over the top of our tangled bodies. "Don't get too comfortable there, Love, we're going to have to clean up soon."

"I know, just give me a couple of minutes."

"I can do that." He says, kissing my forehead and I know I couldn't feel any happier than I do in this moment. I can feel my body relax and I know that I could easily fall asleep, right here using Logan as my pillow. "Come on, let's move before you get any more comfortable than you already are." My body snaps up into a sitting position as his hand lands on my arse with a loud slap.

"Was that entirely necessary Logan?" I ask, as I drag myself off him and fall to the floor beside him.

"It definitely was. It got you moving didn't it? And you can't tell me that you didn't enjoy that, even just a little bit." He says with a smirk.

"That's not the point." I say, in a huff as I get to my feet and start to walk towards the bathroom, his laughter following me.

I step under the hot water and let it flow over my head, down my body. My body aches in the way it can only after two rounds of amazing sex. I wash my hair and rinse, then start soaping up my body, when I feel Logan's presence behind me. "Took you long enough." I say, without turning around.

"I was enjoying the view." He replies, as he pushes me aside gently so that he can step under the water. "Geezus Jules, that water's hot enough to burn the skin off my damn bones!"

"Don't complain Logan, you knew when you stepped under the water what you were getting." He mutters something under his breath that sounds a lot like, 'crazy bastard' and I can't help laughing as I step out of the cubicle. I laugh a little harder when I notice him adjusting the hot water.

"I don't know how you put up with the water that hot!" He grumbles.

"You've been saying that for years now, Sweets and the answer is the same every time you ask it." I laugh as he turns to glare at me.

"It's refreshing." We say at the same time, although I'm laughing and he's grumbling still.

"Refreshing is a *cool* or cold shower Julian, not scalding hot!"

"It wakes me up."

"No, that's what a cool shower does Julian."

"OK, then it relaxes me."

"You don't need to be any more relaxed."

"I think Gavin might disagree." I laugh as I hang up my towel. I'm so distracted with my amusement, that I don't notice that he'd turned off the water and was right behind me, making me jump when he speaks right in my ear.

"I don't give a fuck what Gavin thinks, he's not one of the two men in this relationship." His breath tickles my earlobe sending a shiver down my spine but his body isn't touching mine. "No-one belongs here but you and me, Love. Understand?"

I nod my answer because I don't think I can speak. He's so close that I can feel his body heat but he's not touching me and that's frustrating. Then he reaches out, brushing his arm against mine, as he swipes the towel off the rail and rubs it over his hair, then his chest and the rest of his body. I'm stunned into silence and rooted to the spot. How the hell can drying yourself after a shower be sexy?

"Uhuh." Is the only response I manage to give him.

"Come on Love, let's go order some dinner." He tells me, patting my cheek as he breezes by me and out of the bathroom. "What do you feel like eating?" He looks back at me over his shoulder with a smirk on his face. I know what the dirty bastard is thinking and I'm not going to give him the satisfaction of saying what I know he wants to hear.

"Thai. I feel like Thai food." I say, blinking at him as he bends over right in my line of sight to pick up his phone off the floor, causing my mouth to go dry and my cock to go hard.

"Spicy. I like it." He says, while pulling up the app on his phone to place the order. "The usual?" He asks without looking up.

I nod my answer and then realise he can't see me. "Yes please."

"Are you OK?" Logan asks, looking up from his phone and turning to look at me, concerned.

"Hmmm?" I mumble, he raises an eyebrow at me in question and I give myself a mental shake. "Yes, I'm fine. You're going to get dressed before the food gets here, right?"

"Are you?" Logan asks me smirking, with green eyes glittering in the lights of the living room.

"What? Of course I am." I would never confess to him that I'd forgotten that I was also naked, as I stomped towards my bedroom to find some clean clothes. He follows behind me, like I knew he would, to find himself some clothes to wear. I know he saw my hard cock but for whatever reason, we're both ignoring. It's the thing about being a man that can be annoying, I mean you can't really see if a woman is aroused, but a man, that's easy to spot. Not that I would know, I've never actually been with a woman in any sexual way. "Have you ever been with a woman? You know, sexually?" I ask Logan, suddenly curious.

"Wh-what?" He stutters, stumbling as he tried to step into his sweatpants. "What the hell made you ask *that*?"

"Just curious I guess. I was just thinking how it's obvious when a guy is turned on." I look to the tent that is slowly reducing in my own sweatpants in example. "But it's not so easy from the outside to actually *see* that a woman is and I realised I'm the last person to even think he has any knowledge of that because I've never been with a woman. I just wondered if you had, you know, in your past."

"We've had this discussion Julian, you know I've been with women before. In the past, a long, long time ago. Way before I met you. I was in University and I was still finding out who I was."

"Yeah, I know." I pause because I'm not sure that should ask the question or that I want to know the answer but I ask it anyway. "Is it really different? Do you miss it? Being intimate with women."

"Geezus Julian! It's different but the same. No, I don't miss it and do you want to know why? I don't miss it because it wasn't what I wanted, I never felt satisfied. Ever. I love *you* and I love *our* sex life." He steps closer to me, wraps the hair at the nape of my neck, around his fingers and pulls my lips to his, giving me one hell of a scorching kiss. He drags his lips off mine, leaving me gasping for breath and my cock hard. Again. To rest his forehead on mine. "Let's go clean up the mess in the living room." He takes my hand and leads me back out to the other room and we both, silently start to pick up the discarded clothes, phones and wallets.

"But it's different, right?" I ask, scowling at him while I think about him being not only with someone else, but a woman!

"Yes Julian, it's different." He answers, sighing. "Not better, not really worse either, just different. Before you ask, no, for me it wasn't enjoyable.

Which is why we broke up. I think she knew why it wasn't enjoyable for me."

"But she wasn't your first." It's not a question, more like a statement, causing Logan to sigh and roll his eyes.

"Do we have to go over all of this again? No, she wasn't my first but she was my last. And do you know why? Let me tell you why. Because about six months later, I met this incredible man and while I had been coming to terms with the fact that I liked men more than woman, this guy, he was already there and it was so fucking attractive. It was sexy as fuck that he knew who he was and who he wanted. I was an idiot and kept this guy at arm's length for way too long but I did it. I'm telling you here and now, you should have walked away sooner but I'm so fucking grateful that you didn't, Julian."

"I'm glad Lori knew what was going on and broke up with you." I tell him with a smirk, my words proving to him that we've had this conversation before. Well, not technically about how different having sex is with men and women, but that I know about Lori's existence. "I can't help wonder ..." I don't get to finish my thought.

"Saved by the fucking bell." Logan grumbles, as he walks towards the door to get our dinner. I hear him mumble some thanks to the person delivering our food, then the door closes. "Come on let's eat it while it's hot." He gets plates, while I get cutlery and Logan goes to the fridge to get some bottles of water.

"It smells good." I groan as I take a deep breath and take in all the delicious smells. "Did I hear you talk to two people out there?"

"Yeah, Ben just happened to be in the hallway when I answered the door." I nod, because that's not unusual. "Which reminds me, when I got here earlier I saw him walking out of the apartment and when I questioned him, he said he was checking on something for you." He says it so offhandedly that I'm confused for a minute.

"You mean he was walking out of *his* apartment?" I ask to clarify what he meant.

"No." He shakes his head. "No, I mean he was walking out of *this* apartment. He was locking the door behind him when I stepped out of the elevator."

"Maybe he was just checking the door was locked?" I asked, more hopeful that a grown man should be.

"Nope. When I questioned him, he said that he'd come inside at your request to look for something." He eyes me over the forkful of food he's got paused at his mouth.

"What on earth would I have asked him to look for in *my* apartment?" I ask, astounded.

"A notebook apparently. At least according to Ben that's what it was."

I start shaking my head. "No, nope. I most certainly did *not* ask him to look for anything in here. Why would I when he doesn't have a key? I mean, I know he can't get in so why would I ask him to look for anything, least of all a stupid notebook?" I shake my head again. "Why would I ask him to check anything when I knew you be here soon anyway. I'm pretty sure I would have asked you, if I was to ask anyone, to check on a notebook."

"So, you didn't ask him to come here, on his own?"

"Fuck no, I did not!"

"I think you need to talk to the building manager and ask for the locks to be changed."

"You're right, I'll do that tomorrow."

"Between this and being in random places where you are, he's getting too creepy for me Jules." I nod in agreement and swallow my nerves. "I'm glad you're moving out to Drake Wines with me, the sooner the better but until you do, you have someone else with you at all times. Do you hear me, Jules? Me, Gavin, Caleb, Brady, even Kenna. I mean, Kenna can't fight anyone off in her condition but that doesn't mean that you having one more person with you won't deter him from escalating his creepiness."

Chapter Twenty-four
LOGAN

"Condition? Is Makenna pregnant again?"

"Yeah. They're keeping it pretty quiet for now." I explain. "Caleb and myself know simply because we both picked up on it and they couldn't deny it."

"I'm so happy for them, especially after everything they've been through." Jules smiles.

"Do you want kids?" I ask him.

"It's not something I really thought about, to be honest. I never truly considered it to be in the cards for me but yeah, I wouldn't mind some mini Logans running around the house." He smiles broad and bright at me. "What about you?"

You'd think, after all of the years we were together, that we would have talked about this but we never have.

"Yeah, I wouldn't mind, you know?" I'm a little hesitant in admitting it, although I'm not sure why.

Suddenly, there's a loud crash on the other side of the kitchen wall, that just happens to be the one wall that Jules' apartment shares with Ben's.

"Well, I guess Ben doesn't like the idea of us having kids together." I laugh, trying to make a joke out of it but to be honest, I can't wait to get Jules out of here and away from that guy.

"Maybe not." He laughs, then we finish the rest of our meal in an easy silence, both of us lost in our own thoughts.

OVER THE COURSE OF the next few weeks, Jules makes plans to move out. He asked the building manager to put new locks on the door but as soon as he found out that Jules intended to move out, he refused to change them, telling Jules that he should be more careful about who he gives his key out to next time. I'm furious with the man's cavalier attitude about a tenants safety but Jules begs me to let it go.

"I'm not going to be here for much longer anyway Logan, so what does it really matter?" He asked me and I guess he's right. There's no point getting worked up over something that won't be an issue sooner, rather than later.

"Come on, that's enough for today, let's go out and get some dinner." I say abruptly after one such discussion about it just not being worth it to say anything to Ben.

"You want to go out for dinner looking like this?" He asks, amazed as he looks us both up and down, realising we're covered in dust and packing tape.

"I never said it was going to be fancy, but we need to eat. Let's go get some pizza, we can eat there so that we don't have to worry about cleaning up here."

"Wow, last of the big spenders hey?" He jokes, winking at me. "What kind of lavish date is this? Why Mr Drake, are you trying to get into my pants?" He asks, while batting his eyes at me and I can't help laughing.

"I always want in your pants Jules, that's a given. I feed you so that you've got the stamina and energy to keep up with me. So, come on, move that gorgeous arse so we can get some food."

"You Drake men really like my butt, don't you?" He sends me another wink and I can't help the growl that escapes me as I'm reminded that my brother has seen my man naked.

"Do you have to keep reminding me that Caleb has seen you naked?" I know he's doing it to rile me up. I also know he *knows* it's working and it will every fucking time.

"Yes, I think I do." His laughter so deep, rich and infectious, that it's hard not to laugh along with him but I don't. Instead I glare at him like I mean it, which just makes him throw his head back in an uncontrolled fit of laugher, including tears and holding his stomach.

"You are unbelievable. If I didn't know better, I'd think you enjoyed Caleb seeing you naked." Giving in and joining in with his laughter. Suddenly he stops laughing and looks me dead in the eyes.

"Who says I didn't enjoy it?"

"What?!" The laughter dying in my throat.

"At least now he knows what his brother sees in me."

"You're more than a sexy body to me Jules."

"I know, I was just teasing you. Let's go get this pizza because now that you mention food, I'm starving." Without another word he's got his keys in his hand and he's looking at me from the open door, waiting for me. "Are you coming?"

"Maybe later." I mumble under my breath, as I follow him to the door. When the elevator doors open, Ben is stepping out and he stops, looking between the two of us. I take Jules' hand in mine, holding on tight and lead him into the elevator. Ben can't follow us without looking like the absolute stalker that he is, so he stands there watching us instead, staring at our joined hands. "I can't wait until you leave this place and move in with me, *baby*." I'm speaking to Jules but I'm *looking* Ben in the eyes as the elevator doors close between us and I see the anger all over his face when he realises what I just said. Luckily for him, the doors close before I can do anything about it.

"What the fuck! Why did you do that Logan? I haven't had the chance to talk to Ben yet and let him know I'm moving out!" I pull my eyes away from the closed doors, to look at Jules.

"I can't believe you're worried about *his* feelings about this!" I shake my head.

"How do you know he won't do something even crazier now, you idiot? I was going to tell him but I was waiting until everything was just about done. I had a plan Logan and you just blew it out of the water!" His voice is full of frustration and annoyance.

"Well, now he knows about it, you don't have to talk to him and he has some time to get used to it." I shrug, as the doors open into the lobby and I pull him out of the elevator and out of the building.

"You are unbelievable Logan Drake. Un-freakin-believable!" He's shaking his head in exasperation but he doesn't pull his hand from mine and he's following me to the pizza place. So, I figure he's either not that angry *or* he's really hungry. Either way, I'm glad that I got to let that jackass know that he wouldn't be seeing Jules for much longer.

"Well, you'll always have someone with you, so he can't do anything he'll live to regret if you're never alone." I know it sounds like I'm indifferent about the danger that Jules might be in but the truth is, I'm far from it. I'm worried about him every time I'm not with him. Even more so when I know that no-one else I trust is with him. "You'll be out of there on the weekend, anyway, how much longer were you going to wait to tell him?"

"Right before I left for the last time." I stop as I reach for the door of the pizza place and turn to look at him to check if he's playing with me. The nervous look on his face proves that was exactly what his plan was and I'm astounded. I'm also pissed off but not at Jules, it's obvious now that while he's been pretty blasé about this entire situation, he's actually really worried that Ben might take things too far at some point.

"I won't let him hurt you, Jules, I promise you that."

"I know." His voice is whisper quiet. I guide him inside, find a table to sit at, and after we place our order, I pull him in to my side. I don't care where we are, who will see us, this man needs me and I won't let him down. He takes in a sharp breath, then sighs and leans his head on my shoulder. I decide there and then, we're going home tonight and not staying at the apartment. He needs to relax and he can't do that with Ben lurking around next door.

After we've eaten, we head back to the apartment and I pack us both some clothes, then drive us back to Drake Wines. Jules doesn't argue and that's when I realise just how much stress he's been under these last few weeks.

I resolve to talk to Gavin, Brady, Caleb and Makenna again to make sure they're still on the same page as I am.

Julian doesn't get to spend a minute alone until he's moved out here permanently with me.

Chapter Twenty-five
JULES

I didn't argue with Logan about staying out at Drake Wines because quite frankly, I didn't want to stay at my apartment, even with Logan there with me.

Caleb, Brady and Makenna were over the minute we got here and they were all organising a roster so that I'm not left alone. I couldn't get a word in to tell them that while I was very happy that they cared so much about me, I really didn't need a constant babysitter. None of them would have listened even if I *had* managed to say anything. The Drakes and Harris' close ranks when someone they love is threatened and I guess I just have to accept that. Even as Makenna draws up the roster, I know I can slip away from them, especially Caleb and Brady pretty easily. They've both got other things they need to be doing rather than following me around all day.

After they all finally left, Logan and I sat down to watch a movie, in the dark, snuggled up on the couch but he seems nervous for some reason. He's been fidgeting for most of the movie.

"Can you sit still?"

"Sure." He manages it for all of about ten seconds.

"Are you OK?" I sit up and look at him, shocked to see panic on his face. "Logan, what's wrong?" I reach out to take his face in my hands, forcing him to look at me. "What is it, Sweets?"

"Let's get married." His voice is a little higher pitched than his usual deep grumble.

"I'm sorry, what now?" I ask, sitting back on the couch, putting a little bit of distance between us, which Logan closes in a split second.

"Let's get married Jules." His eyes are darting between mine, searching for something that I don't think he's going to find. The only thing he's going to find is confusion and astonishment to be honest.

"Are you for real right now?"

"I don't mean tonight or tomorrow but soon. I want you to be my husband Jules. I want to be *your* husband Jules."

"What bought this on?"

"You're killing me here Julian, seriously." He closes his eyes but before he does, I catch a glimpse of the pain he's trying to hide from me.

"That's not my intention Logan, not at all. I just feel like this came out of nowhere and I'm trying to understand."

"What's to understand? I love you, you love me and it's not like we've never spoken about it before because we have."

"But marriage? Are you sure you're ready for that?" I need to make sure he wants this, that it isn't just a knee jerk reaction to everything going on with Ben.

"I told you the night I came to ask you for forgiveness that I love you Jules and that this is forever for me and I wasn't joking. You're it for me, I don't want anyone else. I am deeply, unconditionally in love with *you*, Julian Bishop." I can see the pleading in his eyes, the honesty.

"I love you too, Logan but, isn't this moving just a little too fast?" I don't doubt that he loves me, loves me enough to want to be married to me and I know without a doubt that I love *him* enough, that's not the issue.

"It's been too long, Jules." He scrambles off the couch. "Wait right there. Don't move." Then he's gone. I'm not sure I could move even if I wanted to, I'm so shocked by this turn of events.

While he's gone, I ask myself, do I want to marry this man? Do I love him? Do I want to be his husband? Do I want *him* to be *my* husband? Ab-so-fucking-lutely I do, there's no question in my mind at all! That doesn't mean that I don't have reservations about his question coming out of nowhere tonight. Or worrying that perhaps he's only asking because he thinks that's the only way to protect me.

I'm still wondering what's going on and thinking a million thoughts in my head when Logan barrels back out of the bedroom and into the living room. He only stops moving when his legs knocked into the couch, moving it slightly and leaving me holding on to the cushion so I don't fall off!

"Logan." I say, catching my breath. I look at him and realise that he's down on one knee and my entire body freezes, including my lungs when I see the small jewellers box in his hands. "What the?" I whisper.

"Julian John Bishop, will you marry me?" He asks without a tremble in his voice or a hint of uncertainty. Before I can give him an answer, he keeps talking and if I didn't know my answer already, what he says next, seals the deal! "I called your Dad a few weeks ago and asked if he or your Mum would object to us getting married. To *you* marrying *me* and he didn't hesitate or even call out to your Mum, he just said, 'go for it son'. Your Mum messaged me not long after and told me that she loved me and couldn't wait to have another son." The tears in his eyes almost do me in but I hold out. "So, what do you say?" He asks opening the small box to reveal a gorgeous platinum band, with flecks of emerald chips across the top. They're glinting in the light from the TV and I can't help it, I gasp at how beautiful they are and how much they remind me of his gorgeous green eyes.

"Oh Logan!"

"That's not a yes, Love." The panic starting to crawl across his face. "I need an answer Jules. Now if you don't mind, please."

"Yes." My voice is barely a whisper.

"I'm sorry, what was that?"

"Yes." I start nodding. "Yes. Yes. Yes! Oh my, yes of course, Logan!" I throw my arms around his neck, knocking him off balance and making us crash to the floor. When he hits the floor, I use the movement to kiss him, hard but when he pulls back, I chase his lips for more.

"Can I put the ring on your finger now, please?" He asks with a laugh.

"I don't need the ring Logan, it can wait until the wedding." Logan pushes on my shoulders, gently forcing me to sit up in his lap, then he takes my left hand in his.

"I want you to wear it now, please? I have the overwhelming desire to prove to you that this is real, that I mean to marry you as soon as I can. We can use this same ring as your wedding band, if that's what you want but I want, no I *need* you to wear it as a symbol of my commitment to you, to us.

After everything that we've been through, I need this." His speech distracted me from the fact that he slid the ring onto my finger.

"OK." Is all I manage to get out because this man, this man is my everything. He throws the empty box on the floor.

"OK?" He asks, running his hands over my arms, shoulders and up into my hair, scraping my scalp. "IS that OK to wearing the ring *and* marrying me, soon?"

"Yes." I nod and I can feel the tears building, my emotions ready to break. "Hell yes I'll marry you and I'll wear this ring, *your* ring and think of you every time the emeralds shine in the light." I smile broadly and drop my hands onto his chest to steady myself, just as the light changes on the TV and it makes the chips of emeralds shimmer.

"Are you OK, Love?" I don't understand why he's asking me that, until he wipes my cheeks and his thumbs come away wet. I didn't even realise I was crying.

"I'm perfect." I smile through the tears, as he pulls me down to meet his lips. "We're really getting married?" I murmur against his lips and I feel a smile curve across his mouth.

"Fuck yes we are. You're now my fiancé and I'm yours."

"Shit!" I bolt upright in his lap, causing him to groan. I push down on his chest for leverage to get to my feet and I hear the breath leave his lungs with an 'oomph'. "Sorry Sweets."

"Where are you off to in such a hurry?" He asks as he sits up, reaching out for my hand.

"I need to call my parents, they'll be expecting my call. Did you tell them when you were going to ask me? What about Makenna? What about Brady and Caleb? We need to tell them too, right? I need to call Gavin too!"

"Jules, Love, calm down." He gets to his feet, then pulls me in for a tight hug. "Relax. We can tell everyone tomorrow, it's too late to be making phone calls tonight, Love. Why don't we enjoy knowing that we're the only ones who know we're engaged for tonight? Tomorrow the insanity can come at us but for tonight, let's keep it between us and enjoy it."

He pulls me back into his embrace, holding me like he never wants to let go and in this moment, I've never felt more loved or *in love* in my life.

Chapter Twenty-six
LOGAN

There is nothing in the world right now that could make me happier than I am in this moment. I asked Jules to marry me and he said yes! It wasn't at all how I'd planned, it wasn't anywhere near as romantic as I wanted it to be but all that matters in the end is that he said yes.

"You're right of course! It's definitely too late to call my parents and Makenna needs her rest." Jules mumbles into my chest.

"You can scream it from the rooftops in the morning, I promise, Love."

"Are you sure?" He mumbles again but I understand what he says because I understand *him* and I hate that I've cause this uncertainty in him.

"I'll buy you a megaphone if you really want?" I chuckle at my question, watching as his head bounces up and down on my chest.

"I don't need a megaphone Logan, I just need you." He hesitates. "I just need you to be sure. To want people to know about us."

"I want everyone to know." I growl. "Damn it all to hell Julian, I asked you to marry me! I wouldn't have asked you if I didn't want you to be my husband."

"Wanting me to be your husband and telling the world that we're together, well I feel like they're two different things."

"I hate that I've made you feel like this and that you're still insecure and think that I'm not all in this relationship. I am, Love. I know that you can't 'just' get over that feeling of not being enough but I need you to know I'm in this with you for the long haul. I. Am. All. In." I bring his face up to meet mine and I kiss him like it just might be our last, even though I know it won't. "I will love you forever and I *will* shout it out to the world. I don't care who knows because I love you and that's all that matters to me. I just hope that it's enough so that you can put all of your worries and concerns about me and my commitment aside. I just need you to love me Julian."

"I wouldn't have said yes to marrying you if I had any doubts that you loved me, Logan. Believe me. I just wasn't sure you'd want to tell everyone just yet."

"You're not the only one in the room that can't wait to tell anyone who will listen that we're going to be married. I love you, Jules."

"I love you too, Logan." We stand in the middle of the living room, in each other arms, the only light is the flickering of the TV playing the movie that we've forgotten about. "Take me to bed Sweets."

"Anything you want, Love." I pick up the remote and turn off the TV.

"I am *so* tired. It's been a hell of a day, what with packing up my things, trying to dodge creepy Ben *and* getting engaged to the man of my dreams."

"Celebrating in bed it is then." I say, taking his hand in mine to lead him through the dark into our bedroom.

"I'm not sure I have the energy for celebrating unless it's the kind that comes with sleep, Logan, I'm sorry."

"No apology necessary, Love. We've got a lifetime of *celebrating* ahead of us." I kiss his forehead as we reach his side of the bed. "We can start in the morning." I tell him as I start to strip him out of his clothes. I love that he lets me do it.

Pulling back the covers, I watch in the moonlight coming through the still open blinds, as Jules lowers himself down to sit on the edge of the bed. It's then that I see just how tired he really is and I push him gently so that he lies down and pull the covers over him.

"Are you going to join me." He asks and I can hear in his voice just how close he already is to sleep.

"In a minute, I just need to use the bathroom."

"Don't be long." He barely manages to mumble.

"I promise, Love." I drop another kiss on his forehead and then his cheek, before closing the blinds properly and quietly heading to the bathroom. I feel my phone vibrate in my pocket and when I pull it out, I find Makenna's name on the screen.

Makenna: *So, when are you going to ask him big brother?*

I can't help smiling like an idiot. If only she knew that he'd already agreed to become Mr Drake or for me to become Mr Bishop, or we keep our names, who knows and who really cares. Makenna will be so happy when she finds out but that won't be tonight because I'm guessing that my soon to be husband is already fast asleep by now. So, instead of telling the truth, I rely on my reputation of being a grumpy bastard and reply as such.

Me: *I'll talk to you in the morning Makenna!*

I don't even get the chance to put my phone down on the counter before another message comes through.

Makenna: *don't you get grumpy with me! stop using exclamation points, they're obnoxious in messages !!!!!*

Me: *take your own advice. I'm going to bed. Goodnight.*

Makenna: *you can't, you haven't answered me yet*

Me: *I'll talk to you in the morning*

Makenna. *ahh no you haven't answered me yet, so don't you take that tone with me*

Me: *I love you Makenna x*

I know that adding that one x at the end of the message, representing a kiss, will make her wonder what is going on but I can't resist. I also can't resist laughing as I put my phone on silent, her next message or message will come through but I won't hear them. unfortunately, I do need to leave my phone *on* so that I can use the alarm.

I do what I need to do and I can see the screen on my phone lighting up with an incoming message and I laugh all over again, albeit quietly so I don't wake up Jules.

Makenna is going to be so mad in the morning when she works out that I didn't tell her tonight but I don't care. Tonight is for us, even if Jules has fallen asleep.

I walk to the bedroom, *our* bedroom and lean against the door, just looking at him for a few minutes. He looks so peaceful, I don't know what

I have to do to convince I'm in this forever but it doesn't really matter because I've got the rest of our lives to prove it to him.

I can't explain how happy I am that he forgave me and took me back. Not to mention, he agreed to move in here, onto the Drake property *and* he just agreed to marry me!

I strip out of my clothes with a smile on my face and a contentment in my heart that I haven't felt for years, as I wrap my body around his. When he sighs, I fall asleep with a grin on my face.

"**I**s that what I *think* it is Logan Drake?"

I'm startled awake by the high-pitched sound of my sister's voice and Jules jumping in my arms.

"What the hell Makenna? What are you yelling about and why are you in our house?" I groan.

"Don't you start with me, Logan Jack Drake! Is that what I think it is on Jules' left hand?"

I can't help smiling, even as I feel Jules pull his hand underneath the covers. I take his hand in mine and squeeze it.

"Makenna, calm the hell down and let us wake up before you shoot off a million questions would you?"

"Good morning Makenna." Jules mumbles from my arms.

"Good morning Julian. Did I see what I think I saw on your hand *before* you hid it from me?" Makenna demands in a way that *only* my Makenna can and I crack an eye open to find her standing in the doorway, hands on hips and scowl on her face.

"Makenna." I ground out. "Go put on the coffee. If you give us the chance to wake up, we'll be out soon and tell you." I promise, hoping that will get her out of our room long enough for us to get dressed.

I hear her huff but then she stomps out of the room and I can hear her moving about in the kitchen.

"I told you we should have called her last night." Jules says, as he turns in my arms to face me, resting his hand on my chest. A glint of green sparks off his finger and I can't hold back the smile that spreads across my face. "We should get up and tell her the news Logan. *Before* she comes stomping back in here to yell at us again."

"You're right." I say. "And if I know my sister, Brady and Caleb are now sitting in the living room waiting for us as well. Let's get this done, Love." I tap his cheek as much as the covers allow, and even though I know it wasn't hard, it still stung a little. His body jumps with the shock of it, causing our cocks to touch and we both start to get hard.

"We can't stay here Logan." Jules' voice is filled with desire but we both know he's right and neither of us want to be caught having sex by any of my siblings. In fact, I'd rather none of them see either of us naked ever again.

So, instead of ravishing my fiancé like I'd planned on doing this morning, I throw the covers off of both of us and untangle my body from his.

"Let's go, Love."

"You don't have to make it sound like we're walking to the firing squad you know." Jules pouts, stretching out on the bed and stopping me in my tracks. "Logan." I drag my eyes up to meet his.

"You know that's not what I mean. It's a simple case of appeasing my sister so that she can go on with her day and leave us in peace." He gets off the bed and I pull him into my embrace, his left hand landing on my chest and the right on my lower back, holding me tight to his body. "Then, we can celebrate how I intended to when we first woke up this morning." I drop my lips to his and kiss him until both of us a drawing is ragged breaths. It's a promise of things to come, literally, later.

"I love you Logan."

"I love you too, Jules." I drop a light kiss to his lips and pull away before it can become more. "Let's get dressed and get out there." I repeat, for what feels like the hundredth time since Makenna woke us up. A few minutes later, we're both dressed and I look at the love of my life. "Are you ready for this?" I ask him as we both take a deep breath.

"Let's go Sweets." His smile is broad and his eyes are shining. "Let's go tell the Harris slash Drakes that we're getting married."

When we step into the living room, Jules' hand tightens around mine as three sets of eyes look at us expectantly.

"So glad you could all join us this morning." I say to the room, my voice dripping with sarcasm.

"Don't look at me." Caleb protests. "I was blissfully asleep until a few minutes ago when your sister told me that my presence was required here, immediately." He rolls his eyes as Makenna lets out a huff of annoyance.

"My wife called and told me to get here as soon as I could. So, here I am." Brady says, with a shrug of his shoulders when I look at him for an explanation. He's smiling almost as broadly as Jules, so I'm pretty sure Makenna told him her suspicions.

"Now that we're all here, do you two have something to tell us?" Makenna asks, hands on hips and a raised eyebrow. "An announcement of some kind perhaps?"

"As it so happens, we do."

"Spit it out then so that I can get on with my life." Caleb grumbles, then curses under his breath when Makenna clips him over the ear. I'm pretty sure I hear him say she's not allowed to do that anymore but I can't be one hundred percent sure. I look at Jules and he gives me a slight nod, encouraging me to keep going.

"I asked Julian to marry me last night and he said yes." I announce and the room falls silent.

Not quite the reaction I was expecting at all.

Chapter Twenty-seven
JULES

The silence in the room after Logan's announcement is deafening and, if I'm being honest, not quite the reaction I was expecting. A minute of shocked silence? Yeah that wasn't quite what I was expecting at *all*! I look at Logan and he simply shrugs his shoulders, so I'm assuming he doesn't understand it either but as we're looking at each other confused as hell, noise and mayhem break out. Suddenly we're engulfed in three sets of arms and they're all bouncing up and down.

"Oh my god let me look, LET ME LOOK!" Makenna squeals, as she takes half a step back and reaches for Jules' hand. "Oh Jules." Her eyes well with tears as she looks me in the eyes and I can't help the tears that spring to my eyes either.

"Yeah." I know she knows what I mean, we've always understood each other.

"Just like his eyes." She whispers so quietly, I'm pretty sure I'm the only one who heard her. Mainly because the other three are all talking a mile a minute and aren't taking any notice of us.

"Yeah." Is all I can manage again.

Suddenly, Makenna's arms drop from around me and she's standing in front of her brother, holding his left hand in hers. Before she can ask him the question, he answers it for her.

"I asked *him*, for one. For two, that ring on Julian's finger is for *him*. It's to remind him that I am *his*, that he can tell whoever the hell he wants that he's *marrying* Logan Drake. That we belong together and nothing can or *will* change that. It's also his wedding band later when we get married, if that's what he wants." While he's explaining, he pulls me into his side, holding me close. "There will never be another doubt by anyone as to what our relationship is, or where Julian belongs in my life. Ever."

"Nice work brother." Makenna says, while pulling her brother out of my arms and into hers. "Congratulations. To the *both* of you, I couldn't be more happy."

"This isn't about you, Makenna." Logan grumbles at his sister but he has a smile on his face, as he rolls his eyes at her and we all laugh.

"It's always about Makenna Logan." Caleb sprouts, earning him another slap upside the head, only this time he saw it coming and ducks so that her hand only *just* grazes him.

"Alright you two, cut it out, this is about Jules and Logan. You two need to calm down and behave yourselves." Brady admonishes his wife and brother in law but does so with a smile on his face. "Congratulations Jules and Logan. I'm very happy for you both." He says pushing in between the other two to shake our hands.

"Thank you Brady." Logan and I say at the same time.

"Yeah, congratulations Logan and Jules, welcome to the family. Well, you were always a part of the family but you know, now it's going to be official." He launches himself at me and gives me a squeezing hug. "Make sure he earns you every single day." He whispers in my ear.

"What the hell did you just whisper in his ear Caleb?" Logan growls and I can't help laughing.

"I just told him I hoped you appreciated his great arse, that's all." Caleb moves faster than Logan can, mainly because I'm holding Logan's arm, only *just* holding him back from going after his little brother who is making a mad dash for the door. "Congratulations again! I love you both and can't wait for the wedding, which I hope is sooner rather than later. I mean, you've made the man wait for long enough already, don't you think Logan?" He yells over his shoulder as he ducks out of the door before Logan can catch him.

"I'll fucking kill him." Logan storms as he rushes for the door to follow Caleb.

"Sweets, stop." I say, gently touching his arm, as I laugh at Caleb's antics. "You know he only does it to get a reaction out of you, so if you don't react, he'll stop."

"He won't. He likes pushing my buttons." Logan grumbles, still scowling at the door as I pull him back to me and wrap my arm around his waist.

"He does make a valid point though." Makenna says with a smirk.

"Makenna." It's Brady's turn to growl now and I chuckle. "Don't. Leave it alone Baby."

"She won't leave it alone. Neither of them can leave it alone." Logan sighs. "So, before you ask, let me tell you all the details. There are none! I asked Jules to marry me *last night*, Makenna. Not even twelve hours ago, honestly and we haven't discussed any other details, OK? In all honestly, I agree with Caleb, I don't want to wait much longer *but* Jules still has to tell *his* family *and* we still have to sort out the details."

"You don't want to wait?" I ask, surprised. "How soon are you thinking?"

"Love, I would marry you tomorrow if it could be arranged. Hell, I would marry you *today*, if it could be done."

"Well, we can't arrange anything *that* soon but we can manage say, in a month's time. What do you think?" Makenna asks seriously but I can't think. All I can do is look at Logan, searching his face for any signs of reluctance or indecision on his behalf but I can't see it.

"Sweets." I whisper, as Makenna keeps talking in the background and I hear Brady's voice as well but all I can see is Logan.

"It's the truth, Jules." He sighs, closes his eyes and takes a deep breath before opening his eyes once again and continuing. "Caleb's right. I've made you, I've made us *both* wait long enough. We should have done this years ago and if I could make it happen today, I would. But I know I can't and I also know that you'll want to talk to your parents. It's easy for me to want to rush ahead but I don't have my parents to think about. Well, we can both see where my siblings stand on the matter. To be honest, I agree with them but I just want *you* to be happy, so I'll do whatever it is *you* want to do. Just don't let yourself get steamrolled by one Makenna Harris, OK?"

"I promise." I laugh. "So, whenever I want, you'll marry me?"

"Yes."

"No argument, no matter how soon?" I ask, just be sure.

"You won't hear a peep from me. Just give me enough time to get a new suit and I'll be happy."

"A new suit? Three piece, right?" I ask, hopefully. I adore this man in anything he wears but he is devastatingly handsome and fuckable in a three piece suit. "Dark grey preferably." I say, earning a smirk from my soon to be husband.

"I wouldn't think of wearing anything else to marry you, Love." Then he kisses me. Deeply, thoroughly and passionately. That is until we hear a cough and then we're smiling against each other lips.

"That would seem to be our cue to leave Mrs Harris."

"But I have to talk to Jules still. We have things to discuss. We don't have much time if they're really getting married in a month's time, Brady."

"I know Kenna but, how about we let them enjoy the first day of being engaged, together and allow Jules to call *his* family." He wraps one arm around her waist, pulling her into his side and the other reaches up, placing a finger on her lips to stop her from speaking. "It can wait Baby. Let's help them keep Julian safe from creepy Ben and moved in here. Then, *then* you can start talking to Julian about all the details."

"Me too. I get a say too you know, it's my wedding as well." Logan speaks up.

"You better ask your brother for his opinion as well, even though we both know you won't listen to it and he doesn't care that much, as long as he's married to Jules at the end." Brady says, making Makenna laugh as they walk out the door and walk back towards the main house.

"Do you ever wish that you'd taken on the main house?" I ask Logan, more out of curiosity than a desire to actually *live* in it.

"No, not really." He pauses for a second. "Why, would you prefer to live up there? I can kick them out you know, it was my house first." There's dead silence between us before I crack up laughing.

"No, I love *our* house. The one we built."

"Me too."

"Can I ask though, why didn't you want to live in the main house?" My curiosity piqued now. "You don't have to tell me, I'm just wondering why."

"You can ask me anything and I will answer it Jules." Even as he speaks though, I can see that it pains him to answer this one and I feel like I might have pushed him too far. I'm just about to tell him not to say anything when he speaks, quietly. "I just felt like it wasn't my house, my *home*. It held so many memories of my parents, my childhood, you know? Not to mention, it's a house for a family, you know kids running around and I guess I just never saw that for myself."

"You don't want kids?" I ask, not sure how we've never discussed the possibility.

"I would love kids but it's something I've put to the back of my mind because I didn't think it was possible. I didn't want to be a single dad in any form and well, until recently, I didn't see us together like that. That's not entirely true. I *hoped* that we could be but it felt like a pipe dream and I didn't want to get my hopes up."

"And now?"

"Now? Now I want it all with you, Love but I still don't want to live in the main house." He laughs. "Too much work up there, not to mention the siblings all still seem to think they have access to it like they did as kids. We'd never have any privacy." He rolls his eyes and then we're both laughing.

"It's not like your brother and sister don't just walk in here unannounced though, Logan."

"That's true but it also isn't their childhood home, so they don't feel quite as entitled to be in here. Although, I think I might have to change the locks now that you're moving in."

"You know Caleb will just get a copy somehow anyway, so what's the point?" He just growls in response and reaches for his phone that's buzzing. I watch as he scowls at the screen and I wonder what the message says. "What's up?"

"Makenna just reminded me that we have a meeting together this morning that I'd forgotten about."

"Well, go have a shower and get ready for it then, I don't need babysitting you know."

"But I'm supposed to be coming back with you to the apartment to finish up and bring everything back here."

"Go have a shower and we'll sort it out. Go on, go." I push him towards the bathroom. "I'll make us some more coffee and some breakfast. Go on!" I give him one last push and watch as he closes the door behind him. Then I get to work, fixing everything for our breakfast.

Just as I hear the shower turn off, my phone chimes with a message and I know it's Brady before I even pick it up.

Brady: *I can take you back to the apartment this morning and help you pack up the rest of your things*

Me: *thanks I'd appreciate the ride but you don't have to stay*

I wait a few minutes but when he doesn't respond I get back to finishing off our breakfast. Just as Logan strolls out of the shower in a cloud of steam and I forget what I'm doing for a few seconds, until the phone buzzes in my hand again.

Brady: *I don't mind at all*

Brady: *Logan will just make you stay here until he's ready to take you otherwise. No more creepy ben*

I smile at the winky face he added at the end.

"Who's messaging you and making you smile like that? Have you forgotten already that you're *my* fiancé now?" He takes all of four strides to stand in front of me and pull my lips to his, giving me a mind blanking kiss.

"It was Brady." I say breathlessly as he pulls back. "He wanted to let me know that he can take me to the apartment to finish up the packing."

"Oh, that's good." He says nodding.

"Go put on some clothes Logan, I can't concentrate with you like that." I say waving a hand up and down in his general direction.

"It's just a towel, Love." He says with smirk.

"Exactly! Now go and put some clothes on, we both have things to do. You can wait until later."

Logan walks away but I can tell he isn't happy about not being able to celebrate with me yet. When he comes out, all dressed in a suit, no vest today thank heavens because otherwise we would both be late! We eat breakfast together and just talk about things. I try to avoid mentioning Ben's name because I want Logan to head to work and not worry about me going back to my old apartment this morning.

"When are you going to call your folks?" Logan asks me as we clean up the dishes.

"How about now, if you have the time?"

"I always have time for you, Love." He drops a kiss on my forehead as he puts the last dish away. "Let's do it Jules."

Chapter Twenty-eight
LOGAN

I watch as Jules pulls up his Mum's number and takes a deep breath.

"Are you nervous, Jules?"

"About telling them that I'm going to marry you? Yes and no. Let me explain before you make assumptions, please?" I nod and let him continue. "I'm not nervous because I think we're doing the wrong thing, Logan, I am one hundred and ten percent on board with marrying the fuck out of you. I know that they're going to be happy for us, Sweets, that's not the issue either. The issue is, I had kind of conditioned them for this *not* happening and the two of us just being together forever, so they're either going to be shocked in a happy way or an embarrassingly weird way somehow."

I laugh at him because if there's anything I've learned about his parents in all our years together, they're going to have a weird reaction to whatever we tell them.

"Well then, let's find out." I smile wickedly at him. "Do a video call with them, I want to see their faces." Jules sighs and I know that he may be hesitating but he wants to see their faces too. It's quiet as we wait for the call to be answered.

"Hey honey, Julian's calling. How the hell do I get this thing to work again?" We hear his dad yell out and become dizzy from the movement of the camera as he takes it to his wife.

"Ohh hun, you've already answered the call, you just have to look at the damn screen." Her tone is stern but we see the smile on her face. "Ohhh hey there boys, how are you?"

"Good morning Mum, Dad, how are you both?" He sounds nervous and I know his mum picks up on it but it's his dad that asks the question.

"What's up son? What's with the early morning video call? You couldn't give your folks a chance to get cleaned up a little *before* you put us on a camera with Logan?" His dad growls but he shoots me a wink. "I mean, look at him, so handsome and well put together, he makes your mother damn near swoon every time she sees him!"

"Shut up, Harold he does not. I mean, you *are* very handsome Logan but I do *not swoon* over my son's boyfriend Harold!" We both laugh as we watch her slap her husband's arm and he flinches away from her.

"Damn it woman don't hit me so damn hard. That hurts you know, I'm not as solid as I used to be, you've got to be gentle with me these days."

"Oh dear god." Jules mumbles beside me and I can't help laughing. I enjoy spending time with the Bishops, they love each other without reservation *and* they're hysterical. The bonus is, they embarrass the hell out of Jules. "Can you two stop for just one second, please?" Jules pleads with them.

"Sorry son." They both say, while still giving each other a dirty look.

"What is it that you wanted to tell us baby boy?" His mum asks and Jules shakes his head.

"Yes, it must be serious if you're calling first thing in the morning and Mr Handsome is standing right beside you." His mum looks between us and starts to tear up, suspecting something is up but his dad rambles on oblivious to the world around him until Susan slaps him again and tells him to shut up!

"Go on Julian, Logan." Susan encourages.

"So, there's a few things. I know I already told you but I'm moving out of the apartment and into Logan's place out at Drake Wines. Well, that's happening today."

"Ohhhhh I'm so happy for you both." Susan says through her tears.

"He said there's more, shush and let them finish."

"Ummm well, last night. Logan. Ummmmm."

"I asked Julian to marry me last night."

"About damned time young man!" His dad exclaims.

"And?" His mum asks, obviously needing confirmation that the answer was yes.

"And what? Of course I said yes!" Julian says in a high pitched voice and there are a few seconds of silence, just like there was this morning with *my* family and I'm trying to work out why they're all not just instantly happy. Is it just because I was such a jerk for so long that they never expected this day to come? I'm brought out of my thoughts by loud screaming.

"Oh my! That's incredible. Oh my god I'm so happy for you. Both of you! Welcome to the family Logan, although, you've been family for years, now it will be official!" Susan cries.

"Congratulations, both of you. Welcome to the family, like Susan said, officially that is. I'm very happy for you both." Harold is much more sedate in his congratulations but you can see the happiness all over his face.

"Do you have a date yet? Have you thought about where you want to have the ceremony? Of course, it would be perfect to have it out at Drake Wines, among the vines. Isn't that where your sister got married not so long ago Logan? Could you boys do a similar thing? Or do you think that would annoy Makenna? Of course Makenna won't be annoyed by that, she's a gorgeous, generous girl. I bet she's' excited too. Ohhh have you told them yet?"

"Susan." Harold reaches out and takes her hand in his. "Calm down honey, I'm sure they'll give us all the details when they know them."

I look at Jules, who looks a little overwhelmed with his mum's reaction, for permission to tell them what we spoke about with Makenna this morning and he nods.

"We told my family this morning. Makenna walked in and saw Jules' ring and ..." I don't get to finish because there's another high pitched squeal on the other side of the screen.

"Calm down honey!" Harold says but looks at the scene. "I think you're going to give your mother a heart attack!"

"Yes, I have a ring. It's going to do double time as both my engagement ring *and* my wedding band." Jules tells his parents.

"You made the choice?" I ask him quietly and he smiles at me warmly.

"Yes. I want to use it for both. I don't want a new wedding band, this one means more than a new one ever could." When his hand comes up and Susan sees the ring for the first time, she lets out another squeal and I'm not sure Harold's ears can take much more. "Mum calm down! If you're just going to keep squealing, I'll hang up now and you'll just get messages with information in them!"

"You don't have to be mean, Julian John Bishop. That being said, I promise to calm down now." His mum makes the motion of locking her lips and throwing away the key and I can't help laughing.

"Thank you! Right, now to answer *all* of your questions, here we go. Yes I spoke to Makenna this morning and yes Logan and I would love to have the ceremony here, at Drake Wines." His Mum squeaks, until Jules gives her a death glare and she stops. "Brady built a gorgeous arch for their wedding and we would *love* to make use of that as well. It's what I was thinking of and Makenna suggested it, so you're right, she's very kind and thoughtful. As for the date." He looks my way and I know he's asking if I meant what I said earlier.

"The date is as soon as we can get everything organised." I say, smiling at Jules and his Mum gasps. "I think we've been together long enough to not have to wait too long, don't you?" I look at the screen and Susan has tears flowing down her cheeks. "I want to make your son my husband as soon as I possibly can, if you guys are OK with that, that is?" I smile at the screen.

"Absolutely!" Harold says because I don't think Susan could speak around her emotions if she tried.

"Obviously, we'll put you guys up here at Drake Wines. My brother is remodelling a few old cottages that were original buildings out here. We're going to use them for just these kinds of occasions and we would be honoured if you were some of our first guests to use them. Before you argue, I won't take no for an answer and you can stay here for as long as you like."

"Thank you Logan, that's very generous of you and your family." Harold says.

"We're all family now, right? That's what family does for each other. My father wouldn't be impressed with me if I didn't insist that you stay here with us."

"I'm sorry they won't be there to see you get married Logan." Susan says quietly.

"Me too but I know they'll be there in one way or another." Before anyone can say anything more, my phone chimes with a message. "I'm sorry, that's Makenna, I'm going to have to take this. We'll talk again soon to work out what date you're coming to stay."

"Take care, Logan."

"You too, take care." With that, I walk away to call Makenna back.

"Sorry, we were on a video call with Susan and Harold."

"Ohh perfectly understandable. How did they react?"

"Noisily." Is my only response to that. "We'll have a cottage for them to stay in for the wedding, right?"

"Absolutely we will! No matter when it is, even if Caleb has to hire a few more hands to make the building go quicker, they will have a somewhere to stay. If it comes down to it, they have a room at the house."

"Thank you Makenna."

"Pfft. We will make sure they have somewhere to stay, for as long as they want to stay Logan. They're family and that's what we do for family."

"I love you, Makenna." I don't know if I tell my family often enough that I love them and I resolve right then to tell them more often when I hear Makenna suck in a surprised breath.

"I love you too, Logan." She replies, her voice choked with emotion until she coughs to clear it. "Right, OK. Umm, I need to get you here in the office, my office in ten minutes. I just wanted to let you know."

"So that I wasn't late." I laugh at the ridiculousness of her reminder. "When was the last time I was late for a meeting?"

"Well, never *but* you've never been an engaged man before either, so I wasn't sure where your head was."

"I have never intentionally forgotten or missed a meeting Makenna and I don't intend on starting now."

"I know but things were a little exciting this morning, so I thought I'd check in with you." She repeats and I can't say I'm not grateful for her call. "Ohh and Brady can take Jules back to his place, sorry, the apartment and help him get the last few things packed up and ready for us to move it all this afternoon after this meeting is over and done with."

"That will keep Jules happy, he didn't want to hang around here waiting for me."

"Yeah, we kind of figured he'd be going a little crazy knowing that he had things to do but he was still here. Where are you right now?"

"Right here." I say from behind her as I end the call and speak.

"Holy crap! Why does everyone have to sneak up on me?" She demands.

"We don't sneak up on you, Makenna, you just don't hear anyone walking up behind you. You should really get your hearing tested you know? Maybe there's something wrong with a part of your hearing." I say, barely keeping a straight face.

"You know there's nothing wrong with my hearing Logan Drake, you're just a bunch of sneaky arseholes, that's all!"

"Of course that's it!" I say, rolling my eyes. "Come on let's get this meeting started. The sooner we begin, the sooner we can end it."

"In a hurry, Logan?"

"Sure am, I've got a fiancé waiting at home for me now." I say with a shit eating grin that I can feel to the tips of my toes. "Speaking of ..." Just as we step into the meeting, my phone chimes with a message from the man in question, telling me that Brady is going to take him to the apartment to finish up what needs to be done there. I send him back a quick message acknowledging both the fact that I *got* the message *and* that Brady is going with him, while also telling him I'm walking into the meeting right then. I know he'll understand my meaning, I always have my phone on silent when I'm in a meeting but he knows he can call Margot if there's an emergency and she'll come right in and get us.

The meeting takes less time than any of us were expecting and I excuse myself quickly, after saying my goodbyes to everyone, and call Jules to let him know I'll be on my way shortly. When he doesn't answer, I figure he's too busy or can't hear his phone over whatever music he's got playing, loudly, to help him get stuff done.

I quickly duck back home and change out of my suit, into jeans and a t-shirt because we've got packing, moving and cleaning to do today. Jules and Brady won't have had much time to get anything done, so we'll all have to pitch in to help.

When I reach the building, I decide to call him again to make sure he doesn't need anything before I get upstairs but when he answers, he sounds strange.

"Yeah. Ummm hi Logan. Don't come up there's been an issue." He grunts and whispers to someone I assume is Brady, until he then says to me, "It's a real mess up here and I'm going to need more time to clean up."

"Is Ben there with you, Love?" I ask, a strange feeling settling over me.

"Yes, that's what I said, you need to give me more time Logan. I'm just not ready to move in with you, OK?"

"Has he hurt you?"

"No, no. Nothing like that, I just don't think I'm ready."

"I'll be there in two minutes, Jules and I'm calling the police."

"OK, see you later, Logan." Then he ends the call but not before I hear Ben's voice in the background, raging about me not being good enough for Jules and Jules trying to get him to calm down.

I burst in the doors of the building, almost collecting the security guard in the process.

"Mr Drake, please slow down. Is there a problem?"

"Yes, yes there is. Ben, Jules' neighbour has him trapped in the apartment. I need you to call the police."

"You can't go up there Mr Drake, you'll put yourself and Mr Bishop in danger." I spin on my heels and face the man.

"If you think he's so fucking dangerous, then why haven't you done something about him?" I yell.

"Because we didn't have any proof! Innocent until proven guilty Mr Drake."

"You mean, innocent until he hurts my fiancé, right? Call the police, now!" I roar at him, when I see him dial them, I turn and race to the stairs. The elevator will take too long to get here and travel back up, I can get there faster myself.

Chapter Twenty-nine
JULES

I only got off the video call with my parents when Brady walked into the house and interrupted us. My mother wanted to know every last detail, right down to how Logan proposed! Thank god Brady came in when he did, otherwise I don't know what would have happened!

Halfway between Drake Wines and my apartment, Brady got a phone call from the assistant manager at the bar he works at.

"Hey Damien, what's up? Just so you know, you're on speaker because I'm driving." Brady answers the phone, smiling at me.

"Hi Makenna, how are you feeling?"

"Ahh, it's not Makenna, it's our brother in law." Brady says, laughing.

"Oh sorry. How are you Jules?" Damien asks, and I'm shocked he knew exactly who Brady meant.

"I'm great, thanks Damien."

"Logan and Jules got engaged last night, so we have another wedding to organise." Brady informs him.

"That's awesome! Congratulations Jules and please, tell Logan the same and that I said it was about fucking time he made an honest man out of you." We all laugh a little before I thank him once again.

"So, what did you need me for?" Brady asks and they start talking about business. I tune them out because I'm not working and I don't want to think about anything work related.

"Is that OK with you Jules?" I hear Brady ask and I tear myself away from dreamily looking out the car window, thinking about wedding details that I might like and can discuss with Makenna.

"Hmmm. Am I OK with what?" Brady laughs.

"I said, I just have to run by the bar for a few minutes if you don't mind? Then we can head over to the apartment, I shouldn't be long."

"Yeah, of course. You do what you need to do Brady."

"Thanks Jules." Damien's voice says from the speaker, making me jump a little. I hadn't even realise he was still connected!

They keep talking for a few minutes and I zone out again, not wanting to listen and to let them talk freely. When I hear the radio come back on, I know that Brady has ended the call.

"Brady, why don't you drop me at my place? I promise to lock the door and not let anyone in unless their last names are Drake or Harris."

"Logan will *kill* me if I leave you alone for longer than a minute Jules and you know it."

"Logan will never have to know Brady. Seriously, I'm a grown man and I can look after myself! Not to mention I'll be in a building that has security if I need it."

"I don't know Jules, have you ever been on the receiving end of a pissed off Logan? I really don't want that anger thrown in my direction because I let you go into your apartment alone." He sighs, long and resigned. "I'll be ten minutes, max. Come into the bar and we can have a celebratory drink. I'm sure Damien can shake you up a cocktail of your choice." He offers with a smirk.

"I have no doubt that he can, Brady but if you're not going to be long, I'd really rather you drop me at the apartment so that I can start getting things sorted out."

"Jules."

"Brady!"

"I don't want Logan *and* Makena pissed at me if something goes wrong."

"It won't go wrong. The bar is less than a five minute drive from the building, so you can get there and back again in twenty minutes, thirty at the most. They'll never know and we can both get what we need to get done, done." I know he's wavering but I don't plead my case any further, I know the war he's waging within himself and he's right, *if* anything goes wrong, Logan will blame him one hundred percent. Therefore, he carries all that load himself.

"Fine!" He finally gives in, I had a feeling he would. "*But* you keep your phone on you at *all* times and if I call or message you, I get an immediate response. Not even a two second delay, do you understand me? Because even though you might take this all as a bit of over kill and think it's unnecessary, Logan doesn't."

"I know and I'm not saying that Ben isn't weird or that he's not behaving strange lately but I don't think he's going to hurt me Brady, otherwise I wouldn't ask you to do this. I promise to lock the door behind me and not let anyone else in until you get back, OK?"

"Message me when you get inside your apartment, not the building Julian, your apartment."

"I promise."

Ten minutes later, we're pulling up outside my apartment building and I can feel Brady's uneasiness coming off him in waves.

"Thank you Brady, I'll be fine." I tell him as I get out of his car.

"Message me when you get inside." He calls out before I can close the car door.

"I promise." He opens his mouth to speak but I get in before he can. "AS soon as I lock the door when I get inside the *apartment,* I will message you."

Closing the car door, I walk towards the building and the door opens just as I reach it and my heart is in my throat, hoping like hell I'm not about to run into Ben, the same way I have for months now. It couldn't possibly always be a coincidence but it's the security guard at the front desk.

"Good morning Mr Bishop, how are you today?" He asks with a smile on his face. "Ohhh you only have a few days left with us, don't you?"

"I do, Jimmy."

"I'll miss seeing you around, Mr Bishop."

"I'll miss seeing you too Jimmy but life is taking me in another direction and I can't wait." I smile broadly at him.

"As long you're happy Mr Bishop." He hesitates for a second and then continues. "I hope I'm not speaking out of turn but I do hope that direction is with Mr Drake?"

"It most certainly is Jimmy and I couldn't be happier." I flash him my ring and his smile broadens.

"Congratulations to you both."

"Thanks Jimmy." I grin back at him.

I know that Brady was waiting and watching me walk into the building, so I also know, he'll be expecting a message from me sooner rather than later. I get on the elevator and take it to my floor. As the doors open, I look for any signs of Ben lurking, and when I find none, I step off the elevator and make my way to my door. Unlocking it, I walk inside, scan the rooms that I can easily see and decide I'm safe. No-one else has a key to get in there other than myself and Logan. The head of security, Jimmy's boss, assured me that he'd demanded that Ben hand over his copy of my key, which is why the building manager didn't want to replace the locks, much to Logan's dismay and anger.

I send Brady a message that I am safely locked inside the apartment. I smile when he replies immediately, saying he promises to not be longer than twenty minutes.

I'm laughing at the ridiculousness of it all when I hear a noise coming from my bedroom and I head that way without thinking. I mean it could be a cat or mouse, or a cat chasing a mouse, right?

But it's not.

No, when I get to my bedroom, I find Ben standing in the middle of the room, cutting what I assume he *thinks* are Logan's underwear but are in fact *mine.* I speak and as the words leave my mouth, I realise that I should have left the apartment and let security deal with the nutter but I'm so shocked to have caught him in the act that I don't think before I speak.

"What the hell are you doing in my bedroom? And why the fuck are you cutting up my underwear?" I ask much more calmly than I'm feeling.

"Jules. I wasn't expecting you."

"So I can see."

"I didn't know these were yours." He says, defending himself with my underwear in one hand and a pair of scissors in the other.

"Well, I guess that's nice to know Ben but the real question is, why the hell are you in my apartment and how the hell did you get in here?"

"I thought they were Logan's."

"OK."

"I used my key."

"You *have* a key to *my* apartment?" I ask, trying to keep him talking while I try to work out how to get help up here.

"Remember, ages ago, you gave me one so that I could bring in your mail?" He says, with a weird zoned out, creepy smile.

"I do remember that Ben but I also remember you giving me the key back."

"I know I gave you *a* key back but I got an extra couple cut because you never know when you need a spare or two."

"Sure, of your own keys Ben, not someone else's." I state and then realise I made another mistake because I've made him angry.

"You know, I wouldn't have to go to these lengths if you'd just stayed away from Logan, you know, after you broke up. I was just giving you time, space to get over him, before I made my move." Holy fuck, the guy has a screw loose.

"You've always been a good *friend* Ben but I'm sorry, that's all I saw you as, a friend." Another mistake on my behalf. Don't try to placate the raging lunatic Julian!

"That's not true! I see the way you look at me! If it wasn't for *Logan Drake*, I mean what kind of name is that anyway?" He snorts with derision.

"The one his parents gave him?"

"That's not even remotely funny Julian." His anger ramping up as he takes two steps closer to me and I slowly start trying to back up out the door.

I don't move fast enough though and he catches me in the living room. I try to pull out of his hold but he's stronger than he looks and he won't let go! The next thing I know, he's pushing me down to sit on one of my dining chairs and he's tying my hands behind my back. I sit there in stunned silence because I'm not sure how we got here!

"What are you doing, Ben?"

"You're going to sit there and listen to me for a change. I'm going to tell you why Logan Drake isn't good enough for you and why you should be with me instead." I can't speak, I have no words. "I saw that ring on your finger Julian. Is that his?"

I struggle to decide what to tell him and decide, for better or worse, to go with the truth.

"Yes, we're getting married next month Ben." I tell him, hoping that piece of news will make him see sense. Instead, it's like waving a red flag in from of an angry bull!

"No. No, no, no, no. No, I don't accept that. If I can't have you Julian, then Logan doesn't get to keep you either." I swallow and try to think fast, when my phone starts ringing in my pocket.

"It's Logan, Ben. If I don't answer, he's just going to keep calling or come here looking for me." The ringing stops but I know it will start up again because Logan expects me to pick up the phone when he calls and I expect the same when I call *him*.

Ben starts pacing the floor in front of me. I'm not sure how long the silence lasts but when my phone starts ringing again, I know it's Logan again.

"If I don't answer him Ben, he *will* come here, all guns blazing."

"Fine you can talk to him but don't drop him any hints about what's going on here, do I make myself clear?"

"Crystal clear Ben. Crystal." I say, sarcasm and relief dripping from my voice. "You're going to have to pull my phone out of my pocket."

"Right, OK." For a man that wants me all for himself, he sure doesn't seem to want to touch me too intimately. He doesn't even look comfortable reaching into my pocket for my phone. He presses the accept button on the screen just before it cut out for a second time.

"Yeah. Ummm hi Logan. Don't come up there's been an issue." I say into the phone before he can speak. I grunt as Ben kicks my ankle to remind me not to say anything that might make Logan suspect what's really going on. "It's a real mess up here and I'm going to need more time to clean up."

"Is Ben there with you, Love?" Logan asks immediately. I could *not* love this man any more than I do right in this moment.

"Yes, that's what I said, you need to give me more time Logan. I'm just not ready to move in with you, OK?"

"Has he hurt you?" He growls into the phone and my heart breaks a little at his anguish.

"No, no. Nothing like that, I just don't think I'm ready."

"I'll be there in a two minute Jules and I'm calling the police." I can hear his breathing pick up as he picks up the pace to get to me and I just hope that none of us get hurt in the process.

"OK, see you later Logan." I end the call without another word but Ben flies into a rage about me not being honest with him, accusing me of sending Logan code to let him know what's going on.

He's red in the face with rage, telling me how Logan isn't good enough for me and how I'm the only one for him. That I'll only be happy if I'm with *him* and I'm starting to feel sick. I hope the cops get here not long after Logan does because otherwise, I think there might be more trouble than any of us anticipated today.

Chapter Thirty
LOGAN

My legs won't carry me fast enough up these fucking stairs but there was no hope in hell I was waiting for the elevator. Not a fucking chance, I couldn't have handled standing still in there, knowing that Jules needed me.

I bang the door open at the landing to his floor and apologise to the woman who screamed at me. I didn't stop moving though, I kept moving forward.

As I reach Jules' door, I'm already pulling out my keys when I hear the elevator ding, announcing its arrival and the doors opened as I held the key up to the lock.

"Mr Drake, let me." I look over my shoulder to find the maintenance guy standing there with a set of master keys.

"I have a key." I tell him, confused as to why he might be here.

"I mean, let me go in, it might diffuse whatever the situation is in there better." He must see not only the confusion on my face but also the steam coming out of my ears. How dare he think that I can't look after Jules properly! "I just mean, that if you go in there all guns blazing, we might end with a worse situation on our hands. If I go in under cover of checking up on Mr Bishop and making sure that the apartment is in perfect moving out condition, it might be calmer and I can assess the situation. We don't know if he has a weapon or anything, Mr Drake."

I realise that I hadn't even considered that Ben might have a weapon and I'm not sure if I'm more relieved or anxious now that he's brought it to my attention. "Fuck!" I mumble.

"I'm sorry Mr Drake, I didn't mean to cause you any extra worry."

"Logan."

"I'm sorry?"

"Call me Logan. I think we've earned being on a first name basis, don't you?"

"Oh right, of course, Mr, I mean Logan. I'm Harry." He holds his hand out for me to shake it and even though I think it's absurd for the situation we're in, I take it because that's what I do every day. "Let me go in, I'll assess what the situation is and either call you in or come back out, OK?"

"Were the police called?"

"Yes, they're on the way but that doesn't mean they'll be here soon." I nod, knowing he's right.

"OK, you go in first but if I hear anything that I don't like, I'll be in there faster than you can get that key in the lock, do you understand me?" I warn him.

"Perfectly." We don't say another thing, as he pushes the key into the lock and then yells out to let Jules know he's coming in. "Mr Bishop? Are you in here? It's Harry, I'm just coming in to check on your progress and to see if anything needs repairing before you leave."

"I thought you were renovating the apartment?" I hear Jules ask and I breathe a sigh of relief.

"Well, you have me there Mr Bishop." Harry laughs, as he enters the apartment, leaving the door ajar so that I can hear the conversation. "Truth be told, I'm here to make sure you haven't damaged anything while you're packing and moving out."

There's a strange, strangled noise from inside and I can't decide who it was or what it means.

"Surely that could have waited?" Jules says, his voice distant, earning another chuckle from Harry.

"You're right, again, of course but I only do what I'm told to, Mr Bishop." Harry's voice is getting further away and I can only *just* see his shadow on the wall inside the door.

"Don't come in any further Harry." Jules is starting to sound panicked and I inch closer the door, edging it open a little further. "Harry stop! I don't want you to get hurt!" My heart jumps into my throat because Jules is really nervous now.

"I won't get hurt Mr Bishop, you're not going to hurt me." Harry chuckles, again and I'm starting to wonder about the man's sanity. I mean, who laughs in this kind of situation, honestly?

"I won't, no. Not on purpose Harry but accidents can happen."

"Yes, they can but what could you possibly be doing that would cause me harm today Mr Bishop?"

"Jules. Please call me Jules, Mr Bishop is my Dad."

"Sure Jules, whatever you want." The man fucking chuckles again but I can see him from just inside the door and I know he's not actually amused at all. "Now, what could you possibly be doing that could get me hurt, Jules?"

"I ... I've dropped a couple of glasses all over the floor." Jules says in a rush and I know he's lying. "I don't want you to cut your feet."

"Well, Jules, I have shoes on, work boots to tell you the truth and they've saved my feet from a lot worse than broken glass. I'm going to come in the kitchen now and we can talk."

"No!!!!!!!!!!!!!!!" Jules yells but he's too late, Harry is already pushing open the door that I've never seen closed in all of Jules' time living here.

I hadn't realised that I was slowly moving inside the apartment until I hear a crash, Jules squeals and then one of Harry's boots pushes the door open slightly. That's when I realise the man is on the floor, hopefully still alive but I'm guessing he's been knocked out.

Without thinking, I leap the last couple of steps to the door and push it open, hoping to knock Ben off balance so that I can take the bastard down.

What I don't count on, is seeing Jules bound to one of the fucking dining chairs, making me pause for a few seconds, giving Ben long enough to recover and come at me. What he doesn't know, is that he may *think* he has the advantage on me but he doesn't. I spent years going to training with Caleb and we've been fighting each other for years, decades. I've learned to move pretty quick and I dodge out of his grasp.

When Jules screams at me to watch out, I don't look at *him*, I watch Ben to gauge what his next plan of attack is.

"Logan, no!" Jules cries out again. I refuse to look at him, if I do, I won't be able to save either of us!

"You're not good enough for him *Logan*! You never have been but then you went and broke his heart! I could hear his sobs through the walls and then you came back. You were even less worthy of this man and yet, he not only forgave you for stringing him along all these years, but he then *actually* agreed to become your *husband!*" He takes a step over Harry's still unmoving body towards me, I don't move, I'm scared of this guy but I can't let him hurt Jules or Harry any more than he already has. "When I saw that pathetic excuse of a ring on his finger, I knew I had to do something to make him see he was making a mistake."

"What do you mean? What did you do, Ben?" I ask, trying to distract him for long enough for the police or at the very least, security to get up here. I'm still trying to work out why they sent the maintenance guy here instead of security but I have no time to think about that, as Ben takes one more careful step towards me.

"I came in here and started unpacking all his things. Don't you see Logan? He can't leave me, I won't let him! He's mine, forever. You can't have him!" Ben roars, as he lunges for me and I see the knife just as Jules yells out a warning.

"He's got a knife, Logan!" Jules screams, as I dodge around Ben's arm. I don't answer Jules because if I take my eyes or my attention off Ben, well it could spell disaster.

"If I can't have him, then *no-one* gets to have him!" Ben screams, as he suddenly changes direction and moves his attention from me back to Jules. Before I can even move towards him to stop him from touching Jules, a shot rings out and Ben lets out a howl a of pain, then drops to the floor. On his knees, he continues to make his way towards Jules.

"Stop moving you bastard!" Harry groans, getting to his feet. "If you don't stop, I'll shoot to kill you, not just maim you, do you understand?"

"Fuck you!" Ben growls back, shuffling on his knees towards Jules. I go to move forward but a hand comes to rest on my chest, holding me in place. I look from the hand to the man and he shakes his head at me. That's when I notice the gun in his hand and hear the crackle of the hand held radio he had hidden under his jacket.

"I've got this Logan, I promise." His radio crackles to life again but a movement out the corner of my eye catches my attention before I can register exactly what Harry means. "I said stop motherfucker!"

The minute happens in slow motion as Ben lunges at Jules, who in trying to get away manages to topple the chair he's tied to over, hitting the floor hard! Another shot rings out and Ben slumps the ground, groaning in pain. Harry is helping right Jules' chair, as I skid to stop in front it and fall to my knees.

Kneeling in front of Jules, my hands start to move over every inch of his body to make sure he's not injured. Then all of a sudden, he slumps into my arms with enough force to push me onto my arse but I don't mind because Jules is in my arms.

"Hey, Harry you all good in there?" A voice crackles through Harry's radio.

"Backup." He says to us, as he pulls the radio out of its holster to speak into it. "Under control beat cop." A snort fills the room as the radio crackles again.

"You're the beat cop, idiot. Do you need backup?"

"Nah but we're going to need an ambulance."

"One or two teams Harry?" The voice is deadly serious now.

"Just the one, beats. Suspect is going to need some medical attention, everyone else is safe, uninjured and accounted for."

"Copy. Medics are on their way."

Just as he finishes speaking, we hear the door bang open and a voice calling out but it isn't the medics that Harry asked for.

"What the fuck happened in here? Christ Julian, you told me you'd lock the fucking door behind you and you'd be safe! You *said* you were fine when you got in here! I shouldn't have fucking let you come in alone, should have done exactly what Logan told me to. I shouldn't have let you talk me into this! What the fuck, Julian!"

"Hi Brady. Did you get done what you needed to at the bar?" Jules asks from my lap, laughing. Brady looks at me and I'm sure he reads the look on my face because he looks away pretty quickly to focus on Jules.

"Don't 'hi Brady' me. Makenna is going to kill me, if Logan doesn't beat her to it first!"

"Please don't say that right now. I'll have to take it as a threat and I don't think these guys need to go through any more than they already have." Brady looks at Harry like he only just realised the man is standing there. "I'm a cop and you are?"

"This idiot's brother in law."

"Which one?" Harry asks.

"Both." The three of us say in unison and then laugh hysterically, the day's events finally catching up to us all.

Chapter Thirty-one
JULES

After the laughter dies down, the tension between Logan and Brady is obvious. I know that it's my job to diffuse it because I'm the one that put myself in the position that Logan was trying to protect me from.

"Logan." I say, trying to get his attention off glaring at Brady and onto me, because he really needs to hear what I've got to say. "Logan, look at me, please." When he finally does, I continue. "This isn't Brady's fault."

"Well, to be fair it kind of is." Brady says loud enough for the three of us to hear among the noise that is almost overwhelming now that all the medics and police are entering the room, trying to do whatever they need to.

"No, Brady, it really isn't." I'm talking to Brady but I don't break eye contact with Logan. "Brady got a work call on the way here, *he* wanted to go to the bar before coming here and *I* convinced him that I would be OK on my own. He even made me message him when I got inside and locked the door, so that he knew I was OK."

"So what happened then?"

"Yeah, I would love to hear this part of the story too, please Mr Bishop." Harry suddenly appears next to Brady again.

"I wouldn't mind knowing it either, I think." Logan mumbles, not breaking eye contact with *me*.

"I spoke to Jimmy when I came in the building and he asked if I was really going to move out. I told him I absolutely was because I'm going to be a married man soon. He congratulated me and said he was very happy for the both of us." I smile at Logan, who doesn't seem too pleased about it all right now.

"Let's just skip over the pleasantries for now, shall we?" Logan grumbles.

"Right." I cough to clear my throat and then continue. "Brady made me promise to message him when I got inside and locked the door behind me. So, I did that and he replied immediately but that's also when I heard a noise coming from the bedroom. When I reached the doorway, I found Ben standing over the bed with what he *thought* were Logan's underwear but were in fact, *mine* and he was attacking them with a pair of scissors. He didn't notice me straight away because he was so very invested in cutting up said undergarments and the minute he realised I was there, and I saw the look on his face, I know I should have bolted as soon as I found him and called security. Obviously, I didn't and he caught me before I could get out."

"How did he get in?" Harry asks, pushing me to keep going.

"He had a key."

"He *what?*" Logan yells, causing another officer to look over and check with Harry to see if he needed help but Harry shook his head. "What the fuck do you mean, *he had a key*? I thought you said he didn't have one?"

"He got a copy cut." I can't explain it easier than that and I shrug. "Just after I first moved in, I had to go away for work and I asked him to collect my mail for me because I was waiting for an important letter. I got the key back off him when I got home but he'd already made a copy. A few apparently."

"Fucking hell!" Logan mumbles, closing his eyes.

"Has he let himself in here before now? Without your knowledge, I mean?"

"How the hell would he know if it's without his knowledge, officer?" Brady asks, frustrated.

"Well, what I mean to say is, if you think back would you be able to remember a time when things were a little, shall we say, different when you came home to what they were when you left? Even little things like things being in the wrong place, things missing or even things returning?"

"Now that you mention it? Yeah weird things go missing and then return but I hadn't thought anything of it. I sure as hell didn't think someone was coming into my apartment when I wasn't here."

"Except, I recently caught him leaving your apartment and he didn't have your permission to be in here then." Logan adds.

"When was this?"

"Last week. We were staying here so that we could slowly sort stuff out and I came back earlier than Jules one day to find Ben walking out of the apartment and locking the door behind him."

"Did you ask him what he was doing?" Harry asks.

"Of course I fucking did. He said that Jules had asked him to check if he'd left a notebook on the kitchen table. I remember it clearly because I was confused as to why Jules would ask Ben to check when he knew that I would be here soon."

"And you accepted that explanation?"

"What would you have had me do? Call the cops on him? He had a fucking key, it's not like he was breaking and entering. Not to mention, I hadn't spoken to Jules and I didn't know for sure that he *hadn't* asked the creep to check it for him."

"He did ask me later that night when I came home if I had given Ben a key and I said that I most certainly had not, nor had I asked him to enter my home for any reason. That was the night we decided to go stay out at Drake Wines."

"When was that?"

Logan and I look at each other, the realisation hitting us at the same time.

"It was only last night!" We say at the same time.

"Hey Harry." Another officer interrupts. "We've swept the apartment and found a few listening devices. The assailant admitted to planting them months ago as he was being wheeled out by the medics."

Logan's head drops to my shoulder, I can feel the anger and frustration rolling off him.

"Well, that explains how he knew everything that was going on in your life, Mr Bishop."

"Jules. Please call me Jules, Officer."

"OK." He smiles. "Call me Harry. So that means he couldn't hear you through the walls at all, he's been listening to everything that goes on in here for months."

"Fuck." Logan snarls into my shoulder and I'm pretty sure that if Ben hadn't already left the apartment on a stretcher, Logan would be beating the shit out of him right now.

"That's not creepy at all!" Brady points out as if no-one else in the room would agree.

"What happened when Ben caught you, Jules?" Harry asks, ignoring Brady and giving Logan a look that makes him at least *try* to calm down.

"He ummm. He pushed me into the dining chair and tied my hands behind me. That's when he saw the ring and he lost his mind! He started pacing around in front of me and raging about how Logan didn't deserve me, that he wasn't good enough for me. Then my phone rang and he saw Logan's name on the screen. When the phone started ringing again a few minutes later, I convinced him to let me answer. I told him that Logan wouldn't stop calling until I answered and if I didn't answer, then he would come here."

"He let you answer the phone?" Harry asks and I nod.

"Yes but with the stipulation that I didn't give Logan any hints that I was in trouble."

I can't help laughing in response to Harry's question. "It took Logan less than a minute to realise that I was in trouble but Ben, he didn't have a clue that I wasn't just telling the man I love to actually fuck off." I laugh, uncontrollably for a minute, until I realise no-one else is laughing. In fact they all seem to be looking at me like I might have gone crazy. "Anyhoo. Logan picked up that I was in trouble. Asked me if Ben was with me and you know the rest. It really all happened so quickly."

"OK. Thank you Jules. We're done for now but you'll have to come to the station and sign a formal document with your version of everything you just said within the next day or two. So will you Logan." Logan nods to the officer and he nods back.

"Can we pack some more things and leave now?" Logan asks.

"You can't take anything with you today, no, it's all evidence for now. I'll let you know when you can get back in to clean everything up but we are done here for now. So yes, you can head on home as soon as I take down your phone numbers so that someone can contact you when everything is ready."

Logan stands up, taking me with him and he wraps his arm around my waist, pulling me in tight, as he rattles off both of our numbers to Officer Harry. When he's done, we say goodbye and walk out of the front door, Brady close behind us. When the doors to the elevator close, Brady speaks.

"I'm so fucking sorry Jules, Logan. I should have been here." I go to speak but I'm cut off by Logan.

"Yeah, you should have been but what happened here isn't your fault Brady. You wouldn't have stopped it from happening. In fact, he might have tried to hurt you both and then I'd have been really pissed." He rubs the hand that isn't holding tightly onto me over his face in frustration. "I'm not saying I'm not pissed off with you Brady but I also know that Julian convinced you that he was OK. I also know that Ben was planning something anyway, maybe not this exactly because I'm not sure he planned on getting caught in there today but he was going to do something crazy. Let's just be grateful right now that he's the only one who got hurt, OK?"

"OK. I still want you both to know that I'm so fucking sorry."

"We know Brady." I reach out and hold his hand in mine, trying to re-assure him that he did nothing wrong. "Ben is the only one in this situation that did anything wrong."

Then the doors to the elevator open and we walk out into the foyer, where it feels like a hundred people have gathered and are all asking questions. Jimmy and a couple of officers clear a path for us outside to our cars.

The ride back to Drake Wines is silent and I know I have to let Logan come to terms with everything that just happened before we can talk it out. To be honest, I need a few minutes myself to come to terms with the fact that my once sweet neighbour turned out to be a nutjob!

Chapter Thirty-two
LOGAN

The drive home is silent. I don't even turn the radio up in the car. I don't know whether Jules needs time to think and decompress from what just happened but I sure as fuck do.

The minute Officer Harry, also known as 'building maintenance', told us we could leave, I dragged Jules out of there. I was pissed off that we couldn't grab any of his things, I mean it's not like it was *his* fault a crazy man broke into his house to unpack boxes and cut up underwear. I will *always* tell this story as a break-in because that nutjob didn't have permission to *have* a key, but he sure as hell didn't have permission to enter Jules' home without his knowledge.

I growl and Jules reaches over and takes my hand in his. He doesn't say anything though and I can't help wondering what he's thinking about. I can't help thinking about my meeting actually finishing on time and me not getting there when I did. I can't help imagining what the outcome could have been had I been any later than I was.

Damn Brady for not following simple instructions.

Damn Julian for not following my simple fucking request. Don't. Be. Alone!

I growl again. My frustration at the two of them and my anger at Ben's behaviour almost overwhelming me.

"You know you can't blame Brady for what happened today." Jules says quietly as the signs for Drake Wines come in to view and I look in the rearview mirror to see that Brady is still close behind us. He's so close I can see his lips moving and I'm guessing he's on the phone to my sister. My only response to Jules is another growl. "It's my fault. I didn't take the threat of Ben that seriously."

"Jules." I ground out.

"No Logan, I didn't. I thought you were overreacting. I thought you were going overboard and little too 'caveman, overprotective' on me." He says, using his fingers as air quotes. "I truly believed that he was harmless but I realised my mistake pretty quickly today." His voice is full of regret and I squeeze his hand, before letting it go so that I can pull into the driveway to the property.

"What tipped you off, Love?" I ask angrily. "The fact that he was *in* your apartment without your permission, with a key you didn't give him? The fact that you found him in the bedroom cutting up *my* underwear? Or was it when he tied you to a fucking chair and screamed at you?" I know what I sound like but I can barely contain my anger. I know it's wrong to direct it at Julian but I can't beat the shit of the one guy that deserves it.

"They were my underwear, as it turns out." Jules says and when I look over at him, shocked, he smirks at me!

"*That's* what the sticking point is for you? They were actually *yours* not mine, so therefore he's an idiot?" I'm yelling now as we pull into the garage. "I've got a newsflash for you, Love, Ben Sharps is a fucking nutjob. He's insane! Crazy! That man didn't give two shits about whose underwear he was cutting up! He didn't *want* to hurt *you,* Love, he wanted to hurt *me* and if hurting *you* meant hurting *me* you better believe he could justify that in his crazy, fucked up brain!"

"I know, Sweets and I'm sorry." He says quietly as we sit in the car, the only noise the whine and rattle of the door closing behind us.

"What are you sorry for, Jules?"

"I'm sorry that I didn't listen and take the threat more seriously. I'm sorry I talked Brady into letting me go inside by myself but there *is* something I won't apologise for Logan."

"And what, pray tell, is that Julian?" My anger not even close to calming down.

"I'm not sorry that Brady wasn't there. I'm not sorry that he wasn't put in harm's way because of *my* stupidity Logan. I would have never forgiven myself if something had happened to him. Your sister is pregnant, Logan. Do you really wish that he had been there with me and if Ben saw him as an obstacle to remove? Who knows what the fuck would have happened then?" Jules yells at me, gets out of the car, slamming the door behind him and storming inside. A second later, I follow behind him.

"That's beside the point Julian! You put *yourself* in danger, even after I specifically asked you not to. Even after I put in place a way for you to *not* be on your own and fucking vulnerable to this lunatic!"

"And yet, if I had *obeyed* your so called rules, *Logan,* Brady very easily could have been hurt, or worse!" We're both in the living room, facing off with one another and I know that we're not going to agree. Ever, but I need to get this all off my chest. Right here. Right now. Tonight! Otherwise it's going to eat away at me.

"I know!" I scream at the top of my lungs.

"Now, come on guys, you've had a traumatic day, let's not say things you might regret later." Makenna's voice of reason comes from beside me but I didn't even see her there. "The only person to blame for this bullshit is Ben Sharps. He's the one that decided that he had the right to take you away from Logan. He's the one who made the decision to go into your apartment without your permission and be a creepy arsehole." I turn on my sister, ready to scream in rage at her but when I see her resting her hands on her growing belly and Brady steps in between us, I know I've gone too far. My anger disappears in a cloud of regret and sadness.

"You're right Kenna. You are one hundred percent correct but that doesn't make me feel any better. I wasn't there when he needed me the most and I just."

"Yes, you were Logan. In actual fact, you were most definitely there right on time." Kenna soothes me, she's going to be an amazing mother. "Look at him Logan. Turn around and look at the man you love. He's still here and without a scratch on him. Why is that? It's because *you did* make it there in time.

At her words, I sag to the couch, my elbows on my knees and face resting in my hands. The cushion beside me dips and I feel him wrap himself around me. "I just can't." I say through my hands, not looking up. I feel her smaller hand rest on my hand, as she kneels down in front of me.

"I know Logan and I'm sorry it happened at all." She squeezes my shoulder. "We're going to leave you guys alone. I'm sure you have plenty of things to still say but please, do me a favour and be kind to each other. Remember that you *love* each other and the only person to blame for what happened today was a crazy person." She pauses for a second and I take the opportunity to rest my hand on hers. "I can see Caleb rushing over here, so we're going to go cut him off at the pass before he can get in here. We'll see you both in the morning." She pulls her hand out from under mine and I hear, more than see them leave.

"Brady." I hear the door open and their footsteps stop. "I'm sorry. I just, I was scared."

"I know. You have nothing to apologise for." He replies and I know that's not true but I am grateful to my brother in law none the less.

We can hear raised voices, and I know Caleb is arguing with Kenna about not being allowed to come in to check on us. He loves Jules like a brother and I know he must be beside himself, so I promise to send him a message as soon as I can. I might even send a 'proof of life' picture with it just to make him smile.

Jules hands me a tumbler of whiskey and I realise I didn't even notice that he'd gotten up to get it. When he sits back down next to me, I see that he has a tumbler of his own in his hand.

"You *never* drink whiskey." I chuckle, not really feeling amused.

"Well, I thought today warranted something a little different and stronger." He smiles at me, raising the glass in the air. "Here's to life kicking you in the balls some days and you flipping the bird right back!" He clinks my glass with his and then throws back the whiskey like a damned shot! When he starts coughing and spluttering, I can't help the roar of laughter I let out.

"Do you feel better now?" I ask, between breaths and laughing,

"Not really but it'll do." He screws up his face in disgust and coughs again. "Although I think I might switch to a more palatable red wine after that." I laugh again but after a minute, my mood turns sombre again. "Come on Logan, don't go there." He pleads knowing exactly where my thoughts have gone.

"I can't, Jules." I say, shaking my head. I'm not sure whether I'm shaking it tell him no or to get the images of him tied to a fucking chair out of my head. "I can't Jules. You were tied to a fucking chair today Julian, by a lunatic. *A fucking chair!* I could have lost you today and not in a 'I'm behaving like a stupid jerk and I pushed you away', kind of way. No! It could have been a very permanent kind of losing you and I need some time to deal with that, Love."

"I'm still here, Sweets." He says, placing both of glasses on the coffee table, pushing me back into the couch and settling himself in my lap. "I'm right here and I'm not going anywhere."

"Promise?"

"I promise Sweets. I will fight to get back to you, no matter what happens, that I can promise you." He lays down so that his chest is on mine and rests his head on my shoulder. I wrap my arms around him and hold on tight. I can't bring myself to let him go, I need to hold him close to me, to know that's he's here and he's in one piece. No thanks to me.

"I can't believe you thought Officer Harry was the *maintenance* guy. I mean really Logan, he *looks* like a cop!"

"Forgive *me* for not checking the man out! I guess you had more time to do so, seeing as how you were tied up with nowhere to go! I was busy standing out on the landing worrying and wondering what the fuck was going on inside, to care about how the maintenance guy *looked*."

"I'm sorry Logan."

"I know Love." I squeeze him tight.

"No, I mean I was trying to lighten the mood and well, that didn't work. Also, I meant that I'm sorry about today. I'm sorry I didn't listen to you. I'm sorry that Ben turned out to be a complete lunatic and I'm sorry that you were worried about me."

"I'm sorry Ben was a lunatic and I'm sorry I didn't get there sooner but the truth is, Makenna's right." Jules gasps at the admission. "And if you tell her I said that I might tie you back up to that damned chair and let Ben have you!" He kisses the side of my neck and I can feel the smile on his lips. "But she *is* in fact right in the sense that there is no-one else to blame for today's turn of events except for Ben. He put this all into play and we were just his pawns. I'm just glad that it was him that was hurt in the end and that neither you or Brady were injured. I couldn't have lived with myself if either of you had been hurt."

"But you just said ..." I don't let him finish.

"I know what I just said and it's right. Ben is completely at fault but that doesn't mean I don't hate knowing that I should have done more."

"Ohhh Logan. I love you, you stubborn man." He sighs and relaxes into my arms.

"I love you too Julian. Always."

We sit like that, relaxing in the silence and enjoying just holding each other, when my phone vibrates in my pocket. That's Caleb giving in and finally checking in with me.

"Is that a phone in your pocket or are you just excited to have me in your arms?" Jules jokes and I can't help laughing.

"I have to answer him or he won't stop calling. Knowing him, he'll just let himself in here to make sure we're both OK."

"I know. Talk to your brother, I'm just going to the bathroom."

I pull the phone out of my pocket but I don't answer right away. I'm too busy watching Jules walk away from me and thanking my lucky stars that he's in one piece. When he closes the door behind, I finally tap the screen and call my brother back.

"Well geez, thanks for finally taking my call!" He says as a greeting.

"I've had a busy morning Caleb, just in case you were wondering." I say, my voice dripping with sarcasm.

"So I heard. Is Jules OK? Tell me what the fuck happened?"

I don't want to talk about it anymore but I know he'll bug me until I tell him everything. So, I take a deep breath and launch into what I can only hope is the last retelling of the events of today.

Chapter Thirty-three
JULES

I listen to Logan launch into yet another retelling of the events of the day and decide that what I need is to wash the day off but instead of having a shower, I decide a soak in the tub sounds like a better idea. I don't have the mental energy to stand under the water, so I'd rather sit for a while and enjoy the peace.

I'm grateful I don't have to call in to work and tell them I'm not coming in. I don't feel like explaining to anyone else what happened today. Instead, I lie back in the warm water, close my eyes and relax. I can hear Logan's voice rumbling through the closed door but I can't understand what he's saying. Honestly? I don't *want* to hear what he's saying.

A few minutes later there's a soft knock on the door and when it opens before I can say anything, Logan enters but doesn't close the door.

"It's Gavin." He says, waving my phone around in the air. "He wants to talk to you and wouldn't take no for an answer, even when I told him you were resting. I know I *could* just hang up on him but I decided it would be best to check with you first."

"You told him?"

"No. I have no fucking clue how he found out and he refuses to tell me until he talks to *you*." I lift my hands out of the water and dry them on the towel I left on the wooden stool we have next to the tub for books, phones and whatever else one might need for a soak. When they're dry, I hold my hand out for Logan to place the phone in my palm. "You don't have to talk to him Jules."

"It's OK Sweets, I'll talk to him. If I don't he'll just keep calling or messaging until I do." When I don't hear a smart comeback out of the phone, I realise that Logan's put the phone on mute. "Honestly, I'll be fine. You can even stay in here and listen if you want, I don't mind." I'll only end up telling him what we talk about anyway, this cuts out the retelling.

"I'll go get us a drink and then I'll join you." Logan says and then he's gone.

I look at the screen and unmute Gavin.

"Hey Gavin, how are you?" I say as normally as I can.

"Don't you, 'hey Gavin' me! Are *you* OK? What the hell happened today Jules? Are you hurt? Did that crazy bastard hurt you? Are you at Logan's now, well home now I guess. Is he looking after you?" The man barely takes a breath as he asks one question after the other. I don't know how he expected me to answer any of them.

"Slow down Gavin. Take a breath my friend, I can't answer any of your questions unless you give me the chance!" I laugh but it doesn't have any humour in it.

"I'm sorry." He takes a deep, shuddering breath. "I'm just worried about you. Are you OK?"

"I'm fine Gavin, completely uninjured." I assure him.

"That's not quite true." I jump at the sound of Logan's voice because I didn't hear him come back into the bathroom. "Sorry, Love." He apologises as he places two fresh glasses of whiskey on the little wooden stool and pulls it to sit in the middle of the tub.

"What do you mean, that's not quite true, Logan? Jules, did that psycho hurt you?"

"He has some rope burn on his wrists." Logan rumbles.

"How do you even know something happened at all Gavin? I haven't told anyone." I ask him.

"No, you haven't. Why haven't you?"

"Because it *just* happened, Gavin and we've been home for an hour. Don't you think that Jules should be allowed to rest and not have to answer a million questions?" Logan grumbles again and I look up to find him stripping out of his clothes.

"What are you doing?" I whisper, as his pants drop the floor, joining his t-shirt. His underwear falling on top of the pile of clothes.

"Joining you." I hurriedly mute poor Gavin again, this time mid-sentence.

"You can't!"

"Why not?" Logan asks, with both feet already firmly planted on the base of the tub, hot water halfway up his calves. "I'm in here now, are you telling me I can't sit down?"

"No, no I'm not." I admit.

"You better unmute him, you know he's still talking and he'll be pissed that you haven't heard a word." He says, nodding to the phone in my hand, as he slides his gorgeous body into the water, his legs sliding between mine and the wall of the tub.

"Fine but you better behave yourself mister." I point my finger at him in warning and he chuckles.

"I promise to behave, Julian." Just as I unmute Gavin, I hear Logan mumble, 'at least while you're talking to Gavin anyway'.

"Are you there? Jules? What happened? Why aren't you answering me?" Gavin's panicked voice gets louder with every word he speaks.

"Sorry, I was talking to Logan and I had to mute you."

"You could have warned me, Jules." I can hear the pout in his voice.

"You're right and I'm sorry. It was all Logan's fault." I tell him, knowing that Gavin will be more than happy to blame Logan for my behaviour. "I had to put you on mute again, sorry."

"Right. I don't want to know why." He huffs and I can't help smiling for what feels like the first time this afternoon. "So, I asked how are you feeling?"

"Exhausted."

"Which is why he's *supposed* to be relaxing." Logan says loudly.

"When Jilly spoke to her brother just now and he mentioned an incident that required police assistance because of a hostage situation *and* an ambulance, it just sounded like another run of the mill day for him as a cop. Then he mentioned your building and Jilly made him repeat where the incident was. She asked if you were involved and while he told us he couldn't say, it was in your apartment and you were involved. I just knew that Ben had to be involved and I wanted to call and make sure you were OK." His breathing is heavy and I hear Jilly say something to him in the background.

"I'm fine. Logan and the police got there just in time and while yes, I do have some chafing on my wrists, they'll heal in a couple of days and no-one will even know they were there. I'm not the one with two bullet wounds in me and I'm not at the hospital, I got to come home, with Logan."

"So, does that mean you're all moved in there now?"

"Well, no because I couldn't bring anymore stuff over until the cops release the apartment. For now everything is evidence and until they do whatever it is that they need to do with it, that's where my possessions stay. It's OK though because most of my stuff is here already, it's just really a few bigger pieces of furniture and little fiddly things that needed to come over."

"Like my underwear!" Logan grumbles.

"Why is grumpy pants mumbling about *his* underwear?" Gavin asks, amused.

"Ohh well ummm, when I discovered Ben in the bedroom, he was cutting up a pair of jocks that he thought were Logan's but were in fact mine. Logan is still feeling the loss for some reason, even though they weren't his."

"So, you're fine?"

"Yeah. We'll go first thing tomorrow and give our proper statements and sign them or whatever. If we *can* get into the apartment, I'll grab a few things, if not then we'll come home and get on with our lives. We can start to think about our wedding."

"You don't think you should give yourself some time?" Gavin asks quietly, obviously concerned that I'm moving on from this too quickly.

"I won't allow this man take anything away from me Gavin. He doesn't get to make me scared of my shadow, or not live my life the way I want to and the only thing I want to do right now is marry the man I love, as soon as I possibly can. With Makenna's help, I know we can have this organised within a month."

"A month? Are you serious?"

"Deadly!"

"You don't want to wait? Especially after today?"

"Definitely don't want to wait. Especially after today. I want this man to be my husband as soon as we can legally arrange it." I'm staring at the other end of the tub, where Logan *looks* like he's lying back relaxing but I know he's listening.

"Fair enough. If you guys need any help, let me know." Gavin offers.

"As a matter of fact, you can do something for me." I hint, smiling as Logan raises his head off the edge of the bath and looks at me with an eyebrow quirked.

"Oh yeah? That was quick! What can I do for you?" Gavin chuckles and he almost sounds nervous.

"You can agree to be my best man." I tell him and when I hear his shocked gasp, I actually wonder if I've offended him. I nod at Logan, answering his unasked question. I know I could have asked Caleb or Brady and we all would have been quite happy with that but Gavin has been my friend for years, he's always been on my side, no matter what, professionally and personally.

"Are you sure?" His voice is barely a whisper.

"Absolutely but if you're not comfortable ..." I don't get to finish telling him that I would understand if he didn't want to stand up next to me at my wedding because he's screaming into the phone.

"You can't take it back, you already asked me!"

"You haven't answered me yet though." I laugh. I'm so glad to be talking and thinking about something other than Ben and what happened today, to be moving forward.

"I would be honoured to stand up next to you when you marry Logan, Jules. Absolutely!"

"Well, as long as you're sure?" I laugh at his enthusiasm.

"We wouldn't want you to do anything you're not comfortable with, you know." Logan pipes up.

"I mean, I wish you'd chosen a less grumpy arsehole to marry but seeing as how you love him so much, I'm more than happy to stand up with you on the day. I mean, he loves you too, I guess." Gavin's words might sound harsh to an outsider but we can all hear the affection in his tone.

"Love you too, Gav." Logan says loud enough for Gavin to hear.

"As long as you treat my friend there right, we won't have an issue and I will love you because you love him. We have an understanding right?" Gavin demands.

"Gavin!" I can't believe he just very thinly threatened Logan.

"No, he's right. We definitely have an understanding Gavin." Logan answers Gavin but his eyes haven't stopped looking at me and I feel his answer deep in my soul. I've never felt more turned on than in this moment.

"Gavin, I have to go. I'll call you tomorrow after we've been to the police station."

I don't wait for his response, I end the call and blindly attempt to put my phone on the stool but I have no idea where it really lands. I'm too busy watching the sexiest man I've ever known, the love of life, looking for everything calm and relaxed but his cock is hard against his stomach and his eyes are fire.

All I know in this moment, is that I want him, so I go to him.

Chapter Thirty-four
LOGAN

Jules ends his call to Gavin, after asking him to be his best man abruptly, then drops his phone onto the stool we keep next to the tub without taking his eyes off mine. Half a heartbeat later he's sitting in my lap and water is splashing out of the tub, all over the floor.

"Jules." I say his name but I don't know what I'm trying to get across by saying it. Is it a warning that he's making a mess? Or am I asking him what he's up to? Either way, I don't need the answer because we can clean up later and his mouth taking mine is answer enough for me to forget anything and everything else.

"Shut up and kiss me." He mumbles into my mouth. He's so fucking hot when he takes charge, that I don't even give what we're doing or where we're doing it a second thought, I do as he demands and I kiss him until neither of us can breathe properly. "I need you Logan."

"You've got me, Jules." I tell him, leaving a trail of open mouth kisses on the column of his neck, finally nipping at base of his neck where it meets his shoulder. He sucks in a breath at the sting and I run my tongue across the skin to soothe him.

"More." He groans, as he slides his cock up and down mine. "I need more."

Without thinking, I stand up, taking Jules with me. We both step out of the tub, almost losing our balance when we step onto the mat on the floor, as it slides around under our wet feet. Neither of us bother drying off, Jules wraps his hands around the back of my neck, his fingers twisting in my hair and I grip hold of his hips. Taking his lips in a bruising kiss, I turn us both and walk him backwards out of the bathroom, towards our bedroom.

When the backs of his legs bump into the bed, I let us both up for air. "Where do you want me, Love?"

Without a word, he turns us around and gently pushes me back onto the bed. I allow myself to fall back, my hands behind my head and watch him as he wordlessly rolls a condom onto my cock, spreads some lube all over me and climbs up my body, settling himself just over my hard cock, never breaking eye contact.

"I need you Logan." His voice is a soft rasp.

"You have me Jules. Whatever you need, take it." I tell him, knowing he needs permission, even when he's taking charge.

As he lowers himself onto my cock, I can feel his hole spreading around me, taking me in and it feels so fucking good. He rests his hands on my chest to steady himself, closing his eyes against the sensations.

"Touch me Logan." He demands.

"Where do you want me to touch you, Love?" I ask, as I pull my hands out from under my head.

"Anywhere. Everywhere." He begs. He's full of my cock now but he's not moving. I need him to move.

"Do you want me to touch your cock while you ride mine?" I ask, pretty certain I already know the answer.

"God yes!" His words are more like groans than *actual* words and I need no further encouragement, as I settle my fist around his cock and squeeze him, before moving my fist up to the head and running my thumb through the slit that's dripping with pre-cum. He groans loudly and his head drops so far back that *if* his eyes were open he'd be staring at the ceiling.

"Move Jules. Now!" Now it's my turn to demand things from *him*. His head snaps and he looks me in the eyes, his own eyes burning with desire.

"I'll move when I'm good and ready, Sweets." I buck my hips, trying to force him to move but he grips my hips with his knees, stopping me from moving too much. I narrow my eyes at him in frustration, he grins in return. "I'll move when *I'm* good and ready."

"You'll move now or I'll flip us ..." I don't finish my threat of flipping us over because he drags himself up my cock and then slams back down, causing my eyes to roll into the back of my head in pure pleasure. "Fuck!"

"That's the plan Sweets." He says so sweetly I do a double take, until he slides himself up my cock again and pausing with the head resting just inside him. "More?" Like he has to ask and before I can answer, he's riding my cock like it's the only thing he wants to do.

His cock has been gripped in my hand the entire time, so as he finds his rhythm, I find mine as well. He lifts his hands off my chest, leaning back to rest his hands on my thighs as he rides my cock. Hard. I run my hand up and down his cock, matching his rhythm and we're both a jumble of noises and grunts, until we're both coming. Me in Jules' arse and him all over my stomach and chest.

"Fuck!" Jules breathes out and I couldn't agree more, if only I had the thought process to agree with him. He starts to collapse onto my body but I stop him.

"Let me clean up first, Love." We give ourselves another few minutes to catch our breath, then Jules moves off me and heads to the bathroom and I reach for the tissues beside the bed to clean myself up.

Jules saunters back into the room, climbs back onto the bed and we settle in under the covers. Wrapping my arm around his shoulders, I pull him into my side so that he can curl into me.

"Do you think Brady and Caleb will understand?" He asks quietly and it takes a few minutes for my brain to catch up to his meaning.

"You mean you having Gavin stand beside you at the wedding?" I feel him nod against my chest. "Absolutely, Love."

"I don't want to hurt their feelings." I love that he cares so much about Caleb and Brady but I know they'll both be fine with his decision.

"You won't. They might give you a bit of grief about it but they won't mean it. At all. You can have whoever you want standing beside you at our wedding, Love." I tell him honestly. Gavin and I haven't always been on the same page because he's kind of been on the same page as crazy Ben and thought that I wasn't ever quite good enough for his friend. To a degree, I guess he's been right but I couldn't imagine spending my life with anyone else.

"What are you going to do?"

"In regards to what?" I ask, kissing him lightly on the top of his head. "You mean, who am I going to have standing up with me?" I've thought about it a lot in the last couple of months, ever since I decided I wanted to marry Jules.

"Yeah."

"I've been thinking about that ever since I bought your ring." I admit.

"How long have you had it?" He asks, looking up at me through his eyelashes.

"The ring?" I know I'm stalling, I don't know why I don't want to tell him how long I've had the damn thing. I'm a little embarrassed that it's taken me this long to ask him to be my husband. "A few months." I say vaguely.

"How many *months,* Logan?" His chin is resting on his hands, on my chest and looking me directly in the eyes.

"I've had it for about six months." I admit, as I rub my hand up and down his back.

"*Six months*!" I can't say I'm too surprised by his shock at that little revelation. "Why did you wait so long? Weren't you sure?" His questions are barely a whisper.

"I've actually never been more sure of anything in my life than I have about wanting to marry you and be your husband."

"But?" I guess I might as well confess it all now, in this moment.

"I wasn't sure that *you* wanted *me* in that kind of permanent way. I knew I was holding back in a way that I didn't know how to change until you walked away. It took for *you* to have enough and Makenna to talk some sense into me, for me to realise that I couldn't let you go. That I *wouldn't* let you go. Then, I thought I was too late but I still couldn't let go of the ring or the idea of me becoming your husband one day."

"Logan."

"You don't have to say anything Jules. I know we've been over all of this before and it was *my* issues that held me back. I just knew, in that moment while sitting here that night that I couldn't let another minute go by without asking you. Without asking you for *more* and to marry me. In that moment I wanted more commitment from you and to give you more commitment as well." I take a breath and keep talking before he can think about a response. "Before you say anything, I didn't go for it in *that* moment because I didn't want to lose you. I asked you to marry me because I *wanted to be your husband.* I wanted to commit to *you.*"

"Logan." His voice is barely a whisper and yet it's filled with emotion.

"I needed you to understand, now and then, that you mean the world to me Jules." I can see the unshed tears glistening in his eyes and I decide to change the mood. "As for Caleb and Brady, well you've just given them another opportunity to annoy me and fight over who's the best 'brother'." I laugh. Unfortunately, my joke falls flat and does the opposite of what I was hoping it would because Jules is suddenly sitting upright, with his hands on his cheeks.

"Oh no! You're right! This is just going to make them argue over who can stand up with you! What have I done? I should have asked one of them." He says in a panic.

"Julian, calm down." I laugh, still trying to get him to see the funny side. "You wanted to ask Gavin and you did. They'll live with it. You get to have who you want standing next you for *our* wedding. This is a decision you had to make for you and you obviously didn't have to think twice about it and neither did Gavin, which makes him an exceptional judge of character. The boys, they're *my* issue to deal with, Love."

Chapter Thirty-five
JULES

"I don't want you to deal with them though, isn't it *our* problem now?" I ask, knowing I'm pouting but I know I'll get my way. Especially when Logan bends down and kisses me.

"You're right, they *are* our issue now, as is the wedding *but* I want *you* to have what you want and if you want Gavin to stand beside you, then that's what you'll have. Caleb and Brady will deal with it."

"Then we have to work out what we're going to do. I mean, who walks down the aisle? Do we both? Do we meet in the middle? If we walk down the aisle, do we walk alone because baby, your parents aren't here and that seems like it would highlight it and I want you to enjoy the day, not be sad." I kiss him on the chin because that's all I can reach from here. "I saw how it affected all four of you at Makenna and Brady's wedding, I don't want it to stick out like a sore thumb for you at ours."

"It won't, Love, I promise." He sighs and I can feel him getting ready to give me a long explanation of why it won't affect him or us. He's weary already and we've barely spoken about the wedding.

"We don't need to make any decisions today. It's been, shall we say eventful recently and we need to chill for a while."

"No, I want to get this sorted now. We've already started the conversation, might as well finish it." He says with a smile that doesn't reach his eyes. "The thing is, we missed our parents at Makenna's wedding to Brady but we'd all spoken about it as well." It's my turn to sigh.

"Oh, I didn't know." I lay my head back down on his chest, looking away from him so that he can't see the hurt in my eyes at being excluded from that conversation back then.

"I'm sorry." he says quietly into the top of my head, following up his words with a light kiss. "You weren't left out of that conversation intentionally, you weren't actually here the night we had it. You were out of town for work and we were all at the house for dinner. The wedding came up and well, the subject of who was going to walk Makenna down the aisle came up. As you can imagine, Makenna was quite emotional about it and while Brady offered up *his* Dad for the job, neither Caleb or I were happy with that. But then, as usual, Caleb and I couldn't agree to give up the job either. I felt it was my job as the oldest and he felt like he didn't want to be left out of it because he was the youngest." He shrugs and I feel the movement under me. "Brady also wanted us both to stand up next to him as his best men and we couldn't see a solution, until we did."

"You both did both." I say unnecessarily because we were both there.

"We compromised, had a discussion and came to conclusion that made everyone happy." I can feel him nodding on the top of my head, where he's resting his lips. "We can do the same thing with our day, Jules. It won't be difficult, I won't let it. As for who gets to walk down the aisle and how this is all going to work, I don't really care, I just want to end up married to you, so if you have a vision, if *you* know what you want, then that's what will happen."

I don't know how long we lie there, both quietly thinking about our options and weighing them up but when my stomach growls, Logan laughs.

"Come on, Love, let me feed you and then we can talk about it some more."

As we both potter around the kitchen, working together to get dinner ready, we're both thinking about how the day of our wedding can work. We're also working like a well-oiled machine, like we've done this a thousand times before, in this very kitchen because we *have*.

A realisation hits me as we sit down to a meal. "You let me design that kitchen." I say in wonder and shock, looking at Logan across the table and he smiles. It's knowing and gorgeous.

"Of course you did, you helped me design the entire house if you remember correctly." He says, trying to hide a smirk, which leads me to believe he knows exactly what I meant.

"That's not what I meant and you know it! I *mean*. That kitchen is my *dream* kitchen without being a commercial type of kitchen. It's got everything exactly where I want it, where I go to straight away for things and it's got the appliances that I picked out." I'd stamp my feet to emphasise my frustration if we weren't already sitting down at a table we *both* picked out at the store. He wouldn't buy one that I didn't like. At the time I was exceptionally happy to help him and have him listen to my opinion, if not a little surprised. *Now,* I realise what he did. As for Logan, he's just sitting, eating his meal like this is no big revelation and I guess, to him it's really not. He knows exactly what he did! "You're not going to *say* anything?"

"What would you like me to say?" He asks with a smirk but he doesn't stop eating. "Eat your dinner before it goes cold, Love." He says, with a quick glance up at me and pointing to my plate.

"That's all you've got to say for yourself?" I demand, not picking up utensils to eat because that would serve him right for not answering me, right? I'm thinking wrong, as I watch him slowly and gently place *his* cutlery down on either side of his plate.

"What else would you like for me to say, *Julian*? Hmmm ...?" He asks, looking me dead in the eyes and not flinching. "Would you like me to repeat myself and explain it to you one. More. Time?" When I don't answer him or even move, he continues after sighing deeply. "OK then, here goes. When *we* built this house, that's exactly what *we* were doing. Building a house, a home, *together.* This house was *always our home, Julian* and that's why you got the kitchen you wanted. It's also why *we* chose the bed frame and mattress, the dining setting, the couch, towels and everything else, *together.* Do you understand now?"

"I didn't realise." I say stutter over my words.

"Really? Christ Jules! I've already told you, you were part of every damned decision there was to make about this house. The number of bedrooms, where they were put in the floorplan, how big the bathroom was, what the kitchen needed in it. There wasn't one decision that you didn't help with. I made sure of it!"

"You never said." I start but he cuts me off.

"I didn't think I needed to, Jules." He's angry and frustrated now but he sighs deeply and rubs his hands over his face. When he speaks again, he's calmer. "I realise now that I didn't make my intention clear but it took for you to leave me for me understand that. Jules, I built this house, *we* built this house for the two of us to live in it, *together.* It was always my intention to live here, with you, as my husband. I know that I didn't really make that clear before, well everything but I thought that you understood that now. There isn't a part of this house you haven't touched or made a decision about, Love. This isn't just my house, it's our *home.*"

Have I mentioned how much I love this man? "I don't know what to say."

"Can we eat dinner now, before it gets any colder, please?" He grumbles, picking up his cutlery and eating his dinner. I do the same and we sit there in silence, just eating, each of us thinking our own thoughts, obviously and I can't help wondering what he's thinking about. I know what I'm thinking.

He loves me. He's always loved me.

Chapter Thirty-six
LOGAN

"I just don't know how I didn't know." Jules says, as he takes a bite of his dinner and I can't help smiling. I know why he didn't catch on to what I was doing, it was because I asked his opinion and then went with it, most of the time. He was happy that he was helping me but it stings a little that he didn't know *why* I wanted his help.

"Really?" I ask with a smirk that I know drives him nuts, as I finish my dinner and place my knife and fork on the plate.

"Really!" He says, taking another bite.

"You didn't see it because you didn't want to *and* because I never *told* you. It's that simple, Love. I will regret for the rest of my life that I made you feel like you didn't matter to me for any length of time because the truth is, like I've already said, this house was *always* our home, I was just waiting for you to move into it with me. I may not have said the words and made it clear but that was always my intention."

"Wow!" I start clearing away the dishes and when I go to take Jules' plate, he smacks my hand away.

"Come on, Love, it will be cold by now."

"It's not, so let me eat it." I huff out a laugh and leave him to it while I clean up the kitchen and fill up the dishwasher. When I'm done, I grab some dessert out of the fridge and put the mini mousse cakes on individual plates, with a spoon each. What can I say? I'm not bad in the kitchen but desserts can be time consuming and one of the biggest benefits of having Vines here and Leila working there, is that delicious desserts are always close at hand.

"Are you trying to make me fat? You know we have a wedding in a few short weeks, if Makenna has her way, right?" Jules groans when he sees me with the desserts.

"You're not going to get 'fat' after one dessert." He raises an eyebrow at me. "OK, it's more like a few but we're both fit and workout a lot, so we can give ourselves a treat once in a while." He raises his eyebrow impossibly higher at that. "Fine." I concede. "But it's just so easy with Vines and Leila just a few minutes' walk away and forgive me for wanting to spoil my soon to be husband." I say as I sit down opposite him again, hoping to win some points.

"You know all that sweet talking won't always work, Logan Drake." He warns me, as he waves the small spoon around between us. He protests that he doesn't want the dessert but he doesn't hesitate to take a spoonful of it and pop it into his mouth. When he closes his eyes and groans, my cock starts to come back to life!

"So." I say coughing. "I was thinking while we ate about how we can organise this wedding and keep everyone happy." I start to tell him.

"Wait! When did you have time to think about how we could solve the issues around your siblings, Brady and Gavin, while you were explaining to me how ignorant I was about this house?" I laugh but he doesn't seem amused.

"I'm capable of doing more than one thing at a time, Jules." I tell him, my spoonful of dessert hovering in the space between us. "You should know that better than anyone." At my not so subtle insinuation, he blushes and it's the most adorable thing I've ever seen.

"That's." He stumbles over his words, making my cock twitch again.

"Amazing, I know." I roll my eyes but I'm smiling at him. "Here's what I was thinking."

I explain each step to him and hold my breath waiting to see if he's going to agree with me or not. He stares me down for a good minute and I'm worried that I overstepped or he doesn't like the idea. But then his face lights up and his smile is bigger than I've ever seen it.

"That is perfect Sweets! Absolutely perfect. If that doesn't keep everyone happy then I don't know what will. Let's do it." Jules agrees with me and I can't tell you how relieved I am that he's on my side with this now.

"When do you want to tell everyone? I'm guessing as soon as possible because Makenna will be here either later tonight or tomorrow morning to discuss the details of the wedding, you know don't you? She is *not* going to let either one of us take the lead."

"She just wants us to be happy and the day to be perfect."

"I know, Sweets."

"She assumes that I'm going to leave it all up to you and that you're going to then be too stressed about everything going well, instead of getting married and being with me. So, she'll want to take over but I can tell her to cool her jets any time you like Jules. This is *our* wedding every last choice is ours alone to make."

"I'm happy for Makenna to help."

"*But.*"

"No buts, honestly. I still want it to be about *us* and what we want. I just don't want to upset her. I know she's going to want to step into whatever role your Mum might have had because it's Makenna, it's the role she's stepped into since the accident." He's not wrong in that assessment.

"You're right and I can tell her to step back at any time, Love." I reach across the table and take his hand in mine. "Do you want to call them all together tomorrow?"

"Do you think Makenna and Caleb will wait that long?" Jules asks, before spooning some more mousse into his mouth, moaning in happiness and closing his eyes as he licks every last morsel off the spoon. It feels like my cock would be capable of tearing a hole in my pants to get to Jules. "Are you OK Logan?" Jules asks, and I realise he's opened his eyes and looking at me concerned.

"Ahh yup. Sure. If you stop making those noises while you lick the damned spoon I will be." I swallow. Hard.

"Am I distracting you?" He asks, the picture of innocence as he licks the spoon again, wrapping his tongue around the base of the handle, then flattening it on the spoon part, hesitating and drawing his tongue back into his mouth but not before he licks his damned lips as well!

"Fuck!" I mutter, closing my eyes to block out the sight. My cock twitches in my pants, imagining and hoping that he'll do what he just did to the spoon, to me. "Jules." I growl.

"*Logan.*" He growls right back, making my eyes snap open, when they meet his, they're burning with desire.

I'm about to get out of my chair and haul him to his feet when the door opens without warning.

"Hey guys, are you decent?" Caleb's voice rings out as the door slams shut behind him and I growl, louder and from frustration because I won't get to have Jules because my younger brother is a fucking cockblocker!

"Ahh fuck it!" I scrub my hands over my face and Jules chuckles.

"It's OK, it's just Caleb, we'll find out what he wants and then get him to leave."

"It's not that."

"What is it then?" Jules asks, taking my face in his hands, making me look him in the eye.

"I get it now." I say.

"What do you mean? Get what?" The poor man, he's so confused.

"I get why Brady got so pissed at us for just walking into the house without knocking or waiting to be invited." There's a few seconds of silence before Jules throws his head back and roars with laughter.

"Well, I'm glad I didn't walk in to see either of you naked, that sure makes for a nice change." He hesitates for a second before saying, "At least, I *hope* you're not naked because laughter like that isn't good for a man's ego!" He says as he walks in the kitchen, finding us standing next to the table, Jules still laughing, just not quite as loudly.

"We aren't naked." I growled at my brother.

"Yet anyway." Jules says through a wheezing laugh.

"Are you OK Jules? Did the big guy here do something to hurt you? Cause I can kick his arse if I need to you know?" That sends Jules into another fit of uncontrollable laughter but when the door opens and Makenna walks in with Brady close behind her, he really loses his shit and I can't help worrying about his mental health after everything he's been through recently.

"Jules. Love." I say as I bend over to try and look at his handsome face. "Julian! Julian Bishop, you cut this shit out right now!" I demand harshly, knowing that I might sounds like an arsehole to my family but I know it will get Jules' attention. Perhaps not in the way I want with my entire family standing in our kitchen but I'll take what I can get at this point.

"Logan." Jules says, straightening up to his full height, his voice full of lust his eyes full of longing heat.

"Oh my, fuck! You guys and by that, I mean *all* of you in the room, are disgusting. No seriously, why the fuck do you have to all look at each other like that in front of other people. In front of *me,* for fucks sake? Y'all are fucking too horny to function, I swear!"

The four of us look at each other, then back at Caleb and we all laugh, loudly!

"Yeah, yeah, laugh it up you dirty motherfuckers but I'm the one who keeps walking in on y'all having sex in one way or another."

I stop laughing and give him the deadliest look I can muster while still laughing. "Then stop walking into everyone else's house like they're *yours*!" I yell at him. "Have some respect for everyone's privacy Caleb, for fucks sake."

"I *do*!" He yells back at me. "It's not *my* fault you're all sex, all of the time."

"You sound a little frustrated little brother." I smirk at him, trying to piss me off. Why? Because I want them all to leave!

"Fuck you, Logan. I thought you'd be *less* grumpy since you got Jules back *and* he agreed to marry you but noooo. You're the same old grumpy arsehole that pisses everyone around him off."

"Boys!" Makenna says in her stern 'mum' voice that might have worked on Caleb at one stage but doesn't really have much effect on him these days and it's never worked on me.

"Stop!" Jules says loudly but he doesn't yell. "That's enough, *both* of you." He sends a glare my way like I'm the one in the wrong. "Don't say it Logan, just don't."

"Wow! I don't know how you did that but I want to learn." Makenna says to Jules in awe.

"Guess you just have to know what makes him tick." When Jules winks at Makenna, causing her to shiver and scowl, I laugh. "Why are you guys all here?"

"We wanted to check in and make sure you're OK." Caleb says with a pout.

"I'm fine." Jules says and I think he truly is. "We were just making a few decisions about the wedding." My head moves so fast, I swear it's in danger of falling off my neck, why the fuck would he tell them that? Doesn't he know that will make my sister stay here all fucking night?

"Did you make any decisions that you'd like to share?" Makenna asks, following Jules into the lounge room and getting comfortable on the couch. I look at Brady and he just shrugs his shoulders, he knows he's lost his wife to this discussion and he's just along for the ride.

"Well, I asked Gavin to be my best man." I hear Caleb's shocked intake of breath and I can't help smirking as I sit down next to Jules. "I know you three all want to be part of the wedding and I think we've come up with an idea to do just that." He smiles, taking my hand in his and suddenly, I don't care that my family barged their way into our house, uninvited and unwelcome.

The only thing that matters is that smile on my fiancé's face and that he gets to organise a wedding. *Our* wedding, just the way he wants it.

Chapter Thirty-seven
JULES

As I explain our idea for the wedding to Makenna, Brady and Caleb, I see the smile return to Caleb's face and I know that we've done the right thing.

"What do you think?" I ask them but before any of them can answer, Logan speaks.

"Just so you know, this *is* how *our* day is going down, so if you don't like it, learn to live with it because Julian wants it this way and that's what he's getting." Damn the man is hot when he puts his foot down!

"All right grumpy pants, no-one was going to disagree. In fact." Caleb looks to his sister and brother in law, who both nod at him. "I think I can speak for all of us when I say, this is perfect!"

"You're damn right it is and I don't want any arguments from you." Logan says and I don't think he's realised that Caleb actually *agreed* with me!

"I wasn't arguing Logan." Caleb says, holding his hands up in surrender. "I agree. I'm just happy that you two are getting married finally. I want to see you *both* happy brother."

"You're being very quiet." Logan says, looking at Makenna, who is snuggled into Brady's side. "Ohh Kenna." Logan drops my hand and is kneeling in front of his sister in half a second, taking her into his arms. "Don't cry, Sis. This is supposed to be a happy event." We all hear him mumble into her hair.

"I know. These are tears of happiness, believe me." She replies, in a garbled voice that's drowning in tears.

"Believe me when I say, you've made your sister exceptionally happy in the last few days." Brady says, taking his wife out of her brother's arms, and cradling her in his. "This is the perfect solution to who stands with who."

Logan hesitates for a couple more seconds, before coming back and sitting next to me on the couch. I take his hand in mine again and he squeezes it tightly. He knows what's coming and there's a real fear that Makenna might just have a mental breakdown.

"I have one more thing to ask." I don't take my eyes off Makenna as she sits up and looks my way. I noticed that Brady is holding her very closely into his side, obviously expecting a reaction to whatever I say, be it good or bad, he's ready for it. "I want you to help me, help us, to organise everything, if you're up for it that is, Makenna."

There's a minute of silence and I know that Logan and I aren't breathing waiting for her reply. "How long do we have?"

"We have a date in mind but it will mean we get married in less than a months' time from today." I say in a rush. "We've been together for years already and we just don't want to have to wait any longer than we really need to." I explain.

"Oh shit!" Brady mutters, right before Makenna explodes into a fresh bout of sobbing tears.

"Makenna, honey, if it can't be done, if that's too much pressure, it can wait or we can hire someone else to help us do it. I just thought." I don't get to finish what I'm saying before Makenna has leapt out of Brady's arms and landed in mine, pushing Logan out of the way in the process. "Are you OK, Makenna?"

"Fucking hell, Kenna!" Logan says at the same time I'm asking if his sister is OK.

"Oh my god, Jules are you serious?! Of course we can do this in a few weeks. We can get this entire thing all wrapped up in a couple of weeks and ready to go. As long as everyone does what they're told, that is." She scans the room, looking pointedly at the rest of the males in the room.

"You know we're all going to Makenna." Caleb protests.

"I know you will but I'm telling you all now, that to get this done, you need to do what I tell you to when I tell you to do it."

"This *is* still Logan and Jules' wedding ... right? Because I feel like they're the ones who should be issuing the orders around here, not you."

"Caleb!" Brady warns and I love that he sticks up for his wife like that, even with her brothers.

"No, it's OK Brady, he's right. It most certainly *is* all about Logan and Julian *but* if I'm helping to organise the event, then I expect you all to help me with it." She narrows her eyes at Caleb, who narrows his own eyes right back at her and I know, without a doubt, if she oversteps in any way, perceived or real, Caleb is going to be the one who pulls her back. Brady just wants her to be happy and while he might tell her to stop, he won't be overly forceful. As for Logan, he just wants *me* to be happy and if that means doing as Makenna asks, then he'll do as Makenna asks. "So, tell me some details. We can get started on it right away."

"Do you need me?" Logan asks.

"No, you can go now. We'll let you know if we want you for anything." Makenna tells him, vaguely waving a hand in his direction, causing me to laugh.

"I'll go and continue running the family business, how's that?" Logan asks sarcastically but with a smile on his face.

"Well, sure you can do that if you feel the need to but that's why we have staff we trust." Makenna answers with as much sarcasm. "I meant get a drink and sit quietly while the adults talk about what you like." Logan's only response is to roll his eyes as he walks into the kitchen to make everyone a drink.

"So, what are you thinking?" Makenna asks, turning to face me with a notepad and pen in her hand that I have no idea where they came from.

"Well, I need one of the cabins for my parents to stay in." I start.

"Done. Leave it with me, they can stay here as long as they want. I've got the one that Samantha and Tomas stayed in completed. They can stay in that one, which means, they can get here any time between now and the wedding." Caleb smiles at me.

"Thank you."

"That's not a problem at all Julian."

With that out of the way and Makenna scribbling away madly on her notepad over the next hour or so, we get most of the basics out of the way, making us all happy.

"Please tell me you're wearing a new three piece suit for the day?" Makenna asks her brother and Logan's eyes meet mine, there's a glint in them that makes me blush! "You did demand that, right?" She asks me, seeming innocent of the look her brother sends my way. Brady and Caleb aren't as oblivious because I hear *both* of them clear their throats.

"Yes, I did." I admit.

"And you? What are you going to wear?"

"A suit." I tell her. It's simple, easy.

"Right, so we're going shopping then."

"No! No Makenna I don't need a new suit, I have plenty." I tell her because shopping with Makenna, while a *lot* of fun every time, I don't really have the time for it. "We've only got a few weeks Makenna, I can do with one of the suits I already have."

"Is Logan getting a new suit?" She raises an eyebrow at me.

"Well, yes but I want him to have a new black three piece suit to wear." I say, the smile on my lips making Makenna herself smile.

"Black? I thought you wanted him in dark grey?" Makenna asks.

"I did but then I saw the perfect black suit and I'm sure he has a black three piece suit in his wardrobe that 'would do' but it won't. Therefore, *you* get a new suit too." She writes some notes in her magically appearing book. "Don't worry, he's getting the full shopping experience too, just on a different day to you because you don't get to see each other's outfits before the day."

"Makenna, I think we can do away with some traditions, don't you think?" I laugh because it's not like we have a big white dress from anyone. I stop laughing when Makenna throws one of her famous death stares my way. It makes me have no doubt that their children are going to have a healthy respect for that look! "Go ahead."

"Right, so separate shopping trips for new suits." She jots down another note. Ties or bow ties?"

I say, "Bow ties." And at the same time Logan says, "Ties." Makenna's head pops up from her note writing and she looks between us. I'm not sure what she's trying to decide, I think it might be whether to agree with her brother or me.

"Bow ties it is." She says after a few seconds and writes that down. "I think you need a navy blue suit, Jules. It would complement Logan's black three piece suit perfectly."

We hash out a few more details and then say goodnight to them all.

Caleb's the last one to leave and when he pulls me into a tight hug he whispers in my ear, "I'm glad he finally got his shit together. I can't wait for you to officially be my brother. Love you man." He slaps me on the back and then amidst the chorus of goodbyes, I can feel myself tearing up at his sentiment.

As we close the door behind Logan's family, I feel a single tear fall down my cheek.

Chapter Thirty-eight
LOGAN

"**A**re you OK, Love? Do I need to go chase that little turd down and beat the shit out of him?" I ask, as we close the door and I see one lonely tear roll down Jules' face after Caleb's tight embrace.

"No, no arse kicking necessary, Sweets, calm down. You really need to back off a bit from him you know? He's a brilliant and caring man but you and Makenna treat him like he's still the teenager you had to help through the loss of your parents."

"I know." Jules gives me a look that says he doesn't think I *do* know and I reach up to dry his cheek because I don't like seeing him upset. "It's hard to give up the notion that we still have to protect him from the world."

"What are you going to be like if we ever have kids?" I look at him, surprised that he's mentioning kids. "I'm allowed to change my mind."

"Yes, Love, you most certainly are." I kiss him hard on the lips but before it can get too heavy, I pull back. "Come on, let's get some sleep. I have a feeling we're both going to need it to keep up with Makenna for the next few weeks."

"You're not wrong." He chuckles as we walk, hand in hand, to our bedroom. I can't tell you how happy it makes me to know that from now until forever, this will be *our* room.

"Don't you have a shopping trip booked with her tomorrow?" I ask him as we get undressed for bed.

"I do, yes but don't get too smug because you've got one with her this week as well." He's not wrong but until then, I'm holding down the fort here at Drake Wines, along with Caleb. I make the decision to make an effort with letting Caleb take on more responsibility around here because

Jules is right, he is a grown man now, so he should be given new opportunities.

"What did Caleb say to you just before he left?" I ask, as we climb under the covers and I pull my fiancé into my arms, getting comfortable.

"He just said that he was happy for us."

"And?" I ask, because I know that's not enough to get tears out of Jules.

"And." Jules takes a shuddering breath and I almost wish I didn't ask. "He can't wait to officially call me his brother."

"Oh shit!" That'll do it I guess. That acceptance and not just because we're gay but because we're a tight knit family and Caleb has already accepted Jules into the fold.

"Your brother is a good man, Logan Drake and you need to let him know that."

"I will, I promise."

"Good! Now, let me sleep."

"I'm not the one still talking." I joke as I pull him in closer to me.

"Shush, I need some sleep! I'm shopping with your sister tomorrow and we both know that's going to be an all-day experience!"

"Goodnight, Love." I murmur into his neck.

"Goodnight, Sweets. Sleep well."

THE NEW WEEK STARTS as any other week until Makenna arrives on our doorstep mid-week looking for Jules after cancelling their shopping trip earlier in the week.

"Is Julian ready?" She demands, walking into the house without waiting for an invitation.

"Good morning Makenna, why don't you come on in?" I say, closing the door behind her.

"Thanks." She mutters distractedly while looking at her phone.

"No problems at all." My voice dripping with sarcasm that she doesn't seem to notice. I thought I only had to worry about Caleb entering our home without permission but apparently, I have to watch out for our sister as well.

"You're here!" Jules says as he enters the room and gives my sister a hug. "I wasn't expecting you this early, Makenna." He says, kissing her cheek.

"You knew we could expect my sister this morning?"

"Ummm ... only about five minutes ago, sorry, I guess I should have warned you?" His words are an apology but he doesn't *sound* very apologetic to be honest.

"A heads up would have been nice, Love." I say, pulling him in for a kiss that with any luck Makenna wishes she didn't witness.

"OK, you can stop trying to make me wish I wasn't here and let your man go so that we can get out of here." When I pull my lips off Jules' to look at her, I see she hasn't even taken her eyes off her phone to notice what we were or were not doing. "I know you were kissing him because I know *you*, Logan Drake."

"Who are you messaging so early in the day? Is Brady checking in on you?" I ask, ignoring her comment about knowing me.

"I left Brady sleeping." She tells me, finally dragging her attention away from her phone. "Sorry I had to cancel the other day, I just wasn't feeling up to it but I'm good for today, so let's get going." She looks to Jules and smiles warmly.

"OK, let's go."

"Where are you going?"

"To get Julian's suit for the wedding." Makenna informs me as they're walking out the door and Jules gives me one more kiss that's over way too soon. "Don't forget, you're next. Probably next week I think." Before I can answer her, she's swept out the door, Jules not far behind her and they're making their way to her car parked almost right on the doorstep.

I watch as the car disappears down the driveway, while finishing off my coffee and sigh.

I wish Jules and I were shopping for our suits together but Makenna won't hear of it. She wants to keep things as traditional as she possibly can and that means we don't get to see each other's suits. What it does mean is that *Makenna* gets to see them and she gets to make sure that we match without telling either of us what the other is wearing.

The need I have to control everything in my life really hates not knowing what Jules will be wearing but I also appreciate the effort that Makenna is putting in to make our wedding special. I honestly don't know what we'd do without her, she's made it her mission for the next few weeks to help us organise everything and I'm grateful for her efforts, even if they annoy me sometimes.

I spend the day working from home, waiting for the two of them to return home but it's not until early evening when they do and Makenna doesn't come inside, she just drops Jules at the door and heads home.

"Is everything OK?" I ask, greeting Jules at the door with a kiss.

"Yeah, why?' He asks, his eyebrows furrowed in confusion.

"Makenna didn't even come in and that's not like her at all." I say, looking towards the main house where I can see her tail lights disappear into their garage. "Is she OK?"

"Hmm? Oh yes she's fine. We had a long day and she's tired. I think she desperately needed the bathroom too." Jules chuckles and I raise an eyebrow in question, he laughs some more. "You'll find out when it's your turn to go shopping. Which by the way I believe will be early next week."

"So, you got your suit?" I ask, pulling his back to my front and holding him there by pushing on his pecs.

"I did." He says, twisting around to look back at me.

"Am I allowed to know what colour it is? Or is that a secret too?" I ask, before dropping a kiss on his lips.

"I think I can tell you the colour, Sweets."

"Are you sure that Kenna won't sense you're going to tell me and come racing in here to tell us both off?" I laugh, until his phone lets him know he's got a message. From Makenna! "Damn!" I mutter under my breath.

"It's a message from Makenna." He tells me unnecessarily, after pulling his phone from his pocket and starts laughing as he reads the message. "She says, 'and don't tell Logan any details about what we purchased today. Not even the colour of your suit.' Your sister is amazing!"

"How the hell could she possibly have known that was what we were discussing?"

"How could she not, Logan?" He pulls out of my embrace and I let him, as he turns to look at me, his laughter is loud. "She knows you Sweets and she knows that you want to know. You hate not knowing and having control over everything. Why do you think she made the decision to take us shopping separately?"

"Because she's a pain in my arse?"

"No, it's because she wants you to not take everything on. It's our *wedding* Logan, she wants you to be able to breathe and enjoy it."

"I *am* enjoying it." I protest. "We're only a few days into organising, things Julian, how can I have gone too far already? And why is it too much to ask what colour suit, my soon to be husband is going to wear? It would make matching you so much easier."

"That's why Makenna is taking us both shopping." He laughs at me.

"I still don't understand why we have to go separately." I grumble, knowing that I sound like a disgruntled child but I want to be involved in every decision about our wedding. With that thought, I realise exactly what Makenna is doing.

"You just worked it out, didn't you?" Jules laughs as he walks towards the bathroom. "I'm going to have a shower and head to bed."

"What about dinner?"

"I'm not hungry, Sweets."

"Do you want some company?" I ask him but I'm already following him into the bathroom.

"Always but I have to warn you, there's not going to be any fun stuff, I'm exhausted. Your sister is something else when she goes shopping! I barely kept up with her and she's carrying another human around!"

We strip out of our clothes and step under the warm water.

"Did you guys already eat?"

"We ate most of the day, Logan, I barely kept up with Makenna on so many different levels today. She's a powerhouse that sister of yours and if she's not asleep up at the main house already, then she's a better human being than me."

"No-one is a better human being than you, Love." I tell him and I mean it. "You've put up with me all these years and I've been an absolute idiot. I'll never take you for granted ever again."

"You better not." He says with a grin as we wash each other clean, then dry off and crawl under the bed covers. I pull him into my side and let him snuggle into my chest. "Goodnight Logan."

"Goodnight Julian." I kiss his forehead and I feel every muscle in his body relax.

"Hey." His body tenses. "Did *you* eat?"

"I'm fine, now go to sleep." I know he'll be asleep in a few minutes, I give myself a few more minutes after his breathing evens out and he's quietly snoring, to enjoy having his body tucked into mine before I slide out of the bed and pull on some sweats.

As I leave the room, I pull up the messages app.

Me: *are you really not going to tell me what colour his suit is?*

Makenna: *go to bed Logan. You don't need to know everything*

Me: *but I really want to know*

Makenna: *I know but I want you to have a few surprises on the day*

As I read the message from her, I realise she's right. Before I can tell her that, another message comes through.

Makenna: *Trust me big brother. I love you and I love Julian, I won't do anything to ruin your day, I promise*

Me: *I love you too and I trust you with Julian's life. Now get some sleep*

Makenna: *Goodnight Sweets!!*

I laugh, quietly as I warm up some leftovers and sit at the table reading a book on my phone while I eat.

Makenna's right. I need to trust her, I trust her with my life and with business, I need to trust her with our wedding.

I finish up eating and clean up. When I go back to the bedroom I stop in my tracks in the doorway. Seeing Julian spread out across the bed, in our house, with *my* ring on his finger and knowing that in a few short weeks he'll be my husband is a happiness I didn't think I could ever have. But he's right there as proof.

Life is fucking great right now!

Chapter Thirty-nine
JULES

The following week is a whirlwind of work and meeting up with Makenna to discuss and decide all the smaller details about the wedding. I don't think either Logan or I realised just how much would be involved. We just wanted a celebrant who could marry us, while wearing our nicest suits, with our family and close friends to be in attendance and serving them some delicious food and wine to celebrate.

"I don't *want* to go shopping with Makenna." Logan whines and I know he *really* doesn't want to do this because this man, he *never* whines about *anything*. He's always the first person to volunteer to help someone and he never says no when his siblings ask him to do something. Ever. "I don't *need* a new suit, Jules."

"Wanting a new suit and needing a new suit, are two very separate things, Sweets." I grin, not looking up from my laptop.

"I neither want, nor need, a new suit Julian." He grumbles.

"According to your sister, you do." I tell him, still not looking up because I know if I do, I'm going to laugh and that will just piss him off more. "Makenna says we need to start 'fresh' and that means new suits."

"And what do *you* think?" He asks, and my fingers pause over the keys for a second too long. "You don't agree with her either, do you?"

"I don't think it matters either way, Logan *but* this way keeps your sister happy." I tell him, still not looking up from my screen so I don't see him approach me but I can feel him when he gets close.

"It only matters to me what you think, Love. I don't need a new suit if I have one that you prefer already." His body only a hairs breadth away from mine now and I shiver at the closeness.

"I want to make both you and Makenna happy, Logan. Getting a new suit isn't going to kill either of us and to be fair, I don't think she's asking too much. Brady got a new suit for *their* wedding." I argue, still not looking at him, although it's really testing every ounce of my self-control not to.

"He doesn't wear a suit every day, we do."

"Well, if that's your argument, you could also argue that his suits were fresher than any of ours and therefore he didn't need to buy a new one." This time I *do* look up and meet his gaze and I kind of wish I hadn't because I get drawn into his gorgeous green eyes, that are sparking with desire. A desire that we can't give in to because his sister will be here any minute.

"Are you saying I'm old and worn out, Mr Bishop?" He growls, *fucking growls*, so close to my ear I can feel his breath breeze over the shell of my ear but that's the only thing that touches me. I want him to touch me and he knows it!

"If the old man label fits, Sweets." I smile innocently up at him because the truth is, if he so much as leans in, causing any part of *him* to touch *me*, Makenna is going to wish she stayed home!

"You should be careful about who you're calling an old man, *old man*!" He says, stepping away from me as we both hear the door open.

"I'm not that old." I grumble as Makenna enters the room.

"Good morning!" She chimes, a little too chipper.

"What's so good about it?" I grumble.

"What did you do, Logan?" I can't help chuckling at her accusation, as she rounds on her brother with her hands on her hips.

"Why do you think I did anything wrong?"

"Because you're you!" Causing me to laugh a little louder than I meant to and Logan looks at me, his eyes all squinty and cute.

"He called me old." I volunteer when Logan doesn't answer her.

"That's no way to talk to your soon to be husband, Logan! You're supposed to tell him that he's gorgeous and not mention that he's older than you!" She smacks Logan on the shoulder but I can see the smirk on her face as she does it. "He's not *that* much older than you."

"Right, you two can get out of here now." I say, standing up and putting a hand on each of their backs and not so gently encouraging them towards the door. "Don't you have some shopping to do? You need a new suit for the wedding, Logan." He growls at me, even as he allows me to push him towards the door.

"You don't want a new suit?" Makenna stops in her tracks, making us all stop because there's no way I'm getting heavy handed with a woman, pregnant or not.

"Not really, Kenna. I have a wardrobe full of suits." Logan complains.

"Well, I guess we don't have to go shopping then." She says sadly, pouting as she moves towards the door, shoulders slumped.

Logan sighs, closes his eyes and when he opens them, he's got a steely determination in them.

"You know what, Kenna? I think you're right." Makenna stops mid step but doesn't turn around. "I think it would be nice to have a brand new suit to start our marriage off on the right foot. New start, new suit. Right?" He says cheerfully but we can see the pained expression on his face. I rub my hand over my face to cover the smile that's spreading across my lips.

"No, that's OK Logan. You're right, this is your wedding. Yours and Julian's and you should decide what you want." Oh wow, she's good! I think I could learn a thing or two off her, even though I have my own cards to play when it comes to Logan, she's a master! "You should have told me sooner that I was overstepping." She still hasn't turned around to face her brother but she angles her face just so, and I can see the smirk spreading across *her* face.

"No, you're right. I need as much help as I can get and a new suit would be perfect for the wedding. Let's go." He places a hand lightly on her lower back to help steer her out of the door. "We'll see you in a couple of hours, Jules." Logan looks back at me and I smile at him, while moving quickly to give him a quick kiss before they leave.

"See you later Jules." Makenna says over her shoulder, gifting me with a wide grin of the satisfaction of a winner.

"Have fun kids." I say with a wave as they close the door behind them.

Left in the silence, I burst out laughing and end up with tears rolling down my cheeks. Honestly, it wasn't *that* funny but watching Makenna play her brother so damned well was amusing as hell.

Not to mention, I saw them arguing over who was driving and I know that Makenna gave in. I know she let Logan drive because she knows he needs to feel like he's protecting her and his niece or nephew. They might all give each other crap but they would go to the ends of the earth for each other and that's what I love about all of them. Brady included.

I can't wait to become one of them.

Chapter Forty
LOGAN

Shopping with Kenna isn't as bad as I thought it would be. She knows exactly where to go, exactly what she wants and the tailor she takes me to is my own, so I know I'm going to get the suit she wants. Obviously, I have a say in it, but I let her take the reins because I know her reasoning behind wanting to help us as much as she possibly can and I just can't bring myself to ask her to stop.

Over the next week, even though looking at flower arrangements and going to cake tastings isn't my idea fun, I make sure to smile and nod whenever she looks my way or Jules nudges me to prompt an answer out of me. We're just two guys who want to be married, I don't know what all the fuss is about! At the end of the week, Makenna sits us down with Leila to work out the menu.

"We can get a catering service to do this, Leila, if it's too much work on top of the bistro." I assure her, only to get three sets of eyes giving me deadly glares, so I hold my hands up in surrender. "OK. OK, I'm just saying, I don't want to put extra pressure on you. You're a guest at the wedding after all." I stop myself from asking her if she's Caleb's date for the event, even though I would really love to know the answer to that.

"It's fine Logan. I want to do this for you guys, honestly." She assures me, while placing a hand on Makenna's arm to stop her from speaking. "If I thought for one second that service at the bistro would be compromised, I wouldn't even try it but I know that Sara and Georgie have it covered. My brother is coming in to help with everything as well. And you don't have to worry about him either, I taught him everything he knows about baking." She smiles at me and I feel myself relaxing.

"I didn't mean to offend you or give the impression that I don't think you're capable, Leila, I just don't want to put any added pressure on you. You work hard enough as it is in Vines without all of this on top." I explain.

"I know and I appreciate that but you've got nothing to worry about."

"Can we get on with deciding on the menu now, please?" Makenna asks. She's in a mood today and I don't have time to ask her if everything is OK. "We've left it to the last minute as it is. Leila needs some time to get things ordered and set up."

"It's OK Makenna, we have plenty of time." She smiles warmly at my sister and it feels like Leila has taken over the role that Makenna has had the last few weeks. She's calming everyone down and pushing through.

An hour later, with the menu set, Makenna suddenly stands up. "Well, if that's all for today, I'm going to head home."

I stand up and start to walk her to the door, leaving Jules and Leila to talk all things food like they normally do.

"Is everything OK, Kenna?" I ask quietly, as we reach the door.

"Hmm? Oh yeah I'm just tired today, sorry." She doesn't stop walking as she opens the door to leave.

"Makenna." I don't have to use my big brother voice on her very often, so when I do, I usually get results. "Is the baby OK?"

"Yes, Logan, the baby is fine. I'm fine. Everything is fine." I may be a man but I know when a woman says things are fine, they're generally not. Instead of questioning her, I simply raise an eyebrow. She sighs, closes her eyes and when she opens them they're shiny with unshed tears. "Honestly, Logan."

"It doesn't *look* fine." I push.

"Well, it is. When do Mr and Mrs Bishop arrive?" I pull my phone out of my pocket to look at the time, knowing that she's changed the subject perfectly.

"They should be here any minute, actually."

"I'll send Caleb over then when I get back to Vines." Leila says from behind me, making me jump. "Sorry, I guess I should know better than to sneak up on people, if I did that in the kitchen it could end up in disaster." She giggles.

"Yes! You send Caleb over, Leila and I'll see everyone at dinner. Do you want to have it at the main house? There's more space there." Makenna asks, as we all walk out the door.

"OK, but you're not cooking." Jules tells her.

"I've already got dinner for tonight covered." Leila pipes up. "You just have to let me know what time you want it all dished up."

"Oh Leila, you're a gem! Thank you." Jules exclaims, drawing her into a tight embrace, which earns him another giggle.

"You're welcome but I can't take all the credit, I'm just cooking the food, Caleb organised it all." Jules gives me a pointed look, as Leila says her good-byes and Makenna takes off for home.

"I told you Caleb isn't the little kid who needs to be looked after any-more. In fact, he's looking out for you and Makenna." I don't get the chance to respond because his parents choose that moment to pull up outside the house.

After a round of very enthusiastic hugs and excitement, I finally manage to get us all back in the house with a round of coffee to settle everyone down. Yes, I do know that coffee won't necessarily mean they'll calm down but it does mean that they have something else to hold other than me!

Before another round of Susan and Harold telling us just how happy they are for us and how happy they are to have me join their family, Caleb walks in the door! I can't remember a time when I've been so relieved and happy to see my little brother before. I'm even more grateful for him when he works his charm on Jules' parents and convincing them, after Jules promises to drive their car over, to walk over to the cottage so that he can show them where they'll be staying for the next week or so.

When we're left in the silent house, we look at each and sigh. We both know that this is the beginning of the end for at least the next week. We won't be getting a moment of peace or alone time until after the wedding now. With the arrival of Jules' parents today, that means there will be a slow build-up of activity over the next few days until it becomes a madhouse of people and things to get done.

I take Jules' hand in mine and lead him out to his parents car, driving us both over the cottage that Caleb assigned to Susan and Harold. He's done an amazing job on these cottages and I make a mental note to tell him so just as soon as all the craziness surrounding us calms down.

After settling Jules' parents into the cottage, we head over to Makenna and Brady's for dinner. Which is a loud and fun filled evening with the Bishops and my siblings swapping embarrassing childhood stories about us. I act grumpy about all the so called secrets that are being revealed but in actual fact, I couldn't be happier, if not a little sad at the same time. I *am* glad that everyone is getting along though and for that, I'm exceptionally grateful.

I step back for a couple of days, letting Jules spend the time with his parents, while I finish up a few things at Drake Wines. I promised Jules and Makenna that I would stay away from the office this week and next but neither of them said anything about the winery.

It's while I wander through the wine vats that I find myself having an unexpected conversation with Harold.

"He loves you, Logan, with every piece of him." His voice startles me from my own thoughts and as I turn around to face my soon to be father in law, I feel a lightness where I expected dread. A certainty, where I assumed there would be a definite feeling of not being comfortable about having this talk with the father of the man I love.

"I know." I say quietly, nodding my head slightly a few times. "I love him with every part of me, too. I can't imagine my life without him and I don't want to." Harold nods slowly, like he's thinking my words through and assessing them and he never breaks eye contact with me.

"I know we've already had this conversation, Logan but I wanted to have it face to face." I nod my head a few times.

"You need the reassurance." It's a statement, not a question. "I understand."

"We know he loves you, Logan and we know you love our son. That doesn't even come into question."

"What *is* the question then?" I ask, keeping my tone as neutral as I can without sounding panicked or unemotional. I need this to go well, I can't have Jules' parents deciding now, a day or two out from our wedding that I'm not good enough for their son.

"It's not that we think you're not good enough for him, Logan." Harold says like he can read my mind. "It's just that he's our only son and we need to know that he's going to be OK. Before you start telling me you'll never hurt him intentionally, we both know that. We also know that you've had your own set of difficulties over the years, both within the relationship and in your life." I don't know what to say, so I don't say anything, as Harold takes a deep breath and continues. "He's not fragile, Logan but we love him and want him to be safe and happy. I *see* that you make him happy. I also *see* that he makes *you* happy and that, as parents, is all we want."

"I don't know what to say to you that will make you feel better, Harold. All I *can* tell you, is that I love your son. I love Julian with every cell in my body and I *will* spend the rest of our lives together making sure that he is happy, safe and loved." I know I should probably be feeling a little panicked about this conversation but I'm not. "The truth is, I've messed up." I say with a shrug. "Is that easy to admit? Yes, actually because we all mess up but another truth is, Julian is the man I want to spend the rest of my days with. I don't care what those days look like, as long as we're together."

There's a minute or two of stony silence between us and still, I'm not uncomfortable with Harold. I know he needs this and I know, without a doubt, that I need Jules.

"Welcome to the family, Logan."

"Thank you, Harold." We shake hands but then suddenly, Harold pulls into an embrace.

"Let him go Dad! Are you in here harassing Logan? I told you not to do this Dad!" Jules says, his voice a little higher pitched than usual and I laugh.

"It's OK, Love. You're Dad and I were just having a chat. I think we're all good now." I smile at Harold and he smiles back.

"We sure are." He pulls Susan into his side as Jules leans into mine and I drape an arm over his shoulders. "So, who takes whose last name? Do you become a Drake, Julian or do you become a Bishop, Logan?"

"Ohh Harold!" Susan says shaking her head.

"Dad!" Jules says at the same time and I can't help letting out a loud laugh again.

"What? You know you're curious too Susan."

"We haven't decided yet, Harold. We might just keep our names as is." I say shrugging my shoulders. "Or we might go with some hyphenated weird hybrid. Who knows?" That seems to placate him and I lead them out of the winery, heading towards Vines to get some lunch. We're meeting Gavin and Jilly there and then Caleb can show them the cottage they're staying in for the weekend.

"I love you." Jules says quietly into my ear.

"I love you too, Julian." I tell him, leaning in for a light kiss and start laughing against his lips when I hear his Dad raise his voice slightly.

"What? I was curious and well, if you don't ask, you don't know!" Susan shakes her head and Jules rolls his eyes but when he looks at me all I see is happiness. A happiness that pulls at my heartstrings because I wish my parents were here to share in the love.

Chapter Forty-one
The Wedding
JULES

Having my parents stay the week before the wedding has been both a blessing and a curse. And not for the reasons you might think because my parents didn't expected either of us to show them around or spend enormous amounts of time with them. No, instead my Mum made fast friends, even though they already knew each other, with Makenna and helped her out like any great Mum does. And not because Mum and I walked in on my Dad giving Logan one last 'talk' about how much he doesn't deserve me either. It was kind of fun to watch Logan squirm in the hot seat a little bit and I know my Dad was just looking out for both of us, believe it or not because he loves Logan almost more than he loves me!

It's just that, I haven't spent that much time around them since I was a teenager and it feels weird.

Adding to the weirdness, Gavin and his wife, Jilly, also show up a couple of days earlier than expected and while Caleb swears black and blue that it's no hassle that they're here early, I know he's in their cottage when they're out of it, pottering around fixing a few small things for them.

Caleb promises me that they're small things and that guests would probably never notice them but he wants their stay to be perfect and I choose to believe him.

With so many people on the property, even though the property is closed to the public, is overwhelming and strange.

The fact that they're all here for Logan and myself, well that's even more bizarre.

Waking up the morning of our wedding was an even stranger feeling. Makenna wouldn't let us stay at home together, so I went and stayed with my parents in the cottage. I have a feeling that Mum and Makenna schemed this arrangement just so that I would spend more time with my folks.

I can hear my Mum pottering around in the kitchen and I can't help feeling like I'm a teenager again trying to work out how to get out of the house without anyone seeing me. I'm smiling at the memory when my phone chimes with a message from the man who will soon be my husband!

Logan: *can I call you? I need to talk to you*

I can feel his panic from across the other side of the property, so instead of waiting for him to call, I call *him*.

"Julian!" I can hear the stress in his voice and the way he uses my full name.

"Logan. Sweets, calm down, what's wrong?" I ask, sitting up in the bed.

"The ring."

"What ring?" I ask, looking at my finger. I refused to give it to Makenna or Gavin until right before the ceremony.

"*My ring Julian! We didn't end up going to buy me a wedding band!*" I can't help it, I laugh because hearing Logan Drake in such a flustered, panicked state is truly something else. It's something for the history books, that's for sure. Logan never and I mean *never* lets anything get to him. He's always in control of his emotions, unless he's with me anyway.

"Logan." I can hear him breathing heavily into the phone. "Sweets, I promise you don't have to worry about a ring."

"But we were going to go together and choose one and we got so busy that we didn't go." His breathing has become so heavy that I'm worried he's going to cause himself to pass out. "What are we going to do? I know I said I didn't need one but I *want* one now. Do you think I could send Caleb out to get one? No, Brady would do a better job but that would hurt Caleb's feelings and I can't ask Makenna, she's got enough on her plate today."

"Sweets, you don't have to send anyone out to get one. I've got one."

"You're right, maybe Gavin could do you a favour and go?" He rambles on, not listening to me.

"Logan!" I say louder than I should but he's not listening to me.

"You don't have to yell Jules." The annoyance in his voice would be laughable if I wasn't now annoyed with *him*!

"Then stop for a second and actually listen to what I'm saying, Sweets and to do that, you need to calm the hell down." I give him a few seconds to slow down his breathing. "You don't need to send anyone out to get you a wedding ring, Sweets, I got you one."

"You do?" He asks, surprised. "When did you manage that and why didn't you tell me?"

"I picked it out when I went shopping for a suit with Makenna but I only picked it up this week when I took Mum and Dad into town for some lunch and shopping."

"So, Makenna and your parents know what my ring looks like but I don't?" He sounds hurt and I rush to explain that's not true.

"No-one knows what it looks like except myself and the jeweller, Logan." I roll my eyes because this man is unusually needy this morning. "I went into a jewellery store when Makenna went to the bathroom and found the perfect ring for you. She didn't see it but she does know I got it. As for my parents they haven't seen it yet either. Apart from me, you'll be the first person to see it. I'm not even giving it to Gavin to hand over to me in the service."

"Oh."

"Yeah, oh! I haven't taken the ring you gave me off yet either and I won't until I give it to Makenna right before the service so that she can give it to you." There's a few seconds of silence between us and I can hear his breathing settle back into a normal pattern. "Are you OK now?"

"I panicked there for a second." He explains unnecessarily.

"Really? I didn't pick up on that!" I reply, a smile spreading across my lips.

"I'm marrying a sarcastic arsehole, huh?" He grumbles.

"Yeah, I guess you are."

"See you under the arch in a couple of hours, Love."

"I can't wait, Sweets."

"Me either. I wish I could see your face right now. I just want to hold you in my arms and kiss your lips before we do this."

"Logan."

"I know, I know, Makenna would kill me if she found us out but it would *so* be worth it." He laughs and it's nice to hear him relaxed again. "I love you, Julian Bishop. I can't wait to be your husband." He says quietly.

"I love you too, Logan Drake and I can't wait for you to *be* my husband."

"Logan Jack Drake, *who* are you talking to right now?" I hear Makenna ask in the background.

"Maintenance?"

"Are you *asking* me or *telling* me?" She asks, her voice closer to the phone. "Good morning Julian. I hope you're well rested?" I can hear Logan protesting that his sister took his phone right out of his hand.

"Good morning Makenna, I slept like a baby." I chuckle.

"I believe not all babies are created equally in the sleeping department." She retorts. "And on that note, we're hanging up now, see you soon. Love you."

"Love you too, sweet girl." I hear her sigh and then she's gone.

As soon as I hang up, there's a light knock on my door.

"Are you awake, Sweetie?" My Mum asks as she opens the door. "Leila dropped off a delicious looking breakfast. Come out and get some before it goes cold or your father eats it all. He's going to go home a little heavier than when we arrived." She chuckles but I know she doesn't care one bit about it.

"Let me put some clothes on and I'll be right out." I tell her, while not making a move to get out of bed.

"Still sleeping naked I see?" She says with a smile. "I'll get out of here so you can make yourself presentable for breakfast with the parentals then." Then she disappears behind the closed door and I hear her tell my Dad to leave some for me and I can't help laughing again. Maybe I'm just in a happy mood today but listening to my parents back and forth gives me a comfort I didn't know I needed today. I pull on some sweats and a t-shirt, then I walk out into the kitchen for breakfast.

"Good morning, sleepyhead." Gavin says, a little too perky for someone who should have just woken up.

"He's been awake for over an hour already. Anyone would think it's him getting married today and not you!" Jilly says in way of explanation for her husband's liveliness this morning.

"Hey, it's not every week that your favourite person gets married you know and you get to not only attend but stand up beside him."

"And we're all grateful about that." Jilly mumbles as she takes a gulp of her coffee.

These two couples, as well as Makenna and Brady, are exactly what I want in my relationship with Logan. Comfort, love, support and a healthy level of teasing each other.

We spend the next hour chatting and laughing over breakfast before Mum and Jilly send me off to have a shower, with strict instructions to come out smelling wonderful and clean shaven. Which causes me to send a message off to Makenna telling her to *not* allow her brother to shave today. I *like* the longer scruff he's sporting at the moment and I don't want him to change a thing. It's not stubble but it's not quite a beard yet either and I *love* it!

I stare at my phone until I get a smiley face in response to my message, then I put my phone down and do what I need to do.

When I come out of the bathroom, Gavin's leaning against the wall, legs crossed at the ankles, back flat against the wall and arms crossed over his chest. He's already dressed in the charcoal grey suit that Makenna picked out for him to wear today. I start to smile but I stop when I notice the frown on his face.

"What's wrong? Is Logan OK?" I ask, starting to panic.

"Does Logan know how lucky he is that your first thought is to ask if *he's* OK?" Gavin asks without moving. "Your parents are OK too, as is Jilly." He assures me before I can ask about them.

"You can't tell me you wouldn't do the same thing and ask about Jilly, if you were in my place." I know I'm right by the crease that appears between his eyebrows.

"You're right, I would but that doesn't mean I can't give you shit for it." He smirks at me and I want to punch him in the face. I'm not a violent person but I can imagine punching him in the nose right now. "Don't do it. A black eye on your best man won't look good in your wedding photos." His smirk gets wider and I just growl at him as I walk by him to get into the bedroom that's mine for twenty four hours. I can't wait to get back home.

"I'm sure Logan wouldn't mind at all." I tell him as I walk into the room, Gavin close behind me. "I don't need your help to get dressed, Gavin." I tell him, hands on towel covered hips.

"I know you don't but Makenna asked me, well more like demanded, that I be in here as you got ready."

"She won't know if you sit in the other room with my parents."

"You know Makenna, right? I mean she's about to be your sister in law, so I'm assuming you know the woman pretty well after all these years. She'll know." I turn my back to him so that he can't see the smile spreading across my face and to shield my body from him as I pull on my boxer briefs underneath the towel.

"I'm sure she didn't mean that you had to supervise me from naked to clothed. Logan would *not* approve that and neither of them are worried that I'm going to get cold feet."

"You sure? Because I can have you out of the cottage and off the property before anyone even notices." Gavin offers, only half joking I suspect.

"Of course you've got an exit plan in place." I laugh, even though I find the idea decidedly unamusing. I drop the towel to the floor, uncaring as to whether Gavin is looking or not, and pull on the pants of the navy blue suit that Makenna and I picked out a few weeks ago. "Gavin, I need to know that you can stand beside me today and give this marriage your blessing. If you can't, I would understand and there would be no hard feelings if you felt like you needed to step aside." I don't look his way as I reach over to pull the crisp white shirt off the hanger and pull it on, slowly doing up the buttons.

"Jules." He says, then takes a deep breath. "Julian, look at me, please." His tone demanding but not truly forceful. I keep slowly doing up the buttons as I turn to look at him. "I promise, it was a joke, mostly. I will stand up next to you today and I will do it happily, I promise. He's a good guy, Jules."

"Thank you." I say with a smile. "I appreciate you saying that."

"That doesn't mean I won't get you out of here unseen if that's what you want but I have a feeling, we're both here until the bitter end." He holds his hand up to stop me from speaking. "I am *very* happy for you. For you *both*." He amends.

I am more than happy, Gavin. I can't wait to get out there and marry Logan." I sit down on the edge of the bed, and put on my socks and shoes, also picked out by Makenna. Everything is new today, even my underwear, Makenna insisted.

"Are you boys almost ready?" My Mum asks as she opens the door without knocking. "Oh my word! Julian you look so *handsome*! You both do, of course but oh my!" Her hand lands on her chest and I can see tears welling in her eyes.

"Do you know how to tie a bowtie, Mum?"

"No honey, I don't, sorry."

"How about Dad?" I mean, I doubt he's had anywhere he's needed to wear one but stranger things have happened.

"No, I don't think he does."

"Watch out, excuse me Susan, pregnant lady coming to the rescue!" Makenna says as she storms through the doorway and makes a beeline straight for me. "I can tie that for you." Of course she can.

"Why am I not surprised?" Gavin mutters beside me, saying what I was thinking.

"I just did Logan's, I'd show you the proof but I don't want you to see him before the wedding." She tuts like I was trying to pull one over her, instead of her almost offering me a sneak peek of my soon to be husband. While I've been thinking all of that, she's managed to tie my tie for me. "Ohh you look so handsome! You *both* look so damn handsome! You're going to fall in love with Logan all over again when you see him and he's going to fall in love with you all over again too." Tears well in her eyes and when one lonely tears falls down her cheek, she sucks in a breath, wipes her cheek and smiles broadly at me. "Are we ready to go?"

"I have never been more ready to do anything in my entire life." I smile.

"You guys have no idea how lucky you are. No hairdressers, no makeup to get done. Just you, a shower and then you can get dressed!" She's not complaining at all, just trying to change the mood in the room.

"Let's get this show on the road then." Gavin announces, clapping his hands together and ushering everyone out of the room. Before I follow them, I look in the mirror on the wall and smooth out my wrinkle free suit. "Second thoughts?" Gavin asks as he pops his head around the edge of the door.

"Not even one. Just checking I'm all set to go." I grab my suit jacket off its hanger and pat the left pocket to make sure that the ring I bought for Logan is still in there. When I feel the box in there, I resist the urge to open it up and make sure the ring is inside. I've already checked it multiple times last night and this morning, it's in there. "Let's get me married."

Mum, Dad, Gavin and myself make our way up to the main house and wait on the side of the house that Makenna told us we had to. Jilly joins us and gives me a tight hug, before both her and Gavin leave us to wait for the music to start.

"Are you OK son? You look like you're vibrating." My Dad asks.

"I just want to get the service done. I want to be Logan's husband, then I can relax."

"Do you think he'll change his mind?" Dad asks, the worry on his face.

"Not even for a second, I just can't wait to marry the man I love." The music starts and I take a few seconds to hug my parents, then I hold out my arms and they loop an arm each through mine. Then we're walking. The idea being that we'll meet each other in the middle as Logan, Makenna and Caleb walk in from the other side.

As we round the corner, my attention is divided between my parents, all of us beaming at each other with happiness. That is until I catch sight of the group coming to meet us and I suck in a breath!

"Holy fuck!"

"Language!" Mum admonishes and my Dad chuckles. "Although I'll give you a pass on it this once, Logan is definitely a very handsome man and he looks amazing in that suit!"

"Hey!" Dad protests.

"You look pretty handsome yourself honey."

"Thank you."

I can hear them talking but my focus is solely on the man I love. His eyes catch mine and don't break contact, even as we get to the archway where the celebrant is standing. I only break eye contact when both of my parents take me into a tight group hug and then take their seats in the front row. There's a bit of shuffling around as Caleb and Makenna hug Logan, and then take their places beside us, with Gavin and Brady.

Gavin and Makenna stand beside me, while Caleb and Brady stand beside Logan.

"Hi." I whisper.

"Hi, Love." Logan whispers back and even if there was a teeny tiny errant thought about whether this was the right thing to do or not, it floats away on a light breeze.

Logan Drake is everything I want in a man.

"Welcome family and friends, to the wedding of Julian Bishop and Logan Drake." The celebrant starts and I can't hear anything other than her voice, and I can't *see* anyone except Logan standing in front of me.

I'm not sure I could tell you everything that was said but I know that there was barely a dry eye in the garden as we said I do and exchanged vows.

"I now pronounce you, husband and husband! You may kiss your husband!"

Chapter Forty-two
The Wedding
LOGAN

I don't know whether to be annoyed at my sister or tell her to sit her arse down because she's running herself ragged today, but I can't bring myself to tell her off for doing too much. I know why she's doing it, she's trying to distract herself from the fact that our parents aren't here to witness my marriage.

"Makenna." I say her name softly because I don't want her to think for a second that I don't appreciate everything she's done to make our day special but I also want her to slow down. "Makenna, you need to take a breath, Sweetheart." I wrap my hand around her upper arm and pull her into a tight hug.

"I need to keep moving, I have things to do, Logan." She protests into my chest but doesn't attempt to pull out of my embrace.

"You need to take a minute to relax, Makenna." I squeeze her a little tighter but not too tightly, I can't because of her growing belly.

"I've been telling her to slow down for two weeks now but does she listen? No, I'm just her husband and father of her baby, what the hell would I know?" Brady grumbled from behind me.

"She's stubborn, that's for sure but you knew that when you married her." I tell him, resting my chin on the top of Makenna's head and swaying us gently side to side.

"Of course she's stubborn, she's a Drake isn't she?" He declares with a grunt.

"I'd like to defend us, Sweetheart but I don't think I can." I mumble into the top of her head and I feel her laughter before the wonderful sound hits my ears. "They're here Kenna, even if we can't see them and you working yourself to the bone isn't going to make them appear. We just have to accept it."

"I don't know how you do it." She grumbles into my chest.

"How I do what, Sweetheart?" I ask, genuinely confused.

"How do you make it sound so easy. You manage to compartmentalise everything, including the loss of our parents and for all intents and purposes, it seems as though you don't feel their loss today, of all days."

"It's not easy, Kenna." I kiss the top of her head lightly. "Today of all days, it's not easy, believe me. I wish that I'd had the chance to talk to them, to explain and have them know Jules as my boyfriend and my husband but that chance, it's gone, Sweetheart. I can't get that time back and I can't change the past. Does it hurt? Hell yes, it does and I know you understand that on a day like today but the pain isn't any worse today, on my wedding day, than it was yesterday or six months ago or the day after they died. It just is what it is."

"But it's still sad that they're not here. They won't see you married and settled down with the man you love and they won't meet my baby, either." She sniffles and I know she's holding back tears. This isn't what I want with less than half an hour before I marry the love of my life! "I know nothing is going to change, Logan but that doesn't mean I can't be upset about what they're missing. About what we're missing. What my children will miss."

"You're right *but* today is a happy occasion." I pull out of our embrace, holding her at arm's length, my hands on her shoulders. "I convinced Jules to marry me, I can't give him even a second longer than in the schedule to think about the commitment he's making because I'm not letting him back out of this, I need him." I kiss her forehead and gently pass her over to Brady, who pulls her in close and murmurs something in her ear that makes her smile that I'm happy not to know about.

"So, are you ready big brother?" Caleb bounds into the house, breaking the tension with the ease that he always seems to carry with him. An ease that I envy, if I'm being honest.

"I am, yes. *More* than ready actually." I smile, when I notice a little shiver rolling through Caleb because I realise he's thinking about *after* the wedding and just like he doesn't want to think about *how* our sister got pregnant, he doesn't want to know *how* Jules and I plan on celebrating later. "I can't wait until this is all over and Jules and I can have our own private celebration." I wink at Caleb, who visibly shakes this time and closes his eyes while groaning out a 'for fucks sake'.

I look innocently at Makenna as she shakes her head and pulls out of Brady's arms, who is laughing almost hysterically. "I'm going to check in on Jules. You know where to go and what to do, right?"

"Yes ma'am." I say, saluting her. "Caleb and I will be waiting for you in our designated area, that you've drilled into us for weeks now. I promise!"

"Do you want me to come with you, Baby?" Brady asks, concern all over his face and I love that my sister has a man that loves her so damned much because she deserves every drop of his adoration.

"No, Honey, I think I'm capable of walking from Logan's house to the cottage *but* I do appreciate you offering, kind sir." The over politeness earns her a grin the size of which is inhuman, from her husband. It's not that Makenna is rarely nice, it's just that she's such a force of nature from the minute she wakes up, to the minute she falls asleep, and she rarely asks for assistance, that I think when she says stuff like that, his heart probably warms considerably.

"Alright, you two have had your day of declaring undying love for each other, today is for Logan and Julian, so cut out the gooey eyed bullshit for when you're in private would ya?" Caleb admonishes them and when I look his way, ready to thank him, he waves me off.

"Fine! I'm going to check on Jules, I'll meet you two," she points at the both of us, "Where you're supposed to wait until the ceremony starts."

"Yes ma'am." I salute her again and Caleb rolls his eyes at her but he also nods his head, letting her know he understands.

"And I'm going to walk part of the way with my gorgeous wife and then I'm going to check in on all the guests and make sure they're behaving and ready to take their seats." They both come over and give me a hug and then leave.

"I can walk by myself, you know." Makenna says, as the door closes and we don't get to hear Brady's response but we do catch him kissing the living daylights out of our sister before they go in opposite directions to do what needs to be done.

"You know, I might give the four of you a hard time but I'm really happy for you. Especially for you, Logan." Caleb says from behind me and I don't dare to turn around. "I mean, I love Makenna and well, Brady has been my brother from long before they got married, you know?"

"I do." I agree.

"You'll be saying that to Jules soon." I don't hear any amusement in his voice and that causes me to turn around and look at him, for no reason other than to check his face to *see* his feelings, cause this kid can't hide them. "Are you ready for that? I only ask because I know you've struggled with yourself. I know you love Jules, no doubts there, trust me, otherwise I wouldn't *let* you go through with this."

"You wouldn't *allow me*?" I ask, surprised by the determination in his voice and the look of steel on his face!

"That's right. If I thought for even a second that you weren't positive that this is what you wanted, I wouldn't let you go through it because Jules is like a brother to me already as well. Brady and Jules are on the same grounding to me, they were both here to help *all* of us when Mum and Dad died and I won't let you hurt him, Logan. That man is a fucking saint and you better make it your fucking mission to make yourself worthy of him for the rest of your lives."

"I didn't realise you felt that strongly about it, or us, Caleb." I'm shocked at how passionate he feels about my relationship and just how much Jules means to him. "Don't get me wrong, I know you love Jules but I didn't realise you felt this way."

"I just want you to be happy Logan." He says with a shrug of his shoulders. "And Jules makes you incredibly happy, which makes *me* happy but that being said, if you do anything and I do mean *anything* to break that man's heart *ever* again and I swear to god Logan, I will kick your arse! I mean it, seriously, just give me a reason to disown your grumpy arse and I will do it in a heartbeat. That man you're about to marry? He is perfect for you *and* he's a sweetheart. I'm not even sure you deserve him but I'm going to let that slide for now, just don't fuck it up."

"Thanks for the vote of confidence, Caleb." I say with a large helping of sarcasm. "What makes you think I'm the one who's going to screw shit up?"

"You've already done it multiple times Logan and Jules has stuck by you, until he couldn't take it anymore. You just have to make sure you deserve him every day for the rest of your lives and we'll be good brother."

"Well, I guess I know where I stand with you and also, I now understand why Jules has an unwavering affection, loyalty and belief in your abilities."

"It's nice to know that someone has that level of faith in me around here." He mumbles, pushing the toe of his dress shoe in to my carpet, his eyes cast down to watch the progress.

"I have absolute faith in you Caleb." I guess now is the time to at least start that conversation I promised Jules I'd have with my little brother. "I know it's hard for you to see or even understand I guess but I do love you, Caleb and I *do* see you for all the potential you have and skills that you've already got. It's, oh fuck it! It's just hard because you were the youngest when Mum and Dad died and I guess I took on the Dad role, I took it seriously because I didn't want you to throw away your life because of a tragedy. I'm sorry that I've made you feel like I don't believe in you."

"I know you believe in me." He looks up, meeting my gaze and I see a strength in him that I haven't seen before, probably because I've never wanted to. "It's just nice to feel it and hear it sometimes, you know? You're my brother and a kind of father figure as well, I never want to feel like I'm letting you or Makenna down but that doesn't mean I won't take you down if you hurt Jules again. He's been an amazing support to me, even when I haven't asked for it and no-one else has seen it. That man is special and I won't stand by and let him get hurt."

"I've got it. I completely understand." I reach out to grab his upper arms and pull in him for hug that is no doubt tighter than it should be. "I love you Caleb."

"I love you too, Logan." He coughs and pulls out of my arms. "So, are you ready to marry the love of your life or what?"

"I've been ready for years." I confirm, adding a sharp nod.

"Well then, let's get this show on the road then. Makenna will be pissed if we're even a second late to our designated waiting area."

"You're not wrong." I laugh, then we're walking out of the door and towards the backyard of the main house where Makenna and Brady got married last year.

Before I have time to think about what's about to happen, Makenna is standing on my left, Caleb on my right and the music that's the prompt for the service to start and for us to begin the walk towards the arch to meet Jules starts.

"Love you, Logan." Both of my siblings say at the same time. "Let's get married!" I swear to god they've rehearsed this because they are way too in time with each other for them to not have but I don't get the chance to ask them about it because we're moving.

I look up as we round the corner of the house, to look at the arch but all I see is Jules walking towards me from the other side of the house with his parents on each arm and I can see nothing else but him. He looks so fucking handsome and I suddenly wish there weren't any other people here so that I could have him all to myself.

"He's a handsome devil isn't he?" Makenna leans in and asks.

"Too fucking handsome for the likes of you!" Caleb pipes up before I can respond but I don't let either of them into my thoughts. All I can see and think about is Jules and making him my husband.

When we meet each other in the middle at the arch, where Gavin is standing waiting on Jules' side and Brady is standing waiting for me on mine.

'I love you." I mouth to Jules, hoping I can settle some of the nerves I can see in his eyes. When I see him relax a little and mouth my words back at me, I smile.

The celebrant interrupts my thoughts by asking, "Who gives these men away today?"

"We do!" Jules' parent and my siblings chime at the same time with smiles wide enough to split their faces! Gavin and Brady chuckle beside us, as do the rest of the guests, not that there's many.

After that, I couldn't tell you anything else that was said except for our vows because those I wanted to remember forever.

"Do you both have vows written?" The celebrant asks at one point and we both nod. "Now is the time to say them. Why don't you go first Julian?"

"OK." He takes a breath and swallows deeply before taking my hands in his and speaking. "I didn't write anything down because I wanted to speak from the heart, so forgive me if stumble at all." The crowd laughs and I squeeze his hands lightly in reassurance.

"You've got this, Love." I say quietly, earning me the sweetest smile.

"Logan Drake. You drive me insane, in fact I'm pretty sure you've driven me to the point of distraction on so many occasions that I'm surprised we're both here. You make me angry, sad and everything in between but you also always make me feel cherished. I feel loved every time you look at me, every time you speak to me and every time you hold me. I will love you always and I can't wait to grow old with you. Well, older, anyway." Laughter rings out from our audience, and I can hear Makenna's laughter mingled with her sniffling beside me as well but I only have eyes for Jules. "I love you, Logan Jack Drake."

"Logan, do you have a few words you want to say?" The celebrant, Giulia asks and I nod her way then start to speak. I didn't write anything down, I decided to just speak from my heart.

"Generally speaking, I'm a man of few words and rarely express my feelings in front of a crowd, for today and Jules, I'm going to try my best." There's a rumbling of laughter and a snort from beside me but I don't look away from Jules, he is my sole focus, no-one else matters. "You are my soul, my heart and the air I breathe. You are my everything Julian Bishop. I'm sorry that I make your life difficult sometimes and I promise to work on that. I also promise to be a little less grumpy but let's face it, I am who I am. I promise to protect you for as long as I love you, and that means I will always protect. I can't wait to grow old with you and I will love you until my last breath. I love you Julian John Bishop. Always."

"Oh Logan." I hear Makenna say on a shaky, breathy sob but still, I don't turn around to make sure she's OK, she's got Brady, Caleb and Gavin to hold her up if she needs it.

"Can we have the rings now please?" Giulia asks with a kind smile. Makenna hands her the ring I gave Jules a few weeks ago, that she got off Jules when she went to check in on him before the service. He refused to take it off any earlier than that and I love him for it. To my surprise, Gavin pulls a ring out of the small inside pocket of his suit jacket and hands it to Giulia.

"Logan, repeat after me." She says with a smile as I take the ring I bought for Jules from her and push it on to his finger once again, as I repeat the words that promise forever but I couldn't tell you for the life of me what they actually were.

I watch as Jules takes the band from Giulia and he pushes it onto my finger. I don't hear anything. I don't hear the words that Giulia asks him to speak, and I don't hear him repeat them. I'm too busy staring at the platinum band with a thin pale blue inlay, that he slides on to my finger. A pale blue that is almost a perfect match for Jules' eyes. I still don't know how he managed to get this without me noticing but I adore him *and* the ring.

"I now pronounce you married! You may kiss your husband." Giulia declares but I can't move I'm too stunned that we actually made this happen after everything we've been through.

"Kiss him you idiot." Caleb hisses and I can't help laughing, as I clasp my hand behind my husband's head and bring his lips to mine. I don't know if anyone is laughing at my hesitation or Caleb's prompting and I don't care. All I care about is kissing my *husband*.

"OK, keep it PG kids." Gavin says, slapping us both on the back.

"Ladies and gentlemen, let me present Mister and Mister Bishop-Drake!"

"Thank you Giulia." I say, after releasing Julian's lips and turning to smile at her.

"You're welcome, Logan, I wish every wedding I officiated had as much love that you two share." Her smile is warm and sincere. "Now, go and enjoy the rest of your day."

That is exactly what I intend to do as I wrap an arm around Jules' waist and pull him in tight against my side. He curls his arm around my waist and rests his head on my shoulder, as I lead him up to the house. After stopping to be engulfed in a hug from his parents, we walk by the few guests with our families and Gavin walking behind us.

I don't think this feeling of overwhelming love will ever be beaten.

"I love you, Julian." I bend my head down so that I can whisper it in his ear as we walk along.

"I love you too, Logan." He turns his head to look at me and the smile on his face is incredible and in this moment, I feel invincible.

Chapter Forty-three
JULES

After the service, I know we're ushered around the gardens for photos but all I can remember is that Logan didn't leave my side. He touched me in some way, on some part of me, the entire time and I loved every second of it.

"OK, now that those are done, you can all head into what we're calling the reception and mingle with our guests for a while." Logan announces after what feels like the thousandth photo that has been taken of us in all kinds of combinations of family members and friends.

"So bossy!" Makenna grumbles but she's got a smile on her face and I can see that Brady is relieved about getting her to sit down for a few minutes. "I hope you know what you've gotten yourself into with this one, Jules? I mean, it's a little late now and I'm sure *you* enjoy his grumpy, bossy side in ways I never want to know about."

"Makenna." Logan growls out a warning to his sister but she just rolls her eyes at him, completely unaffected by the pointed warning on his face that would have many others tuck their tails between their legs and run in the other direction.

"Logan." She growls back at him, in an amusing impression of her brother and I can't help laughing.

"She's not wrong. Come on everyone, let's leave these two alone for a while." Caleb instructs everyone and has a silent conversation with Brady and Gavin, as all three men gently start pushing everyone, including the photographer towards the marquee that takes up a sizable section of the yard. "You've got about thirty minutes before Makenna sends one of us, meaning myself or Brady, out looking for you both. I'll try to buy you a few more minutes than that but I think you should aim for twenty minutes to be safe. She has this shindig scheduled to the minute."

"Thank you Caleb." Logan says, his voice gruff with emotion that I don't quite understand.

"Don't mention it. No, seriously, I don't want to know." He winks and then disappears with the others and it's just my husband and I standing there, in a mostly secluded area of the garden.

My husband! I can't believe we made it to this day but I can't imagine being any happier.

"How are you doing?" Logan asks, pulling me into his side and resting his lips just above my ear so that he doesn't need to speak loudly. His words, his question, just for me.

"I'm doing great. Couldn't be happier." I turn my head so that I'm looking into his gorgeous green eyes. "How about you? How are you doing?"

"I'm trying to work out when the hell you managed to get this gorgeous ring and how you managed to hide it from me for more than a few days."

"Do you like it?" I ask, suddenly unsure of my choice. "I know we said we were going to choose one together but I saw it the day I went suit shopping with Makenna and I just knew I needed to buy it." I'm rambling, I know I am but I can't stop myself, I'm suddenly so nervous about my choice.

"I love it, Julian and I love you." He takes my face in his hands and pulls my lips to his, for a searing kiss.

"I wanted the blue inlay to remind you of me when you look at it, like the chips of emerald remind me of you every time they glint in the sunlight or I look at them." I explain, suddenly feeling like an idiot.

"It's perfect, Love, absolutely perfect." His lips find mine again, only this time the kiss is tender, almost sweet. Almost. I try to deepen the kiss, I want more, I need more of him but he pulls away from me. "I want to do all kinds of things to you right now, Love but we can't. If we take too much longer Makenna will either come looking for us or send one of the guys out. Caleb warned us and he was right."

"I know." I admit, resting my head on the front of his shoulder. "But that doesn't mean that I want to go anywhere except back home with my husband." I turn my face slightly, giving me access to his neck and I leave a light kiss there, making him groan.

"We can't, Love." He says the words but he doesn't make to move away from where we are.

"I know." I mumble on his neck. "Just a few more minutes." I'm not above begging and I don't think Logan could resist it either.

"Umm guys." There's a loud cough, followed by a very loud sigh. "I'm really sorry but you're needed inside."

"It's OK Gavin, we'll be right there." Logan answers for the both of us.

"I really am sorry, Logan but your sister is about to have a fit if things don't get moving like she's got them planned. It was me coming out here to *ask* you both to come inside or Makenna coming out here to yell at you for putting her plans behind by a few minutes. That sister of yours is a real fire-cracker isn't she? Brady is a brave and strong man!"

"She is but that's my newly acquired sister, Gavin." I warn him as I pull out of Logan's embrace to face him. "She worked really hard to make to-day everything that we wanted it to be and not asked for anything except our happiness in return, so show a little bit of respect. Especially in her own home."

"You're absolutely right and I didn't mean any offence, honestly." Gavin holds his hands up in a defensive manner. "I just meant, she is really on top of the day's events and she would very much like for you two to be a part of those events seeing as how they are in your honour."

"Lead the way then, Gavin." Logan says, tucking his arm around my waist and pulling me in close, as he steers us towards the marquee.

"I truly am sorry, guys."

"We know you are Gavin and we also know that my sister can be a pow-erhouse, so truly, no hard feelings." Logan says.

"There you are! Now you stay out here and we'll make the announce-ment of your arrival." Makenna says in frustration.

"No, Makenna. We talked about this. No announcement, no grand en-trance. Sweetheart, you got your way on a *lot* of things when it came to to-day but this one is not negotiable. Everyone knows why we're here, we don't need a big song and dance to announce that we've arrived at our party. *You* however, my darling sister, can now take a load off and sit down. Relax a little bit and enjoy the party that you organised within an inch of its life, OK?" She looks like she's going to argue with her big brother, until he raises an eyebrow at her, it's an obvious warning, one she seems to know all too well.

"OK, fine!" She scowls and crosses her arms over her chest.

"You're right, I should expect or want you to enjoy the party. I'm a mean older brother, maybe you should go in the kitchen and help Leila and her staff out?"

"Don't even jokingly suggest that Logan." Brady groans in frustration as Makenna looks like she's thinking about getting up. "You and I both know she'll go in there and ask if they need help. They *don't* need help, Baby, they've got it under control. This is Leila's job!"

"Fine!"

"How about I go and check in on Leila and the gang for you?" Caleb offers and I can't help smiling. I have a strong feeling he has an ulterior motive to go in and check on the gorgeous chef.

"OK." Makenna barely finishes speaking, before Caleb takes off, at breakneck speed to go check out things in the kitchen.

"He's got it bad." Gavin says, not realising that he's saying out loud what no-one else in this circle care to think about.

"Fuck!" Logan says under his breath.

"Let's not worry about that tonight." I say. "Let's go talk to the rest of our guests. Makenna, stay here and put your tired but wonderful feet up and make sure Brady waits on you." I smile at them both, knowing that Brady would do anything for his wife.

I lead Logan away and we circle the room, thanking everyone for coming, hopefully giving everyone the same attention. When dinner is served we all sit down to eat with some music playing and the happy chatter of our family and friends.

Not twenty minutes after the last empty dessert dish has been cleared away, Caleb announces that it's time for the first dance and I can't help laughing at the panicked look on Logan's face. He's not much of a dancer, in public anyway and I know he's about to tell Caleb to shove it where the sun most certainly doesn't shine, so I stand up and take his hand in mine. He looks up at me and I smile at him. I see him visibly relax and I know he understands.

I've got him, I won't ever let him fall. Not even when we dance in front of the most precious people to us. As the music starts up and I take him in my arms, he relaxes even further and I'm glad that I can give this to him because he gives me so much and he's so strong for everyone else. I like that I can take this one for him.

"This is our song." He says quietly, as he leans back and looks in my eyes.

"It sure is, Sweets." I say as I sing the words to 'All of me' by John Legend to my new husband, I watch the smile creep across his face.

"You're welcome!" Caleb shouts from somewhere in the crowd, causing everyone, including us to laugh.

Logan opens his mouth to shout back at his brother but I stop him with a quick kiss.

"Leave it, Sweets. He's not wrong, this *is* his choice of song for us and he did a great job of it."

He doesn't get the chance to say anything else because my Mum and Makenna come over and split us up so that we can have a parent dance. I don't think there's a dry eye in the house, when Caleb joins his brother and sister on the dancefloor. It's only a minute before Brady joins them as well and my Dad joins us.

Logan looks over their heads and catches my eye. 'I love you.' He mouths and I do the same back. When the music changes to a more upbeat pace, my parents make their way back to their table and I make the rounds of the room again, stopping to chat with Gavin and Jilly for a while, as the Drake siblings dance together for another song or two.

Chapter Forty-four
LOGAN

Our first dance as married men was amazing. I'm not a dancer in general but I can move when I have to and today was one of those days where I had to. I know that Jules thought that my lack of dancing skills were the cause of my hesitation when called up for our first dance together but the reality is, I knew that at some point in our dance together, it would become the parents dance.

What I wasn't aware of, was that my siblings already had me covered. I should have known better than to think they'd leave me hanging in an awkward situation. When his parents come over mid-way through the song to dance with Jules, I step back and hand him over. I watch them for a few seconds and make to move out of their way, until I feel a hand on my arm and look over to see Makenna standing there with a watery smile on her face.

"Dance with me?" She says and I know I can't say no, so I take her in my arms. "Well, this is slightly awkward." She says with a giggle, that doesn't quite cover the tears, as we try to manoeuvre around her still smallish belly.

We're good, until Caleb joins us as well and then we have to work it all out again but it's worth it.

"Love you guys." I tell them both. I see the emotion on both of their faces but it's the shock on Caleb's that almost takes my knees out from under me. "I should tell you both more often but I want you both to know that I love and appreciate you. Not just for everything that you put in to today, to make sure it was perfect but for every day." The song ends and another starts up but we stay in our own private little bubble for a little longer. I know I need it and I hope that it's comforting for Makenna and Caleb as well.

"Love you too, Logan." Makenna mumbles into my shoulder.

"Love you too, big guy." Caleb says as he thumps me on the back. All three of us with tears in our eyes.

"They loved Jules and they would have been so damned happy about today, you know that, right?" Makenna says quietly.

"They would be proud of you, Logan. We're *all* proud of you. You're an amazing brother." Caleb says, as the song changes to another again and other people start to fill the makeshift dance floor.

"Thank you." I kiss Makenna on the cheek and hand her off to her husband, who takes her in his arms and they slow dance. I grab Caleb by the shoulders and leave a big sloppy kiss on his cheek before he can move away from me. He wipes his cheek clean as he gives me a dirty look, and I know it was more than worth it! I don't know for sure that what either of them said is true but I'd like to at least believe that my parents would have been happy if they were here today.

As I watch Caleb slink off to the bar set up on one side of the marquee, I turn to look for my husband so that I can wrap him up in my arms and take on some of his strength, I don't have to look very far.

"Hi Sweets, how are you doing?" He asks, as he takes my hand in his, placing one on his lower back and the other on his shoulder, he then places his hands on me in the same way, so that we're in an easy slow dancing kind of hold.

"I couldn't be better." I say and I know it's true. Especially now that my *husband* is in my arms.

"Are you sure?" I love that he's concerned but I want to wipe his worries away. Today is about happiness.

"Absolutely. Do I wish my parents were here to help us celebrate? Of course I do! I'd be lying if I said anything else but the fact is, they can't be but that doesn't take away how happy I am today. You've made me a happy man today, Julian Drake."

"You've made me a happy man today too, Logan Bishop." His smile couldn't get any wider and we both laugh at our inside joke. People have asked all day, and leading up to the day, who will be taking whose last name. Neither of us are taking the others name, it's a tradition that doesn't feel necessary to either of us. I would have been happy if Makenna had stayed a

Drake but I'm just as happy that she's chosen to become a Harris because it was *her* choice.

The rest of the night is a blur of talking to our guests, dancing, a few speeches that neither of us wanted or expected and of me asking how long was polite to hang around our own party. All I really wanted after being social with so many people at once, was to take my husband back to our home and have my wicked way with him.

"It would be rude to leave just yet, Sweets." Jules would say every time I asked him and every time I argued.

"But it's *our* party, surely that means we can leave whenever we choose?" Jules would laugh and then move on to talk with someone else, leaving me to follow him because I wasn't going anywhere without him. Not tonight, hopefully not ever.

"You know, you're allowed to unglue yourself from Jules for a minute or two, right?" Caleb my ever smart brother says beside me.

"Did you need something, Caleb?" Not hiding my irritation but that just makes him laugh.

"Yeah, I do actually, if you can tear yourself away from your new husband for a few minutes?" He raises an eyebrow at me in question and I'm trying to work out what happened to the sweet little boy he *used* to be.

"He grew up and went through some shit, Logan, that's what happened to him."

"I didn't realise I asked that out loud." I say, absolutely shocked that I did.

"You didn't, the question was written all over your face. Can we talk for a few minutes, please?"

"Can't this wait until tomorrow, Caleb?" I know he wouldn't be asking me to step away from Jules today if it wasn't important, especially today but I'm not going easily. When he just stands there, waiting for me, I lean in and whisper in Jules' ear that I'll be back.

"Everything OK?"

"Yeah, Caleb wants to talk to me about something. I'll be back soon." I kiss his temple and drop my hand from his back and turn to Caleb. "Lead the way." I wave a hand in between us, indicating I will follow him and he turns, leading us out of the marquee, back into the garden where we were taking photos earlier. I should be surprised to see Makenna and Brady already standing there waiting for us but I'm not.

"OK, what's this about guys?" I'm suddenly nervous about what they want to talk about and I wish that Jules was standing beside me, I could do with the support.

"It's nothing bad, relax, Logan!" Caleb says, rolling his eyes at my obvious discomfort. "You always think the worst, you should relax a little. I really thought marrying Jules would help you chill out a bit, man!"

"Shut up, Caleb, he doesn't know why we want to talk to him, if it was you in this very situation, you'd be stressed out too!" Brady points out and Caleb seems to understand what he means. I'm glad someone does.

"What the fuck is going on?" I demand. "I'd like to get back inside to my husband, I plan on getting out of here as soon as I can."

"We'll be quick, I promise Logan." Makenna tried to reassure me but they're still not spilling the beans, so I wave my hand at her to move it along. "You remember that Pauline and Jeremy gave us a gift from them and our parents at our wedding?" I nod, not understanding where she's going with this. "Well, we weren't the only ones that our parents thought about before they died, in fact, they had a few things still left up their sleeves that we didn't know about until about a week ago." She takes a deep breath and looks at Brady, who squeezes her hand in encouragement.

"Boy, did they have surprises we didn't know about!" Caleb mumbles, earning him a dirty look from both Makenna and Brady.

"The lawyer only read out part of their wills when they died, Logan. He was instructed not to read out the rest until we were ready, until we needed to know."

"OK, what does this have to do with me and today?" I'm confused as all hell. "Your gift was from both sets of parents, the Harris' knew about it and they're the ones who put it all in motion. I'm pretty sure that the Bishops' didn't have any contact with our parents before they died, so we can rule that out." I'm pretty confident that I'm right but by the looks on their faces, might not be.

"I have to admit, your parents were something else." Brady sounds like he admires them for their efforts.

"Apparently Dad was determined to get to know the Bishops. Almost as determined as you seemed to be to keep them away from everyone."

"I wasn't ..." I start but I'm stopped by Harold talking behind me.

"No-one said you were hiding us, Logan but your father was *very* insistent about getting to know us, without letting either of you know about it." Harold, Susan and Jules join our group.

"What do you mean?"

"He called us out of nowhere one day and asked to meet up." Susan says with a kind smile. "He told us that even though you boys thought you were being discreet, he could see the love between the two of you and April agreed with him. They wanted to get know us and see where Julian had come from."

"Jack wanted to know that Julian was good enough for you, Logan." I let out a snort that's not quite laughter and draw Jules into my side.

"If anyone should have been worried about who was good enough for their son, it should have been you guys, not my parents."

"I don't agree with you, Logan but we'll agree to disagree." Harold smiles at me kindly. "Anyway, we shared a few meals with April and Jack before they passed away and we were all pretty sure you two would end up right here, where you are today. Married and happy, so we wanted to do something for you but knew you wouldn't take any money from us, not to help with the wedding or your lives together. We weren't wrong, I mean you asked your guests to donate to charity in place of gifts today."

"We have everything we need." Jules tells his Dad simply.

"So, tell me, what did the four of you come up with then?" My curiosity getting the better of me.

"A honeymoon." Susan announces proudly.

Chapter Forty-five
JULES

"A honeymoon." Susan announces proudly. "Of sorts, anyway."

"What the hell does that mean?" Logan demands, I almost pull him up on his sharp tone but my Mum happily barrels on like he didn't speak.

"We knew you pair wouldn't be impressed with a cash donation of any kind, towards the wedding or honeymoon, so we decided that we would be best to book you something ourselves." Her smile wavers and tears well in her eyes and she takes a breath to continue, my Dad taking her hand in his. "When your parents were killed in that terrible accident, we didn't know what to do about the plans that we'd made together but their lawyer called us and explained that they had written up stipulations for 'just in case' they weren't around for this beautiful event."

"What do you mean?" Logan's voice is barely more than a raspy breath.

"They left a trust, son, that Susan and I had access to, so that our plans could go ahead." Dad explains.

"Jesus Christ!" Logan mutters, I have to say, I agree with him, this is shocking.

"So, Makenna, you said they had secrets, is this it? The one where we've got separate trusts for weddings or honeymoons?"

"I guess so. I mean, I was going to tell you that they had a trust set up for all of us, Caleb included but I had no idea that the Bishop's were involved at *all*." She shakes her head. "I think that came as a shock to all of us?" It's a question, not a statement.

"Don't look at me, I had no clue either." Caleb protests. Then all eyes move to look at me.

"Nope, no clue here. I'm as shocked and surprised as the rest of you that our parents not only met but concocted this plan."

"Well, we're not taking the money, we don't need it." Logan protests. "I don't care what you do with it, leave it in a trust for Makenna's or Caleb's kids, put it into Drake Wines but we're not using it for us."

"The trip is already booked." Dad states. "We didn't go all out and decide to send you to Sandy Cove or anything. It's a simple house, right on the shore of the beach for a week of rest and relaxation for you *both*. I think you've both earned a break, don't you?"

"They sure have." Makenna agrees. "You know you do, Logan. You already know that we have everything under control here because you *were* going away for a couple of nights anyway. Just go and enjoy the break. Isn't that what you said at *our* wedding?"

"I'll think about it." He looks at me and seems to realise his mistake. "What I mean to say is, we'll talk about it and make a decision."

"I'm with Logan. This is a lot to take in, I think the least we can ask for is the night to sleep on it." I eye *both* of my parents, we'll be having words in private later. I can't believe they kept all of this from me. "For now, let's go back to the party, I'm sure our guests are wondering where we've all disappeared off to."

Everyone else moves to walk back to the marquee, including Logan until I don't move making him stop in his tracks because he still has my hand in his.

"Do you want to talk about it?"

"What? Now? No, not really. I mean what do you want to say Jules? My parents went behind my back and I just don't know how I feel about it to be honest. I wish I'd known about all of this when they died or at least before today."

"Would it have made any difference?"

"What do you mean? A difference to what?" He's confused, I can see that but I don't know how he doesn't know what I mean.

"Them knowing. Your parents." I start. "They knew about us, Logan. It's not just something that you've heard from Makenna and Caleb, that they knew and accepted our relationship. This is evidence of the fact that they understood that we've always been ... more."

"I don't know." I knew he'd answer me honestly. "I guess this whole day might have happened sooner. I wouldn't have been an idiot and you wouldn't have walked away because of it." He smirks, trying to lighten the mood. "But the honest truth, Love, is that I have no fucking idea. I can't tell you what would have happened in the past if things had been different. It makes no sense to me to try guess either. It's not what happened, *this* is what happened and I wouldn't change any of that if it meant I didn't end up here. Married to you, the love of my life and having you being a part of my family. Would I have liked it to happen sooner? Sure, I guess so but no, I don't think it makes any fucking difference at all. You want to know why?" I nod yes because I don't think I can speak. "Because I would have ended up fighting for you, anyway. You were always meant to be mine, Love, I'm just sorry I put you through the pain I did to get here."

"I didn't mean to rehash all of that, Sweets."

"I know but it is what it is, Love." He shrugs like it doesn't hurt both of us a little bit still. "I'll spend the rest of our lives making up for it, I promise but right now, I think we need to get back inside. I need to know when we can leave the party and the only way to know that is to go inside. I mean, we could run now but we both know that Makenna will find us and bring us back, then make us stay longer."

"Let's go then." I agree, letting him take my hand and lead me back inside the marquee, where we stay for another hour before Makenna announces that it's time for us to leave. I swear I hear Logan sigh *and* growl in relief. He can stand in a room full of men and women talking about business, without blinking an eye but socialising like he has today? That he finds draining!

I hug my parents goodbye. "We'll talk at dinner tomorrow night." It's both a warning and a reminder.

After a round of goodbyes we leave the marquee to a round of well wishes that are equally filthy as they are sweet, and we're both laughing by the time we reach the house. Logan takes a key out of his breast pocket and I raise my eyebrow in question.

"I locked the house before I left so that Caleb and Gavin couldn't get in here to do anything weird." I huff out a laugh at his innocence because if those two guys wanted to get in here to do something, nothing as simple as a locked door was going to stop them!

He closes the door behind me and then I'm pressed up against it.

"I need you." He breathes as he takes my lips with his. "I need you right fucking now. Husband." That last word is growled but the rest of them are said softly against my mouth.

"Yes, Logan!" Is all I can manage because even just a kiss from him scrambles my brain. The next thing I know, we're in our bedroom and I'm not even sure how he got us here.

"How the hell?" Logan's exclamation draws my eyes to look around room, rather than stare at his handsome face.

"Oh wow!" I knew those boys would find a way in if they really wanted to!

"When the fuck did they find the time to do *this*?" I can answer Logan's question because as I look around the room, I know it couldn't have been *just* those two who did this, they simply hadn't had the time. "They didn't do this alone."

"Leila!" We say at the same time because she's the only one that would have had the time to set up this many candles and rose petals without anyone noticing she was missing. I'm guessing she did it because Caleb asked her to though, which I'm going to distract Logan from thinking about tonight.

"Does it matter? It's done now, Sweets." I pull on his hand until his attention is back on me and see the annoyance on his face replaced with love and lust. "Jacket. Take it off." I demand and I see the heat flare in his eyes as he strips out of his new suit jacket, placing it on the chair that happens to be beside us. I could stand here and look at him in that sexy as fuck vest all night but in truth, I want him naked more than I want him in that vest.

He doesn't wait for further instructions, he starts stripping out of the gorgeous black suit, his eyes never straying from mine. "Get to it, Julian. I want you naked and waiting for me." He demands and now the tables have turned. I love it!

The only sound in the room, is our heavy breathing and the wispy sound of clothing being removed. When we're both completely naked, we take a minute to just drink each other in.

"You are the sexiest man I know." Logan tells me, as his eyes roam across every inch of my body.

"You're not too bad yourself." I laugh, until I see the flash of annoyance flash across his face. Most people would miss it but not someone who watches him all the time. The next thing I know, I'm turned around and pinned against the wall.

"I'll show you not too bad, Julian. Bathroom, now!" It's a hot promise, spoken with determination against my ear as he presses his front to my back, while running his hands down my back and spreading my cheeks for easy access to my hole but he doesn't touch me where I want him to and my hips buck, my body wanting more. "Am I still, *not too bad,* Julian?"

"You're everything, Logan. I need you, now." I beg, not even trying to hide how much I want him. He pushes me to the shower and as steam fills the room, the water isn't the only thing getting hot.

"Don't move. Keep your hands on the wall, unless I tell you otherwise." I groan in protest but do what I'm told anyway.

He presses his front to my back even tighter, which pushes his cock between my legs, rubbing me from my arse crack through to the balls and back again, making me groan loudly. I press my legs together, hoping to create more friction, grateful for the slip from the lube he's already rubbed on himself. I'm not sure when he had time to do it but he did.

His thumb slips into my hole, and his fingers slip around my balls, not coming close enough to even graze my cock. "I'm not going to touch your cock and neither are you." His voice rumbles in my ear, making me shiver, as the little hairs all over my body stand to attention. "Do you think you can come without me touching you?"

"Wh-what?" I stammer out, not really understanding the question. "You *are* touching me."

"Not where you want me to though, am I?" He grinds his hips into my backside and my hips push back without conscious thought from me. His hands roam over my chest and when they reach my pecs, he pauses for a second, then pinches both of my nipples at the same time.

"Fuck!" It's more of a groan than a word!

"That's the plan, Love." He says, while slipping his hand down my side. When he reaches the globe of my arse, he squeezes it. Hard, making me stretch up onto my toes. He spreads my cheeks pressing his finger back into my hole. My head drops back, resting on his shoulder at the sensation. His cock is still sliding between my legs, slowly, deliberately causing *just* enough friction to make my cock stand to attention. My hand moves from the wall, with the clear intent of wrapping a fist around my aching cock. "No touching, Julian!" He grounds out the demand in my ear, while grinding his hips into me.

I jump at his demand but force my hand to move up to take a hold of his neck, my other hand joining in when he doesn't tell me off. I use my position to draw his mouth down to my neck. Dropping my head to the side to give him better access, he does exactly what I wanted him to. He leaves a light bite on my skin, before licking the sting of it away.

"Logan." I ground out in a low, long growl, that honestly I'm not even sure *is* a word at all.

His hands move back to my chest, playing with my nipples, pinching them lightly, while his cock rubs between my legs in an unrelenting, constant rhythm, driving me insane with desire and the need for release. My cock is throbbing and not being able to grip it in my fist to relieve the tension is almost painful.

"Are you ready to come yet, Love?"

"Fuck yes!" I yell.

"Then come for me Julian. Now."

Without another thought I obey his command and come all over the shower wall, my balls emptying harder than I think they ever have. It's until I stop and look down that I realise that Logan's coming between my legs and against the wall as well.

It's the hottest thing I think I've ever seen!

Chapter Forty-six
LOGAN

After cleaning each other and the shower down, we pull back the covers and climb into bed. We're lying in each other arms, chest to chest, legs entwined just enjoying the peace and comfort of each other.

"So, what do you think?" Jules asks. I can feel him looking at me but I keep my eyes closed. I know what he's talking about but I want to enjoy this state of blissfulness before we get into all of *that*!

"About what, Love?" He sighs in frustration because he knows that I know what he means. "Can we not, Jules? Can't we just lie here and enjoy being married for a while *before* I have to digest and think about what my parents have done? What *our* parents did. It's not like your parents are innocent in all of this, either."

"So." He kisses my chest and I can feel his smile on my skin. "You don't want to talk about it yet?"

"No, Love, I truly don't. I want to enjoy our first night together as husbands, not dredge up whatever the hell my parents thought they were doing and the fact that they and your parents kept it all a secret."

"To be fair to the four of them, we were keeping secrets too." I feel his head tilt to look at my face as he pulls away from my chest but I refuse to open my eyes. I'm fucking exhausted.

"Don't Julian. Please." I sigh, knowing I'm being a grumpy arsehole but I just can't. "Not tonight, please. Let's just enjoy us. Just for one night, please? I want to forget that everyone else exists."

"But you'll talk to me about it in the morning?" There's something in the tone of voice that isn't quite hope but I'm not sure what else to call.

"Yes but for now, tonight, it's just us, OK? I seriously need to forget everyone else exists." I grumble.

"Ohh did the poor grumpy bear have to socialise too much today?" He teases.

"You can mock me all you like, Mr Drake but I made you come all over the shower and I'll make you come again later but for now, we sleep."

"I love you, Mr Bishop." He says, smiling against my lips after kissing me lightly.

"I love you too, Jules." My kiss is a little less gentle than his and I leave him gasping for breath. "Now, get some sleep, you're going to need some rest."

"Promises, promises." He jokes as he snuggles in closer to me. "Just us, I promise." He whispers and I finally smile again.

If only we knew what we would wake up to, I might have chosen to have the simple conversation about parents *before* we went to sleep!

I WAKE UP TO THE SUN shining through a gap in the curtains and can't help wondering why there's always a gap when the sun is shining brightly? Maybe that's just when we notice it the most? Who knows but I wake up with a beam of sunshine stretching across the bed, a smile stretching across my face and Jules' tight arse in my crotch.

Running my hand over his hips makes them buck back into me. "Logan." He moans. He's still mostly asleep and this automatic reaction to my touch is something I can't help but enjoy.

"Right here, Love." I murmur in his ear where my lips are resting. "I'm right here."

"Mmmm ..." He moans without opening his eyes. I push my arm under his neck and wrap it around his chest so that I can play with his nipple. My other hand skims over his hip to his cheeks, where I squeeze one and part them for easy access. I slide my cock between his cheeks and he pushes back, begging for more. I take my hand away from him and reach behind me for the lube. I pop open the lid with my thumb and squeeze some over my already hard cock. When I'm done with my cock, I squirt some onto his hole and massage it in for a few seconds, pushing my finger past the initial resistance.

"Fuck!" Jules mutters, pushing back against my hand.

"That's the plan, Love." I say, kissing the back of his neck and smiling. I throw the bottle lube behind me somewhere and ask, "Do I need a condom, Julian?"

"No."

"Are you sure?" We've had unprotected sex before but I really don't want to move away from the heat and sweetness of his body to find one.

"Make love to me Logan." That's all the invitation and confirmation I need. My hand reaches down and pulls his cheeks apart, giving me easy access to his hole and I push the head of my lubed up cock inside, where my fingers were just a few seconds ago. "Logan." My name is more a moan than a word and I love it, I love *him*.

"Play with yourself, Love. Make yourself come with me." I watch as he wraps a hand around his hard cock and we both groan. Our movements though are slow, easy, almost lazy. It's the morning after our wedding and we're in no hurry.

"Logan, Sweets."

"I'm right here." I remind him, squeezing a nipple between my fingers and looking over his shoulder to watch him squeeze his cock a little harder. I bite that shoulder and his entire body shakes.

"Logan." My name is a quiet whisper and I know he's about to come.

"Come for me Jules. Come for me now." I whisper. "Then I can come."

"Come with me Logan, now." We both give two more pumps and then we're groaning out each other's names.

We lie there in the silent comfort of each other's arms for minutes, hours, I don't know and I don't fucking care. This is the first day of married life and I'm not rushing it for anyone.

"I need to clean up, Sweets." I growl when he starts to move, tightening my hold on him. "Seriously Logan, I'm a mess and I need to clean up."

"Just a few more minutes, please?" I beg and he laughs at me.

"One minute, Sweets, then I'm getting up." He warns.

"I'll get you up." I warn myself, making him laugh loudly this time as he throws his head back, resting it on my shoulder.

"You are unbelievable!" He admonishes me but I know he loves it and I know he loves *me*.

'I love you, Jules." I murmur as I leave light, sloppy kisses down his back.

"I love you too, Logan but I'm getting up to have a shower now." I let him up and watch as he walks away from me. "Feel free to come join me." That's all the invitation I need. I throw back the covers that are covering me and jump to my feet. I follow after him and find him already under the steaming hot water.

Much to my disappointment, we're drying ourselves much earlier than I wanted to be because Jules stopped me at the pass every time I tried to initiate something *more*. Telling me that we have other things to do and people to see. He just rolled his eyes at me when I said that I didn't care about the other things *or* the other people and pushed me out of the bathroom.

"Get dressed." He commands.

"This *isn't* how I planned on spending our first day as husbands you know." I pout, trying to get him to feel bad enough that he'd back out of all these supposed obligations but he doesn't. Just like I knew he wouldn't, he's nothing if not responsible and it's one of the things I love the most about him.

"I know but we've got the rest of our lives together to spend them however the hell we want."

"Then let's start how we intend to finish." I suggest, grabbing hold of his hips and pulling him over to me, where I kiss him so indecently that if we'd had an audience they would have insisted on hosing us down. Or leaving. God how I wish everyone would just leave us alone. "We should have done what Makenna and Brady did and left for a honeymoon straight away."

"We're not really *having* a honeymoon though, are we Sweets?"

"We are now, according to our parents." I follow Jules out to the kitchen but instead of him going in to the kitchen, I steer him towards the couch. "Sit. I'll make us both a coffee and decide what we're having for breakfast." He rolls his eyes at me but he does as he's told, which is miracle in itself.

I make the coffee and when I open the fridge to get some milk, I see a stack of plastic boxes with notes on them.

Breakfast for the day after. Love Leila xx

I can't help a quiet, short snort of laughter that escapes me. This girl, woman, is something else. Every container has a note and minimal instructions on it.

"What's so funny?"

"Leila. She's put a few days' worth of food in the fridge for us and each one has a note on it. All of which end with a 'Love Leila', tag."

"She's good people that one."

"I couldn't agree more." I hand him his coffee and sit down next to him on the couch. "So, let's talk."

"About?" He hides his smirk behind his mug.

"Don't be difficult, Love, you know about what!" He laughs at my raised eyebrow, that skilfully accompanies a frown.

"Alright, don't get your knickers in a twist!" He laughs as he puts his mug on the coffee table and I do the same. Then we turn to face each other, each of us taking our time to think about what to say next.

"I think we should take it." Jules says with a cautious smile.

"I think we should go with it." I say at the same time.

"Are you sure?"

"They meant well, even if I wish that they'd gone about things differently, we can't change anything now."

"And you're OK with being away from Drake Wines for so long?"

"It's a week, Jules. I know Makenna and Caleb have things under control here. What they don't, Margot and Leila do."

"Yes, but you, let's face it, Sweets, I love you completely but you're, shall we say, controlling. Especially around here. You like to be in charge and you like to know what's going on."

"I can live without it for a week."

"So, you'll be checking in every day then?"

"Maybe." I smile at him because he knows better than I know myself.

"So, that's a definite yes, of course, Jules." We're both laughing at just how right he is when there's a knock at the door. As I stand up to answer it, I hear a message come through on my phone from Caleb, which makes us laugh even harder. I don't bother to look at the message before heading to the door.

"Nice to know that you can learn from your mistakes, Caleb." I say, still laughing as I open the door. My laughter dies a sudden death when I see who it is. "Lori?"

"Yeah, not Caleb, sorry to disappoint you, Logan." She answers with a warm smile. "I guess he's still the annoying little brother, hmm?"

"Umm what?"

"Well, you said as you opened the door that you're glad he's learned his lesson. I'm guessing he walks in unannounced and catches you in positions no-one wants to be caught in. Am I right?"

"Ahh yes, you are, actually." I stammer out. "What – what are you doing here?" I look back over my shoulder, surprised that Jules hasn't made his way over here to see who it is yet.

"Can I come in please? We really need to talk and I think this is something your husband might be interested in hearing as well." The shock of my ex-girlfriend standing at my door is one thing but her knowing that I got married and to a *man* is something else entirely.

"Sure, come on in." I say as I step aside to allow her to go past me and enter the house.

"Congratulations, by the way."

"Thanks." Is all I can manage as she comes face to face with Jules. My past and my present colliding in a way I never fucking imagined.

"Hi." She says, smiling warmly at Jules. "I'm Lori."

"Hi Lori, I'm Jules." He shakes her offered hand and smiles warmly back her.

"My husband. Julian that is, he's my husband. We got married yesterday." I do not know why I felt the need to tell her all of that. It's not like I owe her an explanation, it's been a hell of a long time since she dumped my arse and left school.

"I know. Congratulations to you both." Her smiles lights up as she looks between both of us, as we naturally gravitate towards each other and I wrap my arm around Jules' waist to anchor myself. "I'm so glad you're happy Logan. I'm very happy that you found the right person to be with and found yourself along the way."

"Thank you." I say again, my own voice sounding weird and stilted even to me. There are a few beats of awkward silence before Jules speaks up.

"Can I get you a drink Lori? Coffee? Tea? Water? Anything at all?" He offers, ever the host and polite one of the two of us. Me, I would have just stared at her until she spoke again.

"I wouldn't mind a drink of water, thanks Julian." She replies, her smile still warm and friendly.

"Coming right up." He pulls out of my embrace, leaving Lori and I standing there looking at each other awkwardly.

"Why don't we sit down?" I suggest, pointing in the direction of the living room and the couches.

"Thanks." She sighs and for the first time since she got here a few minutes ago, I realise she looks really tired. "It's really good to see you, Logan." She smiles as she sits down in one of the armchairs, leaving the couch for Jules and I to sit on.

"It's a surprise to see you, Lori, I have to admit." I smile at her, trying to soften my bluntness but she just laughs.

"Logan!" Jules hisses at me, before handing over a bottle of water to Lori. "Here you go, Lori, I'm sorry about him, he's not quite housebroken." I grunt and the two of them have a chuckle.

"It's OK, Jules, I know what he's like and it looks like he hasn't changed too much, just gotten a little more bear like."

"Of course you do." Jules says quietly and I groan. Could this *be* anymore awkward.

I watch as she struggles to open the bottle, so I take it from her, open it and hand it back.

"Thanks."

"Are you OK, Lori? I'm sorry if I've made you nervous or uncomfortable."

"It's not you, Logan, it's just a side effect of my treatment."

"Treatment? For what?" I ask, even though I'm not sure I want to know the answer.

"Cancer." The silence that comes after that bombshell is something else. I don't think I've ever seen Jules so still or heard him so quiet.

"I'm sorry, Lori." I tell her truthfully. I liked Lori at lot , she's an amazing person.

"Right then. I think I'll leave you two to talk." He starts to stand up but Lori stops him.

"I'd like you to stay, please, Julian. If that's OK with you, Logan? With *both* of you actually?" She looks between us, waiting for an answer that neither of us give her but Jules does sit back down on the couch next to me. "Thank you for staying Jules. I think it will be easier if we're all involved and I know I've turned up out of nowhere, the day after your wedding no less but to be fair, I *have* been trying to get a hold of you for months, Logan." I nod in acknowledgement of the messages and missed calls from her recently. "Honestly, I don't have the time to waste and what I have to tell you, will genuinely effect you both, so it makes sense to tell you together. Plus, like I said, I don't have time to kill here, so I'd rather have one conversation today, than many over the course of days."

"Sure." Jules and I say at once. "I'm sorry Lori. I'm sorry for not answering your calls or messages and I'm sorry that you're sick." I add on.

"It's OK, Logan, I understand. It's not like you were expecting me to call *and* I didn't answer your calls and messages back in the day." She waves away my apology. "I completely understand that you were wondering why the hell your ex was suddenly blasting you from everywhere. Not to mention, you were a little busy the past few months." She smiles at Jules again.

"We have been slightly busy. I screwed up, I had to make amends, then there was a crazy neighbour and then a wedding." I reach out and take Jules' hand in mine.

"But it's nowhere close to what you've had to deal with." Jules says, making me feel like an arse for listing off all the things we've had to deal with recently because none of them can compare to Lori's illness.

"It's all perspective Jules. We're all busy in our ways and we all have our own things to deal with." Lori says, taking a sip of her water, before placing it back on the table. She takes a deep breath before speaking again. "OK guys. Let's get to it, I think the easiest and fastest way to do this is the old fashioned way. Rip off the bandage and get straight to the damn point!"

"That would be preferable, Lori." I tell her, suddenly feeling nervous. I never feel nervous or unsure but I get this feeling that whatever she has to say, will change our lives. She didn't come here just to tell us she's sick, there's no reason for it. "Do you need anything? Can we make you more comfortable?"

"No, I'm fine but thank you for asking. You always have been kind and very thoughtful, if a little grumpy and growly." Lori laughs and when Jules joins her, I frown at them both, which just causes them to laugh at little more.

"OK, enough laughing at my expense, what is it you need to tell us Lori? I'm guessing you didn't come out here just to tell me you're not well. It's not like you have anything to make up for. Me? That would be a different story, according to you two anyway."

"I have a daughter, Logan." Lori says, suddenly very serious.

"I'm happy for you but what does that have to do with me?" I ask confused as hell as to where she's going with this. I know she doesn't have a lot of family but she has her Mum and I know she kept in contact with Jenni after she left school.

"She's almost eight years old." She says, looking at me pointedly.

"OK."

"She's almost *eight* Logan. *Think* about it!" She repeats and just as I'm about to repeat *myself*, I suddenly understand what she's trying to say!

"You mean ...?" I manage to stutter out.

"Yes."

"Ohhhhh." It finally registers with me. "Oh fuck me!" I knew I shouldn't have thought that this would be a nice, easy, simple kind of day.

"Well, yeah, that's how it happened." She cracks a smile and I see the old Lori, from eight or so years ago in her face for a few seconds. "I need your help."

"Anything." I say without hesitation.

Chapter Forty-seven
JULES

It feels like Logan and Lori are having a private, silent conversation between them. It's like I'm not even in the damned room! I have no clue what the relevance of Lori's daughter age has to do with anything but if we can help her and her daughter out, I know we will.

"Are either of you going to explain why the age Lori's daughter has any relevance here?" I look between the two of them, neither of them breaking eye contact with each other, that conversation still happening. "Logan?" When he doesn't answer me I try to get Lori's attention. "Lori? Someone? Anyone? One of you better start fucking explaining!" I yell, making them both jump.

"You and I, we've been together for what? Just over six years, right?" Logan asks, without looking at me.

"You mean me?" I ask, knowing I'm being snippy but he can't even fucking *look* at me!

"Of course!" He snaps.

"Well, it's kind of hard to tell who you're talking to when you seem to only have eyes for one person in the room and that sure as fuck isn't me."

"I'm sorry Jules but I'm trying to understand what's going on myself *and* explain it to you. You need to give me a few minutes to get this clear in my own head, Love."

"Except that you *and* Lori seem to understand the significance here and I'm the one left wondering what the fuck is going on." I take a breath because I realise I've become a little out of control. "I mean, of course Lori understands what's going on but I wouldn't mind being brought into the loop too."

"Are you sure?" Lori nods once. "One hundred percent? Because I'm not explaining this to Jules only for this to not be what I think it is."

"I couldn't be more sure, Logan." She sighs. "I know this isn't the best timing but you left me no other choice when you didn't respond to any other communication. I'm running out of time." He nods once her way and then speaks to me, still not breaking eye contact with her. I shouldn't but I feel completely jealous of the connection they appear to have.

"So, you and I have been together for just over six years, right Love?" I nod, even though he's not looking at me, I know he can see the movement out of the corner of his eye. "And we met about a year after I finished school, where in my final year, I was in a relationship with Lori."

"Yes, I knew you were dating women back then and I knew that Lori was your last *girl*friend." I confirm, still not understanding what he's getting at.

"That final year, Lori left mid-year after breaking up with me, telling me that she wasn't the person for me. I guess she knew what I was trying to not understand about myself back then."

"I knew I wasn't your type, yes." She smirks as she agrees. "I went home for break and found out I was pregnant and I never returned to classes." She explains.

"So, who is your daughter's father?" I ask, although I think I finally understand why she's here.

"I am." Logan says, his voice full of shock and certainty all at one. "Aren't I?"

"Yes." Lori nods once and tears form in her eyes because she knows what the next question is and I know it's going to be hard for Logan to hear.

"Are you sure?" I ask, before Logan can form the question he wants to ask.

"Yes." She answers simply, pulling her gaze away from Logan's and looking at me for the first time since she dropped her bombshell.

"Holy shit!" I mumble under my breath. "Well, there's a wedding present I wasn't expecting!" I say and Lori laughs awkwardly but Logan hasn't moved a muscle beside me. "Logan."

"It's OK, Jules. It's a lot to take in and I understand his shock." Lori makes to stand up. "I'll leave you to digest that for a while. You call me when you're ready to talk some more." She hands Logan a piece of paper with her number on it but when he doesn't reach for it, I take it from her instead. "Thank you." She says quietly. "We're staying in town, so I can be here within twenty or so minutes if you want to chat."

"No." It's the first thing Logan has said since Lori confirmed that he is indeed a father and I have no idea what to say to him.

"I'm sorry? What do you mean, *no?*" Lori demands and it's nice to know that even sick, she'll stand up for herself and her daughter.

"Stay. You'll stay here." Logan announces, before pausing and then asking her, "What do you mean, 'we'?"

"Jenni, Savannah and I are staying in a hotel in the town. It's actually not too far from here."

"Savannah." He says her name on a sigh. "That's her name?" I wonder how he knows her name is Savannah and not Jenni, I don't get the chance to ask because they continue talking.

"Yes." Lori smiles sweetly at me. "Savannah Rae."

"What a gorgeous name, Lori." He chokes out. "Can we meet her?"

"Absolutely."

"Jenni's here?" He sounds so unsure of himself, he's not the man I've always known right now. "Are you sure she doesn't want to kill me?" He laughs but there is no amusement in it.

"She might but she won't. Mainly because I've told her not to but also because she loves Savannah almost as much as I do and she wants what's best for her, which is being with her Dad." Lori explains with a smile and I want to know who this Jenni is and why she'd want to kill my husband. "She's been with us since the very beginning. She helped both of us when my Mum died of a heart attack a few years ago too."

"Did Jenni know why you left school?" Lori looks down at the ground and looks uncomfortable before answering Logan's question.

"Yes."

"And you told her not to tell me?"

"Yes."

"Why? I would have helped you Lori, you know I would have." Logan sounds devastated at the news that Lori made the choice to kept Savannah from him. Lori looks at me, meeting my eyes and not looking away from them as she answers.

"I know. You would have wanted to do the right thing and while that is *very* admirable, I think everyone here can agree that you would have been exceptionally unhappy." She holds her hand up to stop Logan from talking but she's still looking at me. "You would have never met Julian and you wouldn't have found yourself. I know you would have been happy because you had Savannah but that wasn't a life I wanted for you or for me. Or for Savannah to be honest."

"You're right. He was still so skittish when I met him about who he was and how he felt. He would have loved you and Savannah though, in his own way." I smile at Lori, knowing that I've fallen a little in love with the woman that is my husband's ex and mother of his child. I find myself wishing that we had more time together because I think we would have been great friends if given enough time.

"I wanted you to be happy, Logan." She finally takes her eyes off mine and looks at him. "And look at you! You've found the happiness you deserve. A man and a happiness you wouldn't have found if I had told you about my pregnancy."

"Where are you staying?" I ask.

"A hotel in town, why?"

"Tell your friend, Jenni, is it? To pack up your things, you're coming to stay here." I tell her, jumping up from my seat. "Gavin and Jilly are leaving today, they can have that cottage, can't they Logan? If not, they can stay here until the cottage is ready for them!" Logan looks at me like a deer caught in the headlights of an oncoming truck and Lori starts to protest. "I know it might be too soon and I get that it might be too overwhelming for Miss Savannah to meet her Dad, as well as me and the rest of the family but you can't stay in a hotel. I won't allow it. You're not well and we can help. Can't we, Logan?"

"I don't think that's a good idea." Lori says, taking in Logan's still shocked expression.

He doesn't answer immediately and Lori takes his silence as confirmation that he doesn't want them here but I know that's not the truth. I know he wants them here, he's just trying to come to terms with the fact that he's a Dad.

Logan's a Dad!

Chapter Forty-eight
LOGAN

I can't believe I'm a Dad!

Savannah Rae.

While I know I should be more than angry with Lori for keeping my daughter from me for so damned long, I also understand why she did. But I also know I can't let her walk out, not now that I know about my daughter and they're *here*!

"Of course! You'll stay here, with us but I'm warning you, my family can be quite overbearing."

"We can't do that to you, Logan, it wouldn't be fair. You and Julian just got married *yesterday* and I've turned up on your doorstep on what I assume is the start of your honeymoon. I didn't come here to just drop into your life and make a mess. Savannah, Jenni and I can stay in town and wait for you guys to get back before we jump into the fray of families and meeting everyone."

"We didn't really have a honeymoon planned anyway." I wave my hand between in dismissal.

"That's not quite true, Logan –" Jules starts and I know where he's going but all of that can wait if it needs to.

"We can postpone that Jules, can't we?" I look at him and I see the flash of hurt my dismissal causes him before his back straightens and his face becomes calm, devoid of all emotions.

"Of course." His voice cold as ice as he continues. "It's not like our parents planned any of it. Savannah and Lori come first, of course."

"No, we don't." Lori insists and I know she saw the change in Jules. "Guys, I just dropped a massive bombshell on you. I think you need to have a talk, without me here, to sort everything out between you. I'm going to go back to the hotel. You've got my number, call me when you want to talk."

"That's not necessary Lori, Logan's made a decision." Jules says sharply and I know I have to talk to him before this gets out of hand.

"Lori, would you like to go up to Vines? Have a coffee, maybe something to eat if you can stomach it?" I plead with her. I want to meet my daughter!

"I don't think that's a good idea." She starts but Jules interrupts her.

"That's a perfect idea. That way, I can go check in on Gavin and Jilly to see what time they plan on leaving and we can sort out a time to get your things over here, along with Savannah and Jenni of course." Jules stands up abruptly. "Yes! Now come on then. Logan, you can walk her over to Vines and get her comfortable. I'll head over to the cottages and have a chat with Gavin."

"Jules." I start but he's already walking towards the door. "*Julian Bishop Drake, stop right where you are!*"

"No, I'm good, thanks!" He says and keeps walking towards the door.

I won't let another misunderstanding cause a problem between us but before I can say anything else, he's already out the door. "Fuck!"

"I'm sorry Logan, I didn't mean for any of this to happen." Lori says quietly. "I should have waited to talk to you until after your honeymoon. I knew you'd guys just got married yesterday and I took the chance that you would still be here today."

"I'm glad you did and so is Jules, he's just annoyed with *me* right now. I screwed up a few months ago and I promised I wouldn't do it again. I screwed up just now by not having the conversation with him that I need to have." I sigh, while taking a deep breath. "Trust me when I say that man wants you, Jenni and Savannah here. He probably wants it more than I do." I laugh, trying to make light on my statement because I feel like it might be true and I want them here very much.

"And what about you? Do you want us here?" I can't believe she needs to ask!

"Of course I do! I want you all here, even Jenni. I know she's helped you take care of Savannah in my absence." I hesitate because I want to ask something but I'm not sure how or if it's appropriate. If Jules was still here, I'd be able to ask for his opinion. Fuck, I have to go to Jules and explain. "I have to ask and you can tell me to fuck off and mind my own business, obviously, I haven't earned the right to question your parenting choices." Lori laughs.

"You weren't given the opportunity to parent, Logan and that's my fault, not yours." The smile drops from her face. "I want you to know that even though *you* might not have known about your daughter's existence, she has *always* known about *yours*. She's always known who you are. What your name is and where you live. I also told her about Julian. Logan, she *knows* who you *are*. I regret not contacting you sooner and I'm sorry that my illness has pushed me into doing this, truly I am, Logan. I wish I wasn't sick. I wish I had a long life ahead of me where I could watch you and Savannah get to know each other but I don't. I'm not even sure how long I have left and while that scares the absolute hell out of me, knowing that you're here to look after her, to bring our daughter up, that makes me feel better."

"Can I ask a question?" I hesitate because I don't know how this is going to go down.

"Of course. You can ask any questions you want." She smiles at me and it's warm, loving.

"Why tell me now? I mean, I understand *why,* I do but why not give Jenni custody? It makes sense. She's helped you all these years, she knows Savannah and she knows how you would want her bought up. So, why now? Why tell me now?" Lori lets out a quiet laugh.

"Jenni *loves* Savannah, truly she does and don't get me wrong, we discussed the idea after my Mum died and I was first diagnosed." She sighs but the smile doesn't leave her face. "The truth is, you're her Dad and when it comes down to it, she deserves to know you and to have one biological parent in her life. As for Jenni, let's just say she enjoys being able to hand Sav back at the end of the day and not have all the responsibility on her shoulders."

"So, I'm not going to end up in some crazy custody battle with Jenni?"

"No, you won't. Unless something happens to you, Jenni wants to stay the 'fun aunt' who can still visit her favourite niece." She looks down at her hands and plays with her fingers. "Your name is on her birth certificate. She's a Drake, Logan." It takes me a minute to understand what she means.

"I'm sorry? What does that mean?" I'm not a dense man, I run a pretty successful business and have meetings with people all over the damned world but this one sentence? I don't completely understand it the first time I hear it. "Did you just say, she's a Drake?"

"Yes. I put your name on her birth certificate and gave her your last name, against Jenni's advice." She smirks but I can't quite comprehend what she's telling me. "Legally, your daughter's name is Savannah Rae Drake." She says quietly but clearly so I don't miss a damned thing.

"But how? Don't I need to sign something?"

"Not really. I mean I can *name* her anything I want to but your signature would make it one hundred percent official. That you're her father that is, her name is her name."

"I can't believe that."

"I'm sorry, Logan, I know it's a lot to take in and you just got married yesterday and that means you obviously have plans, for today, tomorrow and the future but I need this from you. I need to know that she's safe. I have no-one else and even though you might think the only reason I'm here, telling you that you have a daughter is because I'm dying, I want you to know, to understand, that while that's the motivation behind the *urgency*, I also had every intention of being here. Of telling you the truth about our daughter. Unfortunately, I *am* dying. I don't have many weeks left and I want to know that you two have each other. That Savannah has her dad."

"And Julian." I say, because I need her to understand that I'm a package deal. "You don't just get me anymore Lori, in fact, in the last six years you would have never gotten *just* me, I've been a package deal for a long time. It's official now."

"I know and that's why I'm here rather than trying to call, message and email you anymore. Besides my time constraints, I think it was time that you knew. You're more settled now. You know who you are and who you love. I know you'll still do the right thing all these years later but it will be the *right,* right thing, if that makes any sense at all?" She smiles, a nice warm, comforting smile and I feel guilty because she's not the one who should be comforting me. It should be me comforting her! "I'm rambling and you need to go talk to Jules."

"I'll walk you to Vines first." I reach out to help her stand up and she slaps my hand away.

"I'm not quite there yet, Logan but thank you for the offer." She stands up and starts to walk towards the door. "I can walk myself up to the bistro, I don't need a babysitter, Jenni's not here, so I can breathe without her stressing out for a while. You go find Julian and I'll find your brother. He really is the cutest thing. I wonder if he likes older women."

"Lori, I don't think that's appropriate, do you?" She barks out a loud laugh as I close and the lock the door behind us.

"Not for me you idiot, I don't need the complications. I meant for Jenni."

"No. No you cannot set my little brother up with Jenni, I forbid it. No! Anyway, he has his eyes on someone else. Someone not almost a decade older than him or *Jenni!*"

"It's OK Logan, I was joking." She pats me on the arm, it should be condescending but I know it's not. "Caleb's not her type, he's way too cute and sweet for her."

"I agree." I hesitate as we come to the point where we'll have to go in different directions. "How do you know Caleb?"

"How do you think I knew which house was yours?" She laughs and walks towards Vines, leaving me gaping at her retreating back. *That's* when I remember I've got a message from Caleb on my phone that I haven't checked yet because I assumed Lori was Caleb until I opened the door. I pull my phone out of my pocket to read the message.

Caleb: *your ex, Lori? Yeah she's on her way to your place*

Followed very close by a couple more.

Caleb: *you two are decent right? don't roll your eyes, I've seen some things*

Caleb: *ummm are you guys OK? I can't see any movement from Vines*

Caleb: Logan?

Caleb: Logan?

Me: *We're fine thanks for the warning. You should have* called *not sent me a text. I just sent Lori up to Vines for food and a drink, make sure she's looked after*

Caleb: *Roger that. Glad you all survived whatever it is that she needed to see you for*

Me: *We did*

Caleb: *so do I get to know what she wanted?*

I leave my brother's message unanswered and go in search of my husband. I need to find him. We need to have a conversation and I need to apologise.

My phone buzzes with another message from Caleb but I ignore it and bee line for the cottage that Gavin and Jilly are staying in. When I can see it in the distance, I pull out my phone without looking at Caleb's messages and send him another message.

Me: *How quickly can you have a cottage cleaned and ready for new guests?*

Caleb: *an hour tops. Is Lori coming to stay? I only have the 2 cottages ready Logan.*

An hour tops. I can work with that. I put my phone back in my pocket and pick up my pace to get to the cottage faster. My phone is buzzing in my pocket and I know that Caleb has a million questions but he's going to have to wait.

As I approach the cottage, I see Jules standing out the front, staring out at the vineyard that stretches out across the land that my father paid for with blood, sweat and tears. Just the sight of him standing there, *still* here even though I know he's annoyed with me and we have to have this conversation, makes my entire body relax.

"Jules, we need to talk, Love." I come to a stop just behind him. I don't touch him, but I'm a hairs breadth away. I *know* he feels me there. "I'm sorry, Love. I am so fucking sorry that I made you feel like anything other than my partner, my husband in all of this. Can you forgive me?"

Chapter Forty-nine
JULES

"It was a shock." I say simply without turning around to look at him. Instead I continue to look out over the property that his Dad cultivated into the amazing vineyard that stands before me today.

"It certainly wasn't what I was expecting. Any of it."

I can feel him. He's standing so close to me that I can feel his body heat but he's not touching me.

"So, you didn't know Lori was pregnant back then?"

"No."

"You didn't know she'd had a baby since then?" I need to have all the answers to my questions before we go back to Lori. There's no question in my mind that Lori, her daughter, *Logan's daughter,* and their friend will stay here.

"How would I know? I never answered her calls or messages over the years and I didn't accept friend requests when they came later on either. Lori pretty much told you all of that herself just now, Jules." I know but I needed to hear it from *him.*

"Why didn't you answer those messages, calls and requests?"

"Why would I?" Logan sighs behind me and I feel his breath on the back of my neck. "She was in the past, Love. She'd made it abundantly clear when she left school that she didn't want to see or talk to me. Jenni, her friend, made it very clear that Lori had said she didn't want any contact with me ever again."

"Why would she say that? I mean, I understand her explanation, I do and I think we both know she's right. You would have done the right thing, married a woman you loved but weren't *in love* with to give your daughter a home. You would have sacrificed your happiness for theirs and we would have never met."

"Maybe but that's not what happened, Love and I can't be mad at Lori for how she decided to deal with it all." Neither of us have moved, I still haven't looked at him yet. "If she hadn't done things the way she did, I would have never met *you* and I would have missed out on the best thing that's ever happened to me." His lips brush the back of my neck so lightly, I think I might have imagined their touch.

"Wouldn't finding out that you have a daughter be the '*best thing that's ever happened to you*'?" I ask him and I know my jealousy is showing.

"Not if I couldn't share her with you, Love." This time he *does* kiss me lightly. "Julian, Lori means nothing to me. She's right about what she said when we were together. I went through the motions of being with a woman, it wasn't erotic, arousing or even exciting for me and I guess Lori was either the first woman to feel it as well or the first one to actually *do* something about it. Either way, we were friends prior to dating and I'm not going to regret our relationship or Savannah."

"You get the family you always wanted." I whisper, feeling like a jerk for voicing my own fear.

"Even if Lori wasn't sick, Jules, I wouldn't be making a family with her and Savannah. I'd be making a life with Lori and Savannah *in* it but they'd be joining *our* family, Love."

"Are you sure about that? It's easy to say when there's no other option." I know I'm pushing too far but I need to know for sure.

"Look at me, Jules." He waits for a few seconds. "Turn around and look at me Julian."

"So demanding." I huff out, as I turn away from my view of the vineyard to look at him.

"You love it." A smirk spreads across his handsome face and I can't help smiling back at him. "Do I need to remind you that I married *you* yesterday and not just because you were available and willing but because you're sexy, smart, funny, sexy, intelligent, handsome, edible and I love *you*." His hands move from his sides to grip my hips, pulling me in close to him and he rests his forehead on mine. "My past with Lori is just that, the past, Love. Do *we* get the added bonus of gaining a daughter? Yes *we* do. We talked about having a family and well, this isn't the worst way of having one. At least one of us will share DNA with a child." He pulls back to look me in the eyes. "Is that what you're worried about? That she'll be *mine*? Savannah is *our* daughter, Jules and I can't tell you how blessed I'm feeling right now. It's been a crazy twenty four hours to be honest. I married the love of my life after I thought I'd lost him forever, more than once and then we discover we have a daughter."

"What if she doesn't accept me? Us?" I whisper, finally voicing my biggest fear about this entire situation.

"She might take some time, Jules but she's going to love you as much as I do, if not more. It's just going to be an adjustment for her. It's going to be an adjustment for *all* of us but we'll do it together, I promise."

"I love you, Logan." I know my voice is filled with the uncertainty I feel. "We can make this work, right?"

"Of course we can." Then his lips are on mine and he's kissing me until I can barely breathe.

"I know you guys just got married and you've had a pretty decent bombshell dropped on you this morning but you really should try to keep this kind of display to a minimum. There's going to be impressionable young children walking around the property soon, I mean you're *all* going to have to start watching what you say and do." Logan growls at Gavin's words and I can't help laughing at the two of them but before their wedding truce can fall apart, I speak up.

"Gavin, you may not be welcome out here anymore then." I say trying not to smile and Jilly laughs, loudly.

"He's got you there, Babe. Now, let's head home so these guys can get their guests settled." Jilly says, as she slaps him on the shoulder.

"We were their guests up until a few minutes ago." Gavin grumbles at his wife as she pushes him towards their car.

"Thank you for having us. Your wedding was beautiful, congratulations." Jilly says with a smile while Gavin puts their bags in the back of the car. "Good luck with Lori and Savannah as well, Logan." She touches Logan's arm gently and then gives me a sweet smile. "You're both going to do great. Trust me Jules, you are. You're concerned already about how things will work out, that means you care. You'll do an amazing job. Just give her time to adjust."

"Congratulations. On everything." Gavin mumbles as he joins us again.

"Why don't you guys go on up to Vines and grab breakfast on us?" Logan offers and while Gavin's eyes light up, Jilly looks like she's going to protest. "You're leaving early as a favour to me, Jilly, please say you'll take me up on the offer. It will make me feel better about asking you to leave before we could sit down with you guys after the wedding. You were here for Jules and I appreciate that more than you could know. As you know, we got some surprising news this morning and I appreciate you helping us out once again."

"Thank you, Logan, you're a good man. I can see why Julian loves you so much." Jilly gives us both a warm hug.

"I can't but I can appreciate the situation and I sure do appreciate your kind offer." Gavin smiles.

"I'll send Leila a message and she'll sort everything out before you get there." Logan shakes Gavin's hand and I can see the two of them are having a power struggle with a simple handshake! Jilly and I look at each other and roll our eyes.

"OK handsome, come on. You're dick is bigger than Logan's, you win. Let's get out of their hair so they can sort everything they need to, out." Gavin drops Logan's hand, neither of them flinching and walks over to take me into a crushing embrace.

"He better take care of you, or I'll be back here, pounding him into the ground as fertiliser for the very plants he grows." He says so that only the two of us can hear and I laugh, well as much as can when he's squeezed all the oxygen out of my lungs.

"I'll keep that in mind." I cough when he releases me. "Thank you, Gavin. For everything, it meant the world to me to have you by my side yesterday."

"You're welcome." He grins wickedly as he turns towards his car and Jilly. "I'm willing to do it for your next wedding too." He quips as he gets into his car, only for Jilly to hit him on the arm and tell him off.

Much to my surprise, Logan bursts out laughing. "Are you OK?" I ask him, concerned that the events of the last few hours might have finally sent him over the edge of sanity.

"Of course. I know that it looks like I don't like Gavin and perhaps for a while I really didn't but I truly appreciate the friendship and loyalty he shows you without even thinking about it." He pauses. "Do I appreciate the amount he harasses me to let me know that he's got your back? In a strange way, yes I do. It's nice to know you've got someone else covering you if you ever need it and I think he knows it's warranted. Not these days anyway but he's still doing it and I can respect that."

"I love you, Mr Drake-Bishop."

"I love you too, Mr Bishop-Drake." He kisses me again, only this time I don't lose my breath. "Come on, Love. Let's go talk to Lori at Vines and convince her to move into the cottage." He steers us towards Vines before stopping and turning to me.

"If that's OK with you, that is?"

"What? Oh! Yes, of course. Let's go talk Lori into packing up all their stuff and moving out here. We can't let them stay anywhere else."

He pulls his phone out of his pocket, messaging Leila to let her know that Gavin and Jilly are headed her way for a free meal. It's probably a little too late but he sends it anyway and he gets a response before he can put his phone back in his pocket.

Leila: *Thanks Boss, all sorted*

There's a smiley face on the end and I can't help but laugh because I know Logan thinks they're unnecessary!

"Come on, let's go and talk to Lori." I take his hand in mine and lead him towards Vines.

"Are you sure you're OK with this?" He asks quietly as we near the bistro.

"Which part are you asking about?" I ask with a laugh but stop when he doesn't even crack a smile back. I stop walking just before we reach the bistro door. "All of it? I mean, I knew you had a past, we all do Logan. I also knew about Lori, so if you tell me you didn't know she was pregnant when she left or after, then I believe you. The fact that you've got a daughter you didn't know about, well that's a shock but I think that's a shock to you more than me."

"Tell me about it." He grumbles.

"There's a little girl out there with your DNA and she needs us. I can't even imagine thinking of us *not* taking her in as soon as we can. I will love her as if she were *our* daughter, Logan."

"She *will* be *our* daughter, Jules. She will always have a Mum, obviously but if we do this, we do it together, Love. We *will* be a family." I can tell he means every word but getting a child to accept having two Dads and calling *me* Dad might be a struggle he's not prepared for.

"Come on, let's go talk to Lori and get her to agree to move out here. Then we can talk about how we make all of this work." He smiles at me and it warms my heart so much. I can't burst his bubble of hope by telling him it won't be as easy as he wants it to be.

"Let's do it." I smile back at him and lead the way into Vines.

Chapter Fifty
LOGAN

Walking into Vines, it feels like every pair of eyes in the place is on Jules and myself but I know that's my own paranoia talking.

"Why is everyone looking at us? Do I have something on my face? Maybe it's on my butt? No, they can't see my rear yet!" Jules mumbles quietly beside me. Or maybe not!

"I'm sure it's just because we got married yesterday and they want to wish us well." I say loud enough that eyes duck away to look at anything except *us*.

"What the hell is going on?" I ask Caleb when we reach the table he's sitting at with Lori.

"I'm sorry about that, I think it's my fault." Lori says quietly.

"No!" Caleb says. "People just need to mind their own fucking business." He looks around the room with a scowl.

"I doubt it's your fault, Lori, no-one here knows you." I tell her, as Jules and I join them at the table.

"'They do now." Caleb says. "Gavin and Jilly came in and noticed me sitting here with Lori. They introduced themselves and happened to mention their shock that you've got a daughter. This revelation made me raise my voice and apparently everyone here now knows that you've got a daughter." He sighs. "Sorry, I didn't do it on purpose but it came as a bit of a shock!"

"It was bound to come out eventually. Especially seeing as how Lori and Savannah are going to be living out here."

"We are?" Lori asks, surprised.

"They are?" Caleb asks at the same time, just as surprised.

317

"Yes, so could you get the cottage that Gavin and Jilly just vacated cleaned up and refreshed, please?" I ask Caleb.

"Yeah, I can get the guys onto it right away." Caleb promises, picking his phone up off the table and sending out a couple of messages. "You know you're going to have to go speak to Makenna before she finds out, right? If you don't tell her and someone else does, you're screwed man." I sigh because I know he's right.

"You're right. Family meeting up at the house, let's go." I command, sending Makenna and Brady a message to let them know we're all on our way and with a guest.

Makenna: *who's the guest?*

Me: *you'll find out when we get there*

Makenna: *Do I know them? Haven't we had enough guests?*

I leave her message unanswered because we're going be there in less than ten minutes and she'll find out then.

"Are you ready, Lori?"

"I'm really not sure about this, Logan." She looks pale and unwell as she stands up. I rush to hold her up and Jules rushes to her other side. Together, we get her to her feet.

"Do you need something?" I ask her, worried.

"Yeah." She nods, closing her eyes and breathing deeply. "My meds. I left them in the car."

"Give me the keys and I'll go grab them." Caleb offers, holding out his hand. Lori hands him the keys and he rushes out the door in front of us.

"Come on Sweetheart, we'll get you some fresh air, your meds and a cold drink at Makenna's." I tell her quietly.

"I'm not sure I should be meeting your sister right now, Logan." Her voice barely above a whisper.

"I don't think you want to do whatever this is, in Vines, Lori." I say so that only we can hear it. "Let Jules and I help you to Makenna's and you can rest over there."

"OK." It's just one word but it seems to sap her energy. I look over her head at Jules and we agree. Lori's sicker than she's lead us to believe.

We slowly walk over to the main house after meeting Caleb at Lori's car so that she can take her medications. Leila appears like a vision with a cold bottle of water for Lori and she shares a look with Caleb. They've both realised that Lori's sicker than she's told us too.

"I hope you're feeling better soon, Lori. If you need anything, just let me know." Leila says softly, quietly slipping back into Vines but not before she sends a sympathetic look my way.

Slowly but surely, we walk Lori to Makenna's, who's standing at the front door with it open and waiting for us. I look at the few steps and look over Lori to Jules. He gives me a slight nod, knowing exactly what I'm thinking. She can't make it up those steps on her own. Without a second thought, I lean down and scoop her up into my arms.

"Logan! What do you think you're doing?" Lori squeaks. "You know, you shouldn't just lift a woman up without any notice! I'm not your girlfriend anymore and we haven't spoken in years, so you don't get to touch me like this without asking!"

"You can't get up there on your own Lori, let me help you, please?" I lean down and whisper in her ear.

"I'm not yours to look after anymore, Logan." She whispers, as she cuddles into my chest, wrapping her arms around my neck and closing her eyes.

"You are the mother of my daughter, Lori and for that I will be forever grateful. Which means, I will take care of you as needed and you will accept that help without question." We're inside the house without Lori even noticing. I place her gently on the couch, on which Jules and I take a seat on either side of her.

"Mother of his child? What the hell is going on here?" Makenna asks, looking between all of us for an answer. "One of you better tell me what the hell is going on before I start to panic. That's not good for the baby." She warns, using that baby against me once again and I roll my eyes.

"Makenna, Brady." I look at them both. "This is Lori. My ex-girlfriend from University and yes, you heard me right, she's the mother of my child. A daughter in fact, called Savannah Rae and she's seven years old. To answer your next question Makenna, I found about an hour ago. Was it just an hour ago, Jules?"

"About that, yes." He smiles at me and I really appreciate having the comfort of him being here while I spill everything to Makenna and Brady.

"It came as a bit of a shock but a happy one, that's for sure." I let out a bark of laughter at his complete understatement of the situation.

"Is she OK? Are you OK, Lori? Can Brady get you something?" I bark out another short laugh at her volunteering her husband's assistance but Brady doesn't seem to mind and that's what I love about the guy. He loves my sister unconditionally.

"Anything at all." He confirms with a gentle smile.

"I'm fine, thank you." Lori's smile is weak at best.

"Lori, Savannah and Jenni, Lori's best friend, are going to move into one of the cottages for the next few months." I think multiple months is being generous but I don't say so. "That way, Lori can get some well needed rest, while Jules and I get to know Savannah."

"Can I use your bathroom, please, Makenna?" Lori asks.

"Of course you can!" Makenna says and starts to get up but Jules beats her to it.

"Let me show you where it is, Lori." He offers, while taking her by the hand and slowly leading her out of the room.

"Is she OK?" Makenna asks, the concern evident in her voice.

"No." I say, shaking my head. "She's got cancer. I think she's sicker than she's made out since she got here though, which is why she's here today. The day after my wedding."

"Why hasn't she gotten in touch with you sooner?" Makenna asks, holding tightly on to Brady's hand. I get the feeling he know the answer before I've given it.

"She tried. She emailed me, messaged me on social media and even sent me a text message. I ignored them all."

"Oh Logan!" Makenna whispers but I hear the tears in her voice.

"I'm feeling massive amounts of guilt right now but that's not going to help anyone. What I need to do, is get all their things from the hotel and get them all here. With us to support them and to help Lori live the best last weeks of her life because I think that's all she has left."

"You're right Logan, I didn't tell you the complete truth when we spoke earlier." She coughs and Jules helps her to sit down next to me again. "I've been given weeks. It's why I came here today even though I knew it was shitty timing for you and Julian. I am so very sorry about it too but as you said, you wouldn't talk to me any other way, so I had to just show up."

"We'll go get your stuff and your friend. Do you think she'll be comfortable coming here with Savannah?" Caleb asks, as both him and Brady stand up, ready to move. "We can take my truck. I'm sure what you've got with you."

"We only have our clothes and a few possessions. We didn't bring much, most things are in storage." Lori sighs. "Unless I'm with you, Jenni won't leave the hotel with you guys, especially when she's got Savannah. I'll have to come with you."

"You're not driving." I tell her. "Jules and I can drive you back in your car. Jenni can come back with Caleb and Brady."

"You've become very commanding in your old age, Logan." She says with a worn out smile. "You're going to have to learn to be a little more gentle with our daughter."

"I promise." I smile but I can feel my heart breaking. I wish that I had answered just one of her messages or calls prior to today. The fact is though, I didn't and we *all* have to live with that. "You can call Jenni on the way and let her know what's going on. I do *not* want to walk in there when she's not expecting me. You and I both know she'll try to kill me, whether there's a child in the room or not."

"She's not that bad, Logan." Lori laughs.

"Your car is sitting out the front." Caleb says. "You guys can wait at the gate and we'll follow you there." He nods at Brady, who kisses Makenna in an obscenely graphic manner that as her brother, I don't need to see but it makes Lori giggle, so it's worth it.

We all stand up and Makenna comes over to hug Lori gently. I'm not sure what she says to her but when they pull apart Lori has tears in her eyes and I want to yell at Makenna.

"I promise." Makenna says to Lori, both of their smiles a little sad as tears well up in their eyes. "Anything you need, just ask, you're one of us now."

We say goodbye to Makenna and get ourselves seated in the car, while the guys walk to Caleb's to pick up his car.

I drive up to the gate and sit there idling, waiting to see Caleb's car when Lori speaks, so quietly that at first, I can barely hear her.

"I wasn't expecting that."

"What?" I ask, confused.

"For your family, your sister, to accept me so quickly and easily. To accept Savannah that easily. I was expecting a fight, some resistance to Savannah being yours but you've all just accepted my word for it."

"Should we be suspicious? I mean, the timelines all meet up and everything."

"You didn't even ask for a photo." She lets out a tire laugh. "You can't even say, 'of yeah, she looks like me' because you have no idea."

"You're right. Can we see a photo, please?"

"You can see more than one." She huffs out a rough laugh. "I'll show you a couple but then I have to call Jenni because she would really appreciate a heads up to us all turning up to the hotel."

Lori shows Jules and I photos of Savannah while we wait for Caleb to pull up behind us. I don't notice that he's arrived until he sounds his horn behind me, making all three of us jump.

I wave my hand out of the open window and then pull out onto the road into town.

The conversation between Lori and Jenni certainly is interesting and I find myself laughing at their exchange. I look in the rear view mirror to find Jules smirking as well. This is going to be a very interesting day.

Very interesting indeed. I just hope I'm ready for it!

Chapter Fifty-one
JULES

The drive to the hotel should be uncomfortable but it's not. I feel like I've known Lori for almost as long as Logan has, which is strange considering before today, he barely spoke about her at all.

The phone exchange between Lori and her friend, Jenni, is exceptionally amusing.

"Yes, I spoke to Logan." A pause, with a quick glance at Logan behind the wheel. "Yes, Jenni, he's *fine*." The blush that tints her cheeks says more than the actual words and I can't help chuckling. Logan is a *very* handsome guy, I know he was a gorgeous young man back in his youth.

"Jenni!" Lori growls into the phone. "I'm not asking either one of them that! No! Stop!" There's another pause and she groans, rolling her eyes. "We're on our way to the hotel." Another glance at Logan and I wonder what Jenni's saying, I imagine it might not be great. "Jenni! We'll see you soon, OK? Can you please pack up all our things and make sure Savannah is ready?" She closes her eyes and takes a deep breath. "No, I'm not feeling great. No I'm not driving, Logan is. We'll see you soon." She ends the call and rests her head back on the seat, closes her eyes again and let's out the biggest sigh I've ever heard.

"Is everything OK?" Logan asks, glancing from the road to Lori a couple of times while waiting for her to reply.

"Yes." Her voice is raspy and I'm not sure if she's exhausted, emotional or it's her meds.

"Can I do anything for you Lori?" I ask, resting my hand on her shoulder from the backseat and squeezing it gently. She reaches a hand up and squeezes back.

"No, I'm OK, thank you Julian. She's just worried about me, about us."

"She doesn't have anything to worry about." Logan says, his annoyance very clear in his voice.

"She knows that logically, Logan but she's gotten used to being the only one who looks after us. The good, the bad and everything in between. I can't blame her for being cautious. To be honest, she wasn't for me coming out here to start with but she gave in when I told her why I wanted to come and see you before, well, before the inevitable."

"And why is that? You could have just as easily not come here, never told me about Savannah." Logan doesn't exactly sound angry, he almost sounds hurt. "I mean, you haven't told me before now." Ouch!

"*You* didn't answer any of my communications, Logan." Her frustration is as easy to hear as his pain is. "Look, the fact is, we're here now, aren't we? As for why I'm doing it now, *why* I came here today, the truth is, I didn't want you to find out about your daughter from a lawyer in a few weeks' time. I wanted you to get to know her without all the legal bullshit that will surround you when the inevitable happens. Jenni would take Savannah in, in a heartbeat, in *half* a fucking heartbeat, if I'm being honest but I couldn't do that to her."

"But *could* you do that to me, to us?" There's no venom or anger in his question but I still feel Lori tense under my hand still resting on her shoulder, and I squeeze it gently again to let her know he's not mad or saying no, he just wants to understand.

"Jenni has already done so much for us ..."

"And I haven't? I wasn't given a choice about that, Lori."

"If you let me finish, I was going to say, even though I know I'm in the wrong as much as you and yes, you *are* partly to blame because if you'd answered just *one* message, we would have done this already. That being said, I most definitely could have made this trip a lot sooner and without the looming deadline crashing down us. I'm not saying I'm more innocent than you in this *but* you want an explanation and this is it." She sighs, it's the biggest and deepest one I've heard since we met. "Logan, I'm sorry, OK? I know I could have tried harder. I'm sorry that I've waited until I literally have weeks to live because that's not fair on you or Savannah. I don't see the situation the same way you do and that's simply because you've had less than a day to get used to the fact that you've got a seven year old daughter. One that you'll have sole custody of in a less than a month."

"Lori. Are you sure, Sweetheart?" His voice is quiet and tender.

"Yeah, unfortunately, I am. It is what is, Logan." She shrugs her shoulders like it doesn't matter but we all hear the emotion in her voice. "I got her first seven years and now, you guys get the rest. All I ask, is that you let Jenni stay in her life, that's all I want. I *need* Jenni to be allowed to spend time with Savannah any time she wants. *That* is my only rule, Logan. I need the two of you to settle whatever differences you have for me and for Savannah."

"You have a deal." Logan says, reaching over to take her hand in his. "I promise."

She sighs and a smile spreads across her face. "Now, we just have to convince Jenni to behave!" She barks out a laugh, that turns in to a terrible coughing fit. When she calms down, she turns in her seat to look at me. "I owe you an apology too Julian."

"No, Lori, you don't, truly." I promise her, my voice full of the emotion I'm feeling.

"Yes, I do. Please let me do this, Julian." Her eyes plead with me so I nod, she keeps talking, one hand in Logan's and the other one resting on mine on her shoulder. "I've bulldozed into your life, taken over what should be the happiest time of your life, with this trauma and a daughter you didn't see coming because let's face it, Savannah is your daughter as much as she is Logan's. He may be her biological father but you're going to be her Dad and that's a big deal. So, I'm sorry."

"I'm honoured that you think of me as Savannah's Dad, Lori." My emotions getting the better of me and choke over the word 'Dad', causing Logan to glance back at me, before looking back at the road.

"Lori's not wrong Jules and I'm sorry, I haven't even really stopped to consider how this all affects you as well."

"Oh shit! Had you guys even talked about kids? Damn, that's a very personal question, isn't it? I should know better than to ask questions like that. Let's just blame the medication shall we?"

"You're allowed to ask whatever you want, Lori." I reassure her. "Anything you need to know to put you at ease, you ask it Sweetheart. As for a family, we've talked about it but not in any real way. We wanted one but we hadn't considered how that might happen. I guess we have our answer now."

"That's sweet of you to say but I know I've crashed into your lives like a bull on a rampage in a china shop. Full on and breaking shit everywhere I turn."

"You're not breaking anything, Sweetheart. Nothing at all." I assure her and Logan looks at me in the rearview mirror, giving me a sad smile. We both know that Lori's visit today has cause a ripple effect in all our lives for years to come but I don't think either of us would change that for the world.

We get a daughter. Unfortunately, we lose Lori to gain her.

The rest of the trip is done in silence, each of us settled into our own thoughts and none of us wanting to share. I think Lori has said more than enough and looks exhausted. The trip out to Drake Wines must have taken a lot out of her and I'm surprised Jenni let her drive out there on her own.

When we arrive at the hotel, Lori directs us to the room they've been staying in. The door to the room flies open as Logan turns off the car and a young girl comes flying out to greet us. The driver's side door is flung open and she flings herself into Logan's side.

"Mumma!" When she hits solid muscle, that may or may not have tensed up slightly before wrapping an arm around her.

"Sorry to disappoint you Sweetie but I'm not your Mum." He chuckles.

"No, you're not." A stern voice says from the doorway of the room.

"Jenni." Lori's tone of voice warns.

"Jenni. How are you?" Logan asks, his voice cautious but friendly. Well, as friendly as the grumpy bastard gets, anyway!

"I'm great, just great, Logan." She smiles but it looks fake, even to me. Lori gets out of the car and walks to the doorway, it's only then that I realise that Savannah is still clinging to Logan. Jenni notices too.

"Hi, Jenni?" She looks my way, she almost looks surprised to see me. "I'm Jules."

"The husband." She nods and takes my out-stretched hand, shaking it just the once. "Congratulations. And by that I mean, congratulations on promising to put up with Logan for the rest of your life."

"*Jenni!*" Lori warns from just inside their room. "I told you, behave yourself. None of this is Logan's fault, *none* of it and you know that!" She glances at Savannah, who is still attached to Logan and looks back at her friend, obviously making her point because Jenni deflates. Her anger seems to just disappear.

"Hi ladies. I'm Caleb and this here is my brother, Brady. Who do we have here?" Caleb squats down in front of Savannah, his hand out ready to shake hers. She stands tall, takes his hand in hers and answers him proudly.

"I'm Savannah Rae Drake and I *think* you might be my uncle but if you are, then I don't know who this other guy is." She looks at Brady confused. "Mumma said you only had one brother." She states, looking up at Logan for the answer.

"Well, technically, I do but Brady married our sister ..." Logan starts.

"So, now he's your brother too!" Savannah finishes.

"That's right." Caleb tells her with a smile. "Did you want to come stay with us at our place?"

"Your place? Wouldn't I be staying with Daddy and his husband." She looks over at me through her eyelashes, shy all of a sudden.

"Well, we all live out on the same property, just in different houses." Caleb laughs.

"Really?" Her eyes wide in disbelief.

"Sure do. You can stay with your Mum and Aunt Jenni in a cottage I've cleaned up for you guys. Would you like that?"

"Yes! That sounds like fun."

"How about you take me inside and we can grab your things to put in my truck? Then we can head home and settle in?" Caleb reaches his hand out for hers as he stands back up. Savannah looks up at Logan, who gives her a nod to let her know it's OK. She takes Caleb's hand and they disappear into the hotel room with Brady close behind them, Savannah and Caleb chattering away like they've known each other forever.

"It's nice of you to put us up for a while. We'll pay you, of course ..." Jenni starts but Logan doesn't let her finish.

"It's not nice of us, it's necessary and we did it without a thought. You are *all* welcome to stay as long as you want."

"I won't be there for long, Logan. We don't have long left with Lori." She look at him pointedly.

"We know that Jenni and yet, I'm telling you, you can stay at Drakes Wines, in the cottage for as long as you need. Now and after, well the inevitable. However long you need, whenever you want, you are always welcome. There will always be a cottage or a room made available to you, Jenni. We will not take Savannah out of your life, we promise."

"You're saying *we* a lot." She says with a teasing smile and I see Logan relax.

"That's because Jules and I are a package deal. *We* do things together, as a team and taking in Savannah and Lori will be no different. Letting you in, well that's no different either."

"Do you agree with him, Julian? You haven't said too much." Jenni turns to me and asks.

"I'm behind my husband one hundred percent. This isn't an easy situation for anyone but if we can make it easier in any kind of way, then we will." I tell her, walking over to where Logan's standing and sliding my arm around his waist. "You're Savannah's Aunt Jenni, therefore, you're always welcome at our home."

Her eyes well with the emotions I can see bubbling just under the surface. "Thank you. Both of you." Her voice husky with tears. "I was worried that you'd be mad at her."

"I could have been but I'm not." Logan answers her simply.

I'm so proud of Logan and how he's taken everything that's happened today. He dealt with shock after shock and he never hesitated, not even for a second, to accept this beautiful girl as his. As ours!

"Let's go home!" Caleb says as he carries some of their belongings out of the hotel room, Brady close behind with more and Savannah's bouncing along beside him, carrying a small suitcase.

Savannah gets bundled up into Lori's car in the backseat with me, her Mum and Dad in the front seats. Jenni gets in with Brady and Caleb, and we all head back to Drake Wines.

I'm sure there isn't one person in our little convoy that isn't thinking about what the next few months are going to bring. Our car would be silent except for the fact that Savannah is chatting happily, oblivious to the fact that all of the adults in the car are thinking about what the future holds.

Savannah quietens when we pull into Drake Wines and stares out the window, eyes wide her mouth hanging open in surprise.

"This is all yours?" She asks Logan.

"Not just mine but yes, this is where we live." He pauses to look over at Lori, who nods for him to go ahead. "Your Grandpa built it and now my brother and sister help me to run it. One day, maybe you could help us too?"

"I'm too young to drink wine." We're all laughing as we pull up to the cottage where Makenna is standing in the open door, waiting for us. I'm guessing that Brady let her know we were close.

"Is that your sister?" Savannah asks in a breathy voice.

"Yes. That's Makenna. Brady, who you met at the hotel, is her husband." Logan tells her as he parks the car and turns it off.

"Is she having a baby? Can I go meet her?" Without waiting for an answer, Savannah jumps out of the car and races towards Makenna, stopping just before she bumped into her.

"She's a real firecracker that daughter of yours." I tell Lori and Logan as I get out of the car myself, after grabbing the small bag that Savannah left behind, to take into the cottage for her.

When I reach them, the two girls are talking a million miles a minute and I feel like this whole thing could work. It's a lot to take on when we haven't even been married for twenty four hours yet but I know we can do it. Especially with the way everyone around us is taking Savannah in and loving her unconditionally.

This is going to work! I can feel it.

SETTLING THE GIRLS into the cottage didn't take long with everyone helping out. They didn't really have much and when I asked if they needed other things moved in, Lori told me that she'd sold everything because she didn't want to burden Jenni with the task. Instead, they down-sized to almost nothing.

Unfortunately, it also didn't take long for Lori to succumb to her illness. Within weeks of moving them onto the property, she was gone. I wish we'd known just how close her end was because in the few weeks that I had to get to know her, I understood why Logan went out with her to begin with. Watching someone go through the last days of their life is difficult for everyone involved but in the end, Lori went to sleep and never woke up. It was peaceful.

Savannah took her mum's passing surprisingly well for a kid her age. Lori was an amazing Mum and even though she shielded her daughter from the worst of the treatments *and* the disease itself, she was also very open and honest with her. Savannah was well prepared to lose her Mum. That's not to say she didn't mourn her or have any issues, believe me she did. That little girl slept in our bed for weeks after her mother's funeral, and she was welcome for every one of them. I offered to sleep in her room to give her the time she obviously needed with her Dad but when I moved to get up, she put her tiny hand around my bicep and pulled me back down. I woke up with her plastered to my chest so many mornings, I lost count. That was until one day when she decided that she was sleeping in her own bed and that was that. I kind of miss having her snuggling into me, sleepy and comfortable in the mornings.

Logan didn't take Lori's passing quite as easily as his daughter did and that was hard for me to watch. There wasn't a lot I could do for him except be there for him. I took care of him and Savannah in every way I could to help ease their pain. Logan felt guilt in such a significant measure for not answering any of Lori's attempts to contact him, that his pain at her passing was enormous. He wished for things that he couldn't change.

More time with the mother of his child.

More time with the woman that had actually been his friend *before* she was his lover.

More time to adjust to being a father.

More time to just breathe and settle in to parenting.

None of these things could be changed but my husband, the man who loves to have control over everything in his world, struggled to accept it. His pain wasn't just for himself either. He felt the pain and sorrow for Savannah and tried to take on some for Jenni as well but let's just say Jenni wasn't too impressed with him! I think she felt that she's earned her pain and she wanted to feel it so that she could get past it and learn to live her own life again. She wasn't just mourning the loss of her best friend, she'd been Lori and Savannah's sole carer for months! So, we gave her what was supposed to be our honeymoon. After protesting for *way* too long, we finally got her packed up and sent off in her car for a week away on the coast just to relax, about two weeks after Lori's funeral.

We decided not to go on our honeymoon the minute we found out just how long Lori had left. We were supposed to leave the day after we settled them into the cottage. We changed our mind after a very frank and emotional conversation with Jenni forcing Lori to tell us the truth. Thankfully, Savannah was up at the main house with Makenna, Brady and Caleb, so she didn't have to hear the painful truth. There were many tears and the four of us came out of the heavy conversation with a new respect for each other, as well as an understanding of what we had ahead of us.

Logan and Jenni had a long and difficult talk when they first arrived and they both knew that in order for Lori to have peace in her final days and for Savannah to get through the most difficult time of her young life, they had to put everything out there and get over it. Quickly. Logan understood better than any of us, the pain of losing a parent. Their truce didn't stop Jenni from giving him as much grief as she possibly could, even though I think most of it was done in fun and to break the tension felt by all of us.

Jenni and I have become close since she arrived with the other two ladies. She kind of lives in the cottage now . At least she has when she's not travelling for work. For some reason, known only to her, she doesn't want Logan to know what she does for work. Personally, I think she just loves to have something that drives him nuts. She's always here when Savannah needs her and that's all that matters to either of us though and who knows how long she'll stay here with us? I'm happy for her to stay indefinitely. It's nice for Savannah to have someone to talk to that knew her Mum so well, who she shares memories with, especially on the tough days. And there are still plenty of tough days, we're just all getting better at dealing with them.

I think it almost broke Logan in half to hear it but he never let Lori see just how upset he was. He was strong for everyone but when it was just the two of us, he let the tears fall. Letting himself be vulnerable with me was one of the sexiest things I've ever seen. He's so strong, so in charge, with everything and everyone, I love that he's comfortable enough to show his soft underbelly to me.

He should be able to I guess, we *are* married.

Our wedding feels like it was decades ago, even though it was just a couple of weeks before we had to say goodbye to Lori. Less than a *month* being married to Logan Drake and there was already enough drama to last a lifetime! A daughter he didn't know about, an ex dying of cancer and then they both moved onto the Drake Wines property, along with his ex's best friend.

I feel like we've lived a lifetime together already.

Would I change anything? Yes. I would cure Lori so that she could still be here with us to enjoy watching Savannah grow up because I have no doubt it's going to be a privilege.

Chapter Fifty-two
LOGAN

A few months after Lori died, Makenna gave birth to her twins, it was the happiest day of my life and not just because my sister and Brady got the family they wanted in one foul swoop.

When Makenna was put on bed rest due to complications around her eighth month, we were all worried that she might go into labour early. Savannah spent almost every spare minute, sitting on the bed with her Aunt to keep her company. It was the sweetest thing and it helped Savannah to concentrate on life, rather than death.

It was nice to see Savannah bonding with my sister because even though she still had Jenni, she travelled a lot for work. She was around as much as she could be but I think we all knew it would have to come to end soon. She couldn't live out here forever. Not that I was ever going ask her to leave.

Makenna wasn't the only one Savannah was bonding with though. Caleb and Brady were always taking her somewhere, doing something with her and helping us in so many different ways, I still couldn't quite believe it.

I wasn't sure if Savannah was ever going to settle in here and get used to the idea of having two Dads but she hasn't even blinked. Lori wasn't kidding when she said that she'd already explained who I was to our daughter. She still called Jules by his name but you could see her thinking about whether that was the right thing or not. Neither of us wanted to push her into making that decision, least of all Jules, he wanted it to come naturally or not at all. This kid of mine had already gone through more than most adults had to deal with in a lifetime.

Caleb joined me on the back deck of the main house on the afternoon that Makenna went into labour and quietly asked me, "Is everything OK at home?"

"What do you mean?" I went straight on to the defensive because two men bringing up a daughter always has people asking questions, I just didn't think it would come from family. Especially Caleb.

"I'm just asking how things are going? I know you've all been dealing with some strong emotions." When I didn't respond, he continued. "I had a talk with Savvy earlier, that's all." He said with a shrug.

"About?"

"She was curious. *She* asked if the two of you were happy." He looks at me, pointedly and when I don't answer he sighs and continues talking. "She knows that she was a surprise for you and Jules. She also knows, obviously, that you guys just got married."

"What's your point, Caleb?" I ask, looking him dead in the eyes, because I can't tell what he's thinking.

"She wanted to know if I thought you and Jules were happy that she was in your lives now.."

"And? What did you say?" Ready to pound my brother into next week if he said anything stupid that might have hurt my daughter.

"What do you think I told her? I told her that not only were you two happy she was here, but we were *all* happy she was here. She's family."

"Good. Good." I said, nodding and scowling as this news rolled around my head.

"Relax, Logan. You guys have got this. Savvy is just trying to sort everything out in her head. She's a smart girl, she knows that she has two Dads. She knows that *you're* her father but she also knows that she wants Jules as her *Dad*. Give her a little bit of time and she'll be right there with the two of you. Lori did an amazing job with that little girl!"

Just as Caleb started to walk away, we heard yelling from inside the house and knew that Makenna wasn't happy about something. When we both made it inside, Makenna was standing there with a puddle between her feet and a husband that appeared to be in shock. Caleb took the keys and drove the soon to be new parents to the hospital, while I promised to clean up here and lock up before meeting them at the hospital.

Jules and I made quick work of cleaning up. Savannah wanted to help, so we gave her a few of the smaller jobs to do and it was done in no time at all.

While the lives of everyone in the family changed the day of the twins arrival, our own small family was bonding as well. "Aunty Kenna is having her baby! I'll stay here with Jules so that you can go wait with Uncle Caleb, Dad."

"Are you guys sure?" I asked, directing my question solely at Jules.

"Of course!" He took Savannah's hand in his and a smile that told me he was more than happy that Savannah volunteered to stay with him. It's not that they don't spend any time together but she is almost permanently attached to me some days and her saying she wants to stay with him is a real step forward. For all of us. "We'll be fine won't we sweet girl?"

"Peachy keen, jellybean." She replied with a huge grin. "You go and make sure Aunt Kenna and Uncle Brady are doing fine with the baby and Jules and I will wait for news."

"We'll head home and watch a movie." Jules insisted, pushing me out the door, following close behind after locking up, still holding on to Savannah's hand.

"Are you sure ...?" I don't get to finish my question before they're *both* pushing me towards my car. I get warm hugs and kisses off them both before heading off to the hospital to see my new niece or nephew.

When I arrive I'm surprised to see Leila sitting with Caleb, who is as calm as can be, laughing and talking with Brady's parents. After a round of hugs, we sit in comfortable silence for a while. I watch with interest as Leila and Caleb talk quietly, their foreheads almost touching. She reaches up and gently touches his cheek, before abruptly standing up and announcing she's going home. Caleb looks sad for a few seconds but then that smile that I've come to realise is sometimes fake, returns to his face and he's saying goodbye along with the rest of us.

Not long after Leila leaves, Brady comes bursting into the waiting room and we all jump to our feet. When he announces that they have a daughter, Anna June Harris, Brady's mum bursts into tears and the poor man is surrounded by four bodies hugging him. He breaks out though and his smile is so big it almost makes him look insane and with his next words, I understand why he looks like he's going crazy! They also have a son! Beau Jack Harris!

There's a few seconds of silence and then, a loud roar goes up, earning us a dirty look from the nurse at the desk opposite the room.

Twins! I am *so* glad it's them and not us. We've got one daughter and we didn't have to worry about losing sleep or changing them in the middle of the night. I know that Makenna and Brady are going to make this work and no doubt make it look easy but they won't ever have to do it alone.

Jules and I have been messaging but I call him with the happy news because a message just seems wrong.

"Hey." He whispers when he answers.

"Is everything OK?"

"Yeah, of course." He sounds insulted. "Savannah fell asleep cuddled up with me on the couch and I don't want to move her just yet, that's all." I smile, imaging the two of them on the couch together. I love that we have her in our lives.

"Oh, I'll be quick then. I just wanted to let you know how everyone was and didn't want to text." I chuckle. "We have a new baby girl in the family, Anna June Harris." I tell him and he gasps.

"Ohhhh that's beautiful, Logan!"

"There's more."

"Is everyone OK?"

"Yes, perfect. We also have a young man joining the family."

"What do you mean?" His confusion is adorable and I can't help laughing.

"She had twins, Jules. Beau Jack Harris entered the world much to the surprise of everyone present, including his parents and the doctor."

"Holy crap!" Jules whisper shouts and I know he's woken Savannah up when I hear her sleepy voice but I can't understand what she says. "Hang on, Sweets, I'm going to put you on speaker." A second later my daughters sleepy, sweet voice comes through the speaker.

"Hi Daddy, did Aunty Kenna have her baby?"

"She did, she had twins." I tell her.

"She had *two* babies?" She squeals. "I'm so happy! What are their names? When I can met them?"

"Their names are Anna and Beau." I tell her laughing at her excitement. "Maybe you can come and visit tomorrow, if the babies and Aunt Kenna are up to it, OK?"

"OK, Daddy." She sounds a little disappointed, even as she yawns!

"First, you have to get some more sleep. We can talk about visiting in the morning." I tell her, she agrees and then I have short conversation with Jules, letting him know that I'm going to stay here for a little while longer to see if the new parents need anything and then I'll head home.

Half an hour later, after going in to see Kenna and the babies, I head to *my* family. Quietly, I walk in the door and when I don't see them in the living room, I go to check on Savannah but as I walk past our bedroom, something in the dim light catches my attention and my heart stops beating for a second.

Jules and Savannah are curled up together in our bed, sleeping soundly. My heart can't stand how adorable the two of them look together. I can't believe how much our lives have changed in the last few months.

Moving in together, getting married and now, the family we longed for but didn't dare hope to have.

I feel blessed beyond belief.

"Don't just stand there, Sweets. Come to bed and get some sleep." Jules' sleepy voice says, his back towards the door, he hasn't moved since I walked in. "I heard the door and hoped it was you. I'm too tired to move."

I laugh quietly, so I don't wake up Savannah, again and do as he asked. I strip down to my boxers and pull on my pyjama pants. Then, I crawl in beside the two loves of my life and sleep a restful, happy sleep.

Chapter Fifty-three
JULES

I spent as much time with Lori as I could while she was still with us, getting to know her, sharing her memories and writing a few things down for her so that we could share them with Savannah later. I wanted to know the mother of Logan's daughter so that we could bring her up the way she would have done herself. I felt that bond with Lori by the time she left us and I hoped that it would help me to bond with her daughter as well. I also knew it wasn't going to be a quick, short term bonding and I was going to spend the rest of our lives bonding with that little girl.

Savannah handled herself with such maturity and composure over the days before and weeks after her mum passed away, that I don't think anyone in the family could ever deny that she was Logan's daughter. For not having grown up with him in her life for those first, formative years, she was *very* much like him.

She is our brightest light. We get along amazingly well and have a special bond but I don't think she's going to feel comfortable calling me any form of Dad, any time soon though. She's comfortable with Logan and I being married, that's never been an issue, thanks mostly to Lori and the way she raised her before she came here.

Having Jenni stay on the property has helped Savannah adjust easier as well. Knowing that her Aunt Jen is nearby has been comforting and not just for Savannah. I don't think the truce between Logan and Jenni, is a truce as much as it an actual *true* friendship these days. Not that either of them would admit it!

Savannah is beside herself that she also inherited a set of grandparents. Even though her grandma helped Lori from the beginning to bring her up, she'd never had a grandpa before and my dad was *more* than willing to step in to the role. My mum not far behind him happily fulfilling the role of grandma. Grams and Gramps were over more often than I ever really wanted them here and taking Savannah off on adventures, bringing her home happily exhausted.

Brady's mum and dad adopted her as well, not wanting her to feel left out when they came over to see the twins and became Grams Pauline and Gramps Jeremy. It was a true sight to see both sets of grandparents sitting with the twins and Savannah at Vines having a snack or lunch. The happiness in that one picture was almost overwhelming.

Almost from the minute Savannah moved in, she started asking for a pet. She started with a dog, moved on to a cat, then fish after we said they were too much work. She even asked for a bird, to which my usually stoic and brave husband, said a very sure, no!

With the promise of when we were all settled in properly, we would think about getting a pet, her requests slowed down until they were almost non-existent. She'd given up all hope, when we decided that it might be the right time to get a dog. We'd always wanted one but then other things just got in the way and we'd decided we were too busy with work to be good dog owners. Then, Savannah arrived and we both slowed down at work, mostly. We were definitely home more often, so Logan asked Caleb to start work on building a solid fence around the house.

The conversation went a little like this:

"Yes, Caleb. I want a big yard space for Savannah, the twins and a *dog* to play in."

"You mean you're finally giving in and getting that delightful niece of mine a dog?"

"Yes, Caleb, I am but if you tell her ..."

"What?" He smirked at his older brother. "What are you going to do to me big brother? Are you going to ground me? Maybe you'll take my car keys away from me? Oh, hang on, you can't because I'm an adult now, *Logan*." His laughter was loud but cut short with his brothers promise.

"I'll tell Leila." The laughter stopped so abruptly that it was *my* turn to laugh, as Logan stood there, a wide, sexy as fuck smirk on his face. I swear, if his brother wasn't standing there, I would be jumping the man right this second.

"So what?" Caleb tried to shrug it but the look on his face told us everything.

"That's what I thought. Now, can we just get the fence built while she's visiting with Jules' folks please? Thank you, that would be great."

"She's only going to be gone for a couple of days." Caleb protested.

"I know, which is why I'm pitching in as well." Caleb almost choked on his own spit at Logan's admission. "Don't look so shocked Caleb, I know physical labour and I quite enjoy it, especially when I know it's going to make my daughter very happy."

Once Caleb got over his shock, he moved quick and I got to watch my husband, stripped off to the waist, sweating, build our daughter a fence for her new puppy! It was quite the sight I have to tell you. The shower afterwards was *also* very worth the physical labour! Not having an inquisitive young lady around, who still doesn't like to be separated from one of us for too long, is very liberating. We now understand why parents love date night!

Also, I love my parents for knowing this and giving us some much needed time alone. They are literal saints, I swear.

The morning after the fence is finished and Logan is still sound asleep in bed, I get up to shower. When I walk out into the living room, I find Caleb sitting on the couch.

"Good morning Caleb, to what do I owe the pleasure?" He doesn't do this very often any more. Not since we got married. I'm not sure whether it's because we're married or that Savannah lives here now as well. Either way, it normally means there's something on his mind.

"Is Logan asleep?"

"Sound asleep. Why?" Whatever he wants to talk to me about, he doesn't want his brother to know.

"Is Savvy still with your folks?" His eyes dart towards her bedroom.

"Yes. They should be back soon though." I feel like I need to give him fair warning, if he has something he needs to say to me that he doesn't want anyone else hearing, he should probably move it along.

"I think I'm in love with Leila." He sounds shocked by his own confession and I can't help laughing at the poor man.

"You think?" His eyes widen even more. I cough to cover more laughter and sit down beside him. "I know you are Caleb, I was waiting to see how long it was going to take *you* to realise that. Does she know?"

"No! I don't think so. Do you think so?" He's so cute when he's panicking, I can't believe that Leila doesn't feel the same way. "No, she can't know!"

Before either of us can say anything else, sunshine bursts through the door and Savannah is running into my arms. She squeezes me tightly and tells me she missed me and then she runs into her uncles open and waiting arms. After a minute he lets her go, he looks better than he did just before she arrived.

"You need to go wake up Daddy and ask him." He says with a huge smile as she bolts for our bedroom. My eyes widen, thinking about what she might find, causing Caleb to laugh. His laughter stops abruptly when his brother yells out his name. "I'm out of here. Good to see you again Grams and Gramps." He says to my parents as he bolts out the door.

"That boy is going to damage himself one day." My Dad says, shaking his head. I can't say I disagree with him.

"Thanks for having Sav, we really appreciate it."

"I bet." My mum smiles. "It's never a problem for us, ever. We love having her around."

"Well, thank you anyway." I say hugging them both. "Why don't you guys head up to Vines to grab some breakfast and we'll meet you there as soon as we're ready."

"We'll go have breakfast but you guys stay here. Enjoy having family time we can catch up later."

With another round of hugs and kisses, Savannah comes running out of our room to say goodbye to them too and my heart swells at the sight because even though she's not ready to call me by anything other than my name, she has accepted my parents as grandparents easily. It gives me hope that one day soon, she'll accept me too.

"Come on Jules, we need to make Daddy get out of bed." She takes my hand in hers as runs back into our room, jumps on the bed and giggles as Logan tickles her. He looks over her head and smiles. He's happy, which makes me happy.

I sit down on the bed and we listen, our attention solely on Savannah as she tells us all about her adventures with Grams and Gramps. Logan reaches over and takes my hand in his, he gives it a gentle squeeze but I can't look at him. We're all happy and that's how it's going to stay. It doesn't matter what this beautiful little girl calls me, I am her other parental figure and that's all that matters.

"I love you." Logan says, quietly as Savannah keeps chatting on.

"I love you too, Sweets."

"I love you both!" Savannah says, her smile almost wider than her face. "Are we getting a puppy?"

Logan and I look at each other, then back at our daughter.

"How did you know?" Logan asks.

"Uncle Caleb told me to ask you." She says, shrugging a shoulder. "He said he built a fence for a puppy while I was gone."

Now I know what Caleb whispered in her ear.

"He just can't help himself, can he?" Logan grumbles and Savannah squeals.

EPILOGUE

2ND Wedding Anniversary

LOGAN

It's our second anniversary today and we both took Savannah shopping with us to help pick out presents. Her smile is *so* large this morning as she hands us our coffees, I feel certain that she's played both of us somehow. At almost ten, she's changed so much. Grown so much, both physically and emotionally.

Today we celebrate our marriage and tomorrow we celebrate Savannah and Lori coming into our lives. We decided as a family that both deserved to be celebrated. Our wedding with every member of the family that can make it and Savannah's anniversary as part of our family, just the three of us. The four of us if Jenni can make it as well. She still stays in the cottage every now and then, and even though it was never spoken about, that cottage is never rented out to anyone else, it's always ready and waiting for her to come back to us.

"Gifts! It's gifts time!" Savannah announces a little too loudly. She obviously gets both her ease with the morning and her sunny disposition from her mum.

"OK Sav, sit down before your Dad's head explodes." Jules laughs, as he rests his hand on her arm to calm her. She sits between us which means there's no anniversary passion for us, which means there's definitely no sex in my schedule today either. We couldn't even have lazy morning sex because Savannah woke us up singing happy anniversary to the tune of happy birthday!

Don't get me wrong, I wouldn't trade her for the world but some days, there's not much I wouldn't give for some alone time with my husband.

"I'm sorry Dad." Somewhere in the last year she stopped calling me Daddy and I'm not sure I like it! Before I can answer her, Jaspa, the golden retriever we adopted from a shelter, bounds into the room. "Jaspa! Sit, I'll get your breakfast in a minute." The dog sits, tongue lolling out of the side his mouth, smiling at the girl who feeds him and gives him too many treats. She's the one he listens to the most, he listens to Jules and myself, just not quite as well as he does Savannah.

"It's OK, Sweetie, no harm done." I bend down and kiss the top of her head.

"Gifts! Presents! Come on you two." I look around our daughter to find Jules looking at me with a glint in his eyes. I get the feeling that these two have played me this year.

"Happy second anniversary, Love." I say, as I hand his gift to him around Savannah.

"Happy second anniversary, Sweets." He says, doing the same but I don't let him sit back. I snatch his hand in mine and pull him closer, kissing him until he can barely breathe.

"Guys, I love you but please don't make out like that with me in the middle." With our foreheads pressed together, with our lips barely touching, we laugh. It's not a loud raucous kind of laugh, it's the laugh of parents who don't get a minutes peace. "Open them!" She squeals when I sit back on my side of the couch, leaving Jules a little stunned and leaning towards me a little still.

"Happy anniversary, Love." I say, trying to bring him back to the present ... and the presents!

"Happy anniversary, Sweets." He says, his grin making me want to kiss him again but I don't because I hear Savannah let out a long sigh beside me. I growl and Jules chuckles but we open our gifts. Gifts that we promised not to spend more than twenty dollars on! I don't know why really, except that we both feel like we're so lucky already that we don't need anything.

The sound of ripping paper pulls me out of my thoughts and I tear open my present.

"What the?" I stop myself from swearing, for which I give myself a mental pat on the back.

"What in heavens name is this?" Jules says, as we both sit there staring at the items in our hands. Savannah cracks up laughing, tears rolling down her face, trying to breathe.

"Savannah?"

"Yes?" She asks, between breaths. "Don't you like your gifts? Aren't you supposed to say thank you and smile, Dad?" Cheeky girl!

"Yes, you're right, we are supposed to be grateful for the thought and effort put into buying us gifts." I start.

"But how did you talk your Dad into buying *this*?" Jules finishes. He looks up at me, the question all over his face, 'what the hell, Sweets?'

"I looked up what gifts to buy for anniversaries after I heard Aunt Kenna talking about them because I didn't understand what she meant when she said you had to buy paper gifts for your first anniversary." She says with a shrug. "So, I looked it up on the internet and found out there were traditional and modern gifts. For the first anniversary, which I missed in this case because I didn't know, was paper and clocks. The second anniversary is cotton and china."

"OK, I guess that kind of explains the gifts." I say, trying to be diplomatic and she knows it the little devil because her smile broadens.

"I convinced you both to take me shopping for the other and then pointed you in the direction of either cotton or china."

"Obviously, Sweetheart but why these?" Jules asks, still as confused as I am.

"I chose the most ridiculous gifts to see if you would go along with them and you both did." She loses it again and her laughter is bordering on insanity. What kind of nine year old evil mastermind lives with us?

"It's a cat mug made in a place called *cotton* and some men's handkerchiefs made in *China*." She's laughing again, tears rolling down her face and I look at Jules, who looks like he's five seconds away from joining her. He's trying desperately not to laugh but he doesn't last long before he's rolling around on the floor with Savannah laughing and struggling to breathe.

"You two are crazy!" I announce. "I've never used a handkerchief in my life but I'm about to start!"

My statement just cracks them up even more, so I leave them to their laughter and walk into the kitchen, Jaspa hot on my heels looking for his breakfast.

"It's alright Jaspa, I'll feed you because those two are incapable of it right now." He gives me a bark and wags his tail at me. At least someone makes sense around here.

JULES

Savannah Drake is an evil genius. How she managed to get her dad and I to get such crazy gifts for each other, I'll never quite understand. The only explanation I can offer up, is that we want to see her happy and so, when there's no harm to come from it, we indulge her. Perhaps, too often, if her gift choice is anything to go by.

She gets a real kick out of telling everyone all about it at dinner that night and while Logan is shaking his head and grumbling about her trickery, I can see the affection he has for his daughter all over his handsome face. He's still grumpy and demanding in all the ways that I love but he is a marshmallow when it comes to Savannah.

On the morning of Savannah's arrival anniversary, as she calls it, the sun shines in through the blinds that apparently neither of us closed properly. When Logan wraps his body around mine from behind, I can't help smiling. I never thought we would get here. When I walked away from our relationship way back when, I honestly thought that was it, that we were over and we would never get back together. It feels like a lifetime ago, so much has happened since then but I wouldn't change any of it. If it meant I would be married to Logan and we would have a daughter, then I would go through it all again, over and over to get here.

"Morning, Love." Logan's sleepy, gravelly voice tumbles in my ear.

"Good morning, Sweets."

"God I love you." He sighs contentedly.

"I love you too." I'm about to tell him I've never been happier but then I hear the door open.

"Dad, are you awake?"

"Mmm Hmmmm." Logan mutters.

"Dad, we have a surprise. Remember?" His body stiffens against mine and not in a good way.

"Yes, I remember Sweetpea. Come here and give us a cuddle." He stretches out his arm behind him, inviting her into our bed. She jumps onto the bed and squeezes herself between us, giggling as she does when Logan tickles her.

"Dad." She says quietly after maybe a minute. "Come on!"

"What's so urgent, Savannah that you can't let your Dad wake up for a few minutes?" I smile and crush them both in a hug, causing Savannah to laugh loudly.

"No, Dad has to wake up now! He promised we could do this first thing when you guys woke up and you're awake, so we can do it!"

"Alright, alright. Why don't you go and get everything ready and we'll be out in a minute."

"You need to put on pants, don't you?" Savannah asks as she bounces off the bed and heads towards the door.

"*Savannah Rae.*" He warns but she just laughs louder and leaves us alone.

"She's something else." I laugh.

"That she is." Logan agrees as he sits up on the edge of the bed, pulling on his sweats. He's worn them much more often since Savannah and Jaspa entered our lives. "You don't regret it, do you?"

"Regret what?" I'm confused about what he's asking me as I continue to get dressed.

"Savannah coming into our lives?" It's definitely a question he seems to have wanted to ask for a while. "She appeared so soon after we got married and she came with a lot of baggage, you know? I mean I came with a shit-load of my own baggage and then Lori appeared, Savannah in tow. It was a surprise and a lot to take in. You *seem* to have taken it all in your stride but have you, really?"

"No." I don't even hesitate. "No, I don't regret marrying you and I don't regret that Savannah is now part of our lives. I love that little girl so much, it makes my heart ache. I wouldn't, couldn't give her up even if you asked me to. Is the house noisier? Yes! Would I change it? Not for anything." He seems to relax completely and I feel bad that I didn't recognise that he was so worried about it.

"Good." He nods, pulling a t-shirt over his head. "Let's get out there before Miss Savannah comes back in here to hurry us up."

"What's going on?" I ask as we walk into the living room. "I didn't know you guys were organising anything for today except to spend all day today, just the three of us."

"Savannah organised it, I just did what she asked me to." His smile tells me that he has a secret, one that I desperately want to know.

"You and I don't keep secrets, remember." I push him, knowing why and *when*, we made that promise. His eyes widen at my words but his smile doesn't waiver.

"We don't but this isn't technically a secret. It's more of a surprise, one I hope you're going to love." He doesn't have the chance to say anything more because Savannah is bouncing on her toes in front of us.

"Sit." She points to the couch and I go to sit but Logan doesn't follow me. "Sit!" Savannah demands a little more forcefully this time and I see the smirk spread across Logan's face. He's proud of his daughter taking charge and I can tell you, the apple does fall far from the tree when it comes to these two! Instead of taking a seat next to me, he stands next to Savannah.

"What's going on? Aren't we supposed to be celebrating Savannah, not me?" I am so confused right now. I like to think I'm a pretty smart man and maybe I just haven't woken up properly yet but I am *so* damned confused right now, it's not funny. The two loons standing in front of me seem to be giddy with excitement though."

"I've been wanting to do this for a while now but it never seemed to be the right time. Then Dad and I spoke about it and we agreed. Today was the perfect day for it." She bounces a few times on her toes and claps her hand as if she's excited to see her favourite band. "Sit." She looks at Logan and nods.

"Jules, Savannah has something she wants to talk to you about and ask you. You're allowed to think about it, you're allowed to not answer right away." Savannah growls, she truly is her father's daughter! I can't help laughing at her reaction.

"Savannah doesn't agree with you, Sweets." I say, laughing but stop when I realise they *both* look a little nervous. "What's wrong?" Because now *I'm* nervous about what might be said.

"Jules. Julian." Savannah starts, then swallows, closes her eyes and takes a deep breath. When he eyes open again, they're shiny with tears. "I wanted to ask you a very serious question today." She looks at Logan, who nods in encouragement again. "Today is a special today. One we celebrate together, just the three of us." She clears her throat and continues. "That's why I wanted to do this today. Yesterday was your day, yours and Dad's, today is ours."

"I know all of that, Savannah but you two are making me nervous." I tell them, reaching out to take Savannah's hand in mine. Logan hands me a large envelope, his smile wide and genuine. "What's this?"

"Open it and find out." Savannah says dropping my hand and jumping up and down in front of me. "Hurry."

I open the envelope and take out the papers inside. Reading the first time doesn't help me work anything out, so I go to the next one.

"I want you to be my Dad." Savannah blurts out in a rush of excited, high-pitched words. "I want you to adopt me and be other Dad. I want to be Savannah Rae Bishop Drake."

"Wh-what?" I look at Logan and I wonder for a second if his smile might split his face. Then I look down at the paperwork in front of me but I can't see it, my vision is blurry and I don't understand why.

"Ohh Papa, don't cry." Savannah cries out and jumps into my arms, making me drop the paperwork. "Dad, you said this was a good thing! You *said* he would be happy. You *didn't* say he would cry! He's not meant to cry! I'm sorry Papa, I didn't mean to upset you. I love you!" Savannah takes my face in her hands, bringing my eyes up to meet hers.

She called me Papa! Not Jules or Julian, not Papa Jules, no, it was a plain and simple Papa! I wrap my arms around her, hugging her so tightly, I'm concerned she might not be able to breathe for long but I don't care in this minute. It's wrong, I know but I'm just so happy and I don't want to let her go.

"Is it OK that I call you Papa?" She whispers in my ear, because she's such a caring girl she wants to make sure that she's doing the right thing.

"Yes, my sweet girl." I whisper back, my eyes shut tight trying but not succeeding to hold the tears of happiness at bay. "It's perfect. You're perfect."

When I open my eyes, Logan is staring at us with all the love in the world and a few tears of his own. "I love you."

"I love you too but I can't believe you kept this from me!" This wasn't something cooked up a week ago, they've been onto this for a while.

"I love you both." Savannah says, and then Logan engulfs us both in a warm bear hug.

"It took a few weeks to organise and Savannah struggled to keep it quiet but she did because she wanted to surprise you."

"Are you OK, Papa?" Savannah asks, as she pulls back to look me in the eyes.

"Perfect, Savannah, absolutely perfect sweet girl." Logan looks at me, pride and joy, bursting out of every pore like sunshine. Our little girl has him wrapped around her little finger and I wouldn't have it any other way.

"So, will you? Will you adopt me and can I be Savannah Rae Bishop Drake, Papa?" The hope on her face melting my heart.

"If that's what you want, sweet girl, then yes. I'm happy if you want to stay Savannah Rae Drake though too." I explain not wanting her to pressured into anything.

"You don't want me to have your name too?" Her voice soft and unsure. I pull her into my arms and look up at Logan.

"I want whatever you want Savannah but I would be very proud for you to have my name Sweetheart." I tell her truthfully. She leans back in my arms, looking deeply into my eyes.

"If you're *sure*, sure?" She asks, her hands gripping my cheeks so that I can't look away.

"Two thousand per cent, Savannah. I love you sweet girl."

"I love you too, Papa." Suddenly she spins in my arms to look at her dad. "It all worked out Dad!"

"Just like I told you it would, sweet girl. I knew Jules would adore being your Papa." He says wrapping us both in another warm bear hug. "I love you both more than I could ever put in to words."

"Love you more." Savannah and I chime in together. Then we're all laughing and the dog decides that's the moment he wants to run over and join in.

This is our family. We're not perfect but we *are* perfect together and I wouldn't have it any other way.

THE END

www.ingramcontent.com/pod-product-compliance
Lightning Source LLC
Chambersburg PA
CBHW070049120726
47909CB00002B/332